MALICE AFORETHOUGHT

by Francis Iles

"A finely written analytic psychological tale of crime ... a splendid series of features of English middle class country life with all its malicious gossip and petty foibles."—*Boston Transcript*

"Mr. Iles, intentionally, of course, gives away his grisly secrets as he goes along, and the result is quite as readable as if he hadn't."—*Books*

"(The) ending is a triumph of stage management."—London *Times Literary Supplement*

MALICE AFORETHOUGHT

THE STORY OF
A COMMONPLACE CRIME

BY

FRANCIS ILES

PERENNIAL LIBRARY
Harper & Row, Publishers
New York, Cambridge, Hagerstown
Philadelphia, San Francisco
London, Mexico City, São Paulo, Sydney

A hardcover edition of this book was originally published by Harper & Row, Publishers.

First PERENNIAL LIBRARY edition published 1980.

ISBN: 0-06-080532-3

81 82 83 84 10 9 8 7 6 5 4 3 2

TO

MARGARET

MALICE AFORETHOUGHT

Chapter One

I

IT WAS not until several weeks after he had decided to murder his wife that Dr. Bickleigh took any active steps in the matter. Murder is a serious business. The slightest slip may be disastrous. Dr. Bickleigh had no intention of risking disaster.

Naturally his decision did not arrive ready-made. It evolved gradually, the fruit of much wistful cogitation. And if cogitation, however wistfully nebulous, must have its starting-point, that of Dr. Bickleigh's might be looked for in a certain tennis-party on a hot Saturday afternoon towards the end of June.

It was a party that the Bickleighs themselves were giving. Half Wyvern's Cross was coming to it: all Wyvern's Cross, in fact, that counted. Dr. Bickleigh, coming back to lunch only a few minutes short of two o'clock, tired after a long and strenuous morning's round, found Fairlawn in a state of no little turmoil, and his wife impatiently waiting to get the dining-room cleared.

"Really, Edmund," she greeted him, peering at him disapprovingly through the thick glasses she wore. "Really, I think you might have been considerate enough to get back a little earlier to-day. How can Florence get on with the sandwiches if you keep her waiting to wash up your lunch things like this?" When her husband was late, Mrs. Bickleigh invariably took her meals alone, at their correct times.

"I'm sorry, Julia. I thought I'd better try to get through my list this morning, so as to be free this afternoon."

"Well, of course." Mrs. Bickleigh contrived to reconcile the two apparently irreconcilable necessities by conveying her impression that her husband must have wilfully dawdled by the wayside.

Dr. Bickleigh poured himself out a glass of beer from the bottle by his plate, and carved some cold leg of lamb. He was too tired at the moment to attempt to extenuate himself further; besides, he knew it would be quite useless. He looked sadly at the joint in front of him. There was no knuckle left on it, and the knuckle was the only part he liked. Unfortunately, Julia liked it too.

He began to eat without enthusiasm.

Julia stood over him, sentinel-like. When he made as if to help himself to more beer, she interposed.

"No, Edmund. One glass is quite enough for you on a day like this."

"The hotter the day, the better the drink, my dear," suggested the doctor, but without very much hope.

Julia, who disapproved of facetiousness as much as she disapproved of most other things, only frowned. "You have too much to do to sit here drinking. Besides, you know how beer makes you perspire. Do you want any more meat? Then you had better ring at once."

Dr. Bickleigh rose. He did not point out that, as Julia was standing already, she might perhaps ring the bell herself and save him the trouble. Julia would consider it middle-class manners to ring a bell herself when there was a man in the room to do it instead: and middle-class manners were to Julia what patent medicines were to himself—quite impossible.

Mrs. Bickleigh was eight years older than her husband—forty-five to his thirty-seven. She was also a good two inches taller, for Dr. Bickleigh was an unusually small man.

A somewhat gaunt, erect woman, with frizzy dark hair and a thin-lipped mouth that twisted decidedly downwards at the corners, she had a quite unjoyful as well as a quite unlovely face; and she wore rimless *pince-nez, not* horn-rimmed spectacles, in front of her slightly prominent, pale-blue eyes. The two had been married ten years, and had no children.

When Florence had brought in the remains of a cold gooseberry-pie and departed again, Julia began to give her husband his instructions. "You'd better put the net up first; it sags so during the first half-hour. The new balls are in the cupboard under the stairs; we'll use them, of course, but you can give the old ones a rubbing on the hall mat as well. Then there are the two tables to be taken out, and the chairs, and I think we'll have the bathing-tent up as well in this sun. Then you'll have to ——"

"I don't think I shall be able to get all these things done," interrupted the doctor, with a doubtful air. "I ——"

"My dear Edmund, they've got to be done."

"Yes, but I haven't finished my round yet. Couldn't get them all in this morning. There are two more visits I must make."

Julia frowned. "Who?"

"Mrs. Parrot, and the Holne boy."

"They're not urgent."

"Not urgent, no; but quite serious enough."

"Not so serious as all that," pronounced Julia. "They can wait perfectly well. You can see them after the people have gone."

"But that won't be till after surgery-time, in any case."

"Then you'll have to see them after surgery," said Julia calmly, knocking his evening meal, as it were, out of her husband's mouth. "Have you finished? No, you've no time for cheese. Hurry, please, Edmund."

Dr. Bickleigh reflected that at any rate there would be

a good tea to-day. "Well, well, it's just as well we don't give tennis-parties every day," he said amiably enough, as he massaged his neat little moustache with his napkin and pushed back his chair.

Feeling better for his hurried meal, he put on his hat and went into the garden.

The tennis-posts were of an antiquated pattern, and the handle most difficult to wind as the net began to tauten. Julia had been repeating for several years that they must get new ones next season, but somehow there never seemed to be quite enough money for such an article of sheer luxury; and in any case, as she did not have to wind the net up herself, the matter was not very important to her. The doctor had to lean the whole of his meagre eight-and-a-half stones on the handle for the last turn or two to get the net to the required height. That feat accomplished, he stood back and wiped his forehead. He was not in good condition, and the winding of a tennis-net can be a strenuous business. Then, as always after any physical exertion, he touched carefully the waxed tips of his moustache.

The guests had been asked for half-past three, and it was now already a quarter to the hour. Glancing guiltily at his watch, Dr. Bickleigh hurried up the little bank that bounded the tennis-court on the side nearest the house, turning up the sleeves of his buff-coloured cotton shirt (with two collars to match) as he went. His neat blue coat was already hanging on one of the tennis-posts. Dr. Bickleigh invariably wore a blue serge suit for his work. Country practitioners who made their rounds in old tweed coats and shapeless flannel trousers always seemed to him to be letting down the dignity of the profession. Even to wind up the net and bring out the chairs Dr. Bickleigh wore a spotless grey trilby hat, with a turned-up and corded brim—a hat to which an advertisement-writer could have applied no other word but "natty."

As he brought out and set up the deck-chairs he tried to arrange in his mind the rest of his tasks in their best order. The bathing-tent had beter go up next, for the day was a blazing one and complexions are important things even in the country. Then it would be useless to start with only six balls if Benjie Torr was in the first set, for that morose young man had a gloomily vigorous style, and it was uncanny how he seemed to land balls right in the middle of the almost impenetrable gooseberry plantation in the kitchen-garden. Then the two collapsible tables would need to be up and bearing their quotas of cigarettes, matches, and glasses before the first people arrived, for nothing looks so bad as to bring these things out haphazard afterwards. (Dr. Bickleigh was almost as particular as his wife about things being done in the right way when guests were about.) It seemed to him that everything was just as urgent as everything else.

He was struggling with the bathing-tent when Julia came out of the house and joined him. "You've done the net, Edmund," she asserted; there was no need to ask, as the net was in position to answer for itself, but Mrs. Bickleigh never minded putting the obvious into words.

Dr. Bickleigh paused in his labours to agree that he had done the net.

"It's sagging already. You'd better tighten it up at once."

The doctor hurried over to the post and leaned on the handle. Julia was not satisfied till the net was raised a whole turn beyond what Dr. Bickleigh had secretly imagined to be the limit of his capacity.

Panting slightly, he rejoined her at the top of the bank.

Mrs. Bickleigh was surveying the rest of the court with a cold eye. "The lines don't look at all good. Did you tell Widdecombe to do them this morning?"

"I told him, distinctly. But you know what Widdecombe is, my dear."

"I do," replied Julia grimly. "He's scamped them, as usual." On a Saturday afternoon Widdecombe was no longer available to repair his omissions of the morning.

Dr. Bickleigh scrutinised the lines with an earnest frown. "I think he has done them, though. Yes, I'm sure he has."

"Only once, if at all. Dear me, it's a pity I can't be in a dozen places at once, to see to everything myself." Her tone rebuked her husband for being out on his rounds and unable to supervise the malingering Widdecombe from there. "Well, you'll have to run over them again yourself, Edmund, as soon as you've finished the other things."

"I'll try," said Dr. Bickleigh, a little doubtfully, for he had been wondering whether he would be able to get everything else done in time.

"Try? It must be done."

"Well, if it must, it must," at once agreed the little man, with his habitual amiability. "So I'd better get on with this confounded tent. It's being more of a nuisance than ever, of course."

Mrs. Bickleigh, whose immediate tasks had apparently been disposed of, walked off with her usual purposeful air to the rose-garden. The morning paper was under her arm. It occurred to neither of them that she should relieve her husband's congested time by doing the lines herself.

Before her marriage Mrs. Bickleigh had been a Crewstanton. She was, in everything but name, a Crewstanton still. She showed her husband so several times a day. During their short engagement she had informed her fiancé not once, but several times, with the air of one imparting interesting information, that her grandmother would have no more contemplated sitting down to a meal with her doctor than with her butler, and here was she, Julia, actually contemplating marrying one; it was really, Julia would point out with a short laugh, enough to make that grandmother turn in her grave; and Dr. Bickleigh agreed with her that it was. His wife had reminded him of this singular turn of fortune at frequent intervals ever since, and Dr. Bickleigh continued to express his sympathy for the feelings of the grandmother had she been alive to experience them.

For the Crewstantons, once one of the most important families in north Devonshire, had dwindled shockingly. Sir Charles, the twelfth baronet, had preferred to pay his crushing new taxes by selling piecemeal bits and slices of the wide Crewstanton lands instead of altering his way of living, and now inhabited with his other daughter a small villa on the outskirts of Torquay, where he was sinking angrily into the grave as fast as unlimited whiskey could help him—but not fast enough for his unmarried daughter.

The Crewstanton lands had gone. Three Crewstanton sons, who had been brought up with a valet apiece and unlimited small change, were vegetating miserably, one pretending to manage a banana estate in Jamaica, one making believe to be doing useful work in a surgical bandage firm in Derby, and one (the only one) putting his expensive education to good account by keeping himself in comparative comfort by his skill in bridge, billiards, and poker. Only the fourth, the youngest, had really made a success of his life; he had married a well-known actress, who was able to support him more or less in the style to which he had been accustomed.

Julia, offered the alternative of marriage with a man whom her grandmother could never have entertained at her own table, or joining her younger sister in the *ménage* at Torquay, then being seriously discussed as an impossible but inevitable future, had not hesitated for a moment.

Not that she had ever been grateful to Edmund. That she was thirty-five years old, had years ago parted with any hopes that she might ever have entertained of marriage, and possessed a face not unlike that of her own favourite horse (as her sister Hilda, a candid woman, immediately pointed out on learning of the engagement), weighed nothing against the fact that she was a Crewstanton. Julia had only one criterion, and that was birth. Any gratitude for the marriage—and how much gratitude was due perhaps only Julia could estimate—was owed by Edmund. And for the last ten years it was impossible to complain that Edmund had failed her in that respect.

II

The Bickleighs' tennis-party was to be quite an important event for Wyvern's Cross. In a community of not much more than a hundred souls the principal ones, the super-souls, are collected in a single gathering far less frequently than one might expect. Wyvern's Cross called itself a village, but it was little more than a hamlet; and within a two-mile radius of the cross-roads in its centre there were not more than twenty people whom one (one being Mrs. Bickleigh) could possibly invite to a tennis-party at one's house. On this occasion Mrs. Bickleigh invited them all. The Bickleighs had only one court, but out of those invited at least half did not play tennis at all. An invitation to tennis in rural England does not imply any ability to play the game; the dividing-line between those asked to tennis-parties and those not asked is a social, not an athletic one.

Naturally there was a reason for the unusual size of

this particular party. One does not ask close on twenty people whom one does not like without a reason. The reason was a Miss Madeleine Cranmere. Miss Cranmere had just taken The Hall (bought it outright, in fact, as everyone for miles around knew), after the latter had lain vacant for something like five years, ever since Colonel Swincombe's death and his daughter's discovery that her father's passion for rare bulbs had robbed her of the possibility of maintaining The Hall after he had left it. She had therefore retired to Brighton, where her feelings were unlikely to be harassed by the sight of a bulb again, and left The Hall to be let or sold. And now, after five whole years, Miss Madeleine Cranmere.

That was exciting enough in all conscience; but what made it almost unbearably more so was that Miss Cranmere was not only very rich, but not by any means ill-looking and quite young, and that she actually proposed to live at The Hall quite alone, without even a companion or an aunt. The Vicar, the Rev. Hessary Torr, was reputed to be distinctly concerned about it.

Miss Cranmere had been installed now for nearly a fortnight. Mrs. Bickleigh, as by right, had called at the earliest opportunity, and now she had organised this tennis-party to introduce the girl to such of her neighbours as she would be expected to know.

By a quarter to four the affair was in full progress.

The Torrs, as usual, had been the first to arrive. There were four Torrs—the Rev. Hessary and his wife, his daughter, Quarnian, and his son, Benjie. Where Mr. Torr led, Miss Wapsworthy and Miss Peavy were never far behind; they were the next arrivals. But neither played tennis, and the first set could not be arranged until the two young Ridgeways, Harford and his sister Ivy, made their appearance. Mrs. Bickleigh then deftly split the families (it was always Mrs. Bickleigh who arranged the sets at Fairlawn), and Quarnian Torr and Harford Ridgeway were sent to play Ivy Ridgeway and Benjie Torr. This set had been played at least fifty times before in Wyvern's Cross, and all four players knew that the former pair would beat the latter by six games to two. They always did; but the inevitability never made the least difference to Benjie losing his temper about it in the fifth game.

"Edmund," observed Mrs. Bickleigh, as the players strolled on to the court exchanging the stilted amiabilities of people who know each other exceedingly well meeting on a formal occasion. "Edmund, I know Mrs. Torr wants to see the roses first of all."

"Of course," beamed Dr. Bickleigh.

"Of course," echoed Mrs. Torr, rather less enthusiastically. She had walked up from the Vicarage, and her shoes were new and tight. She would much rather have sat down and rested first.

"You were telling me only the other day what a wonderful show you have this year, weren't you?" she hurried on, having intercepted a disapproving glance from her husband's fish-like but expressive eye. Of course, she remembered now; Hessary had said he wanted a few words with Mrs. Bickleigh privately; this would be an excellent opportunity, before the others arrived. "Yes, I shall be *most* interested. You've got some quite new kinds this year, haven't you, Dr. Bickleigh? Let me see——"

"And perhaps you'd like to take the opportunity too, Miss Wapsworthy, while my husband is free to show them to you properly?" Mrs. Bickleigh cut ruthlessly across Mrs. Torr's garrulity. "I know how interested you are. And you too, Miss Peavy."

Miss Wapsworthy, a tall, thin lady who wore a straw hat trimmed with very red roses on the extreme apex of her head, intimated that she would be glad to make use of such an opportunity, as indeed in social duty bound, though she somehow managed to preserve an air of her own independence in her agreement. Miss Peavy, on the other hand, was frankly intimidated, and looked it.

"Very well, Edmund," said Mrs. Bickleigh, with finality.

The quartette moved off.

In the rose-garden the little doctor pointed out with pride his new *Margaret McGredies* and *Mrs. van Rossems.* Roses were his hobby, and his infectious enthusiasm triumphed over Mrs. Torr's new shoes.

On the court, the third game being still in progress, Benjie Torr had not yet lost his temper. His lanky form, in interesting contrast to Harford Ridgeway's solid stolidity on the other side of the net, was still twisting actively if ineffectually, and had not yet begun to droop in the bitterness of defeat. Nor had the errors of Ivy, who managed to combine on a tennis-court a most pleasingly artless grace of movement with complete ineptitude at the game itself, so that she was both a joy and a grief to watch, had time so far to produce their usual exasperating effect on him. Ivy, in consequence, was playing a good deal better than she would be towards the end of the set.

Seated in state under the umbrella-top of the bathing-tent, Mrs. Bickleigh and the Rev. Hessary Torr were discussing the subject on which he had desired the two minutes of Mrs. Bickleigh's private conversation. "Really, this young woman whom we are to meet this afternoon . . . chrrrm-hrrrm . . . Miss Cranmere . . . It must be nearly four o'clock already."

"She's unpardonably late," said Mrs. Bickleigh resentfully, though several others besides Miss Cranmere had not yet appeared. The only fresh arrival since the set had begun was young Denny Bourne, down from Oxford the day before and very correct in an old Etonian blazer and shining flannels, who was helping Dr. Bickleigh retrieve the balls which Benjie, growing more wild with every minute as the iron of defeat seared deeper into his soul, was now despatching into the gooseberry-bushes with the despondent regularity of a machine-gun.

"One would really have thought on this occasion at least she would have taken the trouble to be punctual." Considering, added Mr. Torr's tones, that she must have known that *I* was to be here.

"You haven't met her yet?"

"No," said Mr. Torr, in his gravest voice. "I thought it better to give her a little more time to settle in before calling." He shook his massive head. "But if rumour is correct, I fear—yes, I fear that she must be a very odd young woman."

"She doesn't appear to be related to the Hampshire Cranmeres," snapped Mrs. Bickleigh, as if that in itself were very odd. "I've never heard of any others."

But Mr. Torr was not to be headed off the main track. "You really did gather that she intends to live at The Hall quite alone? Except, of course, for the servants. Yes, I feared so. A most equivocal position. *Most* equivocal. Chrrrm-hrrrm."

"I agree with you, Mr. Torr. It's not a thing one cares about at all, in this neighbourhood."

"She is quite young, I understand?"

"Quite. She can't be a day over twenty-two. I sounded her—tactfully, of course (I felt it my duty to all of us to do that much)—and I gathered that she has been an orphan for some years. Evidently she has just come into control of her own money, and it's turned her head."

"Very sad," clucked Mr. Torr. "Ve-ry sad."

"Someone will have to speak to her," pronounced Mrs. Bickleigh. "Not obviously (there's no need to be unkind;

doubtless it's nothing but thoughtlessness); but just to let her see what one feels."

"Precisely." Mr. Torr seemed relieved. "Precisely. That, in fact, is just what I had made up my mind must be done, Mrs. Bickleigh. I am delighted to hear you confirm it. The task is not one I should choose, but one has one's responsibilities. In my position . . . chrrrm-hrrrm!" Mr. Torr cleared his throat with grave and sober sonority, as befitted a man in his position.

"But do you think it quite a man's job?" For once Mrs. Bickleigh did not seem so decided. "Wouldn't it be better if . . . ?"

"My wife, you mean?" Mr. Torr's tone was unflatteringly dubious.

"Well, I had rather felt that the responsibility might, in a way, be considered mine. After all, one's upbringing . . . I could hint it to her quite nicely, you see, but without nonsense. I remember that my grandmother once had occasion—Lady Denbury, I mean, not Lady Crewstanton . . ."

Mrs. Bickleigh looked extremely serious. Mr. Torr looked extremely serious too. Their tongues worked busily.

The clacking of them reached Quarnian Torr on the tennis-court as she was about to serve in the final game. To her partner, as he supplied her with balls, she remarked: "Daddy seems to have properly got off with that ghastly woman."

III

Before Mrs. Bickleigh and Mr. Torr could decide who was to voice their displeasure to the unconventional Miss Cranmere everything began to happen at once, as it always does after such peaceful interludes. The set came to an end; the two ladies whom Mrs. Torr had determinedly held in the rose-garden while her reverend lord had his private conversation were at last released, and streaked for the deck-chairs and the shade like two terriers let off the leash; Dennis Bourne and Dr. Bickleigh retrieved the last ball from the gooseberry-bushes and strolled back to the court; and Mr. Chatford arrived, a solicitor who practised in neighbouring Merchester but lived alone, a bachelor, in Wyvern's Cross.

"Well, how shall we play now?" said Dr. Bickleigh, removing his hat for a moment to apply a handkerchief delicately to his brow, but still amiable even towards Benjie. "Let's see. Gwynyfryd hasn't turned up yet, so it looks as if you, Quarnian, and Ivy, will have to play again." Miss Wapsworthy had passed the age when she could appear on a tennis-court; and, though Miss Peavy did not privately think that she had, it had been borne in upon her that others did.

"Here come the Davys," said someone, as a couple came into sight round the angle of the house.

"Come along, Mrs. Davy," called the doctor jovially, waving his racket. "You're just in time. We want you."

"Then you can have a men's four," said Mrs. Bickleigh, in her decisive tones, just as if her husband had not spoken at all. "Mr. Davy and Dennis against Benjie and Harford."

"Rather sit out, if you don't mind," mumbled Benjie sulkily. "Can't hit a ball to-day. Dr. Bickleigh play instead of me."

"Nonsense, Benjie," retorted Mrs. Bickleigh, regardless of maternal feelings. "You only played badly because you were losing."

"You play, Benjie, my boy," Dr. Bickleigh smiled, clapping him on the back. "Enjoy yourself while you're young."

"I'd rather sit out this time, really, Mrs. Bickleigh,"

pleaded Harford Ridgeway, whose solid flesh did look as if it was doing its best to melt. "That set quite exhausted me."

"Very well, Edmund," said Mrs. Bickleigh, accepting this excuse. "You can play, then."

The four men took off their coats, and the others regrouped themselves.

Harford Ridgeway found himself in a deck-chair beside Quarnian Torr, at a safe distance from their elders. He was an engineer, with a post in a large firm at Middlesbrough, now in Wyvern's Cross for part of his holidays.

Quite inevitably the conversation turned in the direction of Mrs. Bickleigh. Harford, a charitable soul, murmured something about the lady not being so bad when you knew her.

Quarnian at once dealt with this suggestion. "My dear Harford, you know perfectly well how she caught poor little Teddy." She explained the process in detail.

Harford shifted uneasily. Quarnian had a raucous voice.

"And anyhow," she summed up, "Teddy's much too sweet for her. He really is rather sweet, isn't he?"

"Is he? I think he's an awful little worm."

"Oh! Well, ask Ivy what she thinks," observed Miss Torr maliciously. "And, anyhow"—she defended her sex—"most people do like him. He's awfully popular round here, you know. You're jealous, that's all."

"Jealous? Good Lord, why?"

"Well, he and Ivy were rather thick at one time. But of course," added Miss Torr hastily, seeing her companion's frown, "that's all over now. Teddy's got eyes for no one but Gwynyfryd Rattery nowadays."

"Gwynyfryd?" repeated Harford in surprise. "But she isn't even here."

"No, and that's why Teddy's looking so glum."

"Oh, rot, Quarnian," said young Mr. Ridgeway, with

the discomfort of the average male before the almost pathological zest for gossip which the English countryside seems to evoke in certain female breasts. "You're making this up."

Miss Torr proceeded, with energy and examples, to rebut this charge.

In the meantime the rest of the party were still waiting, and now with undisguised impatience, for Miss Madeleine Cranmere.

Besides the Davys, a London novelist in search of Devonshire local colour, and his wife, temporary visitors only to Wyvern's Cross, one person alone was indifferent to Miss Cranmere's remarkable absence. Dr. Bickleigh did not care in the least whether she ever came or not. He was waiting, with an impatience that had almost reached bursting-point, for Gwynyfryd Rattery.

IV

At twenty minutes past four Madeleine Cranmere arrived. She had a reasonable explanation. Her car had refused to start, and the combined attempts of her two gardeners and herself, none of whom knew the least thing about dealing with refractory cars, had produced no impression on it until a quarter of an hour ago; then, intimidated apparently by the growing wrath of the head gardener, the car had been cowed into starting as mysteriously as it had before refused.

Miss Cranmere recounted this story with such seriousness, and accompanied it with such a reiteration of earnest apologies, not only to her hostess, but to the other people who really mattered, such as Miss Wapsworthy and Mr. Torr, that the unfavourable feeling which her non-arrival had caused was not only wiped out, but actually gave place to a positively favourable one. Even Mr. Torr, who had been disposed to be quite stiff, found his disapproval thawing before the melting appeal of Miss Cranmere's enormous grey eyes, which mutely implored *his* forgiveness at any rate. She had then undergone the ordeal of introduction to a dozen complete strangers, all ready to be more than critical, with a grave appreciation of the seriousness of the occasion which impressed everyone.

"Miss Cranmere," confided Mr. Davy to Miss Peavy, "is evidently one of those fortunate people who can make every stranger feel that he or she is the person they've been longing in secret all their lives to meet."

"Oh, yes, I do agree," elaborately mouthed Miss Peavy, though the subject of their conversation was at least thirty yards away. "I think she'll be a *great* asset to us. I think she's *so* nice."

Miss Wapsworthy, the third member of the trio, sniffed. It was well known that Adela Peavy was foolish enough to think everyone nice at first sight. But even Miss Wapsworthy did not sniff with quite so much conviction as usual.

The men's four being now over, Mrs. Bickleigh gave the word for tea, and they all trooped into the house together, to crowd with exaggerated cheerfulness into the not very large drawing-room. As they went, Mr. Torr managed to confide to his hostess that Miss Cranmere was very different from what he had expected; very different indeed; quite a sensible young woman; none of the modern flightiness that he had feared; an old-fashioned type of a gairl, such as it was a pleasure nowadays to see. Mrs. Bickleigh went so far as to agree that if any gairl could live alone at The Hall without disgracing the neighbourhood, it really did seem as if Miss Cranmere might be the one.

Gradually people sorted themselves out in the drawing-room. Extra chairs had been brought in from the dining-room, but even then some of the men had to stand. Dapper in his blue coat and white flannels, Dr. Bickleigh was very active. "Edmund!" called his wife if he lingered to exchange more than a bare word with anyone before all were supplied with tea, and back he would dart to collect from the tray in front of her two more cups. The other men were doing their share too, but Dr. Bickleigh carried more cups than any two put together.

"Dr. Bickleigh!" Mrs. Torr shook an arch finger at him across the room. "I've hardly had a word with you all the afternoon. You must come and tell me all the news, you really must. The doctor always knows so much more about what's going on in the parish than the vicar, doesn't he?" This was a somewhat unfortunate remark, for Mr. Torr was notoriously the last person ever to know what was going on under his own nose or within his own circle of duties. The Rev. Hessary Torr was inclined to take himself rather more seriously than his duties.

"Mother putting her foot in it as usual," confided Quarnian to young Dennis Bourne, who was offering her a plate of fish-paste sandwiches with perfect deportment. Young Mr. Bourne raised his eyebrows just a quarter of an inch, and let it go at that. As the only son of Sir John Bourne, the local M.F.H., squirearch and general father of the community, Denny had cultivated the art of eyebrow-lifting to a nicety.

"For instance, how is old Mrs. Brent getting on?" Mrs. Torr was asking hastily, as if conscious herself that her last remark was not altogether a happy one.

"Oh, much better this morning," beamed the little doctor, as he edged through the throng towards her. "In fact, she ——"

"Edmund!"

"Excuse me, Mrs. Torr. Rather a busy moment, just now." He spun round and hurried back to duty.

"*Such* a nice man," prattled Mrs. Torr to Mary Davy, whom she had adopted by now as Best Friend for the afternoon. (Mr. Torr had already appropriated Miss Cranmere, whom he was feeding now with earnest intensity on little pink cakes, which she accepted from him as one being vouchsafed manna from a Being.) "Of course, Mrs. Bickleigh is very nice too," babbled Mrs. Torr, whom that lady frightened half out of her wits and who would willingly walk a mile out of her way in new shoes to avoid her. "Oh, charming. But really, the doctor . . . Well, my dear, I always say that he . . ."

"Will you be like that when you're married, Denny?" giggled Quarnian. "No, don't go; I want another of those. I bet you won't."

"Like what?" coldly queried Dennis Bourne, sadly conscious that his eyebrows for once had failed. Yet three years ago, at Eton, he had only to raise them less than that and . . . Dennis did not like Quarnian. Nor did he like being called Denny, a shameful relic of his nursery days.

"At your wife's beck and call every minute."

"I really can't tell you, Quarnian." And Dennis bore his plate of sandwiches away with the slightly abstracted air of a man about to go and talk with someone about something pretty serious.

The two Ridgeways, as usual in a crowd, had gravitated together, where they would stand side by side and say nothing, Harford stolidly, Ivy a little fearfully.

She was a pretty little thing, in a rather indeterminate way, with lots of fair, very soft hair that curled naturally away from her small head, and big, frightened blue eyes; her figure was slight and delicately boned, and she conveyed an impression of startled fragility in almost ludicrous contrast with her brother's massive stolidity.

From time to time she was unable to resist throwing an

occasional appealing glance in the direction where Dr. Bickleigh was talking with Peter Davy, but the former was evidently too busy with his important guest to be able to come over to them. Mr. Chatford, however, attached himself, and began to make somewhat stilted conversation. He was a dark-browed, intensely shaven man, with a highly professional manner even in private life, who spent his time trying to make himself and everyone else forget that he had originally joined the firm, in which he was now the sole partner, as its office-boy. Being now reckoned the best solicitor in his own district of north Devon, he was in a fair way to succeed in this aim.

To this little group in due course added himself Benjie Torr, addressing himself exclusively to Ivy. By imperceptible degrees, so naturally that nobody but Mr. Chatford could have said how it had come about, the quartette, still talking amicably, split into two pairs, having no connection with each other at all; and one of the two pairs was Harford and Benjie, and the other was Ivy and Mr. Chatford. Mr. Chatford was like that.

Dr. Bickleigh was listening to black-spot, talking black-spot, and apparently thinking exclusively in terms of black-spot. No one could have guessed that all the time his ear was cocked towards the front door, listening for the sound of a car or a bell.

Yet, preoccupied though he was, Dr. Bickleigh had not been too much so to throw an observant eye over the newcomer. No new feminine arrival could escape that.

On this occasion he was frankly disappointed. He had expected a pretty girl; Madeleine Cranmere was nothing of the sort. She was not exactly plain, she was just nondescript. Except for her eyes. They really were beautiful. But her mouth was too wide, her face too sallow, her cheek-bones too high for prettiness, and such of her black hair as could be seen under her hat looked positively dank.

Her figure was good, fairly tall, slender, and straight, but Dr. Bickleigh was shocked to observe that she dressed quite appallingly. Dress was most important, in Dr. Bickleigh's opinion, and for a wealthy young girl to appear on an occasion of such importance in a most uninteresting white frock, obviously not new and looking suspiciously home-made, frankly cotton stockings, a hat that was nothing but dowdy, and nondescript shoes, struck him as little less than an outrage. He dismissed Miss Cranmere as impossible, from all points of view.

"Edmund!" said Mrs. Bickleigh loudly and distinctly. "Mr. Torr has nothing to eat. Do please remember to look after your guests."

Dr. Bickleigh started, broke off in mid-sentence, and hurried across the room to minister to the Rev. Hessary's fleshly needs.

V

Gwynyfryd Rattery did not arrive until the middle of the second set after tea, when Dr. Bickleigh had given up in despair all hope of ever seeing her again. Her excuses were unusual but, to those who knew her father, not unreasonable. Major Rattery invariably insisted on a set of tennis immediately after tea, to keep himself fit. As he refused with equal vehemence to take this exercise anywhere but on his own court and with his own daughter, Gwynyfryd had been unable to leave until she had afforded it to him. That she should not have told her unreasonable parent to whistle for his game if he could not take it at a less selfish time appeared to surprise nobody present except Quarnian.

Physically, Gwynyfryd Rattery was a fine creature. Twenty-four years old, she was tall and well made, and she played a better game of tennis than any other woman in the neighbourhood—a hard hitter with a graceful style. As for her looks, to those who could appreciate them she was not merely striking, but beautiful; her slightly slanting, green-grey eyes, clouds of hair of the real Titian tint, and the milky skin that often accompanies it, were a real joy to look at. They hinted, too, at a full-blooded zest for life which her tennis seemed to confirm. Her manner was in direct contradiction. She minced; she looked down her pretty, straight nose; she was so excessively lady-like that butter would obviously not melt even in her flaming hair.

On Dr. Bickleigh Gwynyfryd had always had a disquieting effect. She frightened him, of course; all girls did that, till he knew them thoroughly. But he could not begin to understand her. He longed to approach her, but could not decide on the way. She seemed utterly sexless, but her appearance made it seem unlikely that she really could be so. Yet Dr. Bickleigh knew that she did not attract the average young man of the district. All the other girls, even Quarnian Torr, seemed to be continually marching in a procession of fresh flirtations, but the name of no youth was ever mentioned seriously by the district scandalmongers in connection with Gwynyfryd's.

Without quite being able to diagnose the cause of this lack of enterprise on the part of Wyvern's Cross's young men beyond the extreme primness of Miss Rattery's public manner, Dr. Bickleigh was able to feel something about her so a-sexual, so frigidly virginal, so repellent in advance of any tentative overtures, that he had simply not dared to put his luck to the trial with her; for it was just this a-sexuality, this cold, intelligent virginity that froze the hearty marrow of the others, which kept Dr. Bickleigh fluttering helplessly round the lamp of Miss Rattery's hair. A dozen times in the last three years he had decided that he would never approach her (he was morbidly sensitive to feminine snubs), a dozen times he had decided afresh that he *must* do something about it—if only once and for all, then once and for all. Meantime he had prepared his path as well as he could by ceaseless attentions when they met in public, a more exquisite deference than he accorded to any other woman, a smile occasionally across a crowded room as if they had some small intimacy in common, a host of other little touches to show Gwynyfryd that he was interested, very respectfully but very intensely, in her good self. And it had seemed to him that during the last month or two Gwynyfryd had responded to this treatment.

Dr. Bickleigh was quite genuine in his feelings. He did not doubt that he was deeply in love with Gwynyfryd, and that she was the one woman in the world whom he ought to have married. The fact that he had been looking for this one woman so long made his discovery of her all the more poignant; the fact that he had been certain so often before of having found her elsewhere did not affect the matter in the least.

He had determined at last to stake his luck, for once and for all, this very afternoon.

His opportunity he had prepared carefully in advance. Under his tuition Gwynyfryd was developing an interest in horticulture. He had arranged to have some *hydrangea hortensia* cuttings ready for her to take this afternoon. That June is not the best time of year to take hydrangea cuttings he had not mentioned. The cuttings were waiting ready in a tool-shed in the farthest corner of the garden.

His heart thumped a little as he said, casually enough, after the greetings and explanations were over and before Gwynyfryd had settled herself into a chair: "By the way, I've got those cuttings ready for you, Gwynyfryd."

"Oo, yerss?" said Gwynyfryd, in her most ladylike tones.

"You'd better take them now, while you're free. Would you like to come along and look them over?"

Not waiting for her answer, he led the way with nervous haste, and escaping his wife's observation, by the shortest route that would take them out of sight of the tennis-lawn. Gwynyfryd followed him. The kitchen-garden, where was the tool-shed, was on the farther side of the house. Dr. Bickleigh did not pause to let Gwynyfryd come abreast of him till he had reached the shelter of the latter.

If Gwynyfryd was surprised that the cuttings should be in the tool-shed instead of the greenhouse she did not show it; she walked in without hesitation as her companion opened the door for her. His heart now thumping so violently as to make him almost breathless, Dr. Bickleigh began in stifled tones to point out the merits of *hydrangea hortensia.* He dwelt on his subject at inordinate length; he repeated himself, stammered, asked foolish, temporising questions; the familiar longing to come to the real point and dread of doing so had him in its grip; he sweated with nervousness.

It was Gwynyfryd herself who finally gave him his cue. "Is that your heart beating?" she asked incredulously. "Ay can hear it from here."

Whether this was innocence or provocation Dr. Bickleigh was in too much confusion to ask himself. He stumbled blindly for the opening. "Well—can you wonder?" he muttered, and tried clumsily to embrace her. In spite of his experience, Dr. Bickleigh had little finesse.

"Dr. Bickleigh!" exclaimed Gwynyfryd in shocked tones. "What are you doing?" She had little difficulty in extracting herself from the little man's clasp, but her alarm seemed unabated.

Dr. Bickleigh followed her as she backed into the farther corner of the tool-shed. He did not know quite what he was saying or doing. "Gwynyfryd—you know I like you frightfully."

"Ay don't."

"Well, I do. You must have seen it."

"Ay—Ay've never thought of you—like that, at all."

"I like you better than anyone I've ever known."

"You say that to every girl."

"I don't."

"You do."

"I swear I don't." A conversation is never so utterly banal as when its participants are at their most tense. "Gwynyfryd!"

"What?"

"Just let me—kiss you."

"Noo!"

"Why not?"

"Ay—don't want you to."

"But why not?"

"Ay would never come between husband and wife," said Miss Rattery, clutching at her primness. She was almost in nervous tears.

"But I like you so dreadfully. Listen, Gwynyfryd: I love you."

"You don't. Ay won't listen, Dr. Bickleigh."

"Oh, don't call me Dr. Bickleigh. Call me Teddy."

"Let me goo, please. You must let me goo."

"Well, just let me kiss you first," repeated Dr. Bickleigh doggedly. Even now he felt his self-respect could be salved if she would do that. He no longer wanted the physical contact, merely the mental satisfaction.

"Ay will not."

"Have you ever been kissed, Gwynyfryd?"

"You've no right to ask me things like that."

"I have. I love you."

"Ay'm gooing." Ignominiously she pushed the little man aside by main force and hurried out of the shed, her face crimson.

"Gwynyfryd! You mustn't —— The cuttings . . . Only give things away."

She took them without looking at him, and they walked back in silence, both breathing as if they had run a long race. The bitterness of defeat—not even glorious defeat, with a slapped face and unwilling lips masterfully kissed, but defeat ignominious beyond words—oppressed the doctor.

"Is it quite hopeless, Gwynyfryd?" he ventured once.

"Ay can't think how you *dared*!" she blazed at him.

By the time they reached the court Miss Rattery had partially recovered her control. Dr. Bickleigh, on the other hand, had come nearer to losing his than ever. A slow anger was burning in him, growing steadily every moment, an all-embracing anger directed as much at himself as at his companion. Gwynyfryd was just a fool. What time and genuine sentiment he had been wasting on her. Come between husband and wife for a kiss, indeed! Good Lord, how he had been taken in. Why, there was more even in Ivy, silly little eternally crying Ivy, than there was in this piece of conceited affectation. And he had thought her sensible, understanding, possessed of brains instead of the usual feminine fluff! Yes, *he* was the fool.

Mrs. Bickleigh had noticed their absence. She knew her husband, and contempt sharpened her voice. "Oh, there you are, Edmund. I've been wanting you."

"Yes, my dear?" To all appearances Dr. Bickleigh was perfectly normal. The two little spots of red that burned on his cheek-bones were too tiny to be noticed.

"They're a ball short. Benjie hit one into the gooseberry-bushes again. Please go and find it at once." She spoke with more than her usual peremptoriness, and her loud, grating voice could not have failed to reach every ear. The men looked most uncomfortable. Each of them had volunteered to look for the ball, and all had been told it was their host's task, and his only. The same thought was obvious now on all their faces: "I'm hanged if I'd speak to a dog like that." Dr. Bickleigh felt his wife's tone and what lay behind it, and he felt his guests' reactions to it. The two tiny spots of colour on his cheekbones spread a little.

And then—Gwynyfryd Rattery laughed.

It was, had Dr. Bickleigh been able to recognise it, only the meaningless laughter of overwrought nerves. But he did not recognise it. What he heard was the mocking of the whole world, the traditional mocking at the insignificant, henpecked husband. And Gwynyfryd, whose respect he had so particularly wanted, whose understanding he had coveted so hungrily, had ranged herself with the mockers.

He turned on his heel, his whole face flaming; and every atom of his varied emotions leapt suddenly into overmastering hatred of his wife. "My God," he muttered to himself, as he strode round the end of the court, his small body taut with anger. "My God, I can't stand this much longer. I wish she was *dead*. My God, I wish I could *kill* her."

Chapter Two

I

To INDICATE Dr. Edmund Bickleigh at the age of thirty-seven it is necessary to lay emphasis first and last upon his size. The smallness of Dr. Bickleigh's stature was responsible for almost everything that he then was, and had been ever since he first realised that he was not going to grow any more and would have to go through life looking up at nearly all men and quite a number of women. His height was five feet seven inches in his boots.

Physical appearance plays a larger part in the formation of character than is always recognised. Some small bodily defect—an unusually large foot, slightly projecting teeth—is quite enough to turn one who would otherwise have been a perfectly normally balanced person into an awkward hypersensitive, and not on this one point alone. Small men are always either perkily bumptious, which generally means an entire lack of imagination, or else quite unnecessarily humble.

In these days of glib reference to complexes, repressions, and fixations on every layman's lips, it is not to be supposed that Dr. Bickleigh did not know what was the matter with him. He could diagnose an inferiority complex, and a pronounced one at that, as well as anyone else. But to diagnose is not to cure. Absurd though he could easily prove it to be, Dr. Bickleigh continued to feel uncouth in the presence of women, insignificant in the presence of men, and an inferior being in every way to each fresh stranger he met. Only when alone could he realise that he was quite as good as anyone else in this world, and possibly a little better.

His upbringing had contributed to this state of affairs. The son of a chemist in a small way in one of the midland towns, Dr. Bickleigh had begun his career by helping in his father's shop. Educated at the local grammar school, with a couple of years to follow at one of the very minor universities, he had then been sent by his father (who all his life had been saving every possibly superfluous penny for this purpose) to a Scotch hospital, where expenses are less than at the English ones. There he had qualified—not brilliantly, but quite competently.

But an L.R.C.P., young Bickleigh was soon to discover, does not necessarily a gentleman make, nor an M.R.C.S. a grandfather. In the atmosphere of the small Devonshire practice which his father bought for him with the last of his savings and a mortgage on the shop as well, and which Dr. Bickleigh had been working up with more than fair success ever since, birth counted for everything and achievement nothing. That he had been able by his own ability to lift himself out of his old plane, and mix on terms of social equality with the kind of people whom he had once served from the other side of the counter, gradually became less and less remarkable; while the fact that he had been born on the wrong side of that counter grew more and more oppressive.

Surrounded by public-school men, he was not a public-school man himself; rubbing shoulders every day with men who had been up at Oxford or Cambridge, he had been up at neither; meeting on his own level nobody who could not produce at least three generations of gentle ancestors, he could carry his own gentility no further back than his own person; married to someone who by all the canons of his friends, his acquaintances, and even the humblest of his cottage patients, was a Somebody, he was a Nobody. The invariable question about a stranger was, "Who is he?" not, "What has he done?" It was the only criterion.

A man with the self-confidence born of physical largeness might have resisted this assumption; might have been driven towards a mental arrogance or simply have laughed at it, according to his possession or not of a sense of humour; Dr. Bickleigh inevitably came to accept it. His father, whose vehemence in the opposite direction might have gone some little way to restore the balance, was dead now, and Dr. Bickleigh lived in continual dread that somebody who had known him and his position might appear in Wyvern's Cross and denounce his son. Even Julia Bickleigh supposed her husband to be at least the son of a doctor, and had never searched a medical directory of ancient date to disclose his perfidy.

What stature and upbringing had begun, marriage perfected. To be informed—not openly, indeed, but by unmistakable innuendo—day in and day out for ten years, and by someone who regards the fact almost as an axiom of existence, that one is a worm, cannot but make a person, inclined already to attach more weight to the opinions of others than to his own, come in time to believe in the idea as firmly as its expositor.

Dr. Bickleigh's reactions to his wormhood were perfectly normal. He accepted it as one accepts a scar on the face. It was a pity, but there it was and it could not be helped. He was not in the least morbid about it. He knew he was popular in the neighbourhood, for instance, worm or no worm, and that pleased him very much; for, like all of us, however superior we may pretend to be about it, he liked to be liked by the people he liked—and he did like most people. He remained more or less what he had always been, a cheerful soul, gregarious, ready to be amused by the simplest means, always willing to do anything for anybody at a moment's notice. With men he got on quite well; with women (to his own recurrent astonishment) better. Dr. Bickleigh had been getting on well with women for over twenty years now, but he was still as astonished about it as he had been when he found himself permitted to kiss his first girl—a giggling creature who implored him to give over, and showed every sign of wanting anything in the world rather than to be kissed by him, yet seemed most strangely annoyed when he acceded to her earnest request to be let go, so that he had to begin the whole nerve-racking business all over again.

To meet him in the ordinary way, then, one would have said that Dr. Bickleigh was as simple, normal a human being as one could find in Devonshire. And so, practically speaking, he was. An inferiority complex, so far from being anything remarkable, is, it would seem, the normal state of affairs; it is its absence which is remarkable, or at any rate the possession of its opposite; for apparently one must have one or the other.

It was only in his relations with women that the little man's bias really found any expression.

Women did not exactly terrify Dr. Bickleigh, but for some reason (traceable, no doubt we should be told, to some incident in infancy) he was far less at his ease with them than with men. He felt more than ordinarily insignificant in their presence. His wife, of course, had a perfect knack, by the mere inflection of a word or lift of an eyebrow, of making him feel quite inexpressibly small; a twist of her lip, and he would know that his evening clothes, so far from improving him, made him look just like a counter-jumper dressed up; a gleam in her eye, and he would realise that his pretensions to gentility were grotesque, that he never had been and never could be anything but an interloper in his own house. But that was a special case. Generally speaking, women were to him, somehow or other by mere virtue of their sex alone, a superior kind of being, simply by being different; for to be different from Dr. Bickleigh was usually, in that particular point, to be superior to him.

The result was curious. He was compelled to pursue them. Sheer masculinity, of which in spite of everything, he had his share, drove him on. He could tolerate his inferiority where other men were concerned, for, after all, the male criterion is almost always a physical one, and the result is out of one's own control; but inferiority to women was unbearable. Perhaps he never realised this with full consciousness, but that made little difference: he pursued women unceasingly, doggedly, and resentfully.

There was little gladness in his hunting. The chase filled him more often with dread than with zest. But he simply could not help himself. Something far stronger than his own wishes seemed to be driving him on. It was an urge rooted so deeply in his primitive masculinity, swollen and strengthened so much by brute-nature in reaction from the timidity of his civilised mind, that he was totally unable to resist it. With every passably attractive woman with whom he was brought into contact he just had to try to flirt. Nearly always a kiss was all that he aimed for, more rarely some closer intimacy. Having achieved it, he was satisfied. His outraged male honour was appeased.

Victory was sometimes sweet to him, more often not. Frequently he did not even want it when it was in sight, but had to take it because it would be impolite at that stage to draw back; and very often because he was simply unable to believe that he could win it until he had actually done so. As a fact, victory usually did come to him (he always thought of it as a victory, never that perhaps the lady had wanted herself to be kissed), but that gave him no more confidence so far as the rest of the sex was concerned: each new affair seemed more impossible of success than the last.

It would be unfair to Dr. Bickleigh to let it be thought that he invariably embarked on these episodes in a spirit of weak revenge, or of sexual adventure either. That may be true of the less important incidents, but his major affairs always had a quite sincere basis. It was that he felt that at last he had met the one woman he really ought to have married. He was not looking for this one woman actively, because, even if he did find her, what would be the use? Julia would never give him the chance of divorcing her, and a country doctor with a practice to consider cannot afford to be divorced himself. It was simply that fate had brought them together. This happened about once in every eighteen months, and each time Dr. Bickleigh discovered with regret that fate had made another mistake.

Of course, it was his unfortunate complex which had brought him into marriage with Julia. Julia was an important person at that time. She was very nearly a Personage. Dr. Bickleigh knew as well as he knew anything that she would never tolerate him in her father's house at all, except on professional terms: but she did. He knew she would never, never condescend to become his friend: but she did. It was inconceivable that she would ever tolerate a few terrified familiarities: but she did. He did not love her; she had no attraction in herself for him at all; he did not even like her much. But if he could actually aspire (he hardly dared even to formulate the thought in his own mind) to *marry* her, just aspire—why, then it would be impossible that he could be an insignificant person at all; on the contrary, he would be highly significant. Of course, it was too ludicrous; not for a moment would Julia even contemplate such a preposterous thing.

But she did: and Dr. Bickleigh found himself even more insignificant than before.

From the beginning they had separate rooms. Julia was not disposed to be a dutiful wife, and Dr. Bickleigh did not particularly want her to be: Julia was the sort of person who would be dictatorial even in bed. So far as his wife was concerned, he had been sexually starved for the last ten years, and a lot may be forgiven a man in such conditions as those—though not, needless to say, by the wife in question.

Once again, then, even including his relations with women Dr. Bickleigh was very little removed from the perfectly average man. The normal man's attitude towards women is far, far more complicated than those women ever suppose, or than theirs towards him—interlaced with totally conflicting likes and dislikes, self-contradictory, altogether much more illogical and irrational than anything of that kind which he has ever deplored in the women themselves.

II

Dr. Bickleigh had a habit which he would have died rather than confess to another living soul. It was both as dear and as shameful to him as a monster-child to its mother. He used to soothe himself into sleep each night with what he thought of as his "visions."

These were the most meticulous mental pictures of some situation of high importance of which Dr. Bickleigh himself was the core and centre. He would roll over on his right side in his single bed, hitch the pillow under his shoulder, curl up a little more compactly in sheer luxury of bodily rest, and then think to himself: "Well, now, what shall we do to-night? What about a little cricket?"

And then for ten minutes he would follow with his

mind's eyes a series of little pictures showing Dr. Bickleigh being selected to play for England in the last test-match to decide the rubber; the papers indignantly asking, "Who is Edmund Bickleigh?"; Australia going in first and making 637; England all out for 46; the follow-on, and nine wickets down for 32; Dr. Edmund Bickleigh last man in, followed by the hoots and jeers of the ignorant crowd; a terrific hit for six right over the pavilion at Lord's; "My God, but this man can hit!"; another, and another, among the frantic cheering of that same crowd, the batting all that day and half the next, with a six every other ball, bagging the bowling all the time; the other man out at last; "Edmund Bickleigh, 645 not out"; "My God, he's actually made more than the whole Australian eleven"; and then Australia's second innings, and their crack batsmen clean bowled one after the other by Edmund Bickleigh's unplayable off-breaks; till England, thanks entirely to Edmund Bickleigh, finally wins by the margin of three runs; "Dr. Bickleigh, you have saved England." But by that time Dr. Bickleigh would be comfortably and happily asleep.

That was his favourite vision, though being summoned to Buckingham Palace ran it close ("Your Majesty, there is only one man in the world who can perform this terrible operation on you with any hope at all, but if it is not performed you will certainly die." "And who is that, Sir Godfrey?" "A brilliant surgeon called Edmund Bickleigh, your Majesty. He elects to bury himself at Wyvern's Cross, in Devonshire, disguising his genius under the guise of a general practitioner; but we who know him know that he is the greatest surgeon of this and all time." "Send for him, Sir Godfrey." . . . "Dr. Bickleigh, you realise? The King's life is in your hands." "I can but do my best, Sir Godfrey." . . . "Marvellous! Stupendous! Not another man could have done it. Dr. Bickleigh, England owes you a debt of gratitude which . . ." "Rise, Lord Bickleigh of Wyvern. . . .").

There were other stock favourites: Wimbledon, Bickleigh's Symphony in C minor, the Bickleigh exhibition at Burlington House ("Bickleigh may owe something of his masterly technique to Rembrandt, but the brilliant manner in which he has transmuted it to his own purposes is all his own. We venture to assert that never before has the world been made to realise what effects are possible to genius armed with a mere palette and . . ."), the Collected Works of Edmund Bickleigh, the Open Golf Championship, the B.B.C. series of Bickleigh concerts, the war ("Field-Marshal Bickleigh, it is known now, enlisted on the day war broke out as a humble private; the first occasion on which he won the V.C. was . . ."), Bickleigh the Great Lover, and the rest of them. And there were the temporary visions, applied to situations of the moment.

On the night before the tennis-party, for instance, Dr. Bickleigh spent a happy fifteen minutes living in advance the scene in the tool-shed on the following afternoon: the masterful shutting of the door, the bold yet respectful and evidently sincere little speech, "Gwynyfryd, you must have seen that my feelings towards you are . . ."; Gwynyfryd's shy delight, "Oh, Edmund—Teddy! Yes, my dear, of course I love you too. I—oh, Teddy, I adore you. . . ." Her yielding, the feel of her slim body in his arms, the scent of her hair, her lips.

That was the last time this particular vision was enjoyed. Dr. Bickleigh never pursued an affair over an initial rebuff. The affair of Gwynyfryd Rattery ended with its beginning, in a violent revulsion. From imagining himself in love with the girl, Dr. Bickleigh now saw her as merely to be despised: not hated, she was not worth that. To the suggestion that Gwynyfryd might have despised him first, his eyes were firmly shut. Even to himself he refused to admit the possibility of lacerated pride (to do so would have been to rub salt into the already smarting wound), and anointed his hurt with the ointment of contempt. The girl was a fool: just a fool. To have credited such a feminine clod with the finer perceptions was now merely amusing. Oh, it was very obvious that Gwynyfryd was certainly not the girl he should have married. Even Julia —well, Julia had sense, at any rate. "Come between husband and wife" for a kiss, indeed. The conceit of the girl! As if a kiss of Gwynyfryd's was so . . .

But the sequel remained. Dr. Bickleigh definitely longed for his wife to be dead.

On the night of the tennis-party a new vision was inaugurated. He saw his life without Julia: the freedom, the expansion, the regained self-respect, the losing of that continual dread of what she might say in front of other people, the incredible peace. It kept him awake for over two hours.

The next night he did the same, and the next.

Gradually life without Julia edged its way into the stock visions. Within a few weeks the details were complete—Julia taken ill, Julia sinking under some malignant disease, Julia on her death-bed, Julia apologising with her last breaths for the hard, cruel woman she had been, Julia dead, Julia's funeral, the house without Julia, the garden without Julia, life without Julia. . . .

For nights and nights he did not play cricket once.

III

Dr. Bickleigh had a great respect for Mr. Torr. Mr. Torr had not married for position, he had that himself and plenty of it; he had married for money—or, at any rate, he had, as it were, absent-mindedly married where money was. Mrs. Torr was the daughter of a neighbouring brewer, and the living of Wyvern's Cross had been in the brewer's gift; it was a fat living, and there was very little work to do for it. Dr. Bickleigh considered that Mr. Torr had made a success of life.

Mr. Torr, too, was a person of some importance. At Oxford his career had been noteworthy. A member of a very small and choice circle, he had been considered on an intellectual level with the most brilliant. Most of the University prizes had fallen to this circle, and Mr. Torr had had his share of them. A remarkable future had been prophesied for him, as for the others. The others had fulfilled these predictions, with the consequence that Mr. Torr could now count as his friends some of the foremost names in literature, art, and the Cabinet. That Mr. Torr alone had dropped into obscurity was never accounted to him in Wyvern's Cross as failure; it was simply that, with the perversity of genius, he had preferred this course.

About a week after the tennis-party Dr. Bickleigh met him in the village street, outside the post-office.

Mr. Torr was evidently pleased about something, for his manner was swelling and vast. Mr. Torr was not unlike his own church organ; fruity in presence always, when in genial mood he would swell to a booming diapason, giving the impression of occupying far more space in matter than his actual physical self could fill.

The post-office in Wyvern's Cross was the grocer's too, and the haberdasher's as well as that, and the ironmonger's besides. One counter served for everything, but you indicated which department you wanted by where you stood at it. Mr. Torr was in the post-office and Dr. Bickleigh was in the ironmongery department, buying a rat-trap for his greenhouse. There was thus the whole of the grocery counter and the gents and ladies' outfitting department between them, yet Mr. Torr somehow overflowed these two and extended right into the ironmongery, squeezing Dr. Bickleigh into the extreme corner, though remaining all the time in the post-office.

"Good morning, Bickleigh. *Good* morning." Mr. Torr conveyed the impression that he had now, by special arrangement with the Almighty, ensured that Dr. Bickleigh *should* have a good morning.

"Good morning," beamed Dr. Bickleigh. It seemed almost a sacrilege to descend to such mundane matters as rat-traps, but he mentioned his requirement to old Mrs. Stinvell behind the counter who kept this multiple store, and she went off, nodding sympathetically, to search mysterious recesses "out to the back." Mrs. Stinvell never seemed to keep what one wanted in the shop itself, and it invariably took her three times as long to overhaul her hiding-places "out to the back" as one would have thought possible. Two persons encountering one another in her shop, therefore, had plenty of time to discuss the weather and their neighbours.

"And how," said Mr. Torr with majestic grace, "is old Mrs. Brent to-day?" He remembered vaguely having heard recently that old Mrs. Brent really was bad this time, and the village clergyman should always keep himself informed about his charges, however humble. Besides, Bickleigh would like to talk about one of his patients; professional men always talk shop.

But Dr. Bickleigh was looking embarrassed. "To-day?" he repeated awkwardly. "Well—she's still dead, you know. I mean, you buried her last week, you remember."

"Chrrrm-hrrrm!" observed Mr. Torr with severity. One gathered that it was tactless of Mrs. Brent to have died in any case, but it was far, far more tactless of Dr. Bickleigh that Mr. Torr should have forgotten all about it.

"Are you—are *you* troubled with rats?" stammered the little doctor hastily, seeking to retrieve his error.

Mr. Torr moved his eyebrows a fraction of an inch up his wide forehead. "I am glad to say that I am not troubled with rats, no." *My* person, added Mr. Torr's tone, always has been free of rats, whatever other people's may be.

This subtle rebuke administered, Mr. Torr appeared to forgive Dr. Bickleigh and resumed most of his former expansiveness. "I called on Miss Cranmere yesterday."

"Oh, yes?" Dr. Bickleigh was not particularly interested. Miss Cranmere had not attracted him, even remotely.

"A most refreshing young woman, I am glad to be able to say. Most refreshing."

"Refreshing?" It was not the kind of epithet which Dr. Bickleigh himself would have applied.

"In comparison with the usual young woman of to-day."

"Oh, I see; yes," said Dr. Bickleigh, and could not help thinking of Quarnian. He had an uneasy feeling that Mr. Torr was doing the same.

But Mr. Torr was not. His voice took on a postively *vox humana* tone. "She promised me a hundred pounds for our restoration fund," he said plummily.

"A hundred pounds?"

"A hundred pounds. Offered it, no less. Naturally one would not introduce the subject on a first call. She herself had admired our church, and noticed the scaffolding on the west front. A most observant young woman. I feel," said Mr. Torr, after communing with his soul for a moment, "that she will be in every way a Credit to Us."

Or in other words, gathered Dr. Bickleigh, who had heard all about his wife's misgivings on the subject, that all objections to Miss Cranmere's living alone at The Hall had now been withdrawn on the part of Mr. Torr.

To do Mr. Torr justice, Miss Cranmere must unwittingly have hit on the one means of effecting this. The church really was close to his heart, and to endow the one was to soften the other; it was of the early Norman period, with a genuine Saxon crypt, and, except for one Perpendicular window in the west end, all that showed above ground was homogeneous in style. His church was the only part of his responsibilities which the Rev. Hessary Torr took really seriously, and he contributed freely to its needs from his own wife's purse.

Dr. Bickleigh went back to Fairlawn with his rat-trap. A hundred pounds to restore a bit of mouldering stonework, while he and Julia could not afford a new tennis-net!

Yes, undoubtedly the Rev. Torr had chosen the wiser policy.

Well, all one could hope was that the woman's health was bad. It looked as if it might be, with that sallow complexion and those hollows under her eyes. She would be almost certain to make him her regular medical attendant; and she ought to be good for some very nice, fat little bills.

But—a hundred pounds!

Ten would have been ample.

IV

It seemed as if the woman's health might be bad. Only the next day Dr. Bickleigh received a summons to The Hall. He wound up his ancient Jowett and trundled off with high hopes.

Dr. Bickleigh had never been inside The Hall before. Its late owner, Colonel Swincombe, had never sent for him, in spite of the knowledge, featly inserted into that retired warrior's mind on the only occasion when the two men had ever met, one year at the Merchester tennis-tournament, that Julia was a Crewstanton; he had his own doctor in Merchester. Now Dr. Bickleigh entered the old house with interest.

It made him catch his breath a little. His visions of Bickleigh the supreme artist were not without some excuse in fact: he did try to sketch a little, in such leisure as he could spare from his roses, and he had a genuine feeling for beauty; old and mellow beauty particularly. The Hall was old and mellow enough, and beautiful enough too: a perfect piece of late Tudor-work, peach-red, gabled, with twisted chimneys and lattice windows, not large but quite unspoiled by any heavy-handed Georgian restorers. Inside there were broad, cool rooms, with low, timbered ceilings, beams, wide open fireplaces, darkly gleaming panelled walls, and carved overmantels with both the Tudor boss and the Jacobean lozenge, which Dr. Bickleigh thought most interesting and unusual.

Madeleine Cranmere met him in the hall and showed him over the ground-floor herself. She appeared delighted to listen to his rapturous enthusiasm, and consulted him on a few points as if he were an expert in the period. He was not, but he knew enough about it to be able to advise her roughly, and was far too flattered by the earnest way in which she listened to gather that actually she knew a good deal more about the points in question than he did. The matter of her health only arose perfunctorily, and was dismissed in a couple of moments: she was inclined to suffer from nervous headaches; could he let her have something to take for them? He promised to make up a prescription for her.

They had tea out on the lawn, under a big cedar. Dr. Bickleigh had other visits to pay, and barely time to get them all in before his surgery at six o'clock, but Madeleine seemed so anxious for him to stay that he had little choice. She admitted to him, with her grave, rather serious smile, that already she was finding life there a little lonely.

At tea they talked about art. It was remarkable how they seemed to agree in condemning the moderns, tolerating the Georgians, and reverencing only the great men of the sixteenth and seventeenth centuries. They agreed, too, that their attitude was not conventional, but based simply on an appreciation of real painting. It was difficult for Dr. Bickleigh to realise that Miss Cranmere really was so young; she seemed to possess the sense and matured judgment of a woman of thirty. From art they passed to other topics, and on each it appeared that their views were identical. It became quite interesting to try to find some point of difference, and most amusing when not a single one could be discovered.

Dr. Bickleigh was delighted. For the first time in his life, apparently, he had come into contact with someone whose mind was in complete sympathy with his own. Expanding, he ventured to hint as much; and his delight grew when his companion confessed that for her too it was a rare joy to be able to exchange intelligent conversation with another person. Most girls of her own age, in Miss Cranmere's opinion, seemed to have developed no further from what they had been at twelve years old, while the young men were even worse. Didn't Mr. Bickleigh agree? Dr. Bickleigh, thinking of Gwynyfryd Rattery, opined that the girls were even worse than the young men. Yes, on the whole Miss Cranmere thought they were.

What pleased Dr. Bickleigh most was the deference which she paid to his ideas. She seemed to hang on his words, nodding gravely her agreement, her big grey eyes alight with intelligent interest. He noticed that when she smiled, the corners of these wrinkled up in a way he found pleasant to watch. He began to try to make her smile more often, for she did not do so very much, and was gratified to find himself able to do so. Not that he was able to reverse his first impression and pronounce her pretty; definitely she was not that. But she was something more vital than merely pretty: her face was a *most* interesting one.

Of course, it came out that Dr. Bickleigh tried to sketch. He admitted it, diffidently but not without pride. Miss Cranmere, it seemed, had been sure that he did something like that. He had given her the impression of being a practiser, not a mere preacher only. Dr. Bickleigh was amazed at her perspicacity.

He came away from The Hall feeling, literally, ten years younger. Younger than that. Younger than when he had first met Julia. And most strangely heartened. It was as if Julia did not count for so much after all. There were things, he had been reminded, a good deal more important than Julia in life—even in his life.

As the Jowett rumbled back to Wyvern's Cross, he took stock of his feelings and this new exhilaration that possessed him. "No," he decided, "I'm not in love with her. I never could be in love with her. She never could attract me in that way at all. And I must never try to flirt with her. That would spoil everything. Whatever happens, even if she gives me the opportunity (which of course she wouldn't), I must never flirt with her."

He hummed a little song. Never had he been so deliciously flattered. Miss Cranmere had not only begged him to come up and make sketches of The Hall and its gardens whenever he liked, but had contrived to let him know that she would feel really honoured if he would do so.

Edmund," Julia greeted him coldly, as he was putting the car away, "why did you not let me know that you weren't going to be in to tea?"

"Because I didn't know, my dear," he told her blithely.

"And you're exceedingly late for your surgery," said Julia, still more disapprovingly, for when Dr. Bickleigh was out she sometimes had to deal with his patients herself, and she detested that. Julia could not pretend that her husband was not a doctor and working for the money that came to him, but she did her best to shut her eyes to the degrading fact by helping him as little in his profession as she possibly could.

"Well," said Dr. Bickleigh surprisingly, "if a man mayn't be late for his own surgery, whose surgery may he be late for?" And with an unabashed smile he walked off to his waiting patients.

Julia looked after him in astonishment.

Chapter Three

I

THERE was a note for him lying on the hall table when Dr. Bickleigh came in to lunch. The housemaid came in to sound the gong as he picked it up.

"Miss Ridgeway left it, sir," she remarked. "She said there was no answer."

"That's right, Florence," nodded the doctor. "It's to remind me of a prescription I promised to write for her, I expect." Dr. Bickleigh always went into unnecessary explanations with servants. It was a habit of which his wife had tried in vain to break him, pointing out that servants never respect an employer who treats them in that familiar way; a good servant does not even like it. Julia herself was exceedingly formal with her servants, and got out of them the very best that was in them; she was an exceedingly capable housewife in spite of her upbringing, and things at Fairlawn ran like clockwork. In consequence, the servants invariably detested her and, quite perversely, adored the doctor. They cannot have been good servants.

"Oh, yes, sir," beamed Florence, and beat a subdued tattoo on the gong so as not to distract her master's reading of the note.

"Yes, just what I expected," he said with a little smile, and crammed the note in his pocket. "Lunch ready, Florence? I must just wash my hands."

With the lavatory door locked, he read the note again.

"My darling Teddy,—What is the matter? Why haven't you written or anything? I waited for you the last three Wednesdays, but you never came. I haven't seen you for nearly three weeks, ever since that tennis-party at your house. And then you hardly spoke to me the whole afternoon. Are you cross with me about something? I must see you this afternoon. I shall be at the cave at 3 p.m. You *must* come, Teddy.

"Your own

"Ivy."

"Damn!" said Dr. Bickleigh mournfully, and went in to lunch.

At ten minutes past three, after a quick glance up and down the road, he was steering the Jowett through the narrow entrance to the quarry.

It was an ideal meeting-place for lovers. Ivy had discovered it, exploring one day on her bicycle—an old stone-quarry, disused these fifty years, its rock-hewn sides covered now with young trees that almost met overhead across its narrow breadth, its flat, rocky floor most accommodating to a car. One came on it quite unexpectedly, through an almost overgrown opening in the rocky wall that bordered one side of the road, and nobody seemed to know anything about it. About six miles from Wyvern's Cross, far enough to be discreet but easily reached by the Jowett and Ivy's bicycle, it had been hailed by both of them as the perfect trysting-place; and when Dr. Bickleigh, scrambling about the uneven sides to the accompaniment of Ivy's terrified expostulations from below, had come across the hidden entrance to the cave, penetrated inside, and discovered an old working driven straight into the face of the rock, perfection had been surpassed.

The cave was about twelve feet above the rock floor, easy enough to reach once a few brushes had been pulled out of the way and slabs of stone lodged here and there to form a rude staircase. Inside, it was about eight feet wide by perhaps fifteen deep, and just high enough for the two to be able to stand upright without knocking their heads. They were enraptured with it. The game of cave-dwellers was inaugurated on the spot, and both set to playing it like the children they felt. The cave was furnished, with a half-dressed block of stone for a table, a couple of others for chairs, and armfuls of sweet-smelling bracken for a divan at the farther end. Ivy even went so far as to grow her bobbed hair from that minute, for no cave-dwelling woman is correct without long hair. With the discovery of a hollow clump of undergrowth on the rocky floor below, where the car could be stowed invisibly, the place was complete.

That had been last summer, and the two had met there every afternoon till the winter, and again in the spring. But only for a short time in the spring. After that Dr. Bickleigh had unfortunately found himself so busy this year that he had been unable to come regularly every week. He had now, in fact, been unable to come once during the previous two months: ever since he had realised the possibilities of Gwynyfryd Rattery.

Ivy was waiting for him. The first thing he saw was the white flutter of her dress through the bushes at the entrance to the cave. He drove into the clump, spinning the operation out as long as he could, and climbed up to the cave. It was inevitable that Ivy was going to cry again.

"Oh, Teddy." There was reproach, welcome, gratitude, and anxiety in Ivy's tone.

"Hullo, Ivy." Dr. Bickleigh made his voice as cheerfully casual as he could, as he parted the bushes and followed her into the filtered green light inside the cave. She held up her face to be kissed, and he kissed her.

She clung to him. "I'd begun to think you weren't coming."

"Sorry I was late. Only a minute or two, wasn't it? Awfully busy, just at present."

"Did you want to come? You didn't." Her eyes searched his anxiously.

"Want to?" Dr. Bickleigh laughed, apparently much amused. "Of course I wanted to, dear." He disengaged her arms gently and sat on the stone table, pulling out his cigarette-case. "But one can't always do everything one wants, you know. At least, a poor, hard-working devil of a G.P. can't." He offered her his case, and, when she shook her head, lit a cigarette for himself.

"If it had been Gwynyfryd Rattery, you'd have wanted to much more," Ivy said slowly, twisting her handkerchief nervously in her hands. "Wouldn't you?"

"Gwynyfryd Rattery! My dear girl, what an extraordinary idea!"

"Everybody's talking about it."

"About me and Gwynyfryd? Why, but it's absurd. I hardly know the girl." Against his will he was being thrown on the defensive already.

"You know her well enough to go away from the tennis-court with her alone for half an hour."

"Half an hour? Three minutes, to give her some cuttings she wanted. Don't be so absurd, Ivy."

"I wasn't the only one to notice it," she persisted. "Quarnian Torr did too. And Denny Bourne. They were laughing about it. Even Julia. You saw how she spoke to you afterwards."

"It's ridiculous. Just because a lot of gossiping girls . . .

And that conceited young ass Denny. . . ." Dr. Bickleigh pulled himself up. It was no good getting hot and angry with the girl. But how irritating she was, and how silly. "You ought to know me better than that, Ivy," he concluded, forcing a smile.

Without warning, she suddenly began to storm. He had never heard Ivy storm before. He had not thought she could. "Then I'll tell you what it is, shall I? It's that Madeleine Cranmere. Oh, yes, I've heard all about it. Everybody's talking, I can assure you. How you go up there every other day, pretending to sketch. *Sketch!*"

"Really, Ivy," Dr. Bickleigh began coldly, "I must say that you ——"

"And you're so busy, aren't you? Much too busy to come here on our Wednesday afternoons. But not too busy to go up there and talk to her."

"I will not have Miss Cranmere's name brought into this—this vulgar discussion, Ivy—do you hear me?" shouted Dr. Bickleigh, white with anger.

For the first time in his knowledge she stood up to him, white too, and trembling from head to foot. "Yes, you will, because I'm going to bring it in. If you can't see through her yourself, it's time somebody told you. I hate her, with her great big eyes and that solemn face of hers. She's deceitful, that's what she is. I wouldn't trust her an inch. She's playing with you, that's all. Just amusing herself, and laughing at you behind your back, I expect. She's a ——"

"Stop!" Dr. Bickleigh's face was so twisted with anger that Ivy did stop, nervously retreating before him till she was standing in the very entrance to the cave.

A horrible thought swept into Dr. Bickleigh's mind: "Push her over the edge! If you thrust high enough she'll turn over in the air and land with her head on that boulder at the bottom. Nobody could ever know." The longing just for one second was so intense that Dr. Bickleigh had actually to clench his hands by his sides to resist it. A red haze seemed to swim before his eyes. The next moment it had all gone, leaving him physically weak and with his anger completely evaporated.

With a shaking hand he put his cigarette to his mouth, and dropped back on to the seat from which he had momentarily risen. "The whole thing's absurd, Ivy," he said quietly. "I've got no interest in Miss Cranmere beyond the ordinary friendly feeling for a patient. You know I do a bit of sketching now and then. Why her permission for me to sketch part of the grounds of The Hall should make you jealous, I really can't see."

It had been an isolated outburst on Ivy's part. She had not the temperament to keep that sort of thing up. Dr. Bickleigh's one furious shout had been enough to make her collapse. Now she was looking at him with wistful eyes, frightened and yet not altogether reassured.

"You really don't like her—better than me?"

"No, of course I don't," lied Dr. Bickleigh with irritation. He did not like lying, even in so good a cause as this.

"Nor Gwynyfryd Rattery either?"

"No, no."

"Teddy—*do* you still like me?" Her lips began to quiver.

"Of course I do, Ivy."

"As much as ever?"

"Yes."

She burst into tears. "Oh, I don't believe you do. You don't! You'd be kissing me, and . . ."

He bent to kiss her, to reassure her, to try to blow on the dead embers of his old feelings for her. She clung to him again, sobbing against his shoulder. He felt supremely uncomfortable, and detested the whole thing; but it takes more moral courage than Dr. Bickleigh had got (and than most men have who are not brutes) to tell a weeping woman that one no longer loves her. As he stroked her soft, fluffy hair with mechanical fingers he wondered, not for the first time, why a woman considers herself insulted by a man if she ceases to attract him. He thought it must be some form of sex-conceit. Women as a sex are so intensely pleased with themselves simply for being women. Dr. Bickleigh, like so many men before him, could not understand it at all.

He wished Ivy would not go on crying; he wished she had the wit to understand that he *was* tired of her and leave it at that, or, rather, that he had been mistaken in her from the first and that she was not, and never had been, the girl he thought her. Oh, God, what a fool he had been to seduce her! And yet she had been most ready to be seduced. Had he seduced her at all? There had been no intention. Somehow it had just happened, inevitably. Besides, in most cases of so-called seduction what initiative there is usually comes from the woman, not the man. In any event, he had been a fool to take what she offered him; and there was going to be hell and all to pay before he could get free. He shuddered at the thought of the tears, the complaints, and the entreaties to come. They were both almost on the edge of the rocky platform. If with one sudden jerk he thrust . . .

He pulled himself up in horror. He must be getting overworked if he could contemplate thoughts like that not even in anger. Ivy did get on his nerves, it was true, and it would be marvellous to be clear for ever of this cloyingness; but still . . .

He loosed her abruptly, walked to the other end of the cave, and lit another cigarette.

Comforted, Ivy repaired the damage to her face so far as she could and began to prattle about the tea she had brought. Dr. Bickleigh watched her set it out on the stone slab, but the old cave-dwelling formalities and jokes no longer amused him, though he did his best to laugh at them; they seemed indescribably childish and pointless; had that sort of thing once really entertained him? Ivy seemed quite happy now, and he was pleased that she should be so; for, after all, when one came down to it she was only a child. That she was in point of fact actually one year older than Madeleine Cranmere appeared to him almost incredible. What was it that Madeleine had said to him at their very first meeting? Oh, yes, that most girls of her own age did not seem to have developed at all from what they had been at twelve years old. That was it, exactly. Mentally Ivy was twelve years old.

So he allowed her to sit on his knee at tea in the old way, though he would much rather she had sat on the opposite side of the table, and show off her hair afterwards. "No, I want *you* to take it down for me, darling. There! It has grown, hasn't it? Lots, since we were here last. Do you like it now it's getting longer?" Ivy was eternally wanting to know whether he liked this or that attribute of hers, invariably a physical one.

He was able to stave off love-making by remonstrating with her over sending the note to his house. It was terribly rash. Julia might have opened it, one of the maids, anyone. Ivy agreed that it had been most foolish, but she simply had to get hold of him, and what else could she do? But why did she simply have to get hold of him? To make certain that he still loved her: and was he quite, *quite* sure he did? No, but *really*? Dr. Bickleigh hurriedly cast round for another less compromising topic.

Perched on his knee, Ivy tried too to rouse his jealousy.

Dr. Bickleigh felt it was rather pathetic, and did his best to give her what she wanted, but it was difficult to appear even interested.

"I could have been somewhere quite different this afternoon if I'd wanted," she told him, with an air of importance.

"Oh? Where was that?"

"Do you want to know? Awfully?"

"I'm dying to know, Ivy."

"I don't think I shall tell you."

"Very well, if you'd rather not."

"You'd be terribly cross," said Ivy wistfully.

"Oho! What's all this about?"

"Will you promise not to be, if I tell you?" Ivy asked, brightening.

"That depends. Anyhow, you've certainly got to tell me."

"Well—it's early-closing day in Merchester, you know."

"Yes?"

"And *somebody* asked me to go out for a car-ride with him this afternoon."

"Somebody in Merchester?"

"Somebody who works there. I nearly went, Teddy."

"Who?"

"Oh, I couldn't tell you that. But I do believe he rather likes me."

After being pressed, as she evidently wanted, she told him that it was Mr. Chatford. Dr. Bickleigh was not surprised. He had noticed how Chatford monopolised Ivy at tea at the tennis-party, and had secretly rejoiced.

"He's a very good fellow, Chatford," he said warmly.

"Aren't you jealous?" said Ivy in dismay, naïvely giving the whole thing away.

Dr. Bickleigh did his best to give an imitation of a

man suffering agonies of jealousy. "Does he want to marry you?" he added, with careful nonchalance.

Ivy tossed her head. "Let him ask me first, and see what he gets. Aren't you going to have another of these rock-cakes, darling? I made them myself. I did truly."

"You might do worse, Ivy," Dr. Bickleigh said slowly.

"You—you don't *want* me to?" exclaimed Ivy. "Oh —oh, Teddy!" Her mouth began to tremble again.

"Want you to? Good gracious, no," said Dr. Bickleigh hastily. "But, darling, you know you and I can never marry, and I mustn't be so selfish as to keep you from marriage altogether. I should simply hate the idea of course—awful!—but I should have to bear it," said Dr. Bickleigh with much nobility, "for your sake."

Ivy was reassured. "I shall never marry anyone if I can't marry you, dear, dear Teddy," she said; but Dr. Bickleigh knew that the idea of Chatford had been planted in her mind; he could only hope fervently that it would fruit.

He kissed her gently.

But when, tea over, Ivy began to kiss him more intently and show signs of shy amorousness, Dr. Bickleigh pleaded a round of urgent visits and made his escape. The sight of her as he left her in the entrance to the cave, with trembling lips that she tried to hide, and an intensity of pleading in her blue eyes which she dared not annoy him by putting into words, made him feel acutely uncomfortable, and stayed with him all the way home; but the panic-stricken longing for flight was on him, and he could not have more pity on her than on himself.

When he came to think about it afterwards, he realised that for perhaps the first time in his life he had refused something that a woman was offering him. But why his friendship with Madeleine Cranmere should cause him to fly in panic from the advances of Ivy he was not clear, though quite certain that this was the reason he had done so. Because definitely he was not going to flirt with Madeleine ever.

But *Ivy* . . .

II

Madeleine Cranmere's loneliness did not last long. Within a week of Dr. Bickleigh's first visit to her she was definitely in the whirl of social life in Wyvern's Cross. The Torrs took her up first of all, led by Mr. Torr in full bay; the Bournes, the Ratteries, the Ridgeways (in spite of Ivy), Miss Wapsworthy, and Miss Peavy followed as a matter of course. Even Mrs. Hatton-Hampstead, Mrs. Hatton-Hampstead of Squerries, the Hon. Mrs. Hatton-Hampstead, who acted as hostess occasionally for her brother, Lord Cornwood, to the Prince of Wales himself (Mrs. Hatton-Hampstead, whose father, *née* Bert Tigley, had acquired so many worsted-spinning mills during the war that the Government had to make him a peer in sheer self-preservation), even Mrs. Hatton-Hampstead, having met Mr. Torr in the village one morning during one of her brief and rare visits to Squerries, left a card at The Hall afterwards: a quite unprecedented honour.

Dr. Bickleigh had availed himself of the invitation to sketch in the grounds of The Hall, though he had not found it necessary to say as much to Julia. During the three weeks that followed his first call he went up to do so on no less than four occasions. On the first three of these, his young hostess was there to welcome him, and, somehow or other, no sketching got done; the fourth time he was unlucky, and had nothing to do but sketch. Apart from that, he saw her several times elsewhere—at tennis at the Torrs' and the Bournes', and when she came to return Julia's call—having casually mentioned to him the day before that she would be coming on the next one. They greeted one another now as old friends.

Ivy's reference to Madeleine as deceitful amazed Dr. Bickleigh. Even after making all allowance for jealousy, the slander was so preposterous. There were things that a jealous girl might have called her, no doubt, with a possible substratum of truth: solemn, too old for her years, dull (to those without intelligences of their own), even on some days plain, and quite truthfully dowdy. But deceitful! If ever there was a limpid clarity of mind and intention, it belonged to Madeleine Cranmere. Dr. Bickleigh had seen that from the first, and so had everyone else who really counted—Mr. Torr, the Davies, even Julia herself. As for the Davies, whose judgment Dr. Bickleigh respected more than anyone else's, Peter was so loud in Miss Cranmere's praises that his wife had pretended to tease him about the jealousy she was beginning to feel. And the very next time Dr. Bickleigh had gone up to The Hall to do his sketching, there was Peter Davy sitting with Madeleine under the cedar and no Mary on the premises at all.

The three had a merry little tea-party (Madeleine was not nearly so serious as usual that day), and, when Dr. Bickleigh gave Davy a lift back to his cottage afterwards, the novelist confided to him that he was studying Madeleine Cranmere with a view to incorporating in his book an entirely new character based upon her. Both men agreed with enthusiasm that they had never met a girl they liked better, nor one more entirely unspoilt by money and attentions, and Peter Davy pointed out how refreshing it was to have contact with a woman to whom sex was not the predominant thing in life.

"In fact, if one is to make any criticism of her at all," suggested the little doctor, diffident in the presence of an expert, "it might be that——"

"Oh, she's not perfect," put in Peter Davy, who had an unfortunate habit of interrupting in mid-sentence, as if his own ideas bubbled up so spontaneously that they had to burst in speech without waiting an instant. "Nobody's that, however they may strike us at first sight."

"No, exactly. But what I meant was, one of her faults is that she *is* sexless. Don't you think so?"

Peter Davy sucked at his pipe for a moment, while his companion cautiously rounded a blind corner in the narrow lane they were following. "No, I don't. I think, given the right man, she has very great capabilities of passion. But her nervous system's very delicately balanced. Crude handling, an initiation not entirely sympathetic, might destroy her capabilities for good and all. It's got to be the one right man."

Dr. Bickleigh preserved an astonished silence. He could not see any capabilities of passion in Madeleine Cranmere at all; it was impossible even to imagine her in passionate mood. In everything she seemed to stand for intellect as opposed to emotion, which was precisely why Dr. Bickleigh had been so impressed by her. For once, he felt his distinguished companion must be wrong.

Not for an instant did it occur to him that, if his companion was correct, he himself might be that one right man.

III

There were two peculiarities of his wife's which irritated Dr. Bickleigh particularly. Quite small things, and not irritating in themselves, but they just happened to get on his nerves. For they were symbolical, in a way, of the difference between them; a perpetual reminder even in his own home. She never used a short word where a long one would do, and her enunciation was distinct to the point of affectation. Where ordinary souls would say: "It doesn' do t' take things casuly," Julia said, "Itt doesn'tt do to take things casu-ally."

One evening at dinner, a week or two after the tea-party at The Hall, she said very precisely: "That gairl, Madeleine Cranmere, is getting herself talked about."

Dr. Bickleigh was both surprised and uneasy: surprised because Julia never took part in any of the local gossip, neither repeating nor even listening to it, and uneasy for obvious reasons. "Really?" he said cautiously, and waited.

Julia produced another irritating trick of hers, and said nothing more. Dr. Bickleigh had to put out a feeler. "The people round here would talk about anyone."

Julia looked at him so meaningly that Dr. Bickleigh shuffled in his seat and bent his attention most earnestly on his cheese pudding; her implication was quite obvious.

Normally Julia made no reference at all to her husband's desultory affairs. He was always in doubt whether she knew anything about the current one or not, but her silence was a relief; though she conveyed the impression at the same time that they were so utterly vulgar as to be beneath her notice. This time, however, there was a meaning edge to her voice.

She condescended to amplify, somewhat surprisingly. "Though no doubt Mr. Davy would expect a little more licence than the rest of us, so far as the normal conventions go." Julia's tone added that in that event she would not be prepared to grant it to him.

Dr. Bickleigh was so relieved that he was able to be indignant. "You don't mean to say they're talking about Miss Cranmere and Davy, Julia?"

"I understand that is so."

"Then it's abominable. Of all the people in the world who . . . Good Lord, what a set of filthy-minded beasts. *Who* are talking? Who told you?"

"Mrs. Torr asked my advice as to whether it was not her duty to hint something to Miss Cranmere." Neither Mr. nor Mrs. Torr ever undertook an unpleasant duty without consulting Mrs. Bickleigh about it first. That Mrs. Bickleigh usually offered to relieve them of it may have been the reason.

"Old scandalmonger! Comes from the precious Quarnian, I expect. I think it's disgraceful. Simply disgraceful."

"You seem very heated about it, Edmund."

Dr. Bickleigh realised that perhaps he was being indiscreet. "Well, who wouldn't be? A nice girl like that. Weren't you annoyed yourself, Julia?"

"Certainly I told Mrs. Torr that I did not think the fact that Mr. Davy had been up to The Hall once or twice to tea need be taken too seriously, in Miss Cranmere's case."

"It beats me how these things get about," groaned Dr. Bickleigh.

"But they do get about, Edmund," said his wife, with so much meaning in her harsh voice that he instantly looked guilty.

"So—so it seems," he mumbled.

There was an uneasy silence. The unhappy conviction grew upon Dr. Bickleigh that his wife had been playing the cat-and-mouse game with him, and still was. The next moment confirmed it.

"Are you intending to try to seduce that gairl, Edmund?" asked Julia without emotion.

Consternation, real anger, and a sickly, choking terror, clogged Dr. Bickleigh's utterance for a moment. "Look here, Julia——" he began in shrill, unnatural tones.

"Oh, you needn't bother to pretend to me," cut in his wife, her pale, prominent eyes contemptuous behind their thick glasses. "I know perfectly well you're not fit to be trusted with any decent gairl. Normally, I think you'll admit, I don't interfere with your amusements. If a gairl is fool enough to be taken in by a man like you, she must learn her lesson. But in this case, I warn you, I will not permit it."

"You've no right . . . How dare you, Julia!" spluttered Dr. Bickleigh with shaking lips, anger gradually displacing even fear as the monstrous imputation grew on him. When for once at any rate he had been so completely sincere, so firmly Platonic! . . . There is only one charge more infuriating than a well-grounded one, and that is one that is baseless. "I think you're absolutely horrible." Never had Dr. Bickleigh spoken like that to his wife before.

"Don't shout, please, Edmund. There is no need to say any more. And you could hardly expect me to believe you if you did. I have told you that I will not allow you to pester Miss Cranmere, at any rate, with your attentions. You had better not go up to The Hall again at all. If she wants a doctor, Dr. Lydston can attend her perfectly well. That will do."

"It won't do," shouted Dr. Bickleigh. "I won't stand this sort of thing even from you, Julia. You can't know the first thing about Miss Cranmere if you imagine for one moment . . . That's just like you frigid women: you're always finding sex or some beastliness everywhere. Horrible minds. . . . Miss Cranmere, let me tell you, is . . ." He trailed off into futile silence, his face working.

Julia was looking at him as at some repellent insect that was not uninteresting in its very repellency. "Edmund, do you imagine yourself in love with this gairl?"

"No, I do not. And I think your beastly insinuations are ——"

"Thank you, I have no wish to hear. You will do as I say about going up to The Hall no longer, and that can close the subject. Have you finished? Ring, please."

Chapter Four

I

DR. BICKLEIGH went up to The Hall the next afternoon.

Madeleine Cranmere had expressed a wish a few days ago to see some of his work, and he had a portfolio of old sketches with him. His mood was an ominous one. Anger with his wife still predominated, and there was mixed with it a certain exhilaration, almost recklessness, in this plain defiance of her orders. In some indefinable way, too, he felt as if by going up to The Hall at the first opportunity he was protecting Madeleine against Julia's beastly insinuations. But there was a curious sinking sensation in the pit of his stomach as he turned his car into The Hall drive.

It was raining, and they looked at the sketches in the drawing-room. Madeleine sat on the chesterfield with the portfolio open on her knees; Dr. Bickleigh sat beside her to explain and comment. They turned through several dozen mementoes of past holidays and scenes round Wyvern's Cross. Madeleine was sparing enough with her praise to make it of real value when she did bestow it. At the end of the collection there were perhaps half a dozen heads, attempts at portraits, imaginary faces. Madeleine examined these with a closer attention.

"You've got a feeling for portraiture," she pronounced, looking at him with her enormous grey eyes.

"Do you really think so?" beamed the doctor. "It's what I like best, of course."

Miss Cranmere sighed. "It's a wonderful gift. I think I'd rather possess it than any other." Her tone implied that Dr. Bickleigh did possess it.

"Oh, but I'm only a dabbler. I can tell you, Miss Cranmere, if I do get a likeness I'm as pleased as Punch about it."

"It must be terribly difficult." She regarded him sombrely, as if mourning over the terrible difficulties of the portraitist. "But all these are likenesses. One can feel it somehow. This one, for instance." She picked up a charcoal drawing of a young girl's head in profile. "How beautiful she must have been."

Dr. Bickleigh looked a little uncomfortable. "Well—as a matter of fact, I sketched that out of my head. No model."

But Miss Cranmere was not at a loss. "That's exactly what I mean. There's vividness in it that makes one feel it *must* be like someone. Just its vitality. If it isn't, that makes it all the more remarkable. You see what I mean?" she added earnestly.

"Yes, yes, of course," at once replied the doctor, who didn't. "Very kind of you to say so."

"You want more practice," the girl said, turning through the sketches again. "That's obvious. If only you could get more practice. . . ."

"So terribly busy," lamented Dr. Bickleigh.

They both looked exceedingly solemn, as befitted two people contemplating the frustration of possible genius. It was obvious that Miss Cranmere was thinking that, if only more practice could have been had, the work of Dr. Bickleigh, R.A., on the line would now be a feature of each year's Royal Academy.

Suddenly she smiled. She had a curious smile. Her mouth widened very slowly, as if stretched against its will and ready to snap back again at any moment like a piece of elastic. The rest of her face, except the corners of her eyes, remained immobile. It was a singularly unbeautiful smile, and gave little indication of real amusement. "Are you in a great hurry now, Dr. Bickleigh? You can stop to tea, can't you?"

"That's very good of you. I should like to very much," said Dr. Bickleigh, who had had every intention of stopping to tea.

"Well, it's still raining, so you can't do any sketching out of doors." Madeleine's eyes searched his, earnest and helpful and not smiling with her mouth at all. "Why not have a little practice now?"

"You mean . . . ?"

"I'd sit for you, if you cared to make a sketch of me, with pleasure." And her tone conveyed delicately that, though the suggestion was put forward half in joke, in case he might not wish to accept it, if he did, Miss Cranmere would feel herself really honoured. "I can get you some paper and things."

"You sketch yourself," cried the doctor.

Miss Cranmere shook her head. "I try, occasionally. But I'm hopeless."

While she was out of the room, Dr. Bickleigh thought, almost devoutly, how in all their conversation on art in general, and his art in particular, she had never said a single word about her own aspirations and accomplishments. Yes, a girl like this was to be met only once in a life-time.

II

Madeleine posed for him on the arm of a chair near the window.

Consciously or unconsciously, her face had assumed its most ethereal expression. It was helped in this respect by the fact that she wore her sleek black hair parted in the middle, like a Madonna. Indeed, so spiritual did she look that, if Dr. Bickleigh could have caught only a fraction of the unearthliness of her expression, his picture might have been labelled: *A Soul in Search of a Body*. Her grey eyes loomed enormous in her face. Dr. Bickleigh thought, rather breathlessly, that he had never seen anything quite so wonderful.

Only the fact that she dressed so badly struck a note that might be considered even faintly jarring. But this particular note no longer jarred on Dr. Bickleigh. That the uninteresting chiffon frock she was wearing only insulted its wearer by having cost so much money and undeniably fitted in the wrong places, he accepted in conjunction with her Madonna-like appearance and accounted to her for a virtue. Here, at any rate, was a girl to whom clothes were not a supreme interest. She treated them with the scorn which, when one could consider it on the right plane, mere coverings for the body undoubtedly deserved. Dr. Bickleigh was charmed by the way her frock bagged where its wearer did not.

Their friendship grew amazingly. There is some bond between sitter and artist which makes both feel that they share in common all sorts of things which just can't be defined, but anyhow they do share them. The conversation had passed with easy inevitability from the general to the particular, and from the particular to the intimate. Without actually saying as much, Dr. Bickleigh had yet somehow informed Madeleine that he was acutely unhappy in his marriage. And Madeleine, equally without putting it into words, had conveyed both her knowledge of this fact and her deep sympathy with the sufferer.

They exchanged other confidences. Taking for granted (between two friends who now knew each other so well) that his wife did not understand the first thing about him,

Dr. Bickleigh confessed sincerely, in response to Madeleine's adroit questioning, that always there had been a void in his life through lack of an understanding comrade (feminine gender) with whom he could share the thoughts and hopes that can be divulged to only one other person in the world, that he knew he was missing thereby one of the sweetest joys life can offer, and that he had practically given up as hopeless any expectation of filling that void. Whereupon Madeleine, radiating grave concern, had hinted (without any questioning) that she too had suffered through lack of just the same thing; that nobody in her family really understood her own delicately balanced mind, with its modest love of beauty and desire to find artistic self-expression, which was why she had been driven to living now quite alone; and what was the use of riches if one had no sympathetic soul with whom to share them?

Each of them spoke with intense seriousness about themselves, about each other, and about life; and each had acknowledged with sober pleasure a kindred spirit in the other.

"You have such a wonderfully understanding nature, Miss Cranmere," Dr. Bickleigh told her, much moved.

"I think there are some people so in tune with one that one just understands them instinctively," returned Miss Cranmere, with a grave, understanding smile.

Sensible of the growing pregnancy of the atmosphere, Dr. Bickleigh worked for a few minutes in silence. His heart swelled as he reflected how wonderful Madeleine was. If only he could have married a girl like her! But it was too late now. Besides, there could be no other girl like her. Madeleine Cranmere was unique.

He felt senselessly apprehensive, of what he did not quite know. Relations never remain stationary. His with Madeleine must either progress or recede. That they should recede was now unbearable; but that they should progress . . .

The portrait, which he had been literally praying might be an astonishing success, was not going well. There was a likeness, but only a surface one. He had not been able to hint at that wonderful sympathy, to catch that look of unearthliness, that sober spirituality, which seemed to characterise Madeleine. It was a flat thing.

In a gust of petulant despair he threw his charcoal into the empty fireplace. "It's no good," he burst out. "I can't get you. Not the real you."

Madeleine did not smile encouragement, as an ordinary girl might have done. She looked at once as if all the burdens of artistic inachievement were upon her too. "May I see it?"

"If you want to. But . . ." He moved away and stared out of the window, disgusted with his failure. Other girls he had drawn had taken it as a compliment when he had confessed himself unable to portray them satisfactorily (why, he had never been able to understand), but of course Madeleine would not be foolish like that. She would just be very disappointed. And too honest to conceal it.

Madeleine walked over to the easel and contemplated the half-finished drawing long and attentively. Dr. Bickleigh's sick anxiety as he waited for her condemnation was almost unbearable. He had long ago forgotten all about their respective ages. It was no longer a man of thirty-seven waiting for the criticism of a young girl of twenty-two, whose powers of judging half-finished charcoal drawings might, to put it at its least, be immature; it was the creator offering the work of his hands to the one person in the world for whom it had been shaped.

"It's clever," at last said Madeleine quietly. The confidence of her tone might have made one suppose that the one thing of which she had made a life's study was the judging of half-finished charcoal drawings. Dr. Bickleigh discovered that he had been actually holding his breath, and expelled it in a surge of relief.

"Do you really think so? I say, that's . . . It's wonderful to hear you say that."

"Very clever," Madeleine continued slowly, still examining the picture, her head a little on one side, her broad white forehead just furrowed, her expressive eyes narrowed. "But, then, I think your work is clever." She spoke without any of that easy enthusiasm which the conscientious craftsman dreads more than the most damning criticism; her words carried the impression of a balanced judgment carefully formed and as carefully weighed after formation. There was not a suspicion of flattery in her flattery.

Dr. Bickleigh could only beam in silence.

"But I don't see what you mean by not being able to 'get' me. I think it's exactly like me."

In his eagerness Dr. Bickleigh came and stood close behind her, studying his work over her shoulder.

"Oh, yes, it's *like* you. But that isn't the point. Anyone with a bit of a knack could draw something that would be *like* you. I was trying to get *at* you. I mean . . . show where you differ from everyone else. Why you're *you*, and could never be anyone who isn't you. No, that's idiotic. It's difficult to explain, but . . . Well, I mean, your expression, that particular look you have, your wonderful . . ."

"I think I understand," Madeleine said gently, and walked over to the window. "And I think you have got *at* me," she added in a low voice, looking out over the rain-drenched lawn, now glistening in a burst of sunshine.

Dr. Bickleigh followed her. His heart was thumping and his mouth had gone dry. "Not the real you," he said. "That's just the one the world sees—the outside, everyday you. I was trying to show the inside one—the one you hide from everyone. Except for a tiny glimpse now and then . . . to some lucky person." I'm beginning to make love to her, he thought desperately; I mustn't—I mustn't; it'll spoil everything; she'd hate it; she'd never speak to me again; besides, what coarseness . . . with *her*. But something drove him on.

Madeleine was still gazing out of the window. "And you imagine . . . there is such a 'me'?"

"I don't imagine," said Dr. Bickleigh hoarsely. "I know." I mustn't, his brain repeated mechanically, to the rhythm of his pounding heart, I mustn't make love to her. I mustn't. "And I think . . . I *think* I've been privileged . . . to catch . . . one or two of those glimpses." His knees seemed to have lost all their strength.

Madeleine did not turn her head. "Perhaps . . . you have," she said, almost inaudibly.

There was a full minute's silence. Dr. Bickleigh's mind whirled hither and thither. She could not mean . . . she did not understand what she was implying . . . he must not, must not, must not . . .

Suddenly a desperate calmness fell on him. He rushed on his fate. "I suppose you know what I'm doing?"

Madeleine turned and looked him full in the eyes. "Yes. I know."

"I'm making love to you."

"Yes."

The next instant she was in his arms.

"Madeleine!"

"Oh, Edmund!"

III

Dr. Bickleigh's first impulse had been to tell Julia that he and Madeleine loved one another. In such an affair as this, subterfuge and concealment seemed out of place.

To hide it from his wife would be to bring it down to the level of those other ignoble little liaisons which he now so bitterly regretted. On the highest peak of exaltation himself, Dr. Bickleigh meant all the circumstances of his incredible new happiness to remain there too.

Rather to his surprise, it was Madeleine who was against this course. It was foolish, she pointed out, to act precipitately. They must be quite, quite sure of themselves before they took any steps which might prove irrevocable. In the meantime, it would be unkind to Julia to cause her more suffering than was necessary.

"We mustn't think of ourselves, dear," she said very earnestly. "We have each other after all, but . . . your poor wife. I know exactly what you feel, and I feel it too; you understand me well enough, surely, to realise that I detest anything underhand as much as you do. But we mustn't consider our own feelings; we must think of hers."

And Dr. Bickleigh agreed that they must sacrifice themselves for Julia's peace of mind. They talked about her a good deal, called her "poor Julia," and were very sorry for her indeed.

Nevertheless, driving home just in time for evening surgery, he regretted the decision. It would have been a wonderful expression of the sober exhilaration that possessed him to walk straight in to Julia and tell her everything; a magnificent gesture. He saw himself breaking the news to her with quiet dignity—no recriminations, no cheap triumph at her expense. But after that the vision faded out. He simply could not see Julia's reactions to his news. She had such a width of choice.

One thing, however, Dr. Bickleigh did determine: he would be as honest with her as he possibly could. Except so far as was necessary to preserve the one vital secret, no lie should pass his lips at all. He actually hoped Julia would give him the opportunity to be honest.

Julia did. As he was hanging up his hat in the dark little lobby at the back of the hall she came out of the drawing-room and looked in her short-sighted way in his direction. "Is that you, Edmund? You were not in to tea." It never worried Mrs. Bickleigh to state self-evident facts. "Where were you?"

"I was at The Hall," replied Dr. Bickleigh. He looked her full in the face for a few moments to give her every opportunity of a reply if she wished to make one, and then walked down the passage and into his consulting-room.

Julia turned back into the drawing-room without a word.

Dr. Bickleigh's mood of unworldly exaltation lasted right through surgery and until the gong rang for dinner. Then it began to ebb a little. But there was enough of it left to enable him to confront Julia, if not with the quiet dignity he had pictured, at any rate with defiance. He recognised the defiance, and it irked him. He had been feeling for the last few hours so very, very far above Julia and all she stood for; it was annoying to find now that he had to face her much as a defiant mouse would face a cat. However superior to any number of cats a mouse may feel in its own hole, it requires a good deal of self-suggestion to maintain this opinion in the presence of the cat. Dr. Bickleigh had to keep on reminding himself of the miracle that Madeleine loved him, and that Julia therefore mattered rather less than nothing to anybody.

Julia, however, did not call his defiance into play. She made no reference to his visit to The Hall. It was as if the scene before surgery had not happened at all. She was not even silent, speaking to him no less and no more than usual. In every respect she behaved in her perfectly normal manner. This made Dr. Bickleigh uneasy. It was unlike Julia, he felt, and therefore ominous; never having defied her commands before, however, he did not know in the least what would be like her on such an occasion. It did not occur to him that, having encountered an unprecedented situation, Julia herself might be at a loss, and uncertain how to deal with it. It never would have occurred to Dr. Bickleigh that his wife was even capable of being at a loss.

The same game of polite make-believe followed them into the drawing-room after dinner. Dr. Bickleigh played it tensely, with growing disquiet, nervously fingering the waxed ends of his little moustache; Julia apparently was not playing it at all. A country doctor does not have so many evening calls as his townsman colleagues (can it be that people are more considerate in the country than in towns?), and Dr. Bickleigh was accustomed to spend his evenings in the drawing-room with his wife, he over a book from the library in Merchester and she with a piece of embroidery or crochet work; Julia did not care for reading. Julia did not care for the wireless, either, so that they had no set; Dr. Bickleigh had often tried to persuade her just to give it a trial, but she was quite sure she would not like it. Now, as she spoke from time to time of this and that, and he looked up from his book to answer her (not being a reader herself, Julia always seemed to make a point of letting anyone else do so for no more than five minutes without interruption), Dr. Bickleigh was wishing that a call would reach him and take him out of this anxious room, out of the house; something serious—a road accident, a milder case even, that would keep him out for some time. But of course no call came.

Only once did Julia make any remark that might be construed as having the slightest reference to the all-important subject. "Edmund," she said abruptly, "I have a very severe headache. Please get me something from the surgery to relieve it."

"Yes, of course." Dr. Bickleigh bounded to his feet, glad of any action, however insignificant. "Aspirin?"

"You know very well that aspirin doesn't suit me."

"Yes, yes; I remember. I'll get you something else."

He went to the surgery and stood there, delaying. A definite dread of going back to the drawing-room possessed him. It was inconceivable that Julia was going to pass over the whole thing like this. No, she was saving it up; playing her damned game of cat-and-mouse; knowing perfectly well what he was feeling. And if she had one of her headaches this evening too . . . Dr. Bickleigh knew those headaches.

He usually treated them with a preparation of phenacetin (the suggestion of aspirin had been a nervous lapse of memory), but to-night . . .

A sudden thought struck him, and he laughed out loud. Taking down a jar of tablets, he shook two out into his palm, dropped them into a measure, added water, and began to dissolve them. There were advantages in being a doctor. A nice little dose of morphia should make Julia far too sleepy to be able to do justice to her subject to-night. He pounded the tablets with a glass rod.

When they were quite dissolved, he paused for a moment. Should he . . . ? No, Julia's powers of resistance were above the normal. Better make sure while he was at it.

He took down the jar again, shook out two more tablets, and dropped them into the measure too. Not even Julia would be able to resist a full half-grain.

Dr. Bickleigh was right. Within twenty minutes Julia found herself so sleepy that she was compelled to go upstairs to bed.

With a smile Dr. Bickleigh pushed aside his book and gave himself up to living through, again and again, the events of the afternoon.

That night he had a new vision ready-made: not merely life without Julia, but life with Madeleine. As a sleep-compelling medium this vision was a failure.

IV

Julia's strange reticence lasted through breakfast the next morning. Her manner during the meal was as ominously normal as at dinner the evening before. Dr. Bickleigh felt, when he left the house for his morning round, that he was leaving a thunderstorm clamped in a small box inside it. He wondered fearfully, and yet with a strange little thrill, how long the clamps would hold. He dreaded the inevitable battle and at the same time almost welcomed it.

He went through his morning's work in a dreamy daze, living only for the afternoon.

So completely had all thought of Ivy disappeared that he did not at first even recognise her when he caught sight of a female figure signalling to him at the side of the road, and pulled up automatically.

"Teddy!" she said mournfully, as he came to a stop abreast of her.

"Why, hullo, Ivy." No little stab of apprehension, no exasperation; seldom can a man have felt more at his ease in the presence of a recently discarded mistress. Dr. Bickleigh was surprised to notice how completely master of the situation he felt. It was a new sensation to him, and a delightful one.

Ivy nervously tucked a stray curl under her small blue hat. "I knew Mrs. Belstone's ill, and I thought you'd be coming this way. I've been waiting nearly an hour."

"Yes?"

"Teddy, I must speak to you."

"I'm very busy, Ivy."

"You're always busy now when I want to see you." Her lower lip began to tremble. Dr. Bickleigh watched it with detached interest. How curious that a lip should wobble rapidly to indicate emotion. It wasn't poetic, it wasn't even pathetic (had he really once thought it was?); it was just ludicrous.

"I really am busy," he said patiently, "but that doesn't say I can't spare five minutes. Jump in. I'll take you on a bit with me."

"We oughtn't to be seen together," she hesitated.

"Jump in." He opened the door for her. Ivy got in, with a glance up and down the road. He let in the clutch and the car moved forward. "Well?" he smiled. "What is it, Ivy?" He felt as if she were a small child. It was a shame to have hurt her, but it had got to be done. He would be as merciful as he could.

"Oh, Teddy."

He pretended to be absorbed in driving along the narrow road, to give her time to collect herself. It was quite plain what she wanted to say: he no longer loved her—*did* he? And this time he was not going to deny it. A clean break had got to be made; a clean, honest break. Any other course now was unthinkable.

Well, may as well get it over. But not in public. They were passing through a small wood now, and Dr. Bickleigh turned the car along a track that led into it. He drove till they were out of sight of the road, and then came to a halt.

"Now then, Ivy."

"Teddy!"

"Yes?"

"Oh, I don't know how to tell you. I don't."

Her hands, in brown suede gauntlets, were twisting in her lap. She had very small hands, and the wide gauntlets at her wrists made them look smaller still. He had adored her tiny hands and feet, and could notice still how pretty they were.

"Tell me? What?"

"Something—terrible." She looked at him with eyes that were really terrified. Some of her fear communicated itself to him.

"What do you mean?" he asked sharply.

"I—I'm—I'm going to have—a baby."

"Nonsense!"

He twisted in his seat and stared at her. She shrank a little away from him.

"I am, Teddy, I am. I ought to know, oughtn't I?"

"Then it isn't mine," he said brutally.

Her eyes swam. She buried her face in her hands, weeping. "Oh, Teddy," she moaned.

"Ivy—who else have you been with?"

She shook her head mutely, and he repeated the question.

"Oh, Teddy, how can you? How *can* you?"

"You must have been."

"I haven't," she choked. "I swear I haven't. I *swear* it."

"Well, it isn't mine. That's certain."

But he believed her. A cold dismay invaded his body; he began to sweat.

This was terrible. Oh, damn the girl, damn the girl, *damn* her! What was to happen now? Little fool; she *would* somehow manage to . . . Presumably he must believe her when she said she hadn't . . . Oh, hell!

And Madeleine . . .

He got out of the car and walked up and down the track, pushing the ends of his moustache into his mouth and biting them savagely, hardly conscious of what he was doing.

"Teddy, I'm sorry."

"Oh, it's all right. I suppose it isn't your fault." But his tone implied that it was.

Ivy began to cry.

As always, her tears, which a few minutes ago he had been ready to tolerate, irritated him almost beyond control. This was a serious business. They had got to thresh it out. It is impossible to get much further if one of the parties to a discussion keeps her face buried in her hands and sobs into them.

"Ivy! For heaven's sake stop that damned crying. How on earth can we talk if you won't keep calm?"

She made an obvious effort to pull herself together, wiped her eyes, and blew her reddened nose. Crying completely spoilt her looks, but she had never learnt not to give way to it. By degrees her sobs died down.

"I don't believe it. It's pure imagination."

Ivy stared sullenly through the windscreen ahead. "Yes, it's easy to say that, isn't it?" He hardly recognised her voice. This was a new Ivy all of a sudden, an Ivy he had never met before. From being helpless and clinging, she had become in a flash like a stubborn bit of tough rubber.

"Well—how do you know?"

"The usual way, of course."

He glanced at her sideways. "If you really are . . ." Suddenly he reached a decision. "All right, Ivy. You needn't worry. It's quite simple. I'll operate."

She started. "An . . . ? But—doctors aren't allowed to."

"Really, my dear girl," he laughed harshly, "sometimes doctors have no choice."

"You might kill me. It's dangerous."

"Not in properly qualified hands. Don't be such a little fool." He was beginning to lose his temper. "There's no danger at all with me. Do you think I'd suggest it if there was? Do use your sense."

"You don't care what happens to *me*."

He shrugged his shoulders and controlled his rising anger. After all, there might he no immediate hurry, though that he must discover. And she would have to consent. But if she was going to be difficult . . . Oh, God, what a mess this was!

He recalled that inspiration he had had on the ledge at the entrance to the cave. It no longer seemed so horrible. Horrible? It was beautifully simple. And there could be no question afterwards. It would be plain that she had been scrambling up the side and missed her footing. And what a solution it would have been. He almost regretted not having had the nerve to do it. The nerve: that's all that is needed.

He looked with something like hatred at her tear-stained face, as she sat there staring stubbornly ahead; and a cold fury seized hold of him. Well, by God, it wasn't too late yet. If the little idiot *was* going to be difficult . . . If there was going to be any question of her coming between him and Madeleine . . . Or even of Madeleine ever hearing . . . Well, she had better look out.

He swung off at a sharp angle into the undergrowth.

"Teddy!"

She had scrambled out of the car and followed him. Her sullenness had gone; there was the old pathetic note in her voice.

"Teddy—aren't you a little bit sorry for me?"

"Yes, yes," he said impatiently.

"You're not. You're cross."

It was all he could do to answer her civilly. "Well, who wouldn't be?"

"If you really loved me you'd be glad."

"Glad you're going to have an illegitimate child?" he said angrily. "Oh, don't be such a fool."

"You don't love me," she sobbed. "You don't. Now I really know. You wouldn't be so unkind. Oh, Teddy. . . . Well, it's lucky I'm not going to have a baby, after all."

"What?" he shouted. "What was that?"

His tone frightened her tears away, but she faced him with a certain defiance. "No, I'm not. I made it all up, to find out if you really do love me or not; because you never would tell me. You're not brave enough, I suppose. Well, now I do know." She laughed hysterically. "So it's lucky I'm—not like that, isn't it?"

He stared at her, his face white, loathing her. "You little —*bitch*."

"Yes, that's right," she cried shrilly. "Call me beastly, vulgar names. I'm nothing now, of course. Not since you met your precious Madeleine. Why don't you call *her* that? That's what she is, and everyone knows it but you. She's just a——"

Something took control of Dr. Bickleigh. Something that made him hit Ivy in the face with his clenched fist, knocking her backwards into a tangle of brambles and smashing back the blasphemy on to her lips. Something that took him striding with set, mask-like face and burning eyes back to the car, heedless of the wailing cries that followed him.

"Teddy! Oh, Teddy, I didn't mean . . . Teddy *darling*!"

He jammed in the gear as if he hardly knew what he was doing, and threw in the clutch. The car leapt forward. He drove at top speed out of the wood and down the road.

Dr. Bickleigh had never laid any but amorous hands on a woman before. His brain, incapable of thought, was throbbing with mixed emotion: half of it was disgust, and half a queer, shouting exaltation.

V

By lunch-time he had stopped trembling.

But he had not forgiven Ivy. On his own account, yes. Considered from that point of view, Ivy was merely pitiable; he was really sorry for her. But the feeling that stayed with him was that Ivy had insulted, not himself, but Madeleine; not merely her futile outburst against Madeleine in person, but his own new standing with Madeleine, his attempts to make himself more worthy of Madeleine, all that Madeleine stood for; it all came back to Madeleine. And that was unforgivable.

Nevertheless, he was glad now, in his sane senses, that there could be no question of that ledge outside the cave; and could shudder to wonder what might not have happened if such a question had arisen. The intensity of his rage with Ivy had frightened himself afterwards. In that mood, heaven alone knew what he might not have done. But it was rather wonderful (he could not help feeling) that the capability for such a mood existed in him at all.

He was rather silent at lunch, answering Julia with such abruptness that she raised her thick eyebrows at him. Afterwards, when he was putting on his hat in front of the hall mirror to start out again, she said: "Are you going to be in to tea to-day, Edmund?"

"No," he answered, without turning round. Then something impelled him to add: "I shall be having tea at The Hall."

He wished Julia would burst out at that. A real hammer-and-tongs row at that moment, such as he and Julia had never had in their lives, would do him all the good in the world while he was still so on edge from the morning; relieve his tautened nerves, afford him something on which to expend his bottled-up energy. Besides, he felt just then ready to give Julia as good as she could give him, and better.

But Julia did not oblige. She merely said: "You will be in to dinner?"

"Of course. Why not?"

"Very well. I shall want to talk to you after it."

That was just like Julia, he thought, savagely cranking up the car (the Jowett's self-starter seldom worked nowadays). She had probably worked out to the minute how many hours of uneasy anticipation he should have.

More than ever he longed for Madeleine.

There were several more visits to pay before he could consider himself free enough to go up to The Hall. He hurried through them, cursing Ivy for having cut so into his morning. It was nearly four o'clock before he drew up before the iron-studded oak front door.

Madeleine was in the hall, obviously waiting for him. They kissed in silence before greeting each other. She was wearing a hat, and seemed to be dressed to go out.

"Dear, I'm so sorry, but I can't stay," she said. "I ought not to have waited so long, but I had to see you first. And I knew you'd come. I'm due for tea at the Bournes'."

He looked his terrible disappointment. "You never told me yesterday."

"I didn't know. Lady Bourne sent her son over with a note this morning."

"Denny? You should have told him you couldn't go."

"But it would have looked so bad."

"Not if you'd got a previous engagement."

Madeleine shook her head. "No, I felt I ought to go. It's a nuisance, Edmund, but we mustn't always think of ourselves, must we? And, anyhow, you've seen me first."

"You're the dearest girl," muttered Dr. Bickleigh, and kissed her again. She was exactly the same height as himself.

"And, Edmund," she said gently, disengaging herself after a moment, "I don't think you must come up here every day."

"But I must see you whenever I possibly can."

"Yes, but not every day. Not nearly every day. People would begin to talk at once."

"Good heavens, let 'em," declared the infatuated doctor. "Don't tell me you're afraid of a bit of cheap gossip, Madeleine."

"I was thinking of you, dear," she told him reproachfully. "Gossip does a doctor so much harm."

"Well, when can I see you?"

In the end it was arranged that Madeleine should be walking in her woods every Monday and Friday, near the lake. On Wednesdays, the day when he had no evening surgery, Dr. Bickleigh should come to the house itself, with his sketching materials as a disguise, and stay for tea. Saturdays and Sundays were no good, because of tennis-parties. Tuesdays and Thursdays must be sacrificed. Dr. Bickleigh grumbled a good deal, but Madeleine was not to be moved.

"And, anyhow," she pointed out, "it will be Friday the day after to-morrow."

"But it's Wednesday to-day. My day for tea."

"You had your Wednesday tea yesterday," she smiled. "You mustn't be greedy, Edmund." He had never heard her so playful before. It delighted him so much that he let her carry the point.

"And now I must go."

They had an impassioned parting.

Dr. Bickleigh drove away gloomily, wishing that Madeleine had not been so firm, wishing that she would let him choose her hats for her.

He felt terribly flat.

To return home was impossible. In the end he drove into Merchester and had tea at a café there, spinning it out as long as possible. The rest of the interval before dinner he spent, with a book he had bought for the purpose in Merchester and disliked as soon as he began to read it, lying in a field half a dozen miles from home. The ground was damp after yesterday's rain, and he had no rug with him.

By the time he did get home his reaction from the nervous energy of lunch-time was complete. He felt utterly worn out, tired, disappointed, and dispirited. So far from standing up to Julia after dinner, he could hardly endure the thought of friction. Definitely, he decided, he could not bear it. And yet it was hardly possible to go out again; while to flee to bed under pretence of being unwell would be worse than useless, for Julia would only follow him up there and he would be more at her mercy than ever. If only she had had one of her headaches today, so that he could get rid of her with the same ease as last night!

He wandered into his surgery and looked gratefully at the bottle of morphia tablets.

Julia. . . . Oh, Lord! She would wipe the floor with him to-night; simply wipe the floor with him. He couldn't stand up to her; couldn't do it. She would try to make him renounce going to The Hall, renounce Madeleine, renounce the only thing in his life worth having; she would bully him into . . .

No, anything was better than that, even flight. Oh, for one of her headaches!

Well, but if one can cure headaches, one should be able to bring them on too. Dr. Bickleigh struck his hands together in excitement. What a marvellous inspiration! *Give* her a headache, and then relieve it for her afterwards—with morphia. Now, what drug would effect his purpose best?

But that was where his inspiration fell down. He could think of not a single drug in his stock which would produce a headache only, accompanied by no other symptoms. Not a single one. He frowned in disappointment. How absurd that there should not be such a thing.

Then a vague memory stirred in him. He concentrated on it, chased it grimly, at last began to disentangle it. There had been a sample. Oh, at least three years ago. Some preparation put up by one of the well-known firms. One out of the hundreds he got in a year, but he had noticed it particularly because it had been so expensive, and because he had seen it noticed a day or two later in the *B. M. J.* It had been designed for—what? Ha, yes: one of the many correctives for uric acid diathesis. And it had been a failure, not only on account of its price, but because—he remembered clearly now—it induced such violent headaches. Now had he . . . ?

He opened the drawer where he kept such of the samples as seemed at all interesting, and searched feverishly.

Tucked away at the back, he found it.

Tiptoe with excitement, Dr. Bickleigh crept into the dining-room. Nobody was there. In front of each place, ready on a plate, was the half of a grape-fruit, ready prepared, with a crystallised cherry in the middle. Hurriedly Dr. Bickleigh produced a folded paper from his pocket and sprinkled its contents over his wife's portion.

Towards the end of dinner that evening Mrs. Bickleigh was attacked by such a blinding headache that she had to ask her husband for something to relieve it at once. The draught he gave her did her no good for the moment, but soon after coffee had been served in the drawing-room she found herself so sleepy that on the doctor's advice she went up to bed immediately, where she fell at once into a sleep so deep that it made her oblivious even of one of the worst headaches she had ever had.

Chapter Five

I

It would be unfair to Dr. Bickleigh's feelings to describe them during these days as an infatuation. All of us suffer at one time or another from those awkward phenomena. Dr. Bickleigh's emotion was on a higher plane altogether than the ordinary mortal's; he never doubted that.

The thought of Madeleine was never out of his mind. If not blazing like a beacon in the foreground, then it was glowing heartfully in the background. It illuminated his every thought and action with a bright, holy light. From a wonderful experience Madeleine had leapt into an obsession with him. Everything else in his life (except Julia, in the evenings) had faded into a pale unreality. Even Julia only existed when he was with her.

He recognised this preoccupation, and compared it, quite sincerely, with the ecstasies of certain well-known saints. But the revelation vouchsafed to himself, he felt, was in one way at least greater than theirs; for, though it is doubtless a miraculous thing that a divine Being should put on humanity, is it not much more miraculous that a human being should put on divinity? If he had said any prayers at all, he would have said them to the spirit of Madeleine.

He stood humbly aghast at the incredible thing that had happened to him. That one who was the incarnation of purity, of unworldliness, of the soul as opposed to the body, should stoop to such gross clay as himself—should reach down to lift him too on to her own exalted plane! And she had lifted him. His old life, with its sordid outlook on money and women, pettifogging details of this and that, lay in tatters about him; with outstretched finger Madeleine pointed the way to broader, nobler ambitions and purer vistas. His old timidity began to vanish: how could he feel inferior to anyone in the world, if Madeleine loved him? Madeleine, with her sweet, chaste kisses that were the physical expression only of a communion of souls.

He did not desire her. He had not thought of her in that way at all. She was simply outside the orbit of gross, fleshly appetites. Every kiss they exchanged (and Madeleine, as befitted one so unfleshly, was sparing with her kisses) was to him part of a breathlessly holy ritual. And he, who had been accustomed to paw every woman the moment he gained her lips, never attempted the smallest familiarity of touch with Madeleine. *Her* body was sacrosanct.

In a word, Dr. Bickleigh had somehow managed to become seventeen again.

On the Thursday evening, depressed at having seen nothing of Madeleine all day and living only for the next afternoon, he had frankly fled. A particularly difficult case had been invented right the other side of Merchester, and Dr. Bickleigh had departed the moment after swallowing his coffee. He stayed out long enough to ensure that Julia should be in bed and asleep before he returned.

On Friday afternoon, bursting with eagerness, he parked his car on the side of the road and made his way into Madeleine's woods.

He found her in a punt on the edge of the lake, drawn up under an overhanging tree. She looked up at him with a face more grave than usual, and did not smile in answer to his joyful greeting.

"Come into the punt, Edmund. No, not this end, dear, please. I want to talk to you very seriously."

His joyful expression wiped off his face as if with a sponge, Dr. Bickleigh sat down obediently at the other end of the punt, full of foreboding.

Madeleine's enormous grey eyes regarded him mournfully. "I've been thinking since I saw you last, Edmund."

"Yes?" Something cold seemed to be clamping itself round Dr. Bickleigh's heart, constricting it.

"It can't go on."

"You mean—us?"

"Yes."

Dr. Bickleigh licked his dry lips. "Why not?"

"It isn't fair. To Julia."

"But—she doesn't care for me, Madeleine. Any more than I do for her."

"She's your wife, though. No, it wouldn't be fair."

"But it wouldn't be fair to us, the other way."

Madeleine shook her head. "No, I've thought it all out. We mustn't go on."

Dr. Bickleigh looked ahead into the darkness. He looked at Madeleine. On her face too was an expression of suffering. How noble she was: how altruistic always. And for Julia!

"I can't give you up," he burst out passionately. "Madeleine—darling, I can't. I wont!"

"You must, Edmund," she returned sorrowfully.

"And when I've only just found you. I can't."

"Do you love me so much?"

Dr. Bickleigh tried to tell her how much he loved her. The process took him to the other end of the punt, beside her. She shook her head mutely, but he caught her to him, and, as his arms closed round her, she yielded. He held her close against him, protesting his inability to give her up, ever, ever. She closed her eyes, and he kissed them gently. She let him kiss her mouth.

"Oh, Madeleine," he muttered despairingly, "you can't really love me, if you can talk about giving me up."

She opened her eyes and looked up at him as she lay in his arms, and said very solemnly: "Edmund, I love you more than life itself. But we must part."

To add to his unhappiness, she began to cry. Not with ugly, silly sobs, like Ivy, but with no sign but the tears actually running down from her eyes. Dr. Bickleigh felt as if he could break the world in pieces to end such grief. He crooned and moaned over her, almost weeping himself.

His ministrations, instead of soothing Madeleine, seemed to have the opposite effect. Her tears grew wilder; she clung to him; her emotion slipped further and further out of restraint; she sobbed as desperately as ever Ivy had. Dr. Bickleigh felt as though his heart were being cut up in small pieces under his eyes. But he was still able to marvel at the depths of Madeleine's love and call himself every vile name for having doubted it.

"We can't part, my darling," he went on repeating inanely. "It would kill us both."

"We must, we must," sobbed Madeleine.

"I'll tell Julia everything."

"No, no! You mustn't do that. Promise you won't."

"But she's not so bad as all that. She'd divorce me."

"Oh, Edmund," wept Madeleine, "I couldn't marry a divorced man." It was the first time marriage had been mentioned between them, and it was not an auspicious welcome.

Between tears they debated the matter. Madeleine continued to swear that she loved him more than life itself, but that she must give him up to Julia because she could never bear to think of herself as responsible for parting a husband and wife, even though they did not love one another and could never live happily together.

Dr. Bickleigh, when emotion allowed him, did his best to deal with the situation. Astonished though he was at the violence of her emotion, he yet tried to reason with her. He pointed out to Madeleine, who was now clinging to him more closely with each reiteration of her decision that they must part for ever, that her concern for Julia, though charming and altogether worthy of her, was quite misplaced. Julia had never shown concern for anyone else in her life: why should she now have the benefit of their own?

There was no longer any question of loyalty or disloyalty to Julia; he did not go beyond the bounds of plain truth, but that at any rate Madeleine must now have. He told her everything. The only result was to make Madeleine weep more unrestrainedly than before.

He emphasised that there must be some good in Julia, and without doubt when she learned the truth she would let him have his divorce. He repeated this several times, but Madeleine remained strangely unconvinced by it. Whatever happened, she continued to say, he must not tell Julia a single word—not a word. They must suffer, but there was no reason why Julia should too. Not one word!

In the case of anyone else Dr. Bickleigh would by this stage have diagnosed incipient hysteria; but with Madeleine, of course, that was impossible.

In the end they parted with nothing really settled, though Madeleine seemed to be taking for granted that they were parting for ever. She had recovered herself more or less before Dr. Bickleigh had to go, and bade him farewell with intensity.

II

Dr. Bickleigh returned home in a state of mental fermentation. He had refused to accept Madeleine's ultimatum. He would not even contemplate accepting it. Life without Madeleine now was unthinkable. If Madeleine took the initiative and fled from him, he would end it.

He even went so far as to sketch out during surgery, between patients, an entirely new vision: Madeleine fleeing to Monte Carlo, selling The Hall, marrying precipitately some soulless brute in her own sphere; the prussic acid in the surgery: the farewell notes, to Julia, to the coroner, to Madeleine: "Madeleine, my own darling, life without you is impossible. Better death. Yet, dying, I send you my . . ."

It was a miracle that he got through surgery without a single wrong diagnosis.

He wished Madeleine had not so expressly forbidden him to say anything to Julia. It was hateful, this underhand business. Once more he felt keyed up to tell Julia everything, like a decent man. She would never understand, of course, but something might come out of the interview. And Julia was still waiting to speak to him about going to The Hall. If she did, he knew he would be unable to stop himself from blurting out the truth, even if only in sheer panic. Julia *must* be stopped from speaking.

He stopped her in the same way as before.

Julia complained of her head towards the end of dinner. Just after pouring out the coffee in the drawing-room afterwards she rose unsteadily to her feet, took a few blind steps forward, and collapsed on the carpet in a dead faint. Her unconsciousness only lasted a couple of minutes, but Dr. Bickleigh had a severe fright. He had given her an overdose; her powers of resistance were not so great as he had supposed. When she came round she was moaning with pain. And for Julia to moan . . .

Sweating with compunction, he ran for his syringe and injected the morphia this time subcutaneously. It relieved her at once, and he helped her upstairs and into bed. When he came down again alone he was shaking all over. He had no love for Julia, but it seemed unfair that she should suffer thus simply in order not to be told.

He kept her in bed for the next two days, although she protested that she was quite recovered. That got him over two more evenings.

On the Sunday there was tennis at the Bournes'. He went alone, taking Julia's excuses with him. He knew he would not be wanted without Julia; but he went. Madeleine was there, and they greeted each other with beautiful casualness. Madeleine took no further notice of him at all, and talked more to Denny Bourne than anybody. Dr. Bickleigh spent a miserable afternoon.

On Monday he went up to The Hall.

Curiously enough, Madeleine, in spite of her expressed determination never to see him alone again, happened to be on her little lake: in a punt: in much the same place as before. She evinced the greatest surprise on seeing him.

The unrepentant man jumped in, beaming with delight, and plumped himself right down beside her.

"Edmund, you mustn't! Have you forgotten what I said? No, I won't let you," said Madeleine, and fell into his arms.

And that was all the reference she made to their last encounter.

Dr. Bickleigh, though a little bewildered, went on to spend a blissful afternoon. Madeleine had never been more delightful, either as companion or lover.

And they were practical too. The sanitation at The Hall

had astonished Dr. Bickleigh. It could never have been improved much since the primitive days when the house was built, Dr. Bickleigh told her that she must really do something about it: it was a scandal; it was unhealthy; it was positively dangerous. Madeleine quite agreed; undoubtedly she must do something about it. Dr. Bickleigh sketched out an alarmed picture of Madeleine expiring of typhoid in his arms. He became extremely distressed and earnest. Madeleine must really do something about it *at once*. Madeleine continued to agree; undoubtedly she must do something about it at once.

It was delightful to discuss these practical details with her. Even sanitation took on a kind of sanctified aspect when considered in relation to Madeleine.

That evening he told Julia.

Thinking it out on the way home from The Hall, he had made up his mind. He wanted to tell Julia badly, both because he detested the concealment and was still as anxious as ever to keep everything connected with this marvellous love on as high a level of purity and honesty as the love itself, and also (as he did not realise quite so plainly) because, having come during the last ten years to rely entirely upon Julia in every difficulty, he needed her help more than ever in this supreme one.

Julia took it incredibly well.

"Now, Edmund," she had said, directly the coffee-tray had been removed, "at last I am able to speak to you. I understand that, in direct contradiction of my wishes, you have been ——"

"Wait a minute, Julia," Dr. Bickleigh interrupted. He got up and stood on the hearthrug, his back to the fireplace. He felt quite calm, and not even nervous. The exaltation he always experienced when he had been with Madeleine was still with him. "I want to speak to you, too. About Miss Cranmere. I want to tell you this. I love Miss Cranmere, and she loves me."

Julia's pale-blue eyes, prominent behind their thick lenses, regarded him searchingly. She was silent for several moments, perhaps in astonishment at the first dignified speech she had ever heard from her husband. At last she said: "I was afraid of this." Her tone was as normal as if she told him to pass the butter.

Dr. Bickleigh felt a little jump inside his chest on the left, and realised that he had not been quite so calm as he imagined. "I'm—sorry, Julia," he said lamely, completely spoiling the effect.

"Well, Edmund, it's no good apologising," returned Julia, with brisk sanity. "Perhaps instead you'll tell me what you propose to do about it?"

But that was just what Edmund did not know. He intimated as much, confusedly.

Julia was still examining him minutely, as if she had hardly ever seen him before. "And how am I to know," she said slowly, "that this is not just another of the ordinary, sordid intrigues in which you have indulged continuously since we married? No, don't bother to deny it. I've known how you were behaving—Irene Sampford, Sybil Whitechurch, the Ryder gairl, Dean Prior's daughter in Merchester, Ivy Ridgeway, even Mabel Christow. I've said nothing, because that sort of vulgarity simply doesn't interest me. But the time has come for plain speaking. How am I to know that this affair with Miss Cranmere is not another of those?"

Dr. Bickleigh coloured. To hear Madeleine's name put on a par with Irene's, Ivy's, *Mabel's* . . . He began to speak hotly.

Julia stopped him. "Very well. I see that you do think yourself really in love with this gairl. And presumably you have had opportunities of discovering that she thinks herself in love with you. Whether you both are or not remains to be seen. Though the acquaintance is rather short, is it not?"

Dr. Bickleigh's mumbled reply seemed to be to the effect that when two people are utterly in tune with each other it does not take years to recognise the fact; it is plain at first sight.

"Love at first sight. I see. Most romantic, at your age," nodded Julia, but her tone was less unkind than her words. "Well, Edmund, I ask you again, what do you wish me to do about this love at first sight of yours? It's unfortunate that you have a wife, but there it is. However, if it's any consolation to you, I will put into plain words what you know perfectly well: that I am not in love with you in the least, and never have been. I married you to escape from an intolerable situation at home, and you are therefore perfectly right in assuming (as of course you do) that I have no moral claim on you at all. So you can speak quite plainly."

"This is awfully decent of you, Julia," exclaimed Dr. Bickleigh, flushing with gratitude and relief. Really, old Julia was . . .

"I may have a few decent feelings, though you have seldom credited me with any," returned Julia without emotion. "Well?"

"Well—I thought you might divorce me." In spite of her invitation to plain speaking, Dr. Bickleigh felt considerable embarrassment. After all . . .

"Yes, of course. I'm afraid my decency doesn't carry me to the point of letting you divorce me. But you realise that such a thing would ruin your practice here immediately?"

"Yes. I'd thought of starting again somewhere else."

"Humph! And I'm afraid you would have to make me an allowance. As you know, I have no money of my own at all. How do you propose to do that, and work up a new practice at the same time?"

"Oh, I don't think there'd be any difficulty about that, Julia."

"I see. You propose to pension off your first wife out of your second wife's money?"

"I—I haven't thought out any details at all yet," stammered Dr. Bickleigh.

Julia smoothed out the black silk on her lap, took off her glasses, polished them on her handkerchief, replaced them, and looked at her husband. "Now listen, Edmund. You can imagine that in the ordinary course I wouldn't listen to this idea of yours for an instant. The reason I do so is because it is Miss Cranmere who is involved. As even you have had the wit to recognise, she is a most exceptional gairl. I won't say anything about her taste in selecting you out of all the men who should be glad to marry her, but I will say that you may consider yourself undeservedly fortunate. I cannot say that I know her at all well. Beyond the calls we have exchanged and our tennis-party here, we have hardly met. But she made a most favourable impression on me. Most favourable.

"In these circumstances, and in view of those of our own marriage, I am prepared to give you your chance. But I must be certain that she is not mistaken in her feelings for you (yours for her I will take for granted). I therefore stipulate that all three of us go on as we are for another year, during which you may see as much of each other as you like: and if at the end of it she still wishes to marry you, then you shall have your divorce."

Dr. Bickleigh, yammering incoherencies, bounded forward and kissed his wife smackingly on the cheek. "Good Lord, Julia, you *are* . . . I say, I never dreamt you'd be so . . . Well, I've always said you were the most sensible woman I knew, but . . ."

Mrs. Bickleigh held up a finger. "But understand this, Edmund. If during that year you attempt to make Miss Cranmere your mistress, even in anticipation of marriage . . ."

Dr. Bickleigh's schoolboy exuberance dropped from him. He drew back in disgust.

Then reason reasserted itself. He looked at Julia only pityingly. After all, she could not help her sort of mind.

III

That was on the Monday. All Tuesday Dr. Bickleigh had to hug his secret to himself. On the Wednesday, just a week after Madeleine had sent him wandering so miserably into Merchester, he set off for The Hall in the highest of possible high spirits. What news to bring her! And what an afternoon ahead of him. He would even stay to dinner, if she asked him.

He turned in at the drive with assurance, and drove up to the house as if he were already its prince consort.

Talk about your Mr. Torrs now. It was with quite a shock that Dr. Bickleigh realised that he really was going to be part owner of this delightful place. Madeleine's wealth, after he had overcome his first feeling of insignificance which the presence of riches always induced in him, had faded quite into the background. Madeleine was Madeleine, and nothing else. But he did not feel it sordid to reflect now that it was exceedingly pleasant that Madeleine should be rich Madeleine too. After all, Madeleine's money was only incidental; though delightfully so. When one cannot afford even a new tennis-net . . .

"Miss Cranmere?" He smiled so happily at the parlourmaid at the door that, in spite of her training, she smiled back.

"I'm sorry, sir. Miss Cranmere is out."

"Out!" He tried to pull himself together. "Didn't she leave a message for me? I—I had—she made an appointment."

The parlourmaid looked most concerned, but no, Miss Cranmere had left no message.

"She must have forgotten all about it," muttered the doctor. "Nuisance. Thank you."

He went home, took off his best suit, put on his oldest, and gardened furiously till tea-time.

Julia looked faintly surprised to see him, but said nothing.

"She had to go out," Dr. Bickleigh felt himself called upon to mumble. "Couldn't get out of it. Left me a note."

Julia continued to say nothing.

On Thursday evening, however, she did say something. She said: "I met Lady Bourne this afternoon. She tells me that Miss Cranmere and Denny are entering for the mixed doubles in the Merchester tournament." It was another of the unexpected things about Madeleine that she played a game of tennis, exceptionally good even in these days of feminine proficiency. "They fixed it up yesterday."

"Yesterday!"

"Yes, Miss Cranmere was playing there yesterday afternoon. Didn't you know, Edmund?"

"Oh, yes. Yes, of course. I'd forgotten." It was a poor attempt. Julia said nothing.

On Friday afternoon Madeleine was waiting for him. He had not meant to reproach her; just utter a mild expostulation. But there was no need. Madeleine at once began to reproach herself. "Edmund, will you ever forgive me?"

"Forgive you, dear? There's nothing to forgive." He climbed into the punt beside her.

But she would not let him kiss her till she had explained properly. "I was terribly disappointed. And I knew you'd think me a beast. I was a beast. A devil!" The extent of her self-vituperation seemed extravagant for so minor an offence. "But I simply couldn't help it, dear. Honestly. I *had* to go to the Bournes'." Her big eyes searched his in appeal for forgiveness. She looked as solemn as if she were confessing to something really dreadful.

"Of course, darling." He wanted to kiss her badly.

"It would have looked so funny if I'd refused. They'd have known I wasn't going anywhere else." Madeleine had apparently not finished apologising yet, although any faint misgivings Dr. Bickleigh might have harboured had long ago disappeared. "I had to go, you see, for both our sakes. Did you hate me very much, Edmund?"

"Good gracious, no. I thought it must be something like that." And, as Madeleine was really looking as if she would not be content unless he did reproach her, he added mildly: "Just wondered why you didn't leave a note, perhaps. That's all."

"Oh, I *couldn't,* dear." Madeleine appeared quite shocked. "What would the servants have thought?"

There is no one more sensitive to other people's opinions of him than a doctor; he has to be, for other people's opinions of him are his bread-and-butter or the lack of it. But Dr. Bickleigh did feel that this was carrying deference to them a little too far.

The next instant he felt guiltily disloyal for having thought so. "Oh, yes; of course. Never thought of that."

"Then you really do forgive me?"

"Of course I do. Though there's nothing to forgive."

At last he was allowed to kiss her.

Dr. Bickleigh noticed with relief that there was no hint in Madeleine's manner of the mood of a week ago. He thought he understood that now: it was just a first reaction on the part of so pure and high-souled a girl to having let another woman's husband make love to her. Certainly her behaviour was being most satisfactory at the moment.

He judged the time propitious to bring out his great news.

"Darling, I've got something wonderful to tell you. I told Julia last night about Us. I thought you wouldn't mind really, and——"

"You told her! About Us!"

Madeleine's voice was shrill, and her face had gone suddenly quite white.

"Yes." Dr. Bickleigh was startled by the abrupt change in her, and tried to hurry on with his explanation. "I hated the idea of anything underhand about Us, you see, and I thought it over and——"

"But I told you not to. You promised not to—you promised."

"No, darling, I didn't," Dr. Bickleigh had to remonstrate. "I very carefully——"

"You did promise!"

"No, really, I——"

"You did! You beast, Edmund! How dare you, when I didn't want you to! You promised not to. It's—it's *horrible* of you." Dr. Bickleigh had attributed Madeleine's change of colour to concern on behalf of Julia: he now saw that it was due to sheer rage.

Madeleine began (there is really no other word for it) to storm at him.

During the next few moments it transpired, and with force, that Madeleine was seriously annoyed. The unfortunate Dr. Bickleigh learnt a number of things about himself which he had always suspected to be true, but had hoped Madeleine didn't. Obviously he had done something not merely foolish, but incredibly mean and underhand—because Madeleine told him so, not once, but several times. His humble protestations that he had only been trying to do the right thing, because he detested any hole-and-corner business in connection with her, carried no weight at all. He was, instead, a cad, a blunderer, and the villain of the piece. Of all this Madeleine, in her new rôle of Truth Stepping out of the Well, informed him with surprising emphasis. Dr. Bickleigh knew that Madeleine could not be wrong and he must therefore be all these things; but he did wish he knew how he had proved it merely by trying for once to be honest.

That Julia had not minded at all, Madeleine brushed aside as beneath notice. Apparently she ought to have minded, and so it had been a piece of outrageous cruelty to tell her.

Altogether Dr. Bickleigh left her that afternoon (or, rather, was left; for it was certainly Madeleine who did the leaving) in a state of considerable bewilderment.

If variety is the spice of love, Dr. Bickleigh might have reflected that he was certainly getting his own well seasoned.

IV

The next day he did not see her, nor the next. Julia preserved a tactful silence in face of his evident moodiness. On the Monday, Madeleine was not on the lake, nor could he find her in the wood. In desperation he went up to the house, regardless of the parlourmaid's possible condemnation.

The parlourmaid, so far from displaying any signs of disapproval, welcomed him like an old and valued friend. Miss Cranmere, she informed him, was in the drawing-room: would he come in? He would, and did.

Madeleine received him sorrowfully, as one uncertain whether to take the lost sheep back into the fold or not. The sheep apologised with humility for his lapse (that he was apologising really for having been honest occurred apparently to neither of them), and went on apologising, so long and so humbly, that in the end Madeleine forgave him for what he had not done and opened the door of the fold once more. "But, Edmund," she told him very gravely before letting him quite in, "if you ever break another promise to me . . . if you make me feel I can't really trust you . . ."

Dr. Bickleigh forbore to point out that he had not broken a promise at all yet, for by this time he had quite accepted the accusation and believed in it as firmly as she did.

The way thus cleared, they were able to discuss Julia's remarkable offer.

Madeleine agreed that it was noble, generous, more than they could ever have expected, anything he liked; but, though showing moderate pleasure, she certainly did not share the doctor's immoderate enthusiasm. He could not understand why. Here was the path being cleared for their feet, and Madeleine could only smile sadly and say how nice it was, and how kind of Julia. He pressed her, but could get no satisfactory answer.

At last she told him.

"Oh, Edmund, I never thought I should have to marry a divorced man."

This point of view astonished Dr. Bickleigh. Why did she mind that? For religious reasons?

Oh, no. It was not a matter of religion. Madeleine hoped she was not so narrow-minded as all that.

Why, then?

"You know people talk so. It's horrid."

"But, my darling, surely you don't mind what silly people say, so long as we're happy?"

"No, dear, of course I don't. But it's not very nice, is it?"

Dr. Bickleigh did not point out that she had already set the Wyvern's Cross tongues wagging by coming to live at The Hall alone, because if her charming innocence on that head were dispelled she would probably import an aunt or something equally in the way. Instead, he tried to soothe her with comforting facts.

"Well, I should have to give up this practice, of course. We can settle down somewhere else where no one will know. Or go abroad, darling. Or anything, so long as we're together and you're happy."

In that case, Madeleine agreed, things might not be so bad; but she remained disappointingly unenthusiastic.

Not that she seemed to love him any the less. Once he had been taken back into the fold the shepherdess withheld none of its privileges. But it was disconcerting that she should interrupt some of their most intimate moments with the wailing cry: "Oh, Edmund, if *only* you weren't married. You don't know how I hate the idea of divorce."

Dr. Bickleigh did know. Madeleine seemed to take pains that he should.

However, she asked him to stay to dinner, and on the whole he spent a very wonderful and holy day.

There was only one other small thing which disconcerted him. Julia had remarked the other evening that a little later on, when things were less tempestuous, she would call on Madeleine and discuss the situation sensibly. When Dr. Bickleigh casually mentioned this after dinner, Madeleine was vehement in her opposition. Such a thing was sordid; it was embarrassing; it was altogether impossible. Dr. Bickleigh, who had thought it most sporting of Julia, and entirely in keeping with the way in which he wished the whole situation to be handled, was surprised, but knew now better than to argue; he hurriedly changed the subject. But he was perturbed. If Julia had said she was going to call, she would call; and if Madeleine, as she protested she would, refused to see her when she did call, what was going to happen? He left the question to look after itself.

Driving home late that night, he was able to see the interview in perspective. Instantly it became plain that Madeleine's dislike of marrying a divorced man was not captious at all, but simply entrancing. Naturally to her flowerlike mind the idea had been an obnoxious shock. But she would get used to it. She must.

V

Julia did call on Madeleine.

She called about a fortnight later. During that time the course of true love had been running more smoothly. Things seemed to have settled down, Madeleine was particularly charming and affectionate, and Dr. Bickleigh had been living in high heaven. The Merchester tournament came and went, and for four days Dr. Bickleigh did not see her at all, for he was too busy to get over there; she and Denny Bourne reached the semi-finals, when they were beaten by a Davis Cup player and his partner, but even then not disastrously. Madeleine could hardly talk about anything else when she saw him next. Dr. Bickleigh, who had no idea that she attached so much importance to games, was charmed by yet another side of his many-faceted young woman. He entered light-heartedly into her mood, and they spent one of the happiest afternoons they had had together.

Julia's call shattered heaven in ugly fragments.

She did not give the least hint that she had been until the evening. Then, as they were sitting in the drawing-room, she looked up from her crochet-work and said abruptly, "Edmund, I called on Miss Cranmere this afternoon."

"Oh, yes?" said the doctor apprehensively. Julia's tone was ominous.

"I rang her up in the morning to make the appointment. She was out, so I left the message. When I got there, the maid said she was ill in bed and could not see me." Julia paused.

"Ill?" echoed Dr. Bickleigh, alarmed.

"As ill as you or I. However, I insisted, and she saw me." From Julia's voice it was possible to gather that she was cutting quite a long story short here. "She received me in a white cotton nightgown," she continued surprisingly, "and a red flannel dressing-gown." She paused again significantly.

"Oh, yes?" said Dr. Bickleigh vaguely, not seeing the significance. Cotton was perhaps not the material he himself would have chosen for a nightgown, but it was only another example of the charming unsophistication of Madeleine's tastes. "Did she?" he added, as Julia still seemed to be waiting for something.

"Well, does that convey nothing to you?"

Dr. Bickleigh, who was not disposed to share his opinion of Madeleine's simple unfleshliness, shook his head.

"Why does a gairl who could afford to have her nightgown of triple ninon and gold *lamé* dressing-gowns wear cotton and red flannel?" demanded Julia sternly. "I'll tell you, Edmund. Because she wants even the housemaid to think her that sort of gairl."

"*What*?" asked the bewildered doctor.

Julia took off her glasses, polished and replaced them, an invariable portent of serious speech. "Edmund, I'm not one to mince my words. What I have to say will pain you, and I am sorry for that; but it has got to be said. My interview with Miss Cranmere this afternoon was most instructive. I don't propose to tell you even the gist of it; certainly not the foolish things that were said; only what it has opened my eyes to. Edmund, I am sorry to have to say so, but that gairl is a hypocrite."

"Julia!" exclaimed Dr. Bickleigh, colouring angrily.

"A hypocrite," repeated Mrs. Bickleigh calmly. "She hasn't the least feeling for you; she is merely amusing herself. She has not the faintest intention of marrying you, even if you are ever free. Did you even know that she is conducting a flirtation with Denny Bourne every bit as violent as the one with you? She is a *poseuse* of the very worst description. She is acting the whole time. If she had her living to make she would be on the stage at once. She is obviously hysterical, and yet at the same time I could detect in her a callous calculation which quite disgusted me. Her selfishness is inconceivable; nothing interests her but herself and her own silly emotions. In short, I should call her utterly untrustworthy, egotistical to the point of mania, and the most dangerous kind of liar there is—the liar who can deceive not only other people, but herself as well.

"Naturally," added Julia, as if anxious to be fair, "I did not discover this all at once. It only dawned on me gradually, and at first I could not believe it. Then I began to test her, and discovered that she was worse than I suspected. It was not a pleasant process, but necessary for both our sakes. I may say that of course Miss Cranmere has no idea of my opinion of her."

Dr. Bickleigh had sat like a small statue, the only sign of his feelings the gradual suffusion of his face. Now he jumped to his feet and, almost out of his mind with rage, leant over his wife. "Look here," he articulated thickly, "if you think that these damned lies of yours are going to make me ——"

"Sit down, Edmund, and don't be childish. You know perfectly well that I invariably speak the truth; lying simply doesn't interest me. This is a shock for you, I know, and I am ready to make allowances. Now listen, please. In other circumstances I should have remained silent and left you to find all this out for yourself, as in due time you will. But I don't consider that in this case that would be fair, because, having altered my decision of a week or two ago, I think you are entitled to the reason for it. In other words, I am not prepared to divorce you for the sake of that gairl."

"Oh—that's what you're getting at, is it?"

"It is, Edmund, and I mean it. It would only mean quite unnecessary unhappiness for you, and when you've got over this infatuation you'll realise that. I'm sorry you should think it pique on my part, as apparently you do; you ought to know me well enough by this time to realise that I should not give way to anything like that. Besides, I am quite prepared to keep my promise in the future. If you ever do meet a gairl, a *nice* gairl, who——"

"Oh, shut up, you——," screamed Dr. Bickleigh, and rushed out of the room.

Julia sat for a moment regarding the banged door; then took up her crochet-work again.

VI

Possessed apparently by some mechanical relict of himself, who performed the normal functions of opening the garage doors, starting up the Jowett, and avoiding the left-hand gate-post after the awkward corner from the stable-yard, Dr. Bickleigh succeeded in making his way without scathe to The Hall. It was a Thursday, and therefore a Madeleine *dies non,* but that did not even occur to him. He drove in a rigid trance of fury.

What he intended to do at The Hall he had no idea. He just had to see Madeleine, and, incidentally, scotch this abominable calumny.

Madeleine was at home, and alone. She rose as he was shown into the drawing-room, and, immediately the door was closed, uttered one word: "Julia!"

Dr. Bickleigh nodded.

"She didn't like me. I felt it. I can always feel that sort of thing. Edmund—what has she been saying?"

Dr. Bickleigh took her in his arms and kissed her. He felt as if he could never let her go. "Oh, nothing much." No need to distress poor Madeleine with what Julia had really said. "I just felt . . ."

"Oh, Edmund, I was wanting you, too. Was she very horrid?"

"We just had a bit of a tiff. Nothing much. Was she beastly to you this afternoon?"

Madeleine's eyes filled with tears. She turned her head away.

"Not very sympathetic."

"You've been crying."

"Yes."

"Oh, my darling."

"But what did she *say*, Edmund?"

"Oh, nothing much, really. Some nonsense about you and young Bourne."

Madeleine looked up quickly. "Denny? What?"

"I don't know. That you'd been flirting with him, or something."

"At Merchester?"

"She didn't mention Merchester."

"Edmund—did you believe it?"

"My darling, of course I didn't."

Madeleine gazed at him, her eyes larger than ever. "Well, I did."

"Flirted with Denny?" Dr. Bickleigh exclaimed.

"Yes; at Merchester. Well, not flirted with him. Just let him be attentive in public. On purpose."

"But, dearest, why?"

Madeleine looked her gravest. "For *your* sake, Edmund. I thought people might be beginning to talk about *us*. So I—well, I'm afraid I rather encouraged poor Denny. People were looking at us quite a lot. I don't think they'll talk about *us* any more."

"My wonderful darling!" It seemed the most self-sacrificing thing he had ever heard. Julia's *beastly* mind . . .

"Are you cross with me?"

"Cross! I could kiss your dear feet. But, Madeleine . . ."

"Yes?"

"You're not—fond of him, are you?"

"Fond of him?" Madeleine smiled tolerantly. Men are so foolish. "Why, he's only a boy."

"Is he fond of you?"

"I think he could be. But I shan't let things go as far as that."

"It's me you really love, isn't it?"

"Yes, Edmund," Madeleine said solemnly. "It's you I really love."

"Really, really?"

"Really, really, *really*."

Dr. Bickleigh released her and began to walk about restlessly. Madeleine sat on the arm of a chair and watched him.

"Darling, I know you do love me, but how much?"

"Quite a lot, Edmund."

"If only I knew how much," he groaned.

"Why?"

"I want to know."

He did want to know. If she did—well, everything else could go to the wall, including Julia. Not that Julia's beastly jealousy had made him doubt Madeleine for an instant, but he had to know how great her love was. A test—he must think of a test that would show him once and for all.

He thought of one. Trembling, he crossed to where she sat and took her hand. "Madeleine," he said, hoarsely, "suppose—suppose I asked you to come away now, just as we are, and—and live with me. Would you?"

Madeleine tilted back her head and looked him full in the eyes. "Yes," she whispered.

"Then you do love me!"

"Yes."

It was his supreme moment.

They clung to one another in a holy embrace.

That night Dr. Bickleigh decided that Julia must die.

Chapter Six

I

EARLY in November, Dr. Bickleigh met Quarnian Torr late one afternoon some miles from Wyvern's Cross. She had been out beagling, and, stopping him, demanded a lift back.

One could always rely on Quarnian for the neighbourhood's news. He had scarcely tucked the rug round her before she began.

"Heard the latest, Dr. Bickleigh?"

"I don't expect so. What?"

"About Ivy?"

"No." Dr. Bickleigh had almost forgotten Ivy. He had not seen her for months. There had been some unpleasant episode. . . . Oh, yes.

Quarnian eyed her companion surreptitiously, and was disappointed to notice his lack of interest. Everybody knew that at one time he had been quite sweet on Ivy.

"She's engaged." Her news was falling disgustingly flat.

"Is she?" said Dr. Bickleigh heartily. "Good. Who to?"

"Mr. Chatford."

"Excellent. Capital fellow, Chatford. Very sound."

Quarnian rubbed her nose. "Shouldn't care for him as a husband myself," she laughed, rather noisily. "Still, there's no accounting for tastes, is there? I dare say he'll suit Ivy well enough."

"I dare say," murmured Dr. Bickleigh absently. He was

thinking that this tidied up the unfortunate Ivy episode very satisfactorily. Lord, what a rotter he had been in those days. Beastly. . . .

"Ivy's awfully gooey, isn't she?" Quarnian was hopefully prodding.

"Gooey?"

"Soppy."

"Oh. Yes, perhaps she is a little."

Quarnian sighed. This was uphill work. She decided to employ more direct methods.

"You used to like her all right, though, didn't you?"

"Yes, quite. Perfectly harmless. Which is more," said Dr. Bickleigh, "than one can say for everyone round here."

"People do gossip a hell of a lot, don't they?" agreed Miss Torr frankly. "They make me sick. Miss Peavy, for instance."

"Miss Peavy?" Dr. Bickleigh had never classed Miss Peavy among the gossips. She seemed altogether too vague. Miss Wapsworthy, perhaps; there was plenty of malice there. But not Miss Peavy.

"Rather. And who do you think she's got her knife into now?"

"I can't imagine."

"Why, Madeleine Cranmere, of all people."

If Miss Torr's object had been to enlist Dr. Bickleigh's interest, she had succeeded. He stiffened visibly. "Indeed?"

"You bet she has," continued Miss Torr with enjoyment, noting her companion's sudden rigidity. "She's saying the most awful things about her. I can't imagine why. I'm awfully fond of Madeleine. Aren't you, Dr. Bickleigh?" she added artlessly.

"I think Miss Cranmere is a very charming young lady. It's disgusting that people should gossip about her."

There was a little silence. Quarnian hugged herself.

She was far too much of an artist to overdo her effects. Dr. Bickleigh's tone had suggested plainly that he did not wish to pursue the subject further, and yet Quarnian hardly thought he would leave it at that.

"What," asked Dr. Bickleigh very stiffly, "is Miss Peavy saying about Miss Cranmere?"

"Oh, a most extraordinary story," replied Quarnian, who thought she could now let herself go. She would have liked a little flirtation with the doctor herself on the way home, but, though she had given him some small encouragement, such as the careful juxtaposition of her knee with his and requiring to have things tucked rather intimately round her, he was obviously not going to oblige; and this was certainly the next best amusement.

"She's saying that Madeleine's in love with a married man, and making the most awful trouble between him and his wife; and that's why she went away so suddenly. She says they want a divorce and the man's wife won't divorce him, and there'll be the most awful scandal when it all comes out, and—oh, lots of extraordinary things like that. I don't believe a word of it, do you, Dr. Bickleigh?"

"Certainly not. It's—it's ridiculous."

"But it's all round the place, for all that," said Quarnian with gusto. "Everybody's talking about it. I think it's disgusting, don't you?"

"And—who is this married man that Miss Cranmere's supposed to be in love with?" asked Dr. Bickleigh, very casually.

"Oh, nobody seems to know that," Quarnian replied, with complete untruth. "I expect there isn't such a person at all, if you ask me. Don't you, Dr. Bickleigh?"

"I think it's abominable. And I shall make it my duty to inform Miss Cranmere of these lies when she comes back." There was a pink spot on each of Dr. Bickleigh's cheek-bones, but he had his voice quite under control.

"Oh, do," urged Quarnian hopefully. "When everybody knows it's Denny Bourne she really likes," she added, more hopefully still.

But this time Dr. Bickleigh was not to be drawn.

He dropped Quarnian outside the Vicarage, and drove straight to Miss Peavy's cottage. Miss Peavy was at home, and received him in a flutter of welcome. She had always liked Dr. Bickleigh.

He marched into the tiny sitting-room and confronted her.

"Miss Peavy, I hear you've been spreading libellous reports about Miss Cranmere. I propose to advise Miss Cranmere to instruct her solicitors. Have you anything to say?"

"Dr. Bickleigh!" Whatever Miss Peavy might have had to say had apparently been struck clean out of her mouth. She worked it, without result.

"You don't deny it, then?"

"*Really*, Dr. Bickleigh. . . . This is . . . I don't understand in the least. Nobody has ever said such a . . . Certainly I have done nothing of the sort. How—how dare you?" Indignation was gradually restoring Miss Peavy's power of speech.

"Then you do deny it?"

"Certainly I do. I—I never spread gossip. I make it a habit. Not to, I mean. Just like Mrs. Bickleigh. This is really quite . . ."

"Then how do you account for the rumours which I hear are circulating about Miss Cranmere?"

"I don't see why I should be called upon to account for them at all," retorted Miss Peavy with spirit. "What rumours?"

"Connecting her name with some married man's, or some nonsense. Do you still deny you've been spreading that?"

"How dare you speak to me like that, Dr. B-bickleigh? C-certainly I d-deny it."

"Then I suppose you deny that you've ever heard such a rumour?"

"I shall do nothing of the sort. I hope I shall continue to speak the truth, even if I am to be insulted like this. Quarnian Torr told me that. I refused to listen."

"Oh, that's your story, is it?"

"Dr. Bickleigh," said Miss Peavy, with unusual dignity, "it's my opinion that you've been drinking."

Dr. Bickleigh disregarded Miss Peavy's opinion.

"Why have you got your knife into Miss Cranmere?"

"I haven't got it. My knife. In her, I mean."

"Do you tell me that you like Miss Cranmere?"

"N-no," squeaked Miss Peavy, but with courage. "No, I don't like her. I never have liked her. I think—I think she's untruthful. And—and if you don't want rumours to go round about her and a married man, you'd better blame the married man, and—and tell him to see that in future there's no cause for them, Dr. Bickleigh. Th-th-that's what you'd better do." And with that she fled out of the room and upstairs to her bedroom, where she hurriedly locked the door.

Dr. Bickleigh, who had had no intention of pursuing her to that fastness, walked out to his car again. He felt pleased with himself. More, he positively glowed. He had struck a blow for Madeleine. That would stop that hag's poisonous tongue, and perhaps a few others as well; he certainly had given her the fright of her life.

Upstairs, Miss Peavy was peeping round the chintz curtain. Breathing very rapidly, she watched the doctor get into his car and drive off.

"*Well . . . !* Well, I . . . I've *never* been so . . . Horrible man! *Poor* Mrs. Bickleigh . . ." said Miss Peavy, mostly in italics, and burst into tears.

II

Madeleine was abroad. She had gone away in the middle of October; in fact, not very long after Denny had returned to Oxford for his last Michaelmas term, and just when Dr. Bickleigh was revelling in having her all to himself; for, though he quite saw the necessity of her spending so much time with Denny, even to the extent of appearing to the gross public to be having an affair with him, and applauded such self-sacrifice on her part, yet it had been nice to have her all to himself. Especially after September.

September had not been an easy month at all. For one thing, the sanitation *motif* had kept cropping up, and it had decidedly lost its sanctified aspect. Madeleine had done nothing about it, and Dr. Bickleigh was beginning to take her drains almost as a personal matter. They were abominable, disgraceful, a sheer danger to the whole household; Madeleine must do something about them *at once*. But Madeleine, displaying unexpected meanness, kept prevaricating, sometimes apologetically, more often testily.

Her attitude towards her drains was typical of Madeleine just then. She had been—well, not difficult, but obviously suffering from the strain of it all. It is impossible to carry on the love-affair of a century at white heat with a man who happens unfortunately to be married to someone else and not feel any strain, as anybody could understand. September was therefore spent by Madeleine in deciding, on alternate days, that Dr. Bickleigh and she must for a hundred thousand reasons give each other up for ever, and that they could never part at all for the one good reason that they loved each other so stupendously. There had been long and earnest discussions in the library at The Hall (gradually the library had been adopted instead of the drawing-room, as more suitable to such momentous business), to a running accompaniment of passionate embraces, ardent protestations, and tears; but the situation remained apparently unaltered one way or the other.

Dr. Bickleigh continued to assure Madeleine that to distress herself on Julia's account was waste of time and trouble, because Julia didn't deserve it. That Julia had changed her mind about the divorce he judged it better not to mention. He did not tell Madeleine that she need distress herself all the less because he had quite decided now to put Julia out of their joint way, because that is not the sort of consolation one very well can administer; he had to content himself with affirming, as one who knew, that things would come all right for them in the end. Madeleine, not being one who knew, continued to kiss him good-bye for ever one minute and plan to elope to Paris with him the next.

In the end she eloped to Monte Carlo alone, to "think things over." It was not the season, she pointed out earnestly, and therefore Monte Carlo would be quite innocuous, even for a high-souled young woman all alone.

While she was away, Dr. Bickleigh wrote to her ardently every day, and about once a week heard from her in return—artless, sincere little notes such as this:

"EDMUND DARLING,—I just loved your letter this morning. I could hardly wait for my coffee and rolls to read it. Edmund dear, remember that you promised you wouldn't let Julia divorce you without letting me know first. Edmund, I do hope I don't have to marry a divorced man. I love you, darling, love you, love you, *love* you.

"Your MADELEINE.

"P.S.—I love you, Edmund."

If these notes did not breathe quite all the reckless passion Dr. Bickleigh might have wished, this was doubtless because Madeleine was such a pure and innocent person.

Well, she would not have to marry a divorced man.

Dr. Bickleigh had not yet decided on his method, but he had formed his decision.

Any idea, however preposterous at first sight, if toyed with for long enough will begin to take on a practical aspect; any ugliness will be lifted by familiarity, if not into beauty, at any rate on to a plane where those relative terms have no meaning. The public monuments of Mr. Jacob Epstein cease to be the most preposterously hideous works of sculpture since the antediluvian days of Ur, and become handy conveniences for sparrows. Murder ceases to be murder at all, and becomes a merciful release.

Of course, Dr. Bickleigh did not think of what he proposed to do as "murder" at all. Not that he consciously avoided the word. He simply could not accept it. Other people "murdered" their wives, but other people's cases were quite different. His case was unique: Dr. Bickleigh was quite sure of that. Julia was impossible; life with Julia any longer was impossible; divorce by consent was impossible, because Julia, having had her chance, had thrown it away, and Julia never changed her mind more than once; divorce in any case would be calamitous, from his professional standpoint; a future without Madeleine was unthinkable; only one course was inevitable. It was quite simple.

Dr. Bickleigh did understand quite well that the world would call that course "murder"; but how could the cloddish world ever understand the peculiar delicacy of his own feelings, or appreciate what Madeleine meant to him? Better that a thousand humdrum Julias should be sacrificed than that Madeleine should suffer a moment: Julia simply did not count, compared with Madeleine: but how could the world ever understand that? Occasionally, in moments of surprised detachment, Dr. Bickleigh did find himself on the world's side of the fence. "By Jove, but it *is* murder." But the thought was invariably followed by an odd little thrill of pride: "Well, then, here's one murderer going to get away with it, anyhow." And the next moment he would see that of course it was not murder at all.

His normal attitude was simplicity itself. In his duties he had put away plenty of pet animals who had passed their usefulness. Now the time had come to put Julia away. That was all.

On one point he was quite determined. Not until he had found the perfect plan, the utterly undetectable method, would he do anything at all. To rush things would be fatal.

His visions took on a new significance. Having contemplated ever since June the fortunate removal of Julia by some opportune disease, the idea of her death was already familiar to him. From that to himself as the cause of it was the smallest of steps. The vision of Julia's death-bed found itself extended backwards; instead of being occupied exclusively with the result, it began to concern itself with the cause. Poison of some sort? A fatality that would be accepted as an accident? Drowning, if managed in some cunning way? During the winter Dr. Bickleigh lived through them all, while his hours of sleep grew less and less.

He did not consider that, so far, he was doing anything at all out of the ordinary. From what he had seen of marriage he did not doubt that most married men spend no small part of their lives devising wistful plans for killing off their wives—if only they had the courage to do it. Where his superiority was going to show itself was in putting his own dreams into action.

That this superiority was indeed his he now took quite for granted. The fact that Madeleine loved him proved it. Madeleine's love lifted him out of the ruck and set him on a pedestal, infinitely lower than her own, of course, but infinitely above the common mass too. The man whom Madeleine loved must be a super-being, capable of anything; and if she loved Dr. Bickleigh, as she did, then a super-being Dr. Bickleigh must be—little though he had suspected it before. Now at last his eyes had been opened to himself.

And, of course, to a super-being murder is merely incidental.

His visions gradually extended now into the daytime. In a scattered country practice such as his the panel is not large, and there are plenty of private patients. Often Dr. Bickleigh had to drive several miles between visits. It amused him now to amble along at the wheel of the Jowett, down lanes and deserted little roads on which one hardly ever met another vehicle, and chew over, point by point, the details of the plan of the moment: so absorbed that his driving was just mechanical, and the salutations of passing acquaintances went as often as not unnoticed. Over and over it again he would go, by night and by day, with a few tiny variations each time which his imagination, uncurbed by repetition, would always supply; following it step by step and incident by incident through imagined weeks, months, and even years, till at last some major flaw would reveal itself to his patience and he would thankfully discard it to look for another. Julia Bickleigh must have died in at least a dozen different ways before her husband, at the beginning of December, found at last the scheme he had been seeking.

It was a wonderful scheme. So obviously fool-proof that very little testing was needed. Whatever happened, it could never be found out. There was the possibility of failure, it was true, but that was well worth risking in view of its other merits. He could never find another plan to come near it.

Curiously enough, it was Julia herself who put it into his mind. Julia had one of her headaches, and asked him for some phenacetin. It was an exceptionally bad one, so he gave her morphia instead, a subcutaneous injection, and told her what it was and why he was doing it. As before, the morphia relieved her at once, and she remarked how much more efficacious it seemed to be than phenacetin. That was all, but it presented Dr. Bickleigh with his plan ready-made.

Four evenings later he proceeded to put it into action. Curiously enough, there was grape-fruit for dinner. Dr. Bickleigh took the coincidence for a lucky omen, and smiled as he dusted the powder over Julia's portion. Julia's headache that night was even worse than the last, and it was she herself who suggested morphia. That too, Dr. Bickleigh thought, was a good augury.

The next evening Julia had another headache, and the next, and the next. On the fourth evening Dr. Bickleigh thought it advisable to increase the dose of morphia a little, and told Julia so, explaining that her powers of resistance to it were getting greater. Julia, white with pain, quite agreed.

It distressed Dr. Bickleigh that Julia should have to suffer like this, but he quite saw that it could not be helped; in any case, it would not be for long. The two were living now on outwardly quite good terms, or as good as they ever had been. Madeleine's name was never mentioned. Julia, who rose above her sex in many particulars, did so in this one too, and, whatever curiosity she may have had to stifle, never asked a thing about the progress of the affair. So far as one could judge, she had simply wiped the whole thing out of her mind. She had not even attempted to stop her husband from going up to The Hall before Madeleine went away, and, though she must have known they were in correspondence, she never once gave any indication of it. Julia was really a most exceptional woman. It was a pity, thought her husband with real regret, that she had got to die.

All through December and January she continued to suffer intermittently from her headaches, and Dr. Bickleigh, solicitous and sympathetic, continued to relieve her with morphia. Early in February she went away for a change to see if that would do her any good, though Dr. Bickleigh did not seem to think it would; they were both right, for, though she had felt much better during her fortnight's holiday and had not had a single headache during that time, they began again immediately she got back.

"You ought to have taken a month," Dr. Bickleigh told her sympathetically.

"Quite impossible," said Julia. "What would happen to the house?" Which of course was unanswerable, even for a medical attendant and husband combined. "Besides," she added, "there is no reason at all why I should be run down." And one gathered that if there was no reason, then it was out of the question that Julia should be run down.

Dr. Bickleigh, it appeared, was inclined to agree with this. "I'm very much afraid it isn't just a matter of being run down, after all, my dear. It looks to me like something organic."

"Well, what?"

"That I can't say. But if these headaches go on, I shall have to take you up to see a specialist."

"You will do nothing of the kind, Edmund," said Julia indignantly.

But the headaches did go on, and Dr. Bickleigh gained his point. They went up to London, with an appointment to see Sir Tamerton Foliott himself.

Sir Tamerton made a most thorough examination of Julia's teeth, her eyes, her ears, and most things that were hers, keeping up all the time a running accompaniment of searching questions. Julia, who had taken a strong dislike to him at first sight, told her husband afterwards that she was sure he would have whisked out her liver and had a good look at that through his eyeglass before putting it back if he could have done so, he talked so much about it. However, Julia had not been manhandled for nothing, for Sir Tamerton was able to say with confidence and precision exactly what was wrong with her. She was eating too much, and the wrong foods: there was an old tooth-stump, which must come out at once; and, while she was about it, she had better have her tonsils out too, as they were most probably the cause of the whole trouble—one of them showed distinct signs of sepsis, definite signs—have a look for yourself, Bickleigh; yes, they should come out without delay.

Sir Tamerton then jotted down a diet for her, tapped his teeth with his gold pencil a great number of times, swung his eyeglass (which he used, though no one would ever have believed it, because his left eye was slightly myopic), passed another reference or two to Julia's liver in a chatty way, as if asking after an old friend who had gone a little downhill and was no longer quite so respectable as one could have wished but whom one wasn't going to be so snobbish as to cut for all that, and finally shook hands most warmly considering that he was getting no fee for all this trouble. He also assured her that in future she would have no headaches, with such conviction that for the moment Julia actually believed him. It was just this conviction coinciding with his patients' wishes which had made all the difference to Sir Tamerton Foliott between Harley Street and Wyvern's Cross.

"But really, Edmund," said Julia, as they walked along Harley street afterwards towards Baker Street Station, "why my tonsils?"

"Tonsils?" repeated Dr. Bickleigh vaguely. He was somewhat engrossed in his thoughts. His opinion of Foliott had gone down. Not that the man could have been expected to diagnose the real trouble, of course; that would have been a clairvoyant's job, not a medical man's; but really, all that stale old stuff . . .

"What could tonsils possibly have to do with headaches?"

"Oh, Sir Tamerton's very keen on tonsils." Dr. Bickleigh's tone implied no censure of Sir Tamerton's hobby; it is well known that specialists must have their idiosyncrasies. "He always advises their removal. Now if we'd gone to Hameldown Beacon, who's nearly as big a man as Sir Tamerton, he'd have gone for your antrum, and paraffin oil."

"If you know in advance what any specialist is going to tell you, why bother to take me to one?" remarked Julia.

"Oh, a second opinion is sometimes very useful," Dr. Bickleigh replied smugly.

They went to Madame Tussaud's.

Dr. Bickleigh had never been in the Chamber of Horrors before. He was much interested.

III

In the middle of March, Dr. Bickleigh put the second part of his plan into action. This was where the possibility of failure lay. Things had to be left entirely to Julia, and if Julia did not follow the course mapped out for her, then all her headaches had been wasted.

For Sir Tamerton, it appeared, had been quite wrong. So far from having no more headaches, she had suffered from them even more violently than before. From being intermittent they had now become practically continuous. Julia was getting white and drawn, and her healthy robustness had quite disappeared. All Wyvern's Cross had noticed the change in her.

Another short holiday at the end of February, just a week taken by her husband's earnest demands, had had no effect at all, in spite of sea air. She had been in such pain the whole time that she could hardly leave the lodgings. Dr. Bickleigh, who had managed to take the week off himself to look after his wife, was loud in his disappointment.

It was not for want of effort that Julia grew worse. The tooth-stump had been removed; she rigidly followed the diet Sir Tamerton had prescribed. Only her tonsils she refused to part with, and in this Dr. Bickleigh strongly agreed with her. The removal of tonsils is a painful operation, and there was not the least need for Julia to suffer unnecessary pain.

During this time morphia had been her stand-by. She had admitted, with an unmirthful smile, that it was the only thing that had kept her from going quite out of her mind. Dr. Bickleigh, really anxious to save her suffering, administered it to her whenever she asked for it, which now was very frequently. To make it effective he had had to double the original dose for the injections, and then treble it, and still more. By the middle of March Julia was having a good five grains a day.

It was then that Dr. Bickleigh judged the time to be ripe.

When she asked for her usual dose one evening after dinner he began to hum and ha.

"But I gave you a grain, my dear, just after tea."

"I know, and now my head's worse than ever."

Dr. Bickleigh stroked his chin and looked very grave. "You know, it can't go on like this. It simply can't, Julia."

"What can't?"

"All this morphia."

Julia turned leaden eyes on him. "What do you mean, Edmund?" She pressed her hand to her forehead and went on looking at him from below it in the same dull way, as if it really did not matter much what he meant.

Dr. Bickleigh had to turn away. "Well it's very bad for you, you know."

"It can't be worse than this."

"No, I mean if you get to rely on it like this, can't carry on without it, well . . ."

"Kindly put into plain words what you do mean, Edmund," said Julia wearily.

"Well, then, to put it bluntly, it'll become a habit."

"Nonsense! If you're hinting that there is a likelihood of my becoming a drug-fiend . . . Really, Edmund."

"Oh, no; not so bad as that. I know you only want it when there's real necessity for it. But for all that, Julia, it's bad for you. Very bad. You must try to do without it."

"That's absurd. If you can't cure me, Edmund, the least you can do is to relieve me. Kindly come to the surgery and give me an injection at once."

"Julia, you must try to bear it." Dr. Bickleigh showed nothing but concern, though his pulses were racing. "Honestly you must. Look at your arm: it's covered with punctures already. It mustn't go on. As your medical man, I must insist. If you want any more injections, you'll have to—to change your doctor. I can't administer any more, for your own sake, Julia."

Mrs. Bickleigh, already at the door, answered in a voice made peremptory by pain, but she found her husband unexpectedly firm. Nor was he to be shaken in the argument that followed, by reason, or by as near as Julia could come to entreaties: no more morphia would he administer to her; if she wanted more, she must change her doctor, though no doctor who knew what she had been having would take the responsibility of giving her more. The discussion was ended only by Dr. Bickleigh going out of the house altogether on a night-call.

He did not get back till past eleven, and went straight to the surgery. His anxiety was so great that he could hardly bear to look at what he had come to see. Had Julia—or not? It was the question he had been asking himself continuously during his two hours of aimless driving that had occupied the place of the fictitious night-call.

If she hadn't, it was not through care on his part. For over a month now he had been administering Julia's injections in the surgery itself. The whole preparation was therefore familiar to her—she knew which bottle contained the morphia, knew the drawer in which he kept the syringe, knew as much about the method of administration as he did himself. No, if Julia hadn't, it was simply that her will was not merely strong, but superhuman.

He pulled open the drawer where the syringe was kept as slowly as if the operation gave him real physical pain, and peered inside. The next moment he straightened up with a sigh of relief. The piece of cotton he had laid across the syringe was definitely gone.

Julia had followed the course prescribed.

IV

At the beginning of April, Madeleine came back to The Hall. From Monte Carlo she had gone to Florence, from Florence to Rome, from Rome half over the rest of Europe. Dr. Bickleigh, guiltily knowing himself responsible for this Odyssey, felt a perfect scoundrel when Madeleine told him how little she had enjoyed it all.

Their meetings were resumed, but the old ardour was not altogether recaptured. Madeleine was nervy. Travel did not seem to have soothed her much in that respect. She asked many awkward questions, too, about Julia's intentions. Was the divorce still pending? Nothing must be done without her own knowledge and consent: could Edmund promise her that he was keeping nothing back? Why did not Julia come to see her again and discuss the whole situation once more? She did want a Bickleigh divorce, she did not want a Bickleigh divorce; they must make a clean break after her long absence, her absence had only brought them closer together than ever. Madeleine's mind was always being made up in contrary directions. Dr. Bickleigh quite understood how difficult it all was for her, and was as distressed over her distress as she was. He also seemed to be running into Denny Bourne at The Hall a good deal more than he liked, but that too he quite understood: Madeleine insisted that he should.

In the second week in April, Dr. Bickleigh began to perfect the final details of his plan. Without saying a word, he had kept replenished the rapidly dwindling stocks of morphia in his surgery. Nothing more had been mentioned about Julia's injections. It was understood that she was managing without them. Actually, he computed, she had raised her allowance to quite six grains a day; which, in view of the constant pain she now suffered, was not excessive.

Dr. Bickleigh felt for her very strongly. Her drawn face and dulled eyes quite upset him; it was terrible that Julia should have to suffer like this, entirely through her own obstinacy. The sooner he was able to put her out of her pain the better. So the next time she was going into Merchester he asked her to get a supply of drugs for him from a chemist's there. The order he wrote out was concerned almost entirely with a large quantity of morphia, and his signature to it was a little shaky. The chemist, however, who knew him well, and Julia too, fulfilled it without hesitation.

Dr. Bickleigh also wrote to Julia's sister, asking her to propose herself for a day's visit and not mention having heard from him, as he had something to communicate to her of the greatest importance and secrecy, and if there were any other members of the family available would they come too, but not Sir Charles himself.

Hilda came, a large masterful woman, accompanied by her brother Victor, the one who found bridge and poker such useful accomplishments for an independently minded gentleman. Victor did not like either Julia or Hilda, and came most unwillingly.

After lunch, Dr. Bickleigh took them into his consulting-room, Julia having gone upstairs to rest, and spoke to them very seriously.

"You notice the change in Julia, of course? I'm sorry to have something most unpleasant to tell you. I thought it only right that her family should know. Besides, the responsibility is rather more than I care to shoulder alone."

"Well, cut the preliminaries, Edmund, and tell us what is the matter," said Hilda, with the family directness, and looked as she always contrived to look when addressing her brother-in-law—as if he really was not there at all.

"Dope," observed Victor laconically, and lit a second cigar. He did not offer his case to Dr. Bickleigh.

"Really," said Dr. Bickleigh, startled, "how did you . . . ?"

"Spotted it the moment I saw her. Seen plenty of cases in my time. No mistaking it, of course. What is it? Cocaine?"

"Morphia," said Dr. Bickleigh, and told them the whole story.

"I should perhaps have been suspicious when she acquiesced so quietly in my discontinuing it," he concluded, in the phrases he had rehearsed carefully beforehand, "but I'm afraid I hadn't realised that it had got such a hold on her by then. I feel very much to blame."

"But when you realised she was helping herself from your supplies, surely you cut them out?" suggested Hilda, addressing the window.

"Of course," replied Dr. Bickleigh sadly. "But she forged my name to an order on a chemist in Merchester, and got a large supply that way."

"Cunning," remarked Julia's brother, without very much concern; apparently the matter did not interest him particularly. "They always are. What you going to do, Bickleigh?"

"Well, that's what I wished to see you about. In my opinion, she should be sent into a home. Only for a limited period, of course. Curative treatment."

"Can you afford it?" asked Hilda bluntly. "It's no good expecting us to help, you know."

"I should be prepared to make such sacrifices as were necessary," said Dr. Bickleigh, with quiet courage.

"I might be able to help a bit," added Mr. Crewstanton sulkily.

"Humph!" said Hilda.

They fell into silence.

"I think," said Dr. Bickleigh, "that I'd like you to see for yourself, Hilda. The punctures . . ."

"Surely there can be no need."

"I think it would be better," Dr. Bickleigh insisted gently. "My position is rather delicate, you see," he added, with truth.

"If you mean, confirm what you've told us, I'll ask her straight out. I don't believe in beating about the bush," said Hilda, to something just on the left of Dr. Bickleigh.

"That would be fatal," the little man snapped, so firmly that his sister-in-law looked for a moment straight at him. "Your brother mentioned how cunning they are in—in this deplorable state. Julia would simply deny it."

"Too ashamed to admit it, of course," nodded Victor.

"But the evidence of the punctures can't be got over. Really, I'd rather you did. You could easily make some excuse. The upper portion of the left forearm."

"Very well," said Hilda, rising. "If you really think it's one's duty."

Dr. Bickleigh opened the door for her.

Victor and he discussed Julia's illness on somewhat stilted terms. Dr. Bickleigh had only met this brother-in-law once before, at the wedding. To his enquiries about his sister's breakdown in health, he replied that he very much feared it to be due to organic changes in the cerebral cortex, in which case things were very serious indeed. The pain would not only continue, but gradually increase. There could be very little hope.

"One mustn't lose sight of the possibility of a cerebral neoplasm, you see; of course, that would induce pressure symptoms, and quite probably metabolic changes leading to cachectic conditions," he explained earnestly.

Victor tried at any rate to look the wiser. "No hope,

eh?" he repeated, flicking his ash carefully on the carpet. "Then in that case d'you know what I'd do? I'd give her her head with this morphia, and let her finish herself off."

"Would you?" said Dr. Bickleigh with interest.

"Far and away the best thing to do in these incurable cases," pronounced Mr. Crewstanton. "After all, why the hell keep 'em alive just to go through a lot of pain?"

"There's a good deal to be said for that point of view," said Dr. Bickleigh unprofessionally.

Hilda came back.

"Oh, there's no doubt about it at all," she said. "Her arm's a mass of punctures."

"I can't tell you how worried I am," said Dr. Bickleigh.

Having, then, no further use for his visitors, he excused himself on the plea of an urgent case and offered them a lift to the station. There was an excellent train to Torquay, it transpired, which they could just catch.

They just caught it.

Dr. Bickleigh drove away from the station yard with the feeling of a good day's work behind him. He had established his evidence, and on top of that it was pretty obvious, judging from the attitude of both of them, that there would be no trouble from Julia's family.

Things could not have been going better.

Chapter Seven

I

Before he killed her Dr. Bickleigh did give Julia a last chance.

Now that it had come to the point, he intensely disliked the idea of killing her. He had, in fact, thoroughly hated the whole thing. It had been almost as much of a strain to him as to Julia. He was not callous, and the daily sight of so much suffering inflicted by himself had got completely on his nerves: it was awful that Julia should have to suffer so. He certainly did not love her; he had not much fondness for her; as an individual he did not like her at all: but he could hardly bear to go on torturing her, as a mere human being, to this extent. It was necessary to drive himself to the administration of the headache-producing medium. He would almost weep as he scattered it into her food.

Three weeks after the Crewstantons' visit he decided that he could stand it no longer. His growing nerviness had made him almost quarrel with Madeleine the day before—well, quite quarrel with her. And over Denny Bourne, of all absurd causes. Five days after the beginning of the summer term, his last term, Denny had been sent down for three weeks for depriving an unpopular don of his trousers and painting his hinder parts scarlet. If the don had not been so unpopular Denny would have been sent down for good, but the rest of the senior common-room, who also did not love their colleague, had felt that a certain justification, and more, was to be found in the existence of the fellow at all. Still, the man was a don, and one cannot have dons going about forcibly disguised as mandrills; so Denny had been sent down for three weeks.

To Dr. Bickleigh's disgust Madeleine seemed delighted with this exploit: that the idea of a trouserless don with a scarlet posterior is about as far removed from the spiritual as one can well get, Dr. Bickleigh pointed out; but Madeleine, though agreeing, and looking for a moment as a nun might on being confronted with such a spectacle, continued to give the impression that she thought Denny really had done something rather clever.

That Denny thought so himself was obvious. Dr. Bickleigh had been forced to be quite rude to him over The Hall tea-table. Then he and Madeleine had nearly quarrelled. Well, quite quarrelled. He had been unable to control himself, and said things to her in front of Denny. And Denny, flushed with impertinent rage, had had the impudence to tell him that if he didn't clear out that minute he'd take him to the stable-yard and do the same to him, then and there, with whatever substitute for red paint presented itself. And Madeleine had sat there with her big eyes and not interfered. Dr. Bickleigh had cleared out.

That was the last straw. An end had got to be made. He made it the next day.

On purpose he lay in wait for Julia's arrival in the surgery, having made a pretence of leaving the house and returning secretly on foot. She came surreptitiously, and jumped violently when he surprised her. The movement added to the aching of her head, and she swayed for a moment.

Dr. Bickleigh put his arm round her waist. He was

wearing his hat and gloves. "Hush," he warned. "Don't want Florence to hear. You were after the morphia, Julia."

Julia nodded defiantly, holding her head. "It's very bad to-day," she muttered. "I must have an injection, please, Edmund."

"Well, it's a long time since I gave you one," he said in a low voice. "Perhaps you might have one."

He filled the syringe, keeping his body between her and his hands, so that she could not see how much he was putting in. Now that the moment had come he felt quite calm. His course lay like a map in his mind, every action noted down. He was surprised at the coolness with which he made his preparations; he had expected to be flustered and anxious.

Pretending to be busy with something else for a second, he gave her the syringe to hold so as to secure her finger-prints on it, just in case.

Julia pushed up her sleeve and held her arm out to him.

"Just half a minute," he said. "Before this takes effect, I want to ask you something, Julia. Will you reconsider your decision about divorcing me? Madeleine and I still love each other, and we want to marry."

"No, Edmund," she replied decisively. "I will not."

"It's been going on for nearly a year now," he pointed out patiently. "I'm not a child. I know my own mind. I ask you, Julia, not as a wife, but as a friend. I'm very much in earnest."

"Edmund, nothing on earth would persuade me to divorce you for that gairl. She's no good. No good at all."

"That's absolutely final?"

"Absolutely."

Julia had had her chance.

Dr. Bickleigh took the syringe from her. With perfectly steady hands he injected into her veins fifteen grains of morphia. His brain seemed to have gone curiously blank.

He felt no emotion at all, no pity, remorse, fear, nor even responsibility. It was as if the conduct of affairs had somehow been taken out of his control and he was following a course from which he had neither physical nor moral powers of deviation. The only thought in his mind was: In twenty minutes Julia will be dead. *Julia. . . .*

"Thank you, Edmund," Julia said gratefully, as he automatically dropped the syringe back in the drawer.

"Go straight upstairs and lie down," Dr. Bickleigh said tonelessly, not looking at her.

"Very well. Oh, yes, there's something I wanted to ask you. Will you——"

"Not now. Some other time." He could not bear to be with her a moment longer. He must get away from her. It was terrible. He had really done it. In twenty minutes Julia would be dead. Dead . . . *Julia!* In spite of its familiarity to his imagination, the thing in practice was inconceivable. And yet he had done it: he had killed her. He escaped from her in something like panic. The power of thought had returned, terrifyingly.

But he did not regret it. Even now he could have saved her, but there was not the slightest impulse to do so. Nor did he lose his head. He got out of the house just as secretly as he had got in; for all that anyone but Julia could know, he had been out on his rounds for the last half-hour. The car even had been left in a road some distance away, carefully chosen in advance; a handy spot, quite a long way round by road, but to be gained in three or four minutes by crossing a couple of fields at the bottom of the garden; and the whole way was sheltered by shrubs and hedges from the windows of the house if one crept in a few places. He had been over the route several times.

He gained the car without the slightest mishap.

In twenty minutes—no, in seventeen minutes now, Julia would be dead. Incredible!

Freedom. . . .

He simply couldn't realise it.

For some reason the engine was sticky and wouldn't start. Not that it mattered now, but it was annoying. The self-starter gave out too, as it usually did no such occasions, and he had to get out and swing her. The engine started at last, and he got back into the car. As he did so, he saw someone topping a crest in the road just ahead. It was Ivy. Excellent. Ivy should help to prove his alibi for him. He was in admirable spirits once more as he waited for her. Really, when one came to consider it, he *had* done something rather notable, put it how you liked.

"Hullo, Teddy," gloomed Ivy. They had met several times since the incident in the wood. It had never been referred to between them.

"Hullo, Ivy. This wretched car. Really, I shall have to think about getting a new one. Suddenly stopped, ten minutes ago. Did you see me swinging her?"

"Yes. I say, Teddy . . ."

"Yes? Oh, by the way, lucky I met you. My watch has stopped. Most awkward. Haven't got the time on you, Ivy, have you?"

"Yes, I have." She pulled down the sleeve of her glove and looked at her wrist-watch. "Just twenty to three."

"Twenty to three, eh? Thanks. Sure that's right?"

"It was right this morning. Teddy . . ."

"Yes?"

"You know I'm engaged now?"

"To Chatford? Yes, somebody told me months ago. Quarnian, I think. Congratulations. Capital fellow, Chatford."

"I don't seem to have seen you for years," Ivy mourned. "Are you glad, Teddy?"

"What, that you haven't seen me? Of course I'm not. I've missed you, Ivy."

"No, that I'm engaged, I mean."

"Oh! Yes, very glad. You'll be happy, my dear. I'm sure you will. And Chatford's a coming man. Well, can I give you a lift anywhere?"

"No, thanks. I'm taking Juno for a walk. Where is she? Juno! Juno!"

"Then I must be getting along. *Au revoir*, Ivy."

"*Au revoir*, Teddy." Her eyes tried to detain him, as usual. Ivy was the kind whose love thrives on blows.

Most useful, thought Dr. Bickleigh with satisfaction as he drove on. But how normal. Ivy just the same as ever, everything just the same as ever. He did not believe he had killed Julia at all. Julia dead. No, it was unbelievable. Julia could never be dead. And yet in twelve minutes now Julia would be dead.

He couldn't believe it.

As nearly as he could compute, Julia died while he was sounding old Mr. Tracey's chest just four miles away.

II

During the afternoon his repugnance from returning home grew and grew. There was a horrible time ahead of him, beginning from the moment he set foot in the house again. Horrible. But it had got to be gone through. Yet minute after minute he kept putting off the beginning of it. No need to hurry things.

As he drove from patient to patient (he had purposely left most of his visits for the afternoon, in order to have plenty to do) his thoughts roved endlessly round Julia—his marriage with Julia, life with Julia, Julia's way of treating him like a small dog, Julia's masterfulness, peremptoriness, rudeness, Julia's quite unconscious habit of humiliating him before other people. He had been afraid of Julia. That he had always acknowledged to himself.

Now he saw, for the first time quite clearly, that he had killed Julia simply because of this fear of her. He had been afraid to run away from her.

That was very curious, and interesting. Dr. Bickleigh, not as a rule given to introspection more than any other person of some imagination, found himself turning over pages of his mind never before perused. Yes, that was quite true. He might have solved his problem so much more simply. He had asked Madeleine, and she had said she would go with him. It was only by way of a test, and he had never intended for a moment to do it, but Madeleine did not know that; she would have gone with him. And they could have lived on her money till he could establish himself somewhere else; their love was above petty considerations of convention like that; no economic difficulties had held him back. Why had he not gone, then? Simply because he could not have found the courage to run away from Julia. He had plucked up enough of it to ask for a divorce by consent; but when that had been refused he had accepted her ruling as always. No divorce: so another way had had to be found.

Dr. Bickleigh smiled to himself. Was this the first time that murder was directly traceable to an inferiority complex? He did not think so.

But really, what a little worm he had been then; there was no getting away from it. And how far from a little worm he was now. Put it any way you like, a successful murder (yes, it was murder: no need to shirk the word), brilliantly planned and flawlessly carried out, lifted one out of the category of worms for good and all.

Would Florence have found Julia yet? . . .

He would go to The Hall for tea. Why not? It was a Wednesday, and he always went to tea at The Hall on Wednesdays. The great thing was to carry on just as usual. And they could always get him on the telephone there. It would not look to suspicious eyes as if he had been trying to keep out of touch.

Not, of course, that there would be any suspicious eyes, but still . . .

That infernal Denny, lounging in the garden as if the place belonged to him. He'd laugh the other side of his face if he did know who it belonged to now—well, practically. Dr. Bickleigh felt quite angry for a moment. Really, it was too bad of Madeleine, on a Wednesday. And infernally awkward, after the *contretemps* of yesterday.

Then his anger disappeared. Things fell into their right proportions. Denny was now utterly insignificant: did not count at all. Only one person counted, and that was himself. He and Madeleine. . . .

What *was* Madeleine worth? He had never liked to ask; nor really bothered; considerations of that sort were beside the main issue. But nevertheless it was a marvellous feeling, that one was going to be actually rich—all the little economies and scrapings finished with for ever; able to afford any whim that took the fancy of the moment; soft living and luxury, owning this magnificent place. He and Madeleine. . . .

Where was Madeleine?

Dr. Bickleigh got out of his car and walked towards the front door. A shout from the lawn arrested him. Denny had got up and was strolling towards him. Damn the fellow! Oh, well, he probably wanted to apologise for yesterday. Dr. Bickleigh would accept that. But a hint must be dropped pretty soon, and more than a hint, if you like. Dr. Bickleigh felt quite equal to telling him in so many words. It was amusing to think that only last summer he had been quite ill-at-ease in the presence of Denny—forced, awkward, bad form, out of it. Lord, what a little worm. . . .

"Come and sit on the lawn," said Denny, rather abruptly.

"I'm sorry," Dr. Bickleigh returned coldly. "I have come to see Miss Cranmere about ——"

"Well, she's out. Come and sit on the lawn. I want to say something to you."

What a parade the boy's making, thought Dr. Bickleigh as he walked with Denny to the chairs under the cedar. Clumsiness of youth, no doubt. Why can't people realise that an apology is even more embarrassing to receive than to offer, and cut it short? A form of egotism.

Funny there had been no telephone message. Florence couldn't have found her yet, obviously.

But would Florence try The Hall? Probably. If he knew anything of Wyvern's Cross, his visits here would be common talk in the kitchen. Well, let them talk.

Poor Julia. It was a relief to think she was out of all that pain at last.

They sat down in two deck-chairs.

Denny stared straight in front of him. "Look here, Bickleigh. . . ."

"Yes?"

"About Madeleine."

All thought of Julia disappeared from Dr. Bickleigh's mind. "Well?"

"She's—a very unusual girl, you know. Extraordinarily sensitive, and all that."

"Yes?"

"I've seen a good deal of her lately."

"Have you?"

"Yes."

The conversation seemed to be languishing.

Denny, for some reason, was remarkably embarrassed—more so than Dr. Bickleigh would ever have expected from such a normally self-possessed young man. And it was an odd way of beginning an apology.

Denny suddenly turned a somewhat flushed face towards his companion. "She doesn't really care for you, Bickleigh, you know," he mumbled.

"What the devil are you talking about?"

"She told me about—you," said Denny, looking supremely uncomfortable; but his eyes did not shift from the other's face.

"She did, did she?" Dr. Bickleigh had recovered his equilibrium. This young cub must have been pumping Madeleine, annoying her. Imagined himself in love with her, no doubt, and had the impudence to be jealous.

"Yes. She—she *doesn't* care for you, you know."

"Indeed?" Dr. Bickleigh was more amused than anything now. This really was rather humorous, in the circumstances. "Who does she care for, then?"

"Me," returned Denny simply, and blushed a deeper tint.

It was all Dr. Bickleigh could do not to laugh in his face. "Really, Denny?"

"Damn it, you needn't smile. I mean what I say. I love Madeleine, and I'm dam' well going to marry her. So now you've got it."

"Well, well," said Dr. Bickleigh. Poor Denny; it really was rather touching. "And what has Madeleine got to say about all this?" he asked tolerantly.

"She hasn't tried to hide from me that she cares too, if that's what you mean," Denny replied in a gruff voice. "She's too straight. She'd have let me kiss her when I went up this term, and you can imagine what that means with a girl like her."

"But you didn't, eh?"

"No, I didn't. Well, I'm glad we've got that straight. Of course, she was carried away by your being so much older," Denny grumbled. "Flattered her inexperience, or something. You sort of swept her off her feet. When she wasn't with you she knew she wasn't in love with you, but when she was you seem to have exercised some extraordinary kind of fascination over her. That's what happened."

"I see," said Dr. Bickleigh, with a small smile. He might have recognised the voice of Madeleine speaking; but he didn't.

There was a little silence.

"Well, I must say," observed Denny, if rather grudgingly, "that you take it dam' well."

"Take what?"

"Why, our engagement."

"Your—what?"

"Our engagement. I told you, I'm going to marry her. We got engaged this morning."

"Nonsense!" Dr. Bickleigh spoke perhaps rather sharply, but otherwise betrayed nothing of the turmoil that had suddenly invaded him.

"Fact. I tried to break it as easily as I could. Afraid it's a bit rotten for you." Denny was no longer embarrassed; he was the proudly possessive male, only held back by good form from being flauntingly possessive. "Here—Madeleine asked me to give you this after I'd told you."

Dr. Bickleigh took the note and broke open the envelope. He had to read the contents through half a dozen times before their meaning was clear to him.

> "EDMUND DEAR,—I have asked Denny to tell you our news. I know you will be terribly upset, but it is the best way out for both of us. You know things could not go on, could they?
>
> "For the last time, Edmund, my love from
>
> "MADELEINE."

He crammed the note into his pocket at last and began to walk rapidly towards the house. "It's no good," Denny said, "if you want to see Madeleine, she's out."

That, thought Dr. Bickleigh, is a lie, a damned lie, a filthy lie, another filthy lie. He walked on.

Denny, who had started after him, stood for a moment in indecision, then shrugged his shoulders and dropped back into his chair. Perhaps better let them have it out and get it over.

Dr. Bickleigh did not trouble to ring the bell. Madeleine, would be upstairs, in her bedroom, waiting, hiding. He got there just as she was locking the door, and forced it open.

"Edmund," she said, looking at him with big, sorrowful eyes, "you shouldn't have tried to see me."

"Look here, Madeleine—this is all nonsense, of course?" Dr. Bickleigh appeared perfectly normal. His face was rather white, and there was a curious spot of red on each of his cheek-bones, but he articulated quite distinctly; almost over-distinctly.

Madeleine, who had looked a little frightened as well as sorrowful, seemed to be reassured. "No, Edmund, it isn't nonsense. I've thought it all out. We couldn't go on. This is the easiest way."

"You don't love Denny?"

Madeleine looked at him reproachfully. "Edmund, need you have asked me that?" She sat down on the edge of the bed.

Dr. Bickleigh went up to her and took her by the shoulders.

"I'll tell you what you're going to do, Madeleine."

"Edmund, you're hurting me."

His fingers sunk deeper into her flesh. The spots of colour on his cheek-bones burned a little brighter. "You're going downstairs this minute to break off this preposterous engagement. To-morrow I'm going to London, to buy a special licence. You'll come with me. We'll be married in three days from now."

"But, Edmund—Julia! Oh, please let me go. You're hurting me terribly."

"Julia," said Dr. Bickleigh, through his teeth, "is dead."

Madeleine looked up into the white face glaring down at hers and began to shriek. "Denny! Denny! Help—help! Denny—he'll . . ." She tore herself free and ran, shrieking, to the window.

But it was not Denny who got into the room first. It was the friendly parlourmaid. She looked from one to the other in anxious bewilderment.

"Your mistress is hysterical," said Dr. Bickleigh coldly. "Get me some cold water, please."

"Yes, sir, but—you're wanted on the telephone, sir. Your housemaid. I—I'm afraid there's bad news, sir."

With Madeleine's hysterical screams ringing through his head, Dr. Bickleigh went downstairs to the telephone.

Chapter Eight

I

Miss Peavy was giving a tea-party.

The preparations had begun yesterday morning. The Crown Derby tea-service had been taken out of the ormolu cabinet in the tiny drawing-room and washed by Miss Peavy's own hands (such an operation could not be entrusted, of course, to Ethel) with, miraculously, not a single resulting breakage. In the afternoon Miss Peavy, her head swathed in a check duster, her small body in a voluminous overall, and her hands encased in white cotton gloves two sizes too large for them, had superintended Ethel's turning out of the drawing-room, with such help as experience and superior strength had to afford. Ethel was only fourteen and heavy of hand; she lived at the last cottage of the village proper, the nearest one to Miss Peavy's, and described herself proudly as Miss Peavy's help. She had been Miss Peavy's help ever since she was twelve (nine to eleven of a morning, and afternoons when wanted special), and in some ways, Miss Peavy thought secretly, she was more of a hindrance; but between the two of them the job was done at last to Miss Peavy's satisfaction.

Then, on the morning of the party itself, there had been a great baking of cakes. Supervised by Ethel in the capacity of critic, admirer, and Hermes ("Now fetch me the baking-powder, Ethel. The small tin at the left-hand end of the middle shelf. No, the *middle* shelf, dear. The *left*-hand end. No, the *small* tin. Never mind, I'll get it myself." "Oo, it ain't in that tin, miss, not now it ain't. It was empty, an' I put the cloves in it. I thought it'd come in handy for the cloves, like. So I put them in it, miss." "Well, where is the baking-powder?" "There ain't none, miss." "Dear, dear, you ought to have told me that before. Really you ought, Ethel. Now you'll have to run up to Mrs. Stinvell and get a tin. Sevenpence, and now my hands are all . . . Where is my purse, dear? I think I left it . . . no, I didn't. Really, Ethel, you should have told me, you know."), Miss Peavy had made a chocolate cake, iced with chocolate, an orange cake, iced with orange, and a great quantity of rock buns and Eccles cakes, not iced at all. And only the rock buns had been what you could really call *burnt*, and those not irrevocably. At least three-quarters, with judicious paring, were made presentable. A most successful morning.

It was to be quite an important tea-party. Mrs. Torr and Quarnian were coming, Janet Wapsworthy of course, Gwynyfryd Rattery, with the Major if she could persuade him, Mr. Torr had promised faithfully to look in if he could find the time, and Ivy Chatford and her husband were actually coming over from Merchester specially. If only *poor* Mrs. Bickleigh were still alive. . . . Only Mrs. Hatton-Hampstead had definitely refused. And Madeleine Bourne, of course; but she refused all invitations nowadays, it seemed. Miss Peavy was secretly relieved that she was not coming.

How lucky it was such a lovely day. Take it all round, Miss Peavy really did think that May was the loveliest month of all. Spring, gloriously fulfilled, budding into summer. . . . But no, they would not have tea in the garden. It would not be fair on the Crown Derby. And Ethel, with the tray. . . .

Fortunately, there would be plenty to talk about. None

of those awkward pauses in the conversation that Miss Peavy so dreaded. For never had there been such a year in the history of Wyvern's Cross. Two marriages and one death. . . . And Mr. Davy's new book, all about the neighbourhood. No, there would be no lack of conversational fodder. There would be gossip, too, of course. Bound to be, with Quarnian *and* her mother there. Miss Peavy hoped they would not get too libellous, but really, gossip had never seemed so rife in Wyvern's Cross before; and the most scandalous things, with but the slenderest foundations—well, no foundations really at all. Miss Peavy would take no part in it herself, nor encourage it; that was her firm rule; but she would hardly be able to check it without being quite rude. And, anyhow, anything was better than those awkward pauses.

The problem of Dr. Bickleigh had been exercising Miss Peavy terribly in this connection. Ought she to ask him, or not? If she did not, would it not look terribly pointed? On the other hand, if she did . . . Even though Madeleine Bourne was not coming. And what would Mr. Torr . . . ? Everybody was talking about Dr. Bickleigh not having been inside the church since his wife died so tragically. *Poor* Mrs. Bickleigh, who would *ever* have thought . . . ? In the end Miss Peavy did not ask him. After all, it was a feminine tea-party really, with such men as might come under specific feminine proprietorship. No, there was really no need to ask Dr. Bickleigh at all.

At four o'clock punctually they began to arrive.

Miss Wapsworthy was the first, very bright in a purple straw hat with pink roses and mauve silk.

"Good afternoon, Janet. So nice of you . . . Isn't it a *perfect* day? Really, we might almost have . . . But I'd made all the arrangements, you see, and it is so . . . Would you like to wash your hands?"

"Thank you, Adela," returned Miss Wapsworthy with some asperity. "I washed them before I came out."

There was more in this exchange than met the ignorant eye. Miss Peavy's cottage was half a mile outside the village, and stood at the foot of the steep slope which began where the hamlet ended. Miss Wapsworthy's cottage, at the other end of Wyvern's Cross, stood on flat land. Miss Peavy, therefore, had a gravitational water-supply to her cottage from a spring half-way up the hill above her. In the village itself there was no pipe-water, and Miss Wapsworthy's cottage shared this disability.

Her water-supply was a great comfort to Miss Peavy. Her soul, heated by other and frictional causes, laved gratefully in its cooling stream. Miss Peavy's cottage, alone among all the others, possessed a water-closet. (Why, even at The Hall they had to . . .)

Miss Peavy never thought of her water-closet as such, but always as "indoor sanitation."

"I invariably," added Miss Wapsworthy pointedly, "wash my hands before I go out to tea." She glanced down at her grey cotton gloves as if to imply that she had come prepared further to keep the members in question free from all contamination while in this particular locality.

"Yes, yes. Yes, of course. Well, then, shall we just stroll round the garden, till the others come? My gloxinias really are beginning to . . ." Miss Peavy temporarily tethered the ends of the tulle scarf.

The two ladies walked in the garden.

Half an hour later the affair was in full swing. So far the gathering was entirely feminine. Not even the dubious masculinity of Mr. Torr was there to leaven it. The Chatfords had not yet put in an appearance. Voices shrill and voices ladylike slashed the atmosphere in vivid ribbons. Characters came up, were seen through, and retired conquered. Reputations littered the ground like snow-flakes.

". . . scarcely to her knees," Mrs. Torr was burbling, in shocked contentment. "Really, I think I know what *my* husband would say if *I* appeared in our church like that. And in a cathedral! Really, you'd think she'd *see* that as the wife of one of the Canons she has a position to keep up, wouldn't you?"

"And fifty, if she's a day," nodded Miss Wapsworthy. "Disgusting!"

"Really, Mrs. Torr," said a lady from Merchester, one of Miss Peavy's childhood friends who had married socially beneath the cathedral set but considerably above its purses. "Really, you don't mean to say you could actually see her—her ——" Even among ladies (real ladies) the existence of such things must only be hinted.

"When she knelt down," replied Mrs. Torr with solemnity, "I could see them distinctly. Distinctly!"

"I must look myself next Sunday," said the lady from Merchester, with as much gusto as if that had not been her sex at all.

"Edged with lace," added Mrs. Torr, as though that were just about the last enormity. As if one could worship the Almighty properly when edged with lace! Even Miss Peavy wondered what the Almighty's views could be on such a frivolous example of His creations.

In a corner, Quarnian and Gwynyfryd were discussing Men.

"Oo, noo, Quarnian," Miss Rattery was saying, with the horrified avidity of the British virgin on matters of sex. "Ay carn't believe thart—rarely Ay carn't."

"He did though. Honour bright. Oh, our Sam's a naughty lad."

"But whay did you *let* him?"

"I wanted to see if he would."

"Well, it seems to me you're as much to blame as he is then," pronounced Miss Rattery fastidiously.

"Who's blaming anyone?" retorted Quarnian, with devastating impartiality.

Having achieved her object, which was the simple one of shocking Gwynyfryd, she turned her attention to the group of her elders round the tea-table. They were now plucking the down of virtue from the perfectly respectable daughter of a Merchester schoolmaster, who had been seen at a local cinema with a Married Man. As Quarnian unfortunately did not know the young woman in question, the gathering heap of white plumage at the ladies' feet did not interest her.

She turned back to Gwynyfryd and yawned without concealment. "Lord, I wish Ivy'd come. This is too dull for words. Haven't seen old Ivy for years. Hardly since she married. Have you?"

"Yes, Ay saw her in Merchester about a fortnight agoo."

"Ask her how she liked being married?" Quarnian asked, with an obscene wink.

"*Noo,* Ay did nert," riposted Gwynyfryd, who invariably grew more affected in proportion as she was really shocked.

"Got a nice house, haven't they?" Quarnian said enviously. "Bill Chatford must be doing pretty well. Not half a bad little nest he's been able to feather for his birdie. Course, he's been saving like mad all the years he lived here. How does Ivy like living in Merchester?"

"Oo, quait well, I think." Gwynyfryd drank a little tea. The forefinger of her right hand was tucked so far under the others that no one could possibly have accused it of being crooked.

Quarnian also drank a little tea, and crooked her own little finger outrageously. When she was Gwynyfryd eyeing it with an expression of intense pain, she spluttered and had to put her cup down. Quarnian had a simple sense of humour.

"Well, has Teddy proposed to you yet, Gwynyfryd?" she asked next. Baiting Miss Rattery was one of the few amusements that Wyvern's Cross had to offer Miss Torr. And Gwynyfryd being twenty-four, while Miss Torr herself was only nineteen (well, practically twenty now), and Gwynyfryd, moreover, intensely disapproving of her twenty-four dignity being assailed by nineteen impudence and yet quite unable effectively to fight back, all added a not unpleasant spice to the entertainment.

"Quarnian, you do say such *things*," lamented Miss Rattery now; but she was ingenuous enough to be thoroughly confused by the question.

Quarnian observed her companion's blush with pleasure, and set about deepening it. "Well, has he kissed you again lately?"

"What do you mean—'again'?"

"Since he did when he took you away to give you those cuttings at their tennis-party last summer. You remember."

"He didn't!"

"My dear Gwynyfryd, don't try to put it on with me," begged Miss Torr, enjoying herself mightily. Gwynyfryd's blush was getting quite interesting now. "Never seen anything quite so obvious in my life. He carefully takes you out of sight instead of bringing the things to you, you're away about an hour, and come back looking all worked up, both of you; and then you tell me—— Oh, Lord, Gwynyfryd, I may be younger than you, but I wasn't born yesterday. Of course he kissed you."

"That he did nert. I never gave him the chance. Horrid little man."

"Oho, so he tried, and you turned him down," cried Miss Torr, in high delight. "Poor Teddy, I only wish it'd been me. *I* don't think he's a horrid little man at all."

"Well, he is," said Gwynyfryd, quite vindictively.

"Poor old Teddy," gloated Quarnian. "Well, now, I

do call that rough luck on him. When everyone knows he only killed his wife to be free to marry you, Gwynyfryd. Well, well, well."

"Quarnian!"

"My dear Gwynyfryd, don't pretend to be shocked. Of course Teddy killed his wife. And I, for one," said Miss Torr judicially, "don't blame him. But if I'd been the coroner, I'd have asked Master Teddy quite a lot of questions."

"Quarnian, how can you say such *things*?"

"What, you don't mean you really think he didn't?"

"Ay think it's simply horrible of you."

"Then I'm not the only one that's horrible. Mother's horrible, father's horrible, half Wyvern's Cross is horrible."

"Ay don't believe it for a minute."

Gwynyfryd was so indignant that Quarnian was driven almost to defend these preposterous mis-statements. She hastily found a grain of truth to inject into the foundations of her imaginative edifice. "Well, I can tell you this, then. Father does think there must have been something funny about Mrs. Bickleigh's death because he says he just can't swallow that story at the inquest of her being a drug-fiend (well, it is a bit tall, isn't it? Teddy really ought to have invented something better), but he doesn't want to make a fuss because he doesn't want a scandal in the parish. So there."

"But Mrs. Bickleigh's sister confirmed the evidence about that, and her brother too."

"Oh, he got round them somehow. I expect they're all in it."

"Nonsense!" Gwynyfryd was really angry. "Ay—Ay think it's *beastly* to go round saying things like that. Quarnian, you're—you're a little beast."

"All right, then." It was Quarnian's turn to become

annoyed. "Call me a liar. I'll jolly well show you. Mother!"

"Noo, Quarnian!"

"Mother!"

"Quarnian, you're not to. Be quiet!"

"Mother!"

Mrs. Torr turned in her chair. "What is it, dear?"

"Gwynyfryd's calling me a liar because I told her father wasn't satisfied with the verdict on Mrs. Bickleigh last year. You remember what he said."

Dead silence cut off the chatter as if it had been sliced off with a knife. The women looked at each other almost furtively.

"N-no, dear," twittered Mrs. Torr, after a long pause. "I—don't remember."

"Yes, you do. He said——"

"That'll do, dear."

But the plucking of the schoolmaster's daughter was resumed only half-heartedly. A chicken, however young and tender, becomes poor fare when a whole banquet, rich, luscious, almost infinite, has been waved for a second beneath one's nose. The last few poor feathers were ripped off mechanically, and four hungry faces confronted Mrs. Torr. In the corner, Gwynyfryd and Quarnian watched their elders, not deceived.

"Miss Peavy," said Quarnian dulcetly, "you were telling me about your gloxinias the other day. May Gwynyfryd and I go out and look at them?"

"Yes, do, dear. They're . . . You'll find them . . . Are you sure you've quite finished? Gwynyfryd, I don't believe you've tried one of my . . . Fresh-baked this morning, I promise you. Quarnian, won't you . . . ?"

"No, thank you; we've quite finished, really. Come along, Gwynyfryd."

The two girls went out, amid the grateful looks of the

others. Tact radiated from Quarnian's lanky form as she slouched towards the door.

Outside, she turned to Gwynyfryd. "Of course they wouldn't say anything while we were in there. But if we went and admired the flowers in that bed there, just under that window, and kept out of sight of the Peavy and the Wop—well, don't you think that was a pretty bright idea, Gwynyfryd?"

"Quarnian, I think you're *horrible*. I wouldn't do anything so mean."

But she followed Quarnian's stealthy progress towards the window nevertheless.

Inside, Mrs. Torr was gracefully giving way before inexorable but practically silent pressure. "How *naughty* of Quarnian. Really, what a thing to say."

"Why wasn't Mr. Torr satisfied?" asked Miss Wapsworthy, who favoured blunt methods.

"Really," said Miss Peavy anxiously, "do you think we *should* . . . ? Isn't it rather . . . ? I mean . . ."

"Well, what do you mean, Odela?" asked Miss Wapsworthy.

"Well, the verdict *was* 'Accidental Death,' wasn't it? And if anyone wasn't satisfied . . . I mean," said Miss Peavy bravely, "isn't it hinting at something quite dreadful?"

Miss Wapsworthy looked round the little circle of intent faces. "Well, and haven't we all been hinting in our thoughts for the last year at something rather dreadful?" she said in her harsh, jerky voice. "Of course we have. And not one of us has had the courage to put it into words. Well, *I* will. I agree with Mr. Torr. I'm not satisfied either." Her tone was a challenge. "It's my opinion that Julia Bickleigh's death was not an accident at all: that she deliberately killed herself because of—well, we all know what."

II

It was past five before Ivy and her husband arrived. Mr. Chatford explained precisely that he had been kept later than he expected by an important client, and had been unable to drive Ivy over earlier.

Ivy, who had hardly been seen in Wyvern's Cross since her marriage, had altered very little. Her fragile figure showed no signs of rounding, and she did not seem to have gained in confidence. Her blue eyes returned constantly to her husband after everything she said, as if seeking his approval for it, and the slight look of timidity in them had increased rather than diminished. She was obviously a little afraid of him. Only her clothes gave any outward indication of the change in her position. The Ridgeways were not well off, and Ivy had always dressed very simply, in tweeds or woollens or home-made little summer frocks. Now she looked rather out-of-place for a cottage tea-party, in a black satin frock with long tight sleeves and a close-fitting black baku hat which, though small and apparently simple, contrived at the same time to be dashing, and sat with an air of incongruity above her rounded, childish face. The ensemble quite certainly did not reflect Ivy's own taste, and one gathered that Mr. William Chatford not only considered that his wife's clothes should stand for a sign of the position in life which he had reached, but had no small part himself in choosing them. Ivy looked more like Bond Street than Merchester.

Miss Peavy, who had not seen her at all since the wedding, welcomed her warmly (Ivy had always been a favourite of hers), and kisses were exchanged. Ethel was summoned to bring fresh tea, and Mr. Chatford, as the only male man, ensconced in the chair of honour.

"Do try one of those Eccles cakes while you're waiting, dear," beamed Miss Peavy. "I made them myself this morning."

"Thank you, Miss Peavy, I'd love to." And, with half a dozen pairs of feminine eyes watching her enviously, Ivy pulled off her small hands the most expensive-looking pair of gloves ever seen in Wyvern's Cross.

"Ivy's looking *so* well," confided Mrs. Torr to Mr. Chatford, in tones of congratulation. "And so smart and pretty. Really, I hardly know her."

"Another of mother's bricks," confided Quarnian to Gwynyfryd. The two girls had returned to the house on the Chatford's arrival.

"This hat?" said Ivy, in answer to a question from the lady from Merchester. "Oh, haven't you seen it before, Mrs. Dunsford? I got it in Paris, on our honeymoon. William gave it to me." She glanced at her husband.

"A model," amplified Mr. Chatford, with obvious satisfaction. The word came oddly in his precise enunciation.

"Charming," pronounced the company dutifully.

There was a pause. Nobody spoke. The pause grew awkward. Miss Peavy looked to Mrs. Torr in appeal. Mrs. Torr did not see her. The pause seemed to have lasted for years.

Miss Peavy plunged. "So lucky you didn't come five minutes earlier, Mr. Chatford," she tittered with nervousness. "We were just . . . Probably quite *libellous*. . . . I expect you'd have had us all arrested."

"Really?" said Mr. Chatford politely. "Then I suppose it would be indiscreet to ask what you were discussing?"

"Oh, very. That is . . ."

"I know when ladies get together the conversation does tend to verge on slander," Mr. Chatford observed humorously. "I trust I was not your subject?"

"Oh, no. Good gracious, no. It was . . . Oh, quite different. Just silly village talk. Gossip, you know. I'm sure we were all terribly shocked as it was to learn that poor Mrs. Bickleigh had taken to . . . But that's very different from suggesting that . . . *Oh!*" Miss Peavy broke off with a little squeak of dismay, conscious of six pairs of horrified eyes regarding her. What *had* she . . . ?

Mr. Chatford, however, appeared quite unhorrified. He chose another Eccles cake with some care and took a modified bite of it. "Oh, yes?" he said, with interest nothing beyond the polite. "So you were talking about Mrs. Bickleigh? Very sad. Very sad indeed. Though rather past history now. Still, as you say, very curious too."

"Oh, Mrs. Torr," Ivy said hurriedly, "I've been meaning to ask you and Quarnian over to tea. You must come soon. Of course, we're only just straight, but . . . Now, what about next Wednesday?"

It was arranged that Quarnian and Mrs. Torr should go to tea with Ivy next Wednesday.

The conversation skated imperceptibly farther from Mrs. Bickleigh.

Soon afterwards Gwynyfryd rose to go. She had promised her father to get back for their usual set of tennis before changing for dinner. Would Quarnian like to come too, pick up Benjie at the Vicarage on the way, and make up a four? Quarnian would. The lady from Merchester went too, to catch the 'bus.

Five minutes later Mr. Chatford gave, as it were, quite casual expression to the topic uppermost in the bosoms of those remaining. "It was strange that you should have mentioned Mrs. Bickleigh just now, Miss Peavy," he remarked. "I had rather meditated raising the subject myself. Or, rather, the subject of Dr. Bickleigh."

"I agree," said Miss Wapsworthy with tight lips. "It's high time it was raised."

"Yes?" Mr. Chatford appeared faintly puzzled. "I haven't seen him once since my marriage. I wanted to ask after him. No doubt you ladies will be able to tell me. How is he bearing the loss of his wife?"

Miss Peavy and Miss Wapsworthy both looked towards Mrs. Torr.

"Well," said that lady carefully, "I think as well as one could have expected."

"Indeed? I'm glad. A very tragic affair. The coroner, I thought, handled it most tactfully."

"Very," almost snapped Miss Wapsworthy.

"I was particularly glad," pursued Mr. Chatford, with the air of one merely making conversation, "that none of the—shall we say?—gossip, which I understand had been coupled with Dr. Bickleigh's name previously, came up in court. No doubt it had never reached the coroner's ears at all; but, if it had, I thought it quite right of him to disregard it."

"Gossip?" queried Mrs. Torr with interest. "Then?"

"Hadn't there been a certain amount of talk about Dr. Bickleigh's perhaps rather indiscreet friendships in the neighbourhood?" replied Mr. Chatford smoothly. "Quite harmless friendships, no doubt; but, for a man in his position, at least indiscreet."

"Oh! Yes. Well, that is—yes, I believe there had."

"Names, even, had been mentioned?"

"Names have frequently been mentioned in connection with Dr. Bickleigh," remarked Miss Wapsworthy acidly.

"Yes; yes, so I feared. No doubt you ladies know whose."

Mrs. Torr, who was not clever at hiding her feelings, looked uncomfortable. From her daughter she had at one time frequently heard Ivy's name mentioned in this connection. She glanced at Ivy, and was shocked to see how white the child's face had gone. So there had been something in it, then. Something rather serious, to account for such apprehension. What an unpleasant man Dr. Bickleigh did seem turning out to be, if only half the things people said about him were true. And she used to think him so nice.

To save Ivy, she plunged for something definite. "I—I've certainly heard Mrs. Denny Bourne—Madeleine Cranmere as she was—I've certainly heard her name coupled with Dr. Bickleigh's. Well, I mean"—Mrs. Torr tried to soften this slander—"they were close friends about then, I believe, though of course she didn't see so much of him after she got engaged to Denny."

"Yes. Ah, yes. Wasn't the engagement announced on the very day of Mrs. Bickleigh's death? Yes. A most curious coincidence."

"Do have some of my orange cake, Mr. Chatford," implored Miss Peavy. "I made it myself, so I can . . ."

"Thank you, I will."

"And Ivy, you're eating nothing."

"I've finished, thank you, Miss Peavy."

"Don't tell me you're going in for this fashionable dieting too. I do think it's so very . . . And really, Ivy, there's no need for *you* to. . . ."

"Oh, no, I'm not," Ivy smiled wanly.

Miss Peavy would have liked to keep the conversation on such an innocuous topic, but Mr. Chatford, it seemed, had not finished with the other. He brushed the thread dangled by Miss Peavy unobtrusively but firmly aside.

"Yes, I'd heard that too. Miss Cranmere, as she was. But I understood that there was someone else, previous to her. Perhaps you've heard that, too?"

Ivy's eyes flickered in appeal over the three faces. It was not necessary. With the rigid sex loyalty of women, all three denied vigorously having heard of a friend of Dr. Bickleigh's previous to Miss Cranmere; though all three knew perfectly well who that friend was reputed to have been. Even Miss Peavy, who never listened to gossip if she could help it, knew that. One does not have to listen to gossip in a place like Wyvern's Cross. It inserts itself into the consciousness somehow, quite irrespective of the ears.

"No," said Miss Wapsworthy, frowning in an effort of memory. "No, I never heard of anyone else. Who was it, Mr. Chatford?"

"Oh, I don't know her name," said Mr. Chatford smoothly, and if he realised that three female breaths were being drawn the more easily he did not show it. "Possibly she never existed. I just heard that there had been another woman. But you know what the gossip is in these small places."

All three ladies did know it, and looked accordingly deprecatory.

"Curious," said Mr. Chatford.

Miss Peavy caught the look in Ivy's blue eyes, and, like Mrs. Torr a moment ago, plunged for something definite. "Oh, I *know* it was Miss Cranmere. Why, I remember one day . . . Really, it was most extraordinary. I—I've never been so insulted in my life." Without quite knowing how it had happened, Miss Peavy found herself embarked on the story of Dr. Bickleigh's visit to her the previous spring. She had never quite forgiven his conduct then, though she had overlooked it on their subsequent meetings; but she had never told a single person about it. Now, as soon as she had got well started, she wished she had done nothing of the sort. But it was too late to recant.

"Well, I never," said Mrs. Torr, suitably impressed.

"Dear me," said Mr. Chatford. "Most injudicious."

"And you never said a word about it to me," accused Miss Wapsworthy, and Miss Peavy looked her guilt.

Ivy said nothing, but went on playing aimlessly with one of her expensive gloves, pulling it again and again through a loosely clenched fist. Mrs. Torr, in an overflow of maternal feeling, thought she looked just like a child dressed up. It was ridiculous to think of her as the wife of that dry stick, Mr. Chatford. Why, there must be over twenty years between them. Did she really love him?

"Well, there's no need to wonder who the 'married man' was, Adela," observed Miss Wapsworthy. "You know perfectly well it was the scandal of the place last summer."

Mrs. Torr shook her head. "I'm afraid it was."

"I confess," mused Mr. Chatford, "that I had not realised how close the 'friendship' must have been." The slightest stress on the word in question enclosed it in inverted commas.

There was a moment's silence, while great issues hung in the balance.

"Close enough," said Miss Wapsworthy, slowly and deliberately, "to turn Julia Bickleigh into a drug-fiend."

Mr. Chatford looked at her searchingly. "I don't quite follow."

"Oh, it's nothing, Mr. Chatford," said Miss Peavy, much distressed. "Just a silly idea of Janet's. Really, Janet . . . I mean, that sort of thing—well, it isn't very nice, is it? Saying that sort of thing."

"We're not considering a nice sort of thing," Miss Wapsworthy returned grimly. "I'll put it another way, then, Mr. Chatford. I'd known Julia Bickleigh for nearly ten years, and I'd be prepared to say with my dying breath that she was the last person in the whole world to give way to any weakness of that sort. There!"

"Then what," said Mr. Chatford quietly, "are you suggesting, Miss Wapsworthy, in view of the evidence?"

"I suggest nothing. I merely feel that I've done my duty in telling you that—and in adding that Mr. Torr, too, was not satisfied with the verdict at the inquest."

"Oh, really, Janet," fluttered Mrs. Torr, "I don't think

you should . . . You really haven't quite the right to—to . . ."

"Right," said Miss Wapsworthy enigmatically, "*is* right."

"What is it you want me to do, Miss Wapsworthy?" Mr. Chatford asked bluntly.

"*I* don't want you to do anything. You're a solicitor. You know whether you should do anything or not; I'm sure I don't. I simply feel that I have rid my shoulders of a responsibility which they are not competent to support by telling you those two things." Who had laid the responsibility on the shoulders in question, Miss Wapsworthy did not add.

"I see." Mr. Chatford uncrossed his knees and leant forward. "Might I ask for another cup of this excellent tea, Miss Peavy?"

The subject appeared to be closed.

On their way back to Merchester some twenty minutes later, Mr. Chatford turned to his wife. "So your pretty story *is* all over Wyvern's Cross, as I expected."

Ivy began to tremble. "Oh, William, I don't think it is, really. They all said . . ."

"They were lying. Do you think I can't tell when a woman's lying or not? You ought to know whether I can, my dear Ivy. Mrs. Torr gave it away with every muscle of her face."

Ivy said nothing.

"No doubt they're all talking about it now. Charming for me, isn't it?" His voice held no tone of anger. Mr. Chatford was never angry. But his dry sarcasm could lacerate Ivy like a knout. "Laughing, no doubt, to think how I've been fobbed off with another man's discarded mistress for a wife. Taken in like any schoolboy. Most amusing, isn't it?"

"Oh, William, don't—please."

"Well, they didn't cut you, at any rate. I suppose we

have that to be thankful for. Your clothes, no doubt. I always said it paid to be well dressed, didn't I?"

They drove on a mile or two in silence.

"And now what's all this about that late lover of yours, eh? Nasty innuendoes. What had they been saying before we arrived, I wonder? That Wapsworthy woman's got something up her sleeve. Torr too, it seems. What do you know about it, Ivy, eh?" He shot the question at her suddenly.

"N-nothing. I don't understand."

"Oh, you don't understand, don't you, my dear? Just as you didn't understand that if I'd known what you'd been before I asked you to marry me, I wouldn't have looked at you again. Eh?"

"Oh, William, please don't bring that all up again." The facile tears crowded into Ivy's eyes. "You know how sorry I am for—for deceiving you."

"No doubt it was because you loved me so much?"

"I do love you, William, I do. If you'd only let me."

"No, you don't," he replied, with unusual fierceness. "You still love Bickleigh."

"I don't," she sobbed. "Truly I don't."

"My God, if I thought you did," said her husband, quite quietly, staring ahead through the windscreen.

There was another little interlude of silence, broken only by Ivy's sniffs.

"Ivy," Mr. Chatford said, not unkindly, "tell me this. I've never asked you before, but it does make a difference. Were you quite innocent when Bickleigh seduced you?"

Ivy caught desperately at the tone. "Yes, quite. I swear."

"Ignorant?"

"Y-yes. Yes."

Mr. Chatford stared ahead.

"William—that does make a difference, doesn't it?"

Her husband patted her knees. His dry skin scraped on the silk.

"It may make all the difference to Dr. Bickleigh," he said, without apparent emotion.

Ivy turned terrified eyes on him, opened her mouth, and then hastily turned her head away.

Chapter Nine

I

DR. BICKLEIGH helped himself to another glass of port. Since Julia died he had been able to afford these little luxuries.

He was thinking of his roses. The two *Marcia Stanhopes* had flowered unexpectedly freely last year; he wished he had ordered a couple more last autumn. Still, the *White Ensigns* he had put in instead would be more reliable. The rose-garden would be better than ever this year. It was quite a pity Julia would not be there to see it: the rose-garden was one of the few points of contact they had possessed.

Poor Julia! Really, thought Dr. Bickleigh for the thousandth time, it had been a merciful release; her life had never been happy. She was probably most grateful to him by now, wherever she was.

He lit another cigarette, and lounged more comfortably in his chair. The open book on his knee slipped aside. Nine o'clock, work finished, and a pleasant, long evening by the fire, all alone (that was the best of early June; one could still enjoy a fire in the evening). He was not in the least lonely; he never did feel so. Dr. Bickleigh was not one of those who rely entirely upon human companionship for their enjoyment.

Nearly thirteen months now. Of late, he noticed with interest, the thought of Julia had been less and less present in his mind. Imperceptibly, he was slipping back to the state of things before he met her. Julia, instead of being his life, was taking on the aspect of an interlude—an interlude, too, firmly and courageously terminated when it became impossible.

That Dr. Bickleigh had been a different man since Julia's death he himself had been the first to recognise. It was extraordinary how that one action had altered his idea of himself. Somehow he could not help feeling that he had vindicated his existence, proved once and for all that he was as capable as anyone else of taking his own line and sticking to it grimly—more capable. What was the phrase? "Something something something, and captain of his soul." That was it, exactly. Captain of his soul.

Poor Julia! How she would have hated being thought of as a mere interlude.

But the interlude had held vital lessons for him. No more marriage—and no more women. One captain of his soul was enough, and that not a female one.

Women . . . Good Lord, *what* an escape he had had with Madeleine. He had never been so grateful to anyone in his life as he was now to Denny. Julia had been right there: he had seen through her in the end. Good God, what a bitch. Just amusing herself. It had been perfectly true. Amusing herself with other people's deepest and most genuine feelings, dragging them in her own muck like the filthy little emotional mudlark she was. How he had been taken in! But what an escape!

Poor Julia? Poor Denny! Already there were rumours. They were living apart; they were contemplating divorce (after eight months!); Madeleine's hysterical tendencies were developing to the verge of mental unbalance (that Dr. Bickleigh could quite believe), the two were seldom seen in Wyvern's Cross now. Yes, poor Denny; how could he, at inexperienced twenty-four, expect to cope with all the failings of the female temperament concentrated and multiplied a hundredfold in one damnable example? Village gossip had condemned such a youthful marriage, Denny's insistence on its early performance, and the Bournes' weak acquiescence; and for once village gossip had been right.

No, no more women. They weren't to be trusted, not one of them. A man should belong to himself, not to some complacent female bear-leader. Dr. Bickleigh had found at last what he had been looking for for the last ten years —the girl he really should have married: and that was no girl at all.

Thank God for freedom, he thought, and toasted its spirit in another sip of five-and-sixpenny port.

Oh, well, reminiscing is a bad thing. He picked up his fallen book and began to read.

The idea of being found out never entered his head. Except for one or two attacks of futile panic round about the time of the inquest, it never had. Why should it? Nothing could ever be proved; nothing could ever even be found out. There never had been the remotest possibility. There had been a certain amount of inevitable gossip, of course; but even that Dr. Bickleigh, for the time abnormally sensitive to atmosphere, had diagnosed as centring round Julia and her enormity. His practice had fallen off a little too, but that was to be expected; now it was nearly back to normal again. He had always been safe, but now the question of safety had almost ceased to apply. There was nothing to be safe about or the reverse. Dr. Bickleigh had practically forgotten that he had ever committed murder: except, of course, in so far as it reflected credit on himself.

The telephone-bell rang, and with a muttered curse he went to answer it. The instrument was in his consulting-room, and, out of long habit, he shut the door before lifting the receiver, though there was not even anyone else in the house. Florence and the cook had gone, and a woman came in from the village now daily.

"Hullo, is that Dr. Bickleigh?"

"Yes. Who is it?"

"This is Ivy speaking. Teddy—I must see you. Can you be at—at our old place at three o'clock to-morrow?"

"Really, Ivy," Dr. Bickleigh expostulated. "Now you're married, I don't think . . ."

"Oh, it isn't *that*." Ivy sounded tearful as usual, and yet urgent too. She spoke in little gasps. "This is terribly important. You must come. Something awful . . ."

"What?" Dr. Bickleigh's voice became suddenly sharp.

"I can't tell you now. Not possibly. Something . . . no, I can't. But you'll be there to-morrow?"

"Yes. Three o'clock."

"Without fail?"

"Yes; without fail."

He rang off.

What the devil was the matter with Ivy now?

Anyhow, he had done with women. Definitely.

II

Ivy was late, by nearly twenty minutes. She drove her car in unskilfully, shaving one side of the entrance. Dr. Bickleigh took the wheel from her, and drove it into the undergrowth beside his own, out of sight, while Ivy apologised. It was William's car. She was not supposed to drive it. She hardly knew how to, and that was why she was so late. She would not have dared to bring it at all, but William had gone to London, and . . .

Dr. Bickleigh groaned in spirit. William had gone to London, and Ivy had demanded a rendezvous directly his back was turned. Was he never to be done with women?

They climbed up to the eyrie, Ivy throwing fearful

glances towards the entrance of the quarry. Evidently she was terrified of being seen.

Dr. Bickleigh, clambering up behind her, noted her appearance at any rate with approval. Ivy certainly did look smart. Like the rest of Wyvern's Cross, Dr. Bickleigh had hardly seen her since her emigration to Merchester. Unlike the rest of Wyvern's Cross, he had hardly thought of her. He was surprised that she had changed so little. It was absurd to think of her as married, and to Chatford. And really, she was looking prettier than ever. Hang it all, she was wasted on Chatford; what did Chatford know, to appreciate a pretty girl? And obviously she was still fond of himself. Hence the rendezvous at the first opportunity. Rather touching, when one came to think of it. Thank goodness he hadn't married her himself; but Ivy married to someone else, Ivy as a married woman, might provide her with the spice of interest which Ivy unmarried had so notably lacked. Well, well, well, there might be possibilities after all.

Dr. Bickleigh arrived at the top of the ascent in a very different mood from that in which he had begun it.

They disappeared inside.

The new Dr. Bickleigh did not hesitate where the old one might have done, even with Ivy. He took her in his arms at once.

She made some small effort to struggle, more with herself than with him. "No, Teddy, you mustn't. I'm married now. Oh, Teddy, please let me go." But, almost before he could have complied, her arms were round his neck and she was straining frantically to him.

"Ivy—dear girl."

"Oh, Teddy, do you still love me? Really? Oh, do say you do."

He said it.

They kissed.

No, Ivy hadn't altered, Dr. Bickleigh mused; but he thought of her as Chatford's wife, and that made her more amusing.

"Look, darling, there's our old couch still there. Do you remember? The divan. Let's sit on it."

"Oh, no, Teddy, we mustn't. . . . Not now. No, don't."

He drew her down on to it beside him. After the barest show of conventional resistance, she yielded.

Dear little Ivy. He really was rather fond of her. And it was nice to be so openly adored. At least, in small and infrequent doses it was.

He took her hands in his and peeled off her gloves, then pulled off her hat and ran his fingers, with complacent proprietorship, through her soft, fair curls. Ivy let him do as he liked with her.

It dawned on him that her thoughts were very much elsewhere. She did not respond, nor was there any answering amorousness in her blue eyes. She did not seem even to be noticing what he was doing. "Penny for your thoughts, dear," he said jocularly.

The look she turned on him was so unexpected that he stiffened in his attitude of the moment. It was one of blank terror. He remembered her words on the telephone and read into them a more literal significance than he had credited to them before. What had Chatford been doing to her?

"Ivy! What's the matter? Something's wrong. Tell me, dear."

She moistened her lips. "I—hardly know how to. It's—terrible, Teddy. Dreadful!"

"What is?" This was something serious: he had never seen Ivy look like this.

"William's gone to London to—to ——"

"Good heavens, not run away from you, has he? Left you?"

"No, no. It's about *you*, Teddy." She began to shiver violently.

"Me?" he said in astonishment. "You mean, he's gone to London about me?"

She nodded.

"Good heavens, what for? On business, do you mean? But he isn't my solicitor. What on earth do you mean, Ivy?"

Her lips were shaking so much she could hardly frame the words. "He's gone to—Scotland Yard."

A sharp pain struck sharply through the left side of Dr. Bickleigh's chest, just as if it had been pierced by a long pin; it was followed immediately by a dull, sickly ache. He stared at Ivy in plain panic, his mouth open, his eyes filmed with fear.

"Oh!" Ivy whispered, and shrank away from him.

Her movement roused him to pull himself together. With a literal physical effort he forced obedience on shaking limbs and quivering nerves. Ivy—must—not—guess.

"Scotland Yard?" he repeated, huskily but fairly evenly. "Good heavens, what for?"

Bit by bit Ivy, amid tears, divulged her news. It was the awful, wicked gossip that had been going round ever since Mrs. Bickleigh died. Teddy didn't know? Oh, yes; it had. Nothing definite had been said, but the circumstances had been considered "queer," and it had been hinted that quite a different story lay behind the verdict, which Dr. Bickleigh could tell if he chose.

"Am I to understand that Wyvern's Cross has been accusing me of murdering Julia?" Dr. Bickleigh asked disgustedly. The news of this gossip was a complete revelation to him. Lot of damned old cats! He'd like to do something to the lot of them.

Oh, *no*; nothing so awful as that. But coming, as Mrs. Bickleigh's death had, right in the middle of all the talk there had been about the doctor and that Miss Cranmere, well, Teddy had already been on the main news-page, and had simply and inevitably been promoted to its leading column, so to speak. From a star of scandal he had become a complete constellation. But only the vaguest hints had been dropped as to cause and effect.

Then, apparently, the whole simmering pot had boiled up, at a tea-party at Miss Peavy's about a fortnight ago, into something very like plain speech. Miss Wapsworthy had been the leading spirit, seconded ably by Mrs. Torr. In the ordinary course it would just have been the usual letting off of feminine steam; but by a misfortune of misfortunes William had been there too, and heard it all. And what is delightful gossip to a village worthy, implied Ivy, is a deadly piece of seriousness to a solicitor. He had gone back to Wyvern's Cross to talk to Mr. Torr about it the very next day. Why Mr. Torr? Because Mrs. Torr had said that her husband had not been altogether satisfied with the inquest last year.

"Blast the silly old hag!" burst out Dr. Bickleigh uncontrollably, white with rage. "Of all the . . . Couldn't Chatford see it was all just the aimless chatter of these damned old women, with nothing else to do but spread scandalous stories about their neighbours? Couldn't he see that?"

"Well, you see," said Ivy timidly, "he—he hates you so, Teddy. I think—you ought to know that."

"Hates me? Good heavens, I've never done anything to him. Why should he hate me?"

"Why, because—because ——"

"My God, Ivy, you didn't tell him about *us*? You did! You damned little fool. I . . ."

Ivy's tears fell thicker and faster. "I knew you'd be angry. But I couldn't help it. He got it out of me. You don't know what he's like. He—he knew I wasn't—good, and . . . I tried not to tell him, Teddy. I swear I did. But you don't know what he's like. On and on . . ."

"All right, Ivy." There was no good in losing his temper with the little fool. He must keep calm: calm. As long as he didn't frighten or antagonise her, Ivy was an invaluable ally; a spy in Chatford's dirty, underhand camp. As long as she thought he loved her, she would . . . "All right, dear." He forced himself to smile, instead of hitting her in the face again as he longed to do—and this time go on hitting her. "Don't cry. I quite see how it happened. And, anyhow, it's done now. No wonder he hates me. And so he's going out of his way to stir up this silly mare's nest, eh? Well, that's all right. Scotland Yard wouldn't listen to him for a minute, of course. Even if he goes there at all. Probably he only said that to frighten you. He can't be such a fool. And, even if they did, two minutes' conversation would clear the whole thing up."

"Would it?" said Ivy, brightening. "Then you don't think it's serious?"

"Serious? Good gracious me, no. How could anything so utterly ridiculous be serious?" His own words were already reassuring Dr. Bickleigh. This might be an infernal nuisance, but it could hardly be serious. "Why, it simply makes me laugh—that's all."

"Oh, Teddy, it's wonderful of you to take it like that, dear. I feel so *ashamed* of William."

Dr. Bickleigh actually did laugh, genuinely. "Why, don't you see, when they hear the circumstances," he pointed out eagerly, "that it's just a case of retrospective jealousy towards the wife's former lover, that'll rob anything he has to tell them of nine-tenths of its value. They'd see through it at once. Just an insane idea of revenge."

"But, Teddy, you wouldn't tell them that?"

"What?"

"About the—the lover. It would be giving me away completely, wouldn't it?"

"My dear Ivy," said Dr. Bickleigh with some impatience, "I don't intend to hang in order to shield your good name. That may be the sort of thing they do in books, but in real life it'd be a bit too much."

"Oh, don't," shuddered Ivy. "Don't talk about hanging. It—it makes me feel dreadful."

"Silly darling," Dr. Bickleigh soothed her, and she clung to him as frantically as if his death-warrant had been actually signed.

Dr. Bickleigh did not want to be amorous any more for the moment. He wanted the history of Chatford's activities to date.

Between perfunctory caresses, he got it.

Chatford had begun by interviewing Mr. Torr. Mr. Torr had had nothing definite to say beyond a vague feeling that the bare facts, as presented in the coroner's court, were improbable; and, if they were true, there must be others to explain them which, whether for good or for bad reasons, had been concealed. That was all he had meant in expressing dissatisfaction with the proceedings: the coroner had not probed deep enough.

Chatford had not told Ivy much about this interview, but he had added that the two had discussed Mrs. Bickleigh's character, which, of course, Mr. Torr knew a good deal more intimately than Chatford himself, and had arrived at the conclusion that, as she must be considered the most unlikely person in the world to give way to such weakness as habitual drug-taking, the apparent cause of this, her headaches, ought to be investigated a good deal more fully. That she had suffered from headaches of the most violent description during the last months of her life had been no secret to her friends; even with her strength of will she could not have concealed them; but the cause had been passed over very lightly in court. Sir Tamerton Foliott's name had been mentioned, but he had not given evidence. Chatford intended to see him.

"But what's the man getting at?" Dr. Bickleigh asked, puzzled. "How is all this going to help anything? What really is in Chatford's mind?"

Ivy told him. Chatford and Mr. Torr and Miss Wapsworthy, all of them suspected something *horrible*: that Mrs. Bickleigh had taken the overdose of morphia deliberately, driven to it by her husband's scandalous affair with Madeleine Cranmere.

"They believe that Julia committed suicide?" said Dr. Bickleigh, half incredulously.

Well, Ivy couldn't say definitely what they believed: they believed in the possibility. And William was determined to drag it all up, so that Dr. Bickleigh's name should be utterly discredited and he would have to leave Wyvern's Cross for ever.

Dr. Bickleigh almost laughed out loud in his relief. So murder was not even in question at all. Why couldn't the little idiot have said so at once, instead of frightening him like that? How funny: he'd never once thought of Julia's death being put down to suicide. It was so utterly unlike her. Mr. Torr as an amateur psychologist was pretty good.

Dr. Bickleigh questioned Ivy further.

Sir Tamerton Foliott was not the only person Chatford intended to interview in London. Madeleine Bourne was there, if not her husband. Chatford was determined to get to the bottom of that affair. There, really, he had hinted to Ivy, was the crux. If Dr. Bickleigh had been as serious in his feelings as Wyvern's Cross had believed (though clearly Madeleine had not been), then Mrs. Bickleigh undoubtedly had a strong motive for suicide. Chatford believed he could get an idea from Madeleine how serious he had been.

Dr. Bickleigh stroked his chin. Madeleine would have no hesitation in giving him away: of that he was certain. Ever since the day of her engagement she had seemed to take a debased delight in prattling of the affair to anyone who would listen; and naturally there had been plenty of willing ears. It had done him a lot of harm in the place undoubtedly; and it was to that, rather than to Julia's death, that he had attributed the falling off of his practice last year. But, even if she did give him away completely to Chatford, what did it matter? It was only her word against his, and Dr. Bickleigh rather fancied that if it came to the point he could discredit Madeleine's word pretty adequately. To prove she was a hysterical subject would be simple; from that to delusions was the merest of steps. And it would be rather delightful to show up Madeleine for the unpleasant thing she really was. Poor Denny!

"But what about Scotland Yard? I thought you said he was going there. Where does that come in?"

Yes, he was. If these interviews, combined with the information from Wyvern's Cross, did show there was a case for investigation, he was going to Scotland Yard to lay it before the police.

"They'll laugh at him," pronounced Dr. Bickleigh with conviction. "What does it matter to anyone now whether poor Julia died by accident or killed herself? It may matter to Chatford, of course, if he could get me drummed out of the place; but it certainly won't matter to the police. Dirty hound, to try and get his revenge through blackening a dead woman's name."

"But, Teddy—aren't you worried?"

"My dear girl, there's nothing to worry about. Of course Julia never committed suicide. That idea's absurd. But of course, too, the authorities won't let your precious husband stir up all this mud over nothing. Naturally I'm not worried."

"I know I should be."

"Well, I'm not. Besides, this is no time for worry, darling, with you here again. Quite like old times, isn't it? Glad to be back?"

"Oh, Teddy, you know I am. Are you? Really, really?"

"You bet I am. You're prettier than ever, Ivy. And aren't you smart too, nowadays? I like your hat. And real silk stockings. Real silk all through, I expect, Mrs. Chatford, eh?"

"No, Teddy . . . you mustn't. No—not now I'm married: it isn't fair. . . . Really, Dr. Bickleigh, I'm surprised at you.—Oh, Teddy. . . ."

An hour later they parted.

Dr. Bickleigh smiled to himself as he drove home. Chatford's activities could really not be taken seriously. And it amused him to have had his revenge on them so promptly.

III

Ivy became invaluable. She kept Dr. Bickleigh informed of everything she knew, and questioned her husband closely on his behalf. As it was impossible for her to use the car after Chatford's return from London, they arranged a rendezvous in Merchester itself, where they met in secrecy and safety regularly twice a week.

On Dr. Bickleigh's instructions, Ivy adopted a subtle line. She pretended to Chatford that she hated Dr. Bickleigh now, and was as anxious as himself to see him driven out of Wyvern's Cross. In this way she got him to part with a good deal more information than he would have divulged to an unsympathetic enquirer.

Dr. Bickleigh thus learnt that Chatford, while getting very little change out of Sir Tamerton Foliott, had got a great deal out of Madeleine Bourne, though mostly small: enough, at any rate, to justify in his opinion the visit to Scotland Yard. Dr. Bickleigh was most interested in this visit, and questioned Ivy thoroughly about it, giving her further questions to put to Chatford later. However, it all amounted to very little more than that Chatford had been received without any great enthusiasm, had seen a chief inspector, to whom he had told his story, and had been advised not without severity that Scotland Yard could not move in the matter, as he should have known, it being outside their province, and, if he was really of the opinion that anything was to be gained by investigation, he had better lay his facts before the proper authorities, who were the Devonshire county police. Altogether, chuckled Dr. Bickleigh with malicious glee, not a very successful interview.

Chatford laid his information before the county authorities.

He was more reticent with Ivy as to the result of that interview, but Dr. Bickleigh was not perturbed. It was all too ridiculous. Except for a growing anger with Chatford and his presumption, and annoyance over the bother that might be caused him, his emotions were not affected. That it would ever come to an enquiry was impossible to believe, and, even if it did, nothing more serious could happen than that he might be censured for negligence in allowing Julia to have access to the morphia after he had discovered her propensities. But it was a nuisance, and Chatford was getting intolerable. Dr. Bickleigh took pleasure in gratifying his hatred by reinstating a none too unwilling Ivy as his regular mistress. Chatford should pay that price for his damned interference.

Not long afterwards a strange man from Exeter was to

be seen pottering about in Wyvern's Cross and chatting casually with the inhabitants. Dr. Bickleigh observed his activities with nothing but amusement, mixed with contempt. A lot of good he could do, collecting village gossip. And, besides, the villagers all liked him; and they had not liked Julia. Dr. Bickleigh thought humorously of writing to Exeter to protest, as a ratepayer, against this waste of time and expense.

The strange man disappeared; and that, it seemed, was the end of that. It was now getting well on in July, and Dr. Bickleigh looked forward to a peaceful remainder of the summer.

But there is never any harm in adding the final touch or two that makes a masterpiece; and one incident particularly pleased him.

"Teddy," Ivy said artlessly one day, "you never told me you once actually asked Madeleine to marry you." The Madeleine theme was a favourite one with Ivy. She loved to question and cross-question him on it, demanding every detail of their intercourse, taking delight in reviving the anguish she had suffered over it and, unknowingly, his too. Dr. Bickleigh wished she wouldn't. He did not want to discuss it at all.

"Didn't I?" he said gruffly, shying as always at the mention of this unwelcome name.

"But you did ask her."

"So she's blabbed that too, has she?"

"Yes, she told William, and he told me. Do tell me about it, Teddy. You must have had a hectic scene, from what she says. And fancy, only an hour or so after I saw you that day in the road. Do you remember? Oh, Teddy, I do think you might have told me. What did she say, really? And all the time . . . Teddy, you're not listening."

Dr. Bickleigh turned from the window. Her words had reminded him of something he had been intending to put to her. "Ivy," he said, very distinctly, as to a small child, "you know when you did meet me that afternoon, I asked you the time?"

"Yes?"

"You told me it was twenty to three, didn't you?"

"Did I? Yes, I believe I did."

"Did you ever find out you were nearly a quarter of an hour fast?"

"No, I don't remember."

"Well, you were. It put me in rather a hole. I was late for a most important appointment. I put in another visit first, thinking I'd got a quarter of an hour more than I had, and it made me late."

"Did it really? I'm awfully sorry, Teddy. Fancy you remembering that."

"Yes," said Dr. Bickleigh, still more distinctly, "when you saw me that afternoon the time was really twenty-five past two." He had always remembered that, just after twenty past two, he had passed two of the villagers as he turned into the very road where he had left the car. "You'd better remember that."

"Yes, I will, darling. But it doesn't really matter, does it?"

"Oh, no; it doesn't *matter*. But—well, I suppose you told Chatford about meeting me that afternoon?"

"No, I don't think I have. I'm sure I haven't. He never asked me. Well, he didn't know, so he couldn't, could he? But I'd nearly forgotten all about it myself, as a matter of fact."

"Yes, so had I. It just occurred to me. Well, if by any chance it ever is mentioned, remember that it was twenty-five past two, not twenty to three. I shouldn't say anything about your watch being fast. No need for complications. Just say that when I asked you for the time, you looked at your watch and told me it was twenty-five past two."

"All right, Teddy. I'll remember."

Dr. Bickleigh smiled on her. How fortunate that Ivy was Ivy.

"Has Chatford told you anything lately, by the way?"

"No, not for a long time now, Teddy."

Dr. Bickleigh kissed her affectionately.

That Chatford was getting more and more reticent with Ivy could be interpreted in only one way: he had nothing to tell. But Dr. Bickleigh's hatred of him did not diminish; if anything, it increased.

Dr. Bickleigh had never hated before in his life. Now he hated two people, Chatford and Madeleine—Chatford the more virulently, but Madeleine the more deeply, with a sick, disgusted loathing. He felt that he had been more humiliated by Madeleine than ever by Julia. Madeleine had taken his most sacred feelings, the most genuine, honest feelings he had ever had, and danced on them. She had exploited every atom of his soul for the gratification of her own unbalanced emotions. And, not content with that, she had, in her astonishing unreticence, taken a perverted delight in slandering him. Dr. Bickleigh knew very well the story that she had been so assiduously putting about, without the slightest provocation, whitewashing her own mean little soul by blackening his: that she, the white flower of trusting innocence, had had her heart besieged by a professional seducer, who by his appalling lies and unscrupulous skill had succeeded in gaining temporary possession of that organ, but, Madeleine coming to her senses just in time, the scales were ripped from her eyes as if by the direct hand of Providence, and the desperate fellow was sent promptly to the right-about. Some version of this story Madeleine had busily poured into all the important ears of the neighbourhood, the Bournes', the Torrs', Mrs. Hatton-Hampstead's, any she could find; and though, of course, she nobly refrained from mentioning a name in connection with it, Dr. Bickleigh had found himself for a time eyed very coldly indeed.

He could still not think of Madeleine without trembling with rage. Denny he no longer honoured by hating; he merely despised that poor creature now. Denny, with his prospective title and eight thousand a year, of course deserved the love of any pure woman.

Ivy was the only one to benefit directly by her lover's present detestation of her late rival. Returning to her after the other, with a celibate pause between to allow things to fall a little into perspective, Dr. Bickleigh inevitably compared the two; and his revulsion of feeling from the latter was enabling him now to appreciate Ivy at a true worth she had not got.

As the summer wore on, this appreciation of Dr. Bickleigh's for his mistress increased more and more. His growing affection warmed her, and she spread the wings of her charming butterfly soul to it; her own love for him had remained surprisingly constant. And, now that the danger threatened by Chatford's retrospective jealousy had disappeared, she became gay and light-hearted. Their bi-weekly meetings were merrier than the old ones had ever been. Tears were a thing of the past. Ivy gained in poise without, however, losing the childishness that was her chief charm to him. She saw that her new smartness pleased him and added to her attractiveness in his eyes, and she exploited this fresh possibility with naïve delight, dressing herself up for him just like a little girl in her mother's hat and furs (and with much the same result), always trying to have some new and interesting articles of clothing on, if only a new shade in silk stockings, and submitting gravely every new hat or frock for his approval.

The attitude which Ivy always contrived to present of hanging on his slightest word exactly suited the new edition of Dr. Bickleigh. He who had been a door-mat himself all his life till in one supreme gesture he had cast off door-mattery for ever, now wanted a door-mat of his own; and Ivy was the ideal door-mat. He began to think very seriously about Ivy. He saw now that he had not been so far wrong after all three years ago when he recognised in her the girl he really ought to have married. Only the recognition was premature; he had not been developed enough to appreciate her; he was still a slave to leading-strings, and missed them when absent. But now . . .

An old vision, three years out of date, was resuscitated, looked over, and found comedy. Once more cricket was pushed aside.

A brand-new vision made its appearance about this time too. A most absorbing vision, which seemed to be continually expanding and expanding, like a rubber pig. The germ of it was in the Ivy vision. For Ivy to become Mrs. Bickleigh the previous elimination of Chatford was obviously required. An inconvenient husband can be eliminated in two ways—by divorce or death. Divorce held this disadvantage—that Ivy would come to him penniless, and he, as co-respondent, would have to leave Wyvern's Cross and set up elsewhere. With Madeleine's money to support him till he got his footing that was simple; in this case it would be impossible. But death held this positive advantage: that not only would Ivy come to him, but as Chatford's widow she would come embellished by Chatford's not inconsiderable possessions. How exceedingly nice, then, from every aspect, if Chatford were to die.

That was the original vision. Its expansion was on these lines: how exceedingly nice if, while death was about, not only Chatford, but Madeleine too, and anybody else obnoxious to Dr. Edmund Bickleigh, were to be happily removed by it.

IV

It was not for some weeks after he had decided to murder Chatford and Madeleine that Dr. Bickleigh took any active steps in the matter. Murder is a serious business. The slightest slip may be disastrous. Dr. Bickleigh had no intention of risking disaster.

Chapter Ten

I

DR. BICKLEIGH read de Quincey on *Murder as a Fine Art.*

He was impressed with Thomas Griffiths Wainewright, but considered John Williams anything but an artist. On the whole, however, he agreed with the author. Murder could be a fine art: but it was not for everyone. Murder was a fine art for the superman. It was a pity that Nietzsche could not have developed de Quincey's propositions.

Dr. Bickleigh had no doubt whatever that in murder he had qualified not only as a fine artist, but as a superman. It was a pleasant sensation. It gave one a feeling of confidence and power. To know that one really could rid oneself of anyone who became impossible . . . The only pity was that the artist in this particular medium should be unable to point proudly to his triumphs. Art for art's sake.

But Dr. Bickleigh still could not think of his own experiments really as *murder*. There was quite a perceptible difference between what he had done, and proposed to do, and murder: though he could not altogether define it.

Still, murder or not, the method had got to receive meticulous attention. Dr. Bickleigh pondered over it closely. Certain broad rules were obvious: the deaths must appear either natural or accidental—anything but designed. Dr. Bickleigh had nothing but scorn for those murderers who despatch their victims in one of the obvious ways—riddled with bullets, sliced with a hatchet, or stuffed full of arsenic—and rely on bad detective work for their escape. His method was to be a great deal more subtle than that.

A great man is one who can not only seize his opportunities, but recognise them. Dr. Bickleigh knew that, and spent some time in looking for his own, turning over in the meantime, just as he had done before, a dozen different plans. When his opportunity—a case of virulent botulism in one of his own patients—did offer itself, Dr. Bickleigh recognised it at once, and paid a visit to the Merchester Public Library. Then he bought an incubator. He was no bacteriologist, but to make a culture of *bacillus botulinus* was simple. Dr. Bickleigh made one.

The more he tested this idea, the better he liked it. Chatford's death would present every natural appearance; there was the case in Wyvern's Cross to prove that contaminated food was circulating in the district; in matters of food-contamination neither Chatford nor Madeleine could be expected to be immune. No suspicion of design could possibly arise. On the other hand, the method, though safe, was uncertain. It was impossible to ensure death. Still, the plan presented so many advantages that this one drawback could not outweigh them. And, if failure did follow, it was always possible to make a second attempt, when their powers of resistance would have been weakened by the first illness; and success then would be almost inevitable.

Dr. Bickleigh invented some legal business, and asked Chatford to tea in a few days' time to discuss it.

To Dr. Bickleigh's annoyance, Chatford proved difficult. He was not Dr. Bickleigh's legal adviser, and, in the curt note which he sent in reply to the doctor's friendly letter of invitation, he intimated quite plainly that he had no wish to become Dr. Bickleigh's legal adviser. Dr. Bickleigh rang him up, and Chatford told him in dry tones that he was far too busy to go out to Wyvern's Cross to tea, but that business (if Dr. Bickleigh persisted) could always be discussed in his office in Merchester. Dr. Bickleigh complained bitterly to Ivy of the way in which Chatford rejected his advances.

And then, suddenly and most unexpectedly, Chatford rang up to say in the most friendly way that he found he was going to be in the neighbourhood of Wyvern's Cross two afternoons later, and would very much like to call in for a cup of tea if that would be convenient. Dr. Bickleigh, delighted, assured him that it would be quite convenient.

He was unable to ask Ivy whether it was she who had brought about this change of heart, for Ivy did not turn up at their rendezvous the next day. Instead, there was a note from her, addressed to the fictitious name in which Dr. Bickleigh had hired the room, to tell him that William had suddenly packed her off at about five minutes' notice to *Spain*, her dear! He had a sister who had a husband who lived in Spain as the representative of a large British engineering firm, and, though Ivy had never met them, they had written out of the blue to ask her and Chatford, or her alone if Chatford could not come too, to go over and visit them at once in Barcelona; and William had insisted on her doing so—simply wouldn't take no for an answer. It was the chance of a lifetime; it would be a great treat for her; she had not been looking too fit lately, and the change would be most beneficial; a hundred reasons. Teddy needn't worry; it wasn't because William suspected anything; that was quite certain, because he had never been nicer. And she would see him again in the autumn, and would miss him terribly, and love him always, and write to him every day, and he was to write to her just as often.

Dr. Bickleigh was sorry, and he did miss her, but he was pleased that such a piece of luck had befallen her, and there was always the autumn, and a rest never did anyone any harm.

He turned the Jowett back from Merchester, and headed for The Hall.

During the last year he had scarcely seen Madeleine at all. They had passed once or twice on the roads, but always contrived not to see each other; and people had had the tact not to ask them to the same gatherings. It was with a curious sense of re-entering the past that he drove up the gravel sweep to the house.

Mr. and Mrs. Bourne were at home. The parlourmaid (the same parlourmaid) hardly knew whether to look welcoming or embarrassed, but succumbed to Dr. Bickleigh's infectious smile. She kept him waiting in the hall for a few minutes before summoning him to the drawing-room.

Madeleine and Denny were at tea. Denny was the only one who showed awkwardness. His face expressed plain hostility. Madeleine, on the other hand, looked merely as if this of all moments was the one she had been awaiting for the last twelve months. Even Dr. Bickleigh, who thought he knew the depths of her duplicity, was surprised. He followed her cue and tried to look the same.

Sitting between them, he hinted delicately at the object of his visit. Without exactly naming it, he suggested that there had been a silly feud, that Wyvern's Cross was too tiny to hold feuds, and that he had come, in frank and manly manner, to insinuate an apology for anything he had done which might not have been approved, and hope that the hatchet might now be considered buried. As he had shrewdly guessed, this situation appealed to Madeleine. She threw herself into it heart and eyes. The two vied with each other in noble exchanges and generous hints. Denny, puzzled and earthily suspicious, might not have been there at all.

Dr. Bickleigh came away with a greater contempt for his hostess than before; if he had cared to take the trouble, he was convinced he could make Madeleine his mistress within a week; he did not care. For he came away also with Madeleine's promise to come, with her husband, to tea the next day.

When he got in, Dr. Bickleigh ran straight upstairs to the attic where, among a litter of oddments, he kept the incubator. He stayed there some time, regarding the happy family inside with a loving eye.

II

Botulism is caused chiefly by contaminated sausages. It may (argued Dr. Bickleigh) be caused just as readily by contaminated potted meat. There were to be potted meat sandwiches for tea.

By Dr. Bickleigh's orders, tea was ready in good time. But the food was not taken into the drawing-room. Nobody should have a chance afterwards to say that he had been left alone with it. Instead, Mrs. Holne's attention in the kitchen was directed for just two seconds elsewhere, and two of the sandwiches were whisked into Dr. Bickleigh's ready handkerchief. Subsequently Mrs. Holne would be able to swear that she had had them all under her direct observation from the time when she cut them to the time when they were carried into the drawing-room under the noses of the visitors. Not, of course, that there would ever be occasion to swear any such thing; but Dr. Bickleigh could not forget now that he was an artist.

As he spread his bacilli on the potted meat upstairs in the attic two minutes later, his only conscious thought was that he must *not* forget to put them back on the plate with their distinguishing marks (a tiny pink smear of potted meat on a corner of the white bread) uppermost. Of Madeleine and Chatford he did not think at all. Now that the affair had gone into action, those two had almost ceased to be human beings to him at all. They had become symbols.

It was going to be a neat business.

Only a tiny smear of the culture was used. The rest was kept in case, improbably, of a second administration becoming necessary. And a minute bit was to be added that night to the jar of potted meat before it was thrown away next day when the news of the two illnesses came through. It is the *little* points that count.

As before, the thing would be utterly detection-proof. How simple murder was, in the right hands.

Murder—well, yes, in a way it *was* murder. . . . How odd.

III

The administration was mere child's-play. Dr. Bickleigh kept the plate of sandwiches on the cake-stand beside him. The two contaminated ones were on the extreme side of the plate. He offered it first to Madeleine and then to Chatford. Both took the sandwich nearest to them. It was as easy as a conjurer forcing a card on a yokel. Dr. Bickleigh could have laughed out loud at their simplicity.

While they all engaged in rather stilted conversation, he covertly watched Madeleine and Chatford eating death. Chatford rushed upon his, caught napping this time for all his dry caution; Madeleine toyed delicately with hers, pretending, of course (the fool!), that her soul was above such earthly things as food and drink. Denny, obviously dragged at her heels, ate in morose silence, looking suspiciously at the food, for all the world as if he thought it might be poisoned. What an idea!

Dr. Bickleigh felt less pity for them than he had felt

for Julia. In a way she had not deserved to die; and these two did. In a way, too, it was Madeleine who had really murdered Julia. At any rate, far more so than himself. Well, Julia was getting her vengeance. As Dr. Bickleigh watched the last morsel of sandwich disappear into her rat-trap of a mouth (yes, positively, in these days Madeleine's mouth was a veritable rat-trap), he experienced a strange sensation: he wanted to roar with laughter, shout, sing, snap his fingers, howl aloud; his chest seemed to be swelling so that he had to keep drawing great breaths to fill it. It was a strange sensation, yet in a way familiar. Suddenly he remembered. It had been just the same when he was driving away from the little wood a year ago, after he had hit Ivy in the face.

He had to talk, chatter nonsense, crack silly jokes. So bubbling with his merriment that the others were infected too. Even Denny laughed. The stiltedness disappeared completely. Dr. Bickleigh, hugging his joy, saw the whole thing amusedly in newspaper headlines. "Laughter at Death-Feast"; "Doomed Guests Joke after Fatal Sandwiches"; "Microbes and Mirth."

As her restraint lessened, Dr. Bickleigh watched too the real Madeleine appear. Her egoism was incredible. It was impossible to keep any topic for more than an initial moment on the impersonal plane; Madeleine could only view it as it affected herself. If cars came up for discussion, with an incipient argument between Denny and Chatford as to the merits of two different makes, Madeleine would intervene with reminiscences of her own surprising skill in driving, and the astonishing accidents which only her own coolness and composure had enabled her to avoid. If the latest play in London was mentioned, Madeleine was led without hesitation to give them anecdotes of the famous actors she had met, and how they had one and all told her that the stage was simply waiting for her to conquer it, offered her immediate engagements as their leading lady, and almost burst into tears on her noble refusal to take the bread out of hardworking (but inferior) actresses' mouths. If anyone anywhere had done anything, Madeleine had done the same thing better. Denny said, more than once, in a weary tone: "Yes, dear. You're wonderful." Dr. Bickleigh was delighted.

But he was careful not to make the mistake of keeping the thing going too long. As soon as reasonably possible, he made the excuse of a couple of urgent visits before surgery to ensure his guests' departure. *Bacillus botulinus* is a tricky fellow, and Dr. Bickleigh did not wish to run the risk of having anyone taken ill before reaching home. To Chatford on the doorstep he made perfunctory excuses. It was a nuisance; Mr. and Mrs. Bourne's unexpected arrival had made it impossible for him to discuss his business that day; Chatford must come out some other afternoon, and they could go into it properly. Chatford quite understood.

Having thus arranged for a second administration in the unlikely event of Chatford being alive to require it, Dr. Bickleigh methodically set about perfecting perfection. It was with an air of slight amusement at himself that he went into the kitchen to interview Mrs. Holne. These details were unnecessary really, of course; but they were half the fun. They made all the difference between a slipshod and a finished piece of work. Dr. Bickleigh knew he was not taking a sordid joy in murder for murder's sake; but he did think that he might allow himself a cynical appreciation of a work of fine art.

Mrs. Holne was a thin, melancholy woman, quite ready at all times to anticipate the worst.

"Oh, Mrs. Holne," Dr. Bickleigh said, with his usual deprecatory smile on invading the kitchen, "are you sure that potted meat was quite all right? The sandwiches tasted just a little bit funny to me."

"Well, it was only opened this afternoon, sir, and it looked fresh enough; but it's bin hot enough to-day to turn anything," Mrs. Holne sighed, "and that's a fact."

"Well, have you got the jar handy? I'd like to have a sniff at it."

Mrs. Holne brought the jar, sniffing at it herself. "It does smell a bit queer, sir, now you come to mention it." Great is the power of suggestion.

Dr. Bickleigh sniffed too. "Very queer. You're quite right, Mrs. Holne. It had better be thrown away. We don't want to run any risks, after that poor Sampford child. I'll drop it in the dustbin myself." Yes, on the whole it seemed to come better to-day than deferring it till to-morrow.

He went out through the back kitchen and did so, smearing the fragment of infected jelly from his culture on it as he went. That fragment would soon infect the whole contents of the pot. What was to happen to the latter after its disposal in the dustbin Dr. Bickleigh did not know, or care. That could be left to look after itself. Meanwhile, there was the sheer artistry of the action.

And that was all there was to be done. How simple it was.

Dr. Bickleigh strolled back to the drawing-room, humming an air from *The Marriage of Figaro*, and strummed on the piano till it was time for surgery. He was self-taught, but he did not play too badly; and it afforded him a good deal of satisfaction.

IV

News came the next morning, from Mrs. Holne. In a village an event has only to take place for everyone in the neighbourhood to know it, apparently almost simultaneously and without visible communication.

"Have you heard the noos, sir?"

Dr. Bickleigh laid his knife and fork across his breakfast bacon and braced himself for the best. "No? What?"

"Mrs. Bourne, sir. Up to The 'All. Took very bad in the night, they say. Had to have Dr. Lydston out from Merchester, an' all."

"Dear me," Dr. Bickleigh clucked, looking properly solemn. "How very dreadful. I hope it isn't serious?"

"Accordin' to what they say, sir, it's about as serious as it could be," returned Mrs. Holne, with mournful relish.

"Now, that's very queer. I was taken quite bad myself last night. Nothing serious, of course, but . . . No, I think you'd better take this bacon away, Mrs. Holne. I don't feel up to it, really. I'll just have a bit of dry toast, and some coffee. Well, really, what a curious coincidence."

Mrs. Holne grasped her cue. "Why, sir, you—you don't think it could 'a' bin that potted meat, do you?"

"Good gracious me, I'd never thought any more about that. I wonder . . . It's quite possible, Mrs. Holne. Dear me, how dreadful."

"Well, it did smell queer, sir, and that's a fact. They didn't say anything about Mr. Dennis being took bad, but what about the other gentleman? Mr. Chatford, sir?"

"I haven't heard anything," Dr. Bickleigh said doubtfully. "And, in any case, we can't be sure, you know, Mrs. Holne. We mustn't jump to conclusions. Of course, if Mr. Chatford *is* . . . But there; we must wait and see."

"Well, glad I am that I didn't touch the stuff, sir," observed Mrs. Holne, taking a reluctant departure. "It's not often I'm spared anything, but at any rate I didn't 'ave any of *that*."

She went out, a firmly established witness.

Dr. Bickleigh smiled gently as he helped himself to

toast. He missed his bacon, but one must be prepared for some discomfort in a good cause.

The annoying thing was that no news came through about Chatford. Most annoying. Twice during his morning's work Dr. Bickleigh called in at Fairlawn to see if any sort of message had arrived, but there was nothing. His suspense grew. It was even more tantalising than, in his pre-marital betting days, waiting for the result of the three-thirty.

After lunch he could stand it no longer. He took up the telephone receiver and gave Chatford's private number.

"I'm sorry," came a female voice over the wire. "Mr. Chatford's ill in bed."

Dr. Bickleigh's heart executed a little triumphant leap. "Ill, is he? I'm very sorry to hear that. This is Dr. Bickleigh speaking, from Wyvern's Cross. I hope it's nothing serious?"

The maid at the other end hesitated obviously. "I—I don't know, sir." There reached Dr. Bickleigh's eager ear the sounds of a whispered colloquy. Asking the cook how much she ought to tell me, he thought.

"Well, what are the symptoms?" he asked impatiently.

Again there was a long pause before the answer was given, but this time Dr. Bickleigh could detect no whispering. "We think he must have eaten something that's disagreed with him, sir."

"Indeed? Now that's very curious. I don't know if you know, but Mr. Chatford was here to tea yesterday, and I was taken bad myself last night; and so, I hear, was Mrs. Bourne, who was here too." No echo of all Julia's attempts at training him reminded Dr. Bickleigh of the reprehensibility of entering into details with servants. "I'm beginning to fear that it must have been something we had here. Will you run up and give Mr. Chatford my compliments and tell him that I shall be in Merchester this afternoon and would like to call in and see him? Not in a professional capacity, of course; but if he wouldn't mind my examining him, really for my own peace of mind . . . Will you tell him that?"

"Yes, sir. Hold on, please?"

As he waited, Dr. Bickleigh congratulated himself on the inspiration. That he was committing a heinous breach of professional etiquette worried him not at all. As weighed against the tremendous advantage of insinuating himself as secondary medical adviser to Chatford, that meant nothing at all. Why, the man would be completely in his hands. If he did not die of this first administration, a second would be even easier; and a third, if necessary, and a fourth. Not, of course, that a third would be necessary.

And besides, he would be able to diagnose botulism at once, and get that fact established from the beginning. That he came straight from a similar case of his own would make such a startling diagnosis perfectly feasible (Lydston would miss such an unusual possibility almost certainly). Everything fitted in. Dr. Bickleigh felt no more emotion over Chatford than he had yesterday; the man had got to be put out of the way, and the more simply the better.

But the return of the maid brought a check to his plans. "Mr. Chatford's compliments, sir, but Dr. Lydston's got his case in hand, and he's afraid he's too ill to see anyone else."

"I see," said Dr. Bickleigh smoothly. "Then just give him my condolences." But his hand was shaking with anger as he hung up the receiver. That had been a snub direct. Damn the fellow! Of all the infernal impudence. . . .

Dr. Bickleigh felt it to be sheer presumption on Chatford's part to refuse opportunities in this way of being neatly polished off.

He went along to his consulting-room and sat down to think the situation over. The more he pondered it, the more desirable did it seem that he should gain access to Chatford's bedside. Not merely desirable: imperative. Why, the fellow might recover otherwise, and then the whole business would have to be begun again from the beginning. He would hardly be able to use the same plan twice, too, and he could never find another so perfect as this one. It was inconceivable that Chatford should be allowed to recover.

As for Madeleine, Dr. Bickleigh was by now not nearly so emphatic. It would be nice if the creature were to die, and he would be doing the world a service (and, incidentally, Denny) by ridding it of her; but if the improbable happened and she did nothing of the sort—well, let her live. She should have her chance. But Chatford . . . he was impossible. Dr. Bickleigh was overcome for a moment with a sense of awe as he sat at his table in judgment: awe of himself and this tremendous power that he had grasped. He saw himself from the outside, a small, grim figure, meting out life or death. . . . Had he once really accepted himself as insignificant? Really?

His plan formed itself. A natural anxiety possessed him to find out exactly how bad Madeleine was. That could be fitted in. He would go up to The Hall that afternoon and see her. There should be no difficulty about that. He was sure he could rely on his standing with the parlourmaid to induce her so far to forget her training as to show him straight into Madeleine's bedroom. After all, he was a doctor. Then he would go boldly to Chatford's house in Merchester the next morning, armed with the authority of Madeleine's reception of him, and . . .

The small, grim figure stiffened; the mild blue eyes glinted stonily. Once inside Chatford's house . . .

V

That evening Dr. Bickleigh received a most unexpected visitor.

He had had a successful afternoon, in a way. That is, Denny had been out and he had penetrated without difficulty to Madeleine's bedside. Madeleine had not seemed in the least pleased to see him (he guessed that the parlourmaid would be in for a bad five minutes after he left), and, with a pose of prudery verging on the indelicate, had kept the girl in the room with them during the whole of his ten minutes' stay.

In the same spirit of purity incarnate she had refused to let him make the least examination, even to the extent of taking her pulse, and her embarrassment was so exaggerated as to appear something like panic; one would have thought she had never had a doctor in her bedroom before, or any being in trousers at all, and she a married woman. Good God, hadn't the fool the very faintest idea where to draw the line? It isn't necessary to simulate terror in order to indicate a clean mind. Dr. Bickleigh had looked down at the cocoon-like form wrapped in protective bedclothes and thanked heaven sincerely for his escape. Poor young fool of a Denny!

But there success had left him; for Madeleine was not nearly so ill as he had hoped. Not nearly so ill, in fact, as she ought by every right to have been. Not only not at death's door, but a mile out of sight of it. It was very disappointing. But that, Dr. Bickleigh had reflected philosophically, is the worst of those food-germs: they are so hopelessly unreliable. Still, he was a fair man. He had decided that Madeleine should have her chance, and he would not go back on his decision. Madeleine could live.

But it was very much to be hoped that Chatford had not been affected so lightly too.

Dr. Bickleigh was thinking, when his visitor arrived, that now more than ever it was imperative for him to get into Chatford's bedroom the next morning.

There being no servant in the house at night, Dr. Bickleigh had nowadays to answer the door himself in the evenings. On the doorstep stood a large, solid man, with a benevolent face, a heavy moustache, and a bowler hat inappropriately gilded with the last rays of the setting sun. He was a stranger to Dr. Bickleigh.

"Yes?" said the doctor in some surprise. Strangers are rare in Wyvern's Cross. "I am Dr. Bickleigh. Do you want me?"

"Just a few words, if you don't mind, doctor," returned the large stranger, with a deprecatory air. "Here's my card. Perhaps you won't mind if I come in." Without waiting for permission, he came in, though still with the same apologetic look.

Dr. Bickleigh, his surprise growing, took the card. The next instant his heart seemed to jump right up into his throat and lodge there, for on the card he read: "Chief Inspector Russell, C.I.D., New Scotland Yard."

Fortunately it was dark in the hall, and Dr. Bickleigh, fighting down a sudden, nauseating panic, was able to shut the front door on his confusion. Almost the next moment the worst of his terror had been dispelled by sheer reason. On whatever mysterious quest this man had come, of course it could not be because any suspicion had arisen concerning himself. That, at any rate, was out of the question.

It could not have been more than ten seconds before he replied, in a perfectly normal voice: "Of course, Chief Inspector. Come along to my consulting-room."

Seated in his own chair, with the Chief Inspector in that reserved for patients, Dr. Bickleigh felt his full confidence return. He could almost have laughed at the remembrance of that moment of foolish panic as he pulled out his cigarette-case and offered it with a friendly smile over the table. "You smoke, I expect?"

"Well, thank you, sir," said the Chief Inspector, extracting a cigarette from the packed case with a deftness which the largeness of his fingers would not have led one to expect. "I don't mind if I do." He produced matches from his pocket.

"Now, what is it you wanted to see me about?" Dr. Bickleigh asked, when the cigarettes were alight. "No trouble among any of my patients, I hope?"

Rather a good touch, that.

"No, sir. Oh, no, nothing like that." The big man seemed quite ill at ease. Watching him, Dr. Bickleigh felt his own confidence increase. He was going to be more than a match for this blundering policeman. It was to be the rapier and the bludgeon once more. "No trouble among your patients. Rather more personal than that, I'm afraid, sir."

"Indeed?" Dr. Bickleigh was nothing but frankly puzzled. "Personal, eh? What on earth . . ."

The man from Scotland Yard did not seem to know quite how to proceed. Dr. Bickleigh's contempt for him grew.

"Well, you know, sir, we have to look into these rumours," he apologised. "Just as a matter of form. I'm really sorry to have to bother you with it, but there it is. So if you wouldn't mind answering a few questions . . ."

"What rumours?" No, that was a mistake. Of course one could not live in Wyvern's Cross and not know that rumours existed, or what their purport was. Dr. Bickleigh corrected himself neatly. "Why, good gracious, you don't mean . . . ?"

"Afraid so, sir," mumbled the Chief Inspector. He might have been apologising for all the malicious gossip of rural England. "Unpleasant for you; and unpleasant for me, too, having to rake it all up. But I'm sure you'll be sensible and see that."

"Oh, of course. But really!" Dr. Bickleigh laughed quite naturally. "Well, it's too preposterous, you know. Of course, I won't pretend not to know that there have been the most atrocious rumours about my poor wife. *De mortuis nil nisi bonum* doesn't hold good in villages like this, you know."

"No, sir; probably not," agreed Chief Inspector Russell vaguely. "And of course I've no doubt it's all a mare's nest; but there you are."

"But in any case, Chief Inspector, does it *matter*? That's what I don't quite understand. My poor wife's dead now. Whether her death was accidental (as, of course, really was the case), or whether, as this infernal gossip suggests, she may have deliberately taken her own life, what does it *matter*? No amount of investigation is going to bring her back to life."

Chief Inspector Russell adopted a somewhat guiltily confidential air. "Well, sir, I needn't tell *you* how jealous these coroners are of their privileges. You've had plenty of experience of that, I dare say. And if they think there's been a mistake made, or some evidence didn't come out which ought to have done—well, you know as well as I do, sir, that they've got the powers and they will use them. So there you are."

Dr. Bickleigh nodded. There seemed something of a *non sequitur* somewhere, but the Chief Inspector was looking so very apologetic, and as if his task were so distasteful to him, that Dr. Bickleigh thought it better not to press for the connection. "Of course. I quite understand."

"That's right. I was sure you would, sir. So if you'll just let me put my questions, simply as a matter of form, I've no doubt that'll be the last you'll hear of the matter."

"Certainly, Chief Inspector. But talking's dry work, you know. I've got some whiskey in the dining-room. I'll bring the decanter along before you begin."

The Chief Inspector lifted an enormous hand. "Not for me, if you please, sir. I never touch it."

"You don't?" said Dr. Bickleigh incredulously.

"Well, not when I'm on a—when I'm working," qualified the other. "Makes me too muddled, and that's a fact."

"I'll bring the decanter, anyhow. Perhaps you'll reconsider it later."

As he went in search of the syphon and glasses, Dr. Bickleigh allowed his secret smile full play. The situation was really too delightfully ironical. Here was this absurd Inspector making laborious enquiries as to the possibility of Julia having committed suicide, when the real truth, right under his nose, was about the last thing in the world he was suspecting. What would he say if Dr. Bickleigh told him that truth straight out? "No, Chief Inspector, my wife's death was not accidental. It was deliberate. But she didn't kill herself. I killed her." He would refuse to believe it, of course; probably say something facetious about doctors having to have their little joke, but they couldn't pull *his* leg: he was too old a bird for that. Good God, what was Scotland Yard coming to? As a taxpayer, Dr. Bickleigh felt quite indignant.

He returned to the consulting-room prepared actually to enjoy himself. The situation was not merely amusing; it was in a way exciting too. He felt a strong temptation to make it more exciting still; play with fire, drop subtle hints that this comic-opera detective would never understand. But of course he must not do anything of the sort; that would be inartistic over-elaboration.

The Chief Inspector was engaged in studying a fat black note-book. He waited till Dr. Bickleigh had mixed himself a drink (purposely not at all a stiff one); then he began.

For a mere matter of form, Dr. Bickleigh felt, his enquiries were remarkably searching. Not that it mattered, of course, for there was a ready answer waiting for every possible question. But it all seemed very unnecessary.

First of all, Julia's illness was gone into at great length: how it began, her symptoms, the visit to Sir Tamerton Foliott, her two holidays, every detail. Dr. Bickleigh, smiling inwardly, again brought out his remarks about cerebral cortices and cachectic conditions which had served so well for Victor Crewstanton, but this time they were laboriously entered in the Inspector's black note-book. Dr. Bickleigh began to yawn.

Then they went on to the question of morphia. Dr. Bickleigh explained exactly what had happened, how he had refused to administer any more injections, and why, and the distressing sequel to that refusal. It was perfectly plain sailing, for he had only to tell the truth.

"I see," quite agreed the Inspector. "And you never realised she had begun to help herself?"

"Indeed I did," retorted Dr. Bickleigh. Of all the obvious traps! "I noticed that my stock of morphia was dwindling, and there was only one explanation."

"But you did nothing about it?"

Really, this was too puerile. "Naturally I did, Chief Inspector. Do you imagine I wanted to encourage my wife in such a dangerous practice? I locked it up."

"'Locked morphia up,'" repeated the Chief Inspector, entering the fact. "And what happened then, sir?"

"If you must know," Dr. Bickleigh replied with apparent reluctance, "she forged my name to an order for a large quantity on a chemist in Merchester. It—it is exceedingly painful for me to have to tell you all this."

"Naturally it is, sir. Naturally. And I needn't say I don't like having to ask you. By the way, you haven't got that order still by any chance? Didn't recover it from the chemist and put it by, I suppose?"

"How curious you should ask that." Dr. Bickleigh positively beamed. "As a matter of fact, that's exactly what I did. I queried it, of course, when the bill came in; and the man showed me the order. I didn't say anything to *him*, but I did get it back. Just to be on the safe side, you know."

"Of course. Very wise of you, I'm sure," assented the Chief Inspector with much heartiness. "Now, could I just have a look at that document, sir?"

"Certainly. I'll get it at once. In fact, I believe it's in one of these drawers."

He found it.

The Chief Inspector examined it closely. "I think I'd better keep this, if you don't mind, sir," he said, and, without waiting for a reply, tucked it carefully away in a large pocket-book.

"Not at all," said Dr. Bickleigh, who in any case had not the least objection.

The Inspector went on to something apparently quite irrelevant—Dr. Bickleigh's movements after lunch on the fatal day. Noticing the doctor's eyebrows rise, he hinted in deprecatory tones that there were vague but scandalous suggestions of negligence somewhere; and, though it was obvious that Chief Inspector Russell himself did not attach the faintest importance to such an outrageous idea, he was unfortunately precluded by his duty from treating it with the scorn they demanded.

With just the right amount of indignation, Dr. Bickleigh detailed his movements—how he had gone out almost immediately after lunch, what he could remember of the visits he had made, his meeting with Miss Ridgeway at a moment when he was having a little trouble with his car, his subsequent actions, ending with a visit to The Hall, where his housemaid had been able to catch him with the terrible news. Anxious to afford the Chief Inspector every help, he turned up his day-book to see if any corroboration was to be found there. By a coincidence which both men agreed to be most lucky, there was actually, for that day only, a detailed time-list of the visits he had paid. Dr. Bickleigh explained that he remembered now having entered it up that evening in an attempt to distract his thoughts from the tragedy that had overtaken him. The Chief Inspector, alternating between sympathy and apology, copied the extract meticulously into his note-book.

"Well, surely that's all I can tell you which can have any possible bearing on my poor wife's death," Dr. Bickleigh sighed, when the copy had been made. "Now, Chief Inspector, let me offer you that drink again."

"No, thank you, sir. It's very good of you, I'm sure, but——" The Chief Inspector looked quite uncomfortable. "Well, sir, to tell you the truth, I haven't quite finished yet, if you'd be so good."

"There's something else you want to ask me?"

"Something else I'm afraid it's my duty to ask you," corrected the Chief Inspector gently. "I don't know if you've heard it, but there's an idea going about that your poor lady's death wasn't due to morphia at all." The Chief Inspector looked his distaste at voicing such a shocking rumour.

Dr. Bickleigh had no need to act his astonishment. "What? I don't understand. Of course it was due to morphia."

"The suggestion is," apologised the Chief Inspector, "that it was due to arsenic, covered by a dose of morphia."

"Arsenic? Nonsense! It's quite out of the question."

"But you keep arsenic by you, sir, of course?"

"Only Fowler's solution; and a very large quantity of that would have to be drunk to cause death."

"There isn't any white arsenic in your surgery, or elsewhere, to which she could have had access?"

"Certainly not. The whole idea's ludicrous."

Chief Inspector Russell made a note. "But you have arsenical weed-killer on the premises, no doubt?"

"No, I haven't. There's been no arsenic in or near this house ever since I've been in it, except the small quantity of Fowler's solution I keep in the surgery. You can take it that the suggestion's simply absurd, Chief Inspector."

"So I fancied, sir. But you'll understand that I had to put it to you, just as a matter of form." The Chief Inspector folded up his note-book and stowed it away. "Well, I think that's all, sir. Quite satisfactory, of course. In fact, I'm sorry to have troubled you."

"This idea of arsenic," Dr. Bickleigh puzzled. "I simply can't understand it. There'd be no question of accident there, I take it; and if the suggestion is that my poor wife deliberately took the stuff . . . It's such a painful death, you see. The wife of any medical man would know that. So why should she, even if she had wanted to—to do away with herself, when there was morphia ready to hand?"

"I don't understand that myself, sir," admitted the Chief Inspector, "and that's a fact."

"Anyhow, you'd better see Dr. Lydston, in Merchester. I called him in at once. He'll tell you that the appearances were perfectly consistent with death from morphine poisoning and nothing else; certainly not arsenic."

Out came the note-book again. "Thank you, sir. Dr. Lydston. Yes, perhaps I'd better. You called him in, you say? I see. But he hadn't had your lady under his observation, I take it, during her illness?"

"Yes, indeed he had," retorted Dr. Bickleigh, not without triumph. "I'd called him in for a consultation only a short time before my wife's death. I was puzzled about her illness, you see, and the treatment Sir Tamerton Foliott recommended didn't seem to be doing her any good."

"Quite so. And there was no post-mortem, I understand?"

"No, the coroner didn't think it necessary. The cause of death was quite obvious, you see. And of course I had confided to Dr. Lydston the—the unfortunate habit my poor wife had formed, so that was no news to him."

"Yes, quite so, sir. Then the real nature of her illness was never discovered?"

"No, not definitely." Dr. Bickleigh was getting simply bored with all this old history. "But Lydston and I agreed that her headaches must have been due to a cerebral neoplasm of some sort, or tumour on the brain, as I said just now. In any case, it wasn't worth opening the body to find out, as that was not the cause of death."

"No, of course not. I see, sir. Well!" The Chief Inspector rose ponderously to his feet. "Oh, yes. I was nearly forgetting. Would it be putting you to a lot of trouble just to let me have a look in your surgery, doctor, and show me where you kept the syringe and all that? Just to establish that your poor lady had easy access to them, you understand."

"Yes, quite. No, none at all. Come along, Chief Inspector."

Hardly troubling to conceal his smile, Dr. Bickleigh led the way to his surgery. What on earth the fellow expected to gain by . . .

It was somewhat abstractedly that he showed the man from Scotland Yard what he wanted to see. Dr. Bickleigh was pondering a certain course of action, bold perhaps, but not unsubtle. There was little time to make up his mind, but it was enough. He made his decision.

"Chief Inspector, I told you I couldn't pretend to be ignorant of these vile rumours. I can tell you further that I'm not ignorant of their source."

"Sir?" The Chief Inspector looked puzzled.

"Oh, yes, I know perfectly well where they come from. A man named Chatford, in Merchester. A solicitor. He dislikes me strongly, has a grudge against me; and he's set these beastly ideas about to try and do me a bad turn."

"Is that so, sir?" The Chief Inspector's voice expressed nothing but concern.

"I should like to ask your advice: ought I to take steps against him for criminal libel? The facts, you see, are these." Dr. Bickleigh went on to give a very succinct account of Chatford's cause for his grudge; nor did he trouble to hide the fact that Ivy had so completely given her husband away, and barely refrained from adding in plain words the poetic revenge that he himself had subsequently taken on his traducer.

"What ought I to do, Chief Inspector?" he asked confidentially. Dr. Bickleigh did feel quite confidential with the man now. He was a fool, but he wasn't a bad fellow by any means. And it was interesting to talk on more or less intimate terms with a real detective from Scotland Yard. "You can see for yourself that this kind of thing can't be allowed to go on. The man's mouth must be stopped."

The Chief Inspector was interested, distinctly interested. He put a few questions. Dr. Bickleigh answered them with manly frankness. Ivy's character lay in ribbons at their feet.

"Well, doctor, if you take my advice you'll do nothing for the time being. You don't want to drag the girl into the witness-box to admit adultery, which is what it would lead to. If you're right in saying that these rumours do come from him, well, he's had the matter taken up officially and an enquiry made, which is what it seems he wanted, and I don't see what more he can do. It's my opinion he'll drop it now. If he doesn't . . . But, anyhow, if I were you I should wait and see."

"Thank you, Chief Inspector. Yes, perhaps that would be best. Anyhow, I'm glad you know now that it's entirely due to him that you've had to waste your time like this." Dr. Bickleigh concealed the vindictiveness he was feeling under an aspect of duty done.

Chief Inspector Russell leaned back against the surgery counter and looked denser than ever. "Still, it's a bit of a puzzler, doctor. If what you say is right, what's his idea? Even if it could be established that your poor lady did make away with herself, that's only going to bring up a lot of mud about her. How does he think he's going to get at you that way?"

"His wife says his idea is that if suicide could be proved, you see, I should have to leave the place."

"But why, sir? I don't see that at all."

"Oh, well various things might come out, you know." Dr. Bickleigh grinned knowingly. "We doctors have to be like Caesar's wife if we're to keep our practices. Anybody else can enjoy himself occasionally and people only smile; but a doctor—good gracious me, no!"

Chief Inspector Russell actually winked. Broadly. It was very evident that with the stowing away of the note-book he had put off the official and become the genial (if somewhat stupid) soul that he really was at heart.

"Well, I won't say I'm not rather in that position myself,

doctor. But still, if one likes the ladies enough, one can always find some means, eh?" He winked again.

Dr. Bickleigh chuckled delightedly. That was the sort of thing he had been brought up to before he had had to don this damned gentility; a regular tang of his youth, as unlike Wyvern's Cross as it was like Nottingham. A wave of kinship with this large, human man, so mistakenly trying to be a detective, surged over him.

"Well, it's hard for a man to get on without them, I must say."

Innuendoes thickened the surgery air.

"And," said the Chief Inspector, with an envious air, "I dare say a doctor has his opportunities, more than some of us."

"Well, if he doesn't, he can always make them, can't he?"

They laughed wickedly.

"And ladies in the country must have something to occupy their time, I expect."

Dr. Bickleigh saw his opportunity to be rather cunning. "Yes, and nobody but one's patients takes that sort of thing seriously, you know. Why, my poor wife . . . Yes, Chief Inspector, I lost a real, understanding friend in her. A wonderful woman. I can tell you, there aren't many wives who have the sense to let their husbands—well, amuse themselves, and know it means nothing."

"She did that?"

"Yes, indeed she did. She was one of the few really sensible women I've ever met." Dr. Bickleigh looked extremely serious. Inwardly he was thinking: And that knocks away even the ground for suicide. It was too easy.

"Well, well." The Chief Inspector was looking suitably serious too. He roused himself with an effort. "Well, I mustn't keep you any longer, doctor. It's been most good of you to answer my questions so frankly. And you understand, I'm sure, that I only had to do my duty."

"Yes, of course. Perfectly. And there's nothing more I can do for you?" asked Dr. Bickleigh expansively. "I'm quite at your disposal."

The big Chief Inspector seemed struck with this offer. That was very kind. Yes, since the doctor was so good, he would like to have a look over the house. Just as a matter of form, of course. It would help him with his report.

Dr. Bickleigh agreed at once. It would be most amusing.

They went over the house together. Although the suggestion had not come from him, the man from Scotland Yard made a thorough job of it while he was about it. Dr. Bickleigh, secretly much entertained, stood by while his visitor opened cupboards, peered into wardrobes, even looked under the bath; though what he expected to find there remained a complete mystery.

"You're making a regular search-party of it, Chief Inspector."

"Never do a thing by halves, doctor," replied Chief Inspector Russell genially. "That's our rule. It gives us a lot of trouble, but it saves us more in the long run."

Dr. Bickleigh felt he was obtaining an interesting insight into the methods of Scotland Yard. They did not impress him.

The Chief Inspector penetrated even into the attic. He led the way up the last flight of stairs, and Dr. Bickleigh could not have stopped him had he wished. Not that he did wish. It could not matter in the least. So he carefully refrained from discouraging remarks, and followed with an air of eager helpfulness.

His visitor stood in the middle of the room and looked round at the litter of tools, test-tubes, photographic appliances, wireless parts (since Julia's death Dr. Bickleigh had made wireless, and the manufacture of sets for it, something of a winter hobby), and general oddments, with a look of humorous dismay. "Lucky I'm not making a real search-party of it, sir. It'd take half a day to go through all this."

"My hobby-room," explained the doctor.

On a table already loaded with other impedimenta stood the incubator. The Chief Inspector's glance did not even hover there as it swept in plain bewilderment round the room. The situation appealed to Dr. Bickleigh. Here under the man's very nose . . . Well, really, if this was the best that Scotland Yard could do! He was almost tempted to say casually: "And that thing over there's an incubator, you know." Probably the man did not even know what an incubator was. In any case, it would convey nothing to him.

"You go in for scientific experiments then, doctor?" suggested the Chief Inspector, eyeing the test-tubes.

"Oh, just a little research-work occasionally. I've always been interested in it. Of course, a country G.P. doesn't get much chance. But one does what one can."

The Chief Inspector advanced to the table on which the instruments lay (not the incubator-table), and picked up a Bunsen burner rather as if it were a Mills bomb. "Chemistry, eh? Now, that's a thing I never knew anything about."

"No? It's quite fascinating. I'll tell you what I've been doing." Dr. Bickleigh explained how he had been amusing his leisure moments by passing chlorine through a solution of sodium thiosulphate.

"Oh, yes," said the other vaguely. "I believe I've heard of that. Have to use arsenic for that, don't you?"

"Certainly not," Dr. Bickleigh replied sharply. What was this arsenic *motif* that kept cropping up? "I told you downstairs, there's no arsenic in the house at all except the Fowler's solution in the surgery. What is the idea about this arsenic?"

The Chief Inspector looked distressed. "Oh, *that*. No, I wasn't thinking of that, doctor. Just getting a bit mixed in my chemistry, that's all. Well, it's good of you to have shown me round like this. I think I've seen all I wanted."

They parted genially, the Chief Inspector still refusing a drink.

Dr. Bickleigh returned to his consulting-room and mixed himself another, a stiffer one this time. He felt extremely pleased with himself. It had been an amusing evening.

But what a ridiculous pother to make over a question of possible suicide already over a year old. Red tape, no doubt.

Well, anyhow, that would be the end of Chatford.

In more senses than one.

VI

He woke up in the middle of the night, sweating with terror.

It was all up. They knew he had killed Julia. They were going to prove it. They wouldn't rest till they had got him—hanged him. It was all up.

Everything showed it. His brain was clear now. Everything was ghastly plain. How could he not have seen it before?

Would they have sent a man down from Scotland Yard just on a case of suspected suicide? Of course not. It was murder they suspected. *Murder*. What was he to do?

The Devonshire police had found out something. They had called in Scotland Yard. And Scotland Yard never let go. Good God, what *was* he to do?

Everything showed it. The Chief Inspector had refused

to drink with him. That proved it, didn't it? Refused to drink with him. That was final. A policeman never refuses to drink with anyone except a man he intends to arrest. Final.

All those hints about jealous coroners had been bunkum. All the suggestions about suicide just soft soap, to put him off his guard. That geniality a pose, to lure him into giving himself away. And, good God, he *had* given himself away. Hopelessly. What hadn't he said? Got confidential, hinted at woman-chasing, showed his vindictiveness towards Chatford. Oh, given himself away disastrously. It was all up.

How could he have been such a *fool*? He had made the fatal mistake: underrated his opponent. The man had pretended to be a numbskull, and he had been taken in. And had thought it amusing! Oh, God, it was he who had been the fool.

Everything showed it. The account of his movements. They wouldn't have wanted that if it was just a case of suicide, would they? Of course they wouldn't. They *knew* it was murder. And the man had taken that order on the Merchester chemist away with him. Away—to prove that it was in his own disguised handwriting, not a forgery at all. *Away*—and he would never be able to get it back and destroy it. That piece of paper was going to hang him.

And that arsenic. What did that mean? Something mysteriously dreadful. They thought he had poisoned Julia with arsenic, and somehow they were going to prove it. But he hadn't—he hadn't. God, this was awful. He was going to be hanged for something he had never done. Arsenic! What did it mean?

Hanged! He was going to be hanged—hanged—*hanged*. By the neck, until he was dead.

Oh, why had he killed Julia—why—why? It had been so *silly*. So ridiculously unnecessary. Why had he done it—why? Oh, if only she was still alive. He wanted her so badly. Unbearably. What *was* he to do?

He sat up in the bed, a stiff, erect little figure in pink cotton pyjamas, his hair half on end from sleep, and rocked backwards and forwards, his knuckles to his mouth.

If *only* he hadn't done it. If only Julia were still *alive*.

"Oh, *oh*," moaned Dr. Bickleigh, and began to cry.

Chapter Eleven

I

The next morning Dr. Bickleigh's confidence had completely returned. The despair of the night had been a natural reaction, at a time when the vitality is at its lowest, from the knowledge that Scotland Yard really were interesting themselves in Julia's death. Remembered in the friendly light of day, it seemed like a nightmare, and almost as preposterous.

Of course, murder was not suspected. How could it be? There were simply no grounds for suspicion. Chatford had made a fuss, and, since he was a solicitor and presumably a man of weight, the Home Office had been bound to look into his mare's nest, even to the extent of sending a man down from London to make out a report. How fortunate that he had told the Chief Inspector Chatford's reason. That proved him so much of an interested party that his ridiculous accusations simply lost all weight.

Of course, too, the Chief Inspector had been satisfied. It was incredible that he could have been so friendly had he not been. He would have been stiff and official if he had thought he was investigating a case of murder; not genial and apologetic. Scotland Yard apologising to a suspected murderer! Not likely.

And even (reasoned Dr. Bickleigh over his eggs and bacon) if the impossible did happen, had happened, and the possibility of murder ever had been raised—well, what did it matter? Nothing could ever be proved, in the case of Julia any more than in the cases of Chatford and Madeleine. Not a thing. He was on velvet. Really, Dr. Bickleigh could hardly understand why any murderer, who took the merest intelligent precautions, should ever be brought to trial at all. But, of course, that was it: the fools did not take intelligent precautions, because they hadn't the intelligence.

Chatford?

Wouldn't it be advisable to let well alone? Chatford might be dying, in which case excellent; but, on the other hand, he might not, and one hardly wanted to commit a murder right under the nose of a Scotland Yard detective. (Yes, if Chatford did die now it really would be murder. Most curious.) But yet again, could he in justice to himself let Chatford off? By every canon Chatford deserved to die. As long as Chatford lived . . .

It was most difficult.

And then there was Ivy. Good gracious, yes, he had been almost forgetting Ivy. Ivy, bringing with her as Chatford's widow all the excellent possessions that Chatford had so industriously massed together. Ivy, an independence at last. . . .

Now that would be a revenge worthy of himself.

Oh, yes; Chatford must die.

But Scotland Yard should not be bothered. Not in the least. Chatford should die a nice, ordinary natural death. Poison? Absurd. The silly man ate some bad potted meat, you know. Well, if people will do these things they must expect to take the consequences. Wasn't there a similar case in Wyvern's Cross? A child named—oh, yes, Sampford. Yes, of course. Botulism, they called it, didn't they? And now Mr. Chatford the same. Well, well.

Dr. Bickleigh could hear the words actually on the worthies' lips. He smiled unconsciously as he finished his coffee and neatly dabbed with the napkin at his little waxed moustache.

Now, then. Chatford. . . .

II

But to see Chatford was apparently not quite so simple as Dr. Bickleigh had reckoned.

At the house he met with a blank refusal, and a door very nearly slammed in his face. Mr. Chatford was rather worse to-day, and far too ill to see anyone; and, before Dr. Bickleigh could even speak again, bang! the door closed by the agitated maid right on his words.

Well, no use trying that again, Dr. Bickleigh reflected temperately as he climbed into his car. Chatford was evidently determined not to be seen, by him or anyone else. Unfortunately, however, for Chatford, Dr. Bickleigh was equally determined to see him; and where this regenerated Dr. Bickleigh had made up his mind to anything . . .

He drove through the streets of Merchester, a consciously grim figure of death. Chatford need not hope to escape that way. If direct methods failed, subtlety always remained.

Dr. Lydston was out. Dr. Bickleigh, growing grimmer every moment, hung about in Merchester until the other could not possibly be out any longer. Then he went back. This time he was more lucky. Dr. Lydston had just come in to lunch.

Dr. Lydston received him quite effusively for a man normally so restrained. "Ha, Bickleigh. Excellent. Haven't seen you for quite a long time. How are you? Yes, I was expecting you."

"Expecting me?"

Dr. Lydston's tall, spare form seemed to coil itself

round his consulting-room chair in an effort to find a comfortable position. He cleared his throat very loudly. "Yes, that . . . H'm! I understood you referred him to me. Most awkward. Very—h'm!—distressing. Of course I confirmed . . ."

"Oh! Oh, yes. He came, did he?" At last Dr. Bickleigh understood the other's embarrassed references. He had been so absorbed in his present business that he had quite forgotten about the Scotland Yard man. Well, the fellow would not have got much change out of Lydston. After all, Lydston had given his own opinion on Julia's case; and he had his professional position to consider. Not, of course, that Lydston could tell the police anything even if he wanted. Death had been perfectly consistent with morphia poisoning, because death had been due to morphia poisoning. What more could one want? Still, all that mattered less than nothing now.

"Yes, that's right. I referred him to you. But that isn't what I've come about now. Look here, Lydston, I'm bothered. I hear Chatford's been taken bad. You're his medical man, aren't you? How does he strike you?"

Dr. Lydston seemed to be weighing his answer with his usual caution before he gave it, looking thoughtfully at Dr. Bickleigh through his spectacles and then hastily looking away again. "Well, he's in a pretty bad way," he said at last, and twined himself a little more impossibly round his chair.

"Really dangerous?"

"Decidedly, I should say."

"Yes, but how much so? Likely to prove fatal?"

Dr. Lydston looked at him thoughtfully again. "Possibly. Possibly not."

Dr. Bickleigh subdued his irritation. Silly old creature; why couldn't he say straight out what Chatford's chances were? However, he was in a bad way, anyhow. But not quite bad enough. Just a little edging nearer the precipice. . . .

"Well, I'm worried. He came to tea with me the other day, you know. Day before yesterday. The Bournes were there too. Four of us. Well, three out of the four were taken bad in the night. Really, I'm afraid . . ."

"Bourne wasn't taken ill."

"No, he was the only one who wasn't."

"Oh! You were, then?"

"Yes, I was. Quite violently. Fortunately, however, I must have eliminated most of the poison, and——"

"Poison, eh?" interrupted Dr. Lydston quite sharply, looking at Dr. Bickleigh now over his spectacles instead of through them. "You suggest you were poisoned?"

"Well, surely. Pretty obvious, isn't it?"

Dr. Lydston joined the tips of his long fingers and contemplated them with apparently earnest admiration. "And what do you imagine was the nature of this poison?"

"Oh, I don't know. Some food poison, I suppose." It was Dr. Bickleigh's turn to be cautious. "That's just what I wanted to see you about. I don't want to butt in or anything like that, you know, but how are you treating the case?"

Dr. Lydston's professional dignity was clearly upset. "Well, really," he began stiffly.

Dr. Bickleigh hastened to eradicate an unfavourable impression, and put on his most winning smile. "That sounds awful cheek, coming from me to you, but I really am interested. I was caught myself, you see, and it was a literal case of 'Physician, heal thyself.' And yesterday I called to enquire about Mrs. Bourne (just a friendly visit, of course) and saw her for a few moments, as perhaps you've heard." Yes, the old fool would certainly have heard, so he had better be smoothed down over that too. "I know you attend her, so I was careful not to verge on the professional; but out of sheer interest I asked her a few questions, and her symptoms were certainly identical with mine; and presumably with Chatford's too." He paused questioningly.

"The cases certainly do present points of resemblance," admitted Dr. Lydston.

Pedantic old fool! "Yes. Well ——!" Dr. Bickleigh smiled again, most disarmingly. "The fact is, I wondered whether I could possibly be of any help. Chatford's case certainly sounds the most serious of the three, and—well, I did cure myself, didn't I?"

"Are you suggesting that I call you in for a consultation?" asked Dr. Lydston precisely.

"Something like that, perhaps." Dr. Bickleigh dissembled his eagerness. "I know it's a most unprofessional thing to suggest, but, after all, we're all more or less friends, and . . . Well, I really do think I could be of help."

"How did you treat yourself?"

"Oh, well . . ." Dr. Bickleigh laughed. "I'd much rather hear your own suggestions."

"Um!" Dr. Lydston deliberated. "Chatford called me up in the middle of the night. He was in a good deal of pain, so I gave him an injection of morphia, and ordered hot applications to the abdomen. Later on I recommended a colon wash-out of normal saline, and made him up a prescription of bismuth and soda with hydrocyanic acid."

Dr. Bickleigh nodded. "Yes. Treatment on normal lines, in fact."

"I saw no reason to advise anything else," replied Dr. Lydston stiffly.

"No, quite. But in my case . . . Oh, well, I won't

bother you with that. But seriously, Lydston, I should very much like to have a look at him, out of sheer professional interest. Surely you could stretch a point and take me with you? What about this afternoon?"

"H'm! Somewhat irregular, isn't it? And, in any case, I could do nothing without the patient's consent."

"Oh, Chatford wouldn't mind," said Dr. Bickleigh easily.

"He might object most strongly," remarked Dr. Lydston drily. "No, Bickleigh, I'm sorry. I think it would be too irregular."

"Oh, come," persuaded Dr. Bickleigh. "Stretch a point, Lydston. He won't mind."

Dr. Lydston, however, seemed to have made up his mind at last. He rose. "I'm afraid it isn't a thing I could agree to. In fact, I don't care about it at all. I'm sorry."

"Oh, very well," Dr. Bickleigh smiled. "After all, it doesn't matter in the least. And no doubt you're quite right to be so old-fashioned, Lydston; in questions of etiquette as well as treatment." Two little spots were burning on his cheek-bones.

The two parted without shaking hands.

Dr. Bickleigh drove away rigid with fury. The damned old fool! If he didn't look out it would be his turn next. It had been a sheer insult—a reflection on his own professional competence, nothing less. Dr. Bickleigh fingered through the cloth the little phial in his trousers pocket. Lydston had better look out; he didn't seem to realise what sort of a man he was dealing with.

And if the two of them thought they were going to keep him out of that bedroom . . .

In his consulting-room, Dr. Lydston, after staring at his blotting-pad for five minutes, pulled the telephone towards him.

III

After all, there could have been no conspiracy to keep Dr. Bickleigh out of the bedroom. He had hardly finished his belated lunch an hour later when his telephone bell rang.

It was Dr. Lydston. "Oh, Bickleigh, I've been thinking over what you suggested. I couldn't do anything without Chatford's consent, of course, but I've just put it to him and he has no objection at all."

"Oh, yes," said Dr. Bickleigh, with a mighty effort of indifference.

"And I must confess," proceeded Dr. Lydston in his precise tones, "that the case does present certain puzzling features. So if your offer still holds good . . ."

"You're inviting me in to a consultation?"

"Yes, in a way . . . Yes, certainly."

"How would three-thirty suit you?"

"Admirably."

"Very well. I'll be there."

Dr. Bickleigh's exultation was so great that his hand shook as he hung up the receiver. Chatford was delivered into his grasp.

He went into the surgery. Since the morning a better idea had occurred to him.

With meticulous care he prepared a capsule, his thoughts darting brightly from one rosy realisation to another. Revenge was sweet . . . but Ivy was sweeter . . . rich, widowed Ivy . . . yes, riches were sweetest of all. And, with Chatford out of the way, those ridiculous enquiries must collapse; their mainspring would have been removed. Though, for that matter, they must have collapsed already. (Had he really in the middle of the night taken them seriously? It was curious to remember now. Most interesting how lowered vitality depressed the brain. Triumph of matter over mind.) The Chief Inspector would be back in London by now, his report of a mare's nest in his pocket. In a way it was rather a pity. It would have been amusing to remove the instigator of it under his very nose.

How utterly undetectable murder could be made. It was amazing. Why did not more intelligent people take it up? Perhaps they did, and one never heard of it. But Dr. Bickleigh could not quite believe that. Surely he was unique.

At three-thirty exactly he stepped blithely out of the Jowett in front of Chatford's house. Two minutes later his goal was triumphantly reached.

Chatford was in a bad way. That was quite evident. He lay inertly in bed, obviously in a state of extreme collapse, and seemed hardly conscious. Dr. Bickleigh stood for a moment looking down on him, and could hardly control the muscles of his face.

"I'll take his temperature," he said in a low voice.

"No need," Dr. Lydston replied, in equally hushed tones. "I've just taken it." He beckoned Dr. Bickleigh into a farther corner. "Seems to have just taken a turn for the worse," he whispered. "Since I rang you up. Temperature's jumped up to a hundred and two point eight."

Dr. Bickleigh nodded. "I'd better make a cursory examination."

"I shouldn't advise disturbing him, just at the moment. I can tell you anything you want to know."

"Well, what are the other symptoms?"

"Oh, what one would expect: tongue slightly furred, considerable abdominal pain, cramps in the lower limbs, and, of course, vomiting and diarrhœa."

"Pronounced?" Dr. Bickleigh asked sharply.

Dr. Lydston hesitated. "Well, perhaps not so pronounced as one might have expected, no."

"Any paralytic symptoms?"

"I—don't think so. Well, possibly. I haven't particularly noticed."

Dr. Bickleigh looked his contempt at such inefficiency. "Well, have the pupils been dilated?"

"Yes." Dr. Lydston seemed to brighten. "Oh, yes. Decidedly."

"And you've been treating him just with a bismuth and soda mixture, with hydrocyanic acid?"

"And bismuth salicylate. Fifteen grains every four hours."

"I see. And what's your diagnosis?"

"In my opinion," said Dr. Lydston, somewhat defensively, "acute gastro-enteritis, resulting from food poisoning."

"Yes," Dr. Bickleigh said gently. "I don't agree with you, Lydston."

"No?" Dr. Lydston was surprised.

"No. From what I've seen of him, and from what you tell me, I should say it was a clear case of botulism."

"Botulism!" It was plain that the idea had not entered Dr. Lydston's head at all.

"Yes. Of course, I was practically sure from my own case, and Mrs. Bourne's. But they were really too light to be certain. That's why I wanted to see him. I'm pretty certain where the infection came from, too. We had potted meat sandwiches for tea, and—well, really, there was no other possible vehicle."

"Good gracious. But that ought to be ascertained, Bickleigh. Is the rest of the potted meat still in existence?"

"No. I thought the sandwiches tasted a little funny at the time, and I went out to the kitchen afterwards and smelt it." Dr. Bickleigh explained how he and Mrs. Holne had arrived at the conclusion that the pot had better be thrown away.

"Dear, dear." Dr. Lydston stroked his lean chin. "Botulism. No, I must confess that never occurred to me. In fact, I've never had a case before at all."

"Ah, that's where I scored," Dr. Bickleigh pointed out. "I had a case in Wyvern's Cross. Unfortunately, it proved fatal, but it gave me the experience. I attribute the promptness with which I was able to cure myself entirely to that."

"No doubt, no doubt. Well, what do you advise, then?"

"A full dose of jalap and cream of tartar," replied Dr. Bickleigh promptly. "And, in view of his condition, the sooner it's administered the better. Luckily I brought one with me."

"You did?" said Dr. Lydston with interest.

"Yes. I was practically certain, you see, and I judged that speed would be advisable. Here it is." Dr. Bickleigh drew a small pill-box from his trousers pocket and extracted the capsule with its fatal content of culture-jelly. "I'd better administer it at once." How incredibly easy it all was.

"I'll administer it, I think," said Dr. Lydston, a little stiffly.

With a hidden smile at the childishness of this exhibition of professional jealousy, Dr. Bickleigh handed the capsule over. All the better. Let Lydston kill him. It made the situation still more amusing.

Dr. Bickleigh watched the administration with calm pleasure. He felt no more compunction than before, in his own drawing-room. Chatford was not the sort of person to arouse that.

With his usual preciseness, Dr. Lydston half filled a tumbler with water and approached the bed. "I want you to take this," he said gently, and Chatford's eyes slowly opened. He had not the strength to raise his head, and Dr. Lydston had to support it and put the capsule in his mouth for him. It took several efforts and sips of the water before Chatford intimated that it had gone down. As Dr. Lydston carefully laid the head on the pillows again Dr. Bickleigh turned away and looked out of the window. He had to do so, to hide a small smile of triumph which he simply could not suppress. Well, that was the end of damned Chatford and his mischief-making. Heigho for Ivy, and independence at last.

Now that the thing was done, his senses seemed strangely intensified. He turned back from the window and looked round the room as he had not done before, and seemed to take everything in at one sweeping glance —the big double bed in which the sick man lay (Chatford was evidently old-fashioned; it was always the man on that question who was the old-fashioned one), the cup of arrowroot on the bedside table, the medicine-bottle of milky-looking fluid on the mantelpiece, the tumbler and two smaller bottles (surgery bottles, too) on the washstand, the very feminine dressing-table with its wing-mirrors. . . . How very curious to reflect that this was Ivy's room as well as Chatford's. Most curious.

Abstractedly he strolled, with unconscious professional instinct, towards the washstand. Why surgery bottles? And labels indicating their contents, too. Most unusual. "Sod. Carb. Sol." "Tinct. Ferr. Perchlor." And the bottle on the mantelpiece; but the contents of that were not stated.

"Well, I think we'd better leave him," suggested Dr. Lydston.

Dr. Bickleigh, who had no further object in staying, quite agreed.

Downstairs, the two chatted for a moment about the case and Chatford's chances of recovery, which they agreed in putting none too high. Dr. Bickleigh asked whether

Mrs. Chatford had been sent for, and was told that everything necessary and possible had been done. He prepared to say good-bye.

But Lydston, it seemed, was positively loath to let him go. Not out of Chatford's house. They both left that briskly enough. But then it appeared that Lydston had not brought his car, and Dr. Bickleigh had to give him a lift home; and, as if overcome by gratitude for this service, Lydston pressed him so strongly to stay to tea that, eager though he was to get away, it was simply impossible to refuse. Dr. Lydston explained earnestly that his wife was out, and seemed to think this still another excellent reason for Dr. Bickleigh staying to tea. And afterwards he had so many questions to ask about botulism and food-poisoning in general, and a dozen other subjects, that it was past five o'clock before Dr. Bickleigh got away.

When finally he was allowed to escape, he drove back to Wyvern's Cross in a kind of trance of satisfaction.

IV

It was only when he had got home and put the car away that a query which had been lying submerged in his mind rose to the surface. Why on earth tincture of perchloride of iron?

He took down the *Materia Medica* in his consulting-room bookshelf and looked it up. The next moment he laughed out loud. The combination of ferric perchloride and sodium carbonate, with the tumbler, on the wash-stand, the arrowroot, the demulcent drinks, and the milky-looking stuff on the mantelpiece (obviously calcined magnesia)—why, it was as plain as pikestaff. That old fool Lydston had been treating Chatford for arsenical poisoning!

Well, after all, the symptoms are identical with those of gastro-enteritis.

So that was why he had come round so suddenly. Wanted to see if he himself would diagnose the same thing. How extraordinarily funny. Lydston had suspected arsenical poisoning, and——

Dr. Bickleigh's mirth ended sharply. Arsenic! That was where the arsenic *motif* came in. Nothing to do with Julia at all. Good heavens, but surely they could not suspect. . . .

He dropped into a chair, literally. His knees had suddenly lost their strength. They *did* suspect.

They *must* suspect. Why else should the Chief Inspector have questioned him so closely about arsenic? They suspected him of having administered arsenic to Madeleine and Chatford. That reference to gossip about Julia had been just a blind. The man had been trying to trap him into an admission of possessing arsenic.

But how could they suspect such a thing? Chatford's symptoms were not unlike those of arsenical poisoning, it was true; but the presence or absence of arsenic in the body could be ascertained in a moment by any competent analyst. And the analyst's report would have been negative. So how could they suspect?

Dr. Bickleigh leaned forward over the table, his head on his hands. He must keep calm. He must think this properly out.

They had suspected arsenical poisoning, but they might not have suspected himself as its administrator.

No, that would not do. The Chief Inspector would not have questioned him like that if he had not been suspected as the administrator.

Well, then, they *had* suspected him of administering arsenic, but they couldn't do so any longer because by now they must have got the analyst's report that there was no arsenic in the eliminations. What would they be thinking now, then? Obviously, that the illnesses had been due to natural causes. That their suspicions had been unfounded, beastly, lying. They *must* be thinking that. There was nothing else to think.

And that was why Lydston had changed his mind. Lydston would have been in the confidence of the police. He would have known of the suspicion. Naturally, then, he had refused to let him see Chatford this morning. But, after he had left, Lydston had heard of the analyst's report and realised that arsenic couldn't be in question at all; the illness was perfectly natural. And he had called Dr. Bickleigh in, not only to get a helpful opinion, but in a way to make amends for the baseness of . . .

Wait a minute, though. Suppose the whole thing had been a trap. Suppose that, arsenic being out of the question, Lydston and everybody else had been puzzled as to what really was the matter with Chatford: the analyst could find no poison, but they persisted in their beastly idea that Dr. Bickleigh had poisoned Chatford. Supposing they had called him in with the hope that he would give himself away and tell them what the trouble really was. And, good God, that was exactly what he had done: diagnosed an obscure disease like botulism, without a proper examination of anything . . . given himself right into their hands.

Wait a minute again, though. No good getting flustered. Supposing that really was the truth—well, what did it matter? He was competent to diagnose botulism. And botulism was a natural disease. No question of poison there. His idea all along had been to establish botulism as soon as possible. That couldn't be wrong now, could it?

No, not possibly. How could the establishment of botulism possibly be wrong?

Oh, God—the capsule. The capsule that he had pretended to contain jalap and cream of tartar.

But Lydston had administered it. Chatford had swallowed it. He had seen him with his own eyes. That definitely precluded the possibility of a trap. And of suspicion too. Good heavens, yes. They wouldn't have invited a suspected man in and calmly administered anything he brought with him, would they? No, that was final.

What a hell of a relief. And what a hell of a stew he had been getting into over nothing at all. He really must look after his nerves. This sort of thing was really silly.

Oh, God, though . . . *Suppose Lydston hadn't administered it at all.*

Suppose he had been only pretending. And Chatford had been only pretending too. Suppose the thing *had* been a trap, arranged by the police, in the hope that Dr. Bickleigh would bring something for administration which they could get their filthy hands on, and so find out the cause of the trouble that way. And that was exactly what he had done. He had walked straight into it.

It was all up.

Absolutely all up. How they must be chuckling now. What was he to do?

Oh, God. . . .

Dr. Bickleigh banged on the table with his fist. This was getting too absurd. Of course nothing of the sort had happened. It was this damned imagination of his. Chatford had swallowed the capsule. He had seen him with his own eyes.

Had he seen him? He lived the scene through, staring intently down the table. Yes: Chatford must have swallowed it. *Must* have.

Very well, then. That was enough of this silly panicking. It was no good going on like this. Nobody suspected anything. And, even if they did, it didn't matter;

because they would never be able to prove anything. Neither about Julia nor anything else. He had covered his tracks too well for that.

But there was no harm in taking reasonable precautions. The incubator, for instance. That might prove an awkward piece of evidence. It would not be wanted any more. Better destroy it, just in case.

And there's no time like the present.

He jumped to his feet, his overstrung nerves welcoming action.

As he passed through the hall, Mrs. Holne called to him from the kitchen, "Are you ready for your tea, sir?"

"I've had it, thank you, Mrs. Holne."

"Very well, sir. Oh, and the man came about the cistern, sir, and he said . . ." Mrs. Holne's words faded into silence as he ran up the stairs, two at a time. What man about what cistern? He could not be bothered with cisterns at the moment. When you've got a job in hand, do it.

He threw open the door of the attic and advanced confidently—till a sudden realisation brought him up short in his tracks, with blanched face and incredulous eyes.

The incubator had gone.

V

That evening three men came to see Dr. Bickleigh.

He received them calmly, for he had known they would be coming. Every moment of the interview before him, every possible development, he had gone over again and again in the interval that had been allowed him. Now that the time had come he was surprised to notice how cool he was.

Chief Inspector Russell entered first, then another equally large man, and then a tall, military-looking man who shut the door behind them. Dr. Bickleigh, a minnow among these Tritons, looked at them enquiringly.

The Chief Inspector indicated the second man. "This is Superintendent Allhayes from Exeter, doctor," he said, with the greatest geniality. "He's got something to say to you."

"Yes?" said Dr. Bickleigh politely, and looked puzzled. But his heart had given a sudden jump. Surely they were not going to . . . "Look here, come into my consulting-room, won't you?"

Superintendent Allhayes, a stolid man, intimated that perhaps that might be a sound move. The quartette trooped into the consulting-room. The third man stationed himself by the door in an unpleasantly ominous manner.

Superintendent Allhayes began to speak. He spoke in a curious, sing-song voice, with his eyes half closed. Quite obviously he had learnt his words off by heart. Dr. Bickleigh felt a foolish wish to giggle, he looked so funny.

"Enquiries have been made concerning the recent illnesses of Mrs. Madeleine Bourne and Mr. William Chatford after taking tea with you here on the 14th instant. They were taken ill shortly after they left you on that date with violent sickness and other symptoms. These symptoms agree with the symptoms of gastro-enteritis, such as might be caused by contaminated food. Acting on instructions from me, Detective-Sergeant Tanner of Scotland Yard made a search this afternoon of your dust-bin. In it he found a half-consumed jar of potted meat, which has since been shown to contain germs which might have caused such illnesses. It is therefore necessary to enquire whether, and if so how, and by whom, this contaminated potted meat might have been added to the food partaken of at your tea-party. It has occurred to me, therefore, that you might like to make a statement regarding your own actions on the 14th instant, why Mr. and Mrs. Bourne and Mr. Chatford were asked to tea, as to what you know of this contaminated potted meat, and any other observations which you might like to make and which might throw light on the matter; but I must add that anything you say will be taken down in writing and may be used in evidence hereafter." He stopped, and looked at Dr. Bickleigh with eyes suddenly quite open.

"Certainly I'll tell you anything I can," Dr. Bickleigh replied easily. He was feeling quite weak with relief. Not a word about Julia! Not a single word. They must have decided to drop that. Seen that it was hopeless. Well, what could they have proved, in any case? Nothing. As for this other matter—well, somehow or other that seemed very small beer compared with Julia. Besides, Chatford wasn't dead yet.

"There's a good deal too much of this contaminated food going about." He had decided already to feign complete ignorance of the grim implications in the Superintendent's words. His attitude should be the perfectly normal one of a doctor in consultation with the police on a matter of public welfare. That would be far the best. Besides, it was inconceivable that they could arrest him. Even including the incubator, they had no real evidence at all. They were only trying to frighten some admission out of him. Well, they had come to the wrong man for that kind of thing. "I was afraid there was something wrong with that particular jar as soon as I smelt it. But perhaps you'd like me to begin at the beginning?"

"If you please," said the Superintendent, and nodded towards the door. Detective-Sergeant Tanner came forward, seated himself at the table, and produced some sheets of paper and a fountain-pen. "Now, doctor."

Dr. Bickleigh, in a perfectly collected manner, began to

speak. "The jar of potted meat was bought by my housekeeper, Mrs.——"

"Excuse me, doctor," interrupted the Superintendent. "If you wouldn't mind beginning by saying that I cautioned you before you said anything. Just to be on the safe side for me."

"Certainly," Dr. Bickleigh agreed amiably. "Of course. 'I should like to say first of all that——' "

"Suppose you began something like this. " 'I, Edmund Alfred Bickleigh, having been cautioned by Superintendent Allhayes that anything I may say may be used in evidence hereafter, wish to make the following statement.' "

"That will do very well," nodded Dr. Bickleigh, leaning against the mantelpiece.

Detective-Sergeant Tanner at the table wrote busily.

"Got that?" Dr. Bickleigh asked. " 'The jar of potted meat was bought'—no, better say: 'The jar of potted meat which has since proved to be contaminated was bought by my——' "

"Sorry to interrupt, doctor," remarked Chief Inspector Russell in friendly tones, "but what about putting that in later, when you come to it? I should suggest you begin by giving an account of your acquaintance with Mr. Chatford and Mr. and Mrs. Bourne."

"Is that really necessary?"

"Well, it'd look better, don't you think?"

"Just as you like. Though it seems rather irrelevant to me. Well, then: 'I have known Mr. Chatford for some years. He was——' "

"Relations always friendly?" remarked the Chief Inspector, studying the ceiling with apparently great interest.

"Perfectly."

"Well, I should mention that."

" 'Our relations have always been perfectly friendly; and——' "

"Until his marriage, eh?"

"How do you mean?"

"You were telling me last night he married an old flame of yours," said Chief Inspector Russell most jovially.

"Oh, well." Dr. Bickleigh smiled. The Chief Inspector smiled too. Only the stolid austerity of Superintendent Allhayes failed to relax before this human touch. "But that didn't affect our relations with each other in the least."

"Oh, come, doctor. Not when you were still sweet on her yourself?"

Dr. Bickleigh's smile broadened. So that was the motive they were trying to hang on him, was it? Remove Chatford, and Ivy would be free. Clever of them to have got more or less the right one. But not so clever as he could be in demolishing it completely. Come, the ordeal was not going to be so bad if they couldn't produce anything better than this. "But I wasn't," he said gently. "Not in the least. If I had been I should have married her myself. My wife was no longer alive at the time of Mr. Chatford's marriage, you must remember. 'Our relations have *always* been perfectly friendly, and have continued so till the present day.'"

"Oh, but one minute, doctor," said the Chief Inspector reproachfully. "You really can't put it quite like that, can you? Not when you were telling me last night how he hates you, what with that grudge you mentioned and so on. You can't say the relations between the two of you have remained friendly till the present day."

"Oh, well, put in 'on my part.' That's perfectly true."

Detective-Sergeant Tanner looked up enquiringly. "'Have continued so on my part'?"

"Yes."

It went on.

The officers had arrived at twenty minutes past nine. At

a quarter to one Dr. Bickleigh suggested an adjournment till the following day, or rather, till later in the same day.

"I'm sorry, doctor," returned the Superintendent unsmilingly. "It's our rule that statements must be taken straight through without a break."

"But we shall be here till daybreak at this rate, if you keep on questioning every single thing I say."

"Oh, really, doctor," protested Chief Inspector Russell. "Come now, sir, you can't say that. We only make a suggestion occasionally, to see you do yourself justice."

"Oh, yes, that's very likely, isn't it?" Dr. Bickleigh snapped. "Well, if we must go on, I suppose we must; but, anyhow, I'm going to have a drink and some biscuits. I'll get the decanter."

"Now that's what I call a really good idea," observed the Chief Inspector with enthusiasm. "I'll give you a hand."

"Oh, I can manage; no need for you to bother."

"It's no bother at all, doctor," returned Russell almost affectionately, and accompanied Dr. Bickleigh out of the room.

At ten minutes past three the statement was finished. At Superintendent Allhayes' request, the Sergeant read it through, in a flat, entirely expressionless voice.

"I, Edmund Alfred Bickleigh, having been cautioned by Superintendent Allhayes that anything I say may be used in evidence hereafter, wish to make the following statement:

" 'I have known Mr. Chatford for some years. Our relations have always been perfectly friendly, and have continued so on my part till the present day. Mrs. Bourne I have only known for about two years. She was a friend of my wife's, and I used to see her a good deal when my wife was alive, but since her marriage I have scarcely seen her at all. Mr. Dennis Bourne I have known for about ten years, but never very well. I had not invited Mr. Chatford to tea on the 4th; he suggested it himself. I had invited him previously, to discuss a legal matter of some fishing rights in which I am interested, but he had been unable to come. I did invite Mr. and Mrs. Bourne on the 14th. My reason was that there had been a slight coolness between us, which I thought too petty to continue, and I wished to put an end to it. I invited Mr. and Mrs. Bourne after I knew Mr. Chatford was coming, because I thought his presence would ease things and the legal business was not so important that it could not wait a few days.

"'On the day in question, Mr. and Mrs. Bourne arrived first, and I took them into my garden and showed them my roses. Mr. Chatford arrived at about 4.40 p.m., and we all then went into the drawing-room, where tea was at once served. The food was on plates on a wicker cake-stand. The food consisted of buttered buns, potted-meat sandwiches, and a cherry cake. I remember Mr. Chatford said that he was very fond of potted meat sandwiches, and he ate several of them. We all ate the sandwiches, but Mr. Chatford ate most. Mrs. Bourne ate least. So far as I remember, everybody partook of all the food that was present. No sandwiches were left on the plate. I fancied I detected a slightly unpleasant taste in one of the sandwiches I ate, but I did not remark on it. I did not attach any importance to it. I remember Mr. Chatford saying that he was working very hard at the time, and that his wife had gone to Spain for a holiday and he wished he could have gone with her. As a medical man I consider that, if he was in a state of exhaustion through overwork, he would be especially liable to an attack of gastro-enteritis if any irritant were introduced into his stomach. This is my opinion now. I did not know before he told me that he was overworked.

"'All the food which was served had been prepared

by Mrs. Holne, my housekeeper. She had bought the jar of potted meat, but I cannot say where. She cut and prepared the sandwiches, and to the best of my knowledge they were not out of her observation from the time she made them till we all arrived in the drawing-room for tea. I did not ask her this, but in the ordinary course of her duties it would be so. After my guests had gone I was speaking to Mrs. Holne on some other matter, and mentioned to her that I had thought one of the sandwiches tasted peculiar. I asked her to fetch me the pot. She did so, and we both smelt it. It seemed to both of us to smell a little bad. Mrs. Holne seemed to think this more strongly than I did. I still did not attach very much importance to the fact, but to be on the safe side I suggested that the unconsumed portion of the contents had better be thrown away. I threw it in the dust-bin myself. I am not in the least surprised to learn now that the potted meat has been found to be contaminated and unfit for consumption. I can suggest no other explanation of how it came to be so beyond the obvious one that it was in that state when bought.

"'I am interested in chemical and similar experiments. Such research-work as a practitioner in general practice can undertake has always been a hobby of mine. I was reading recently an account of how the gas-masks used for our troops in the war were manufactured, and this caused me to experiment with passing chlorine through a solution of sodium thiosulphate. I have never conducted any experiments involving arsenic. I have never handled arsenic in any form except the Fowler's solution which I keep in my surgery. In connection with my experiments I ordered an incubator a few weeks ago from Messrs. Rabbage & Co., Wigmore Street, London. I do not know the exact date. It was about the time that I had a case of botulism under my observation here. My purpose in ordering the incubator was to conduct certain experiments in bio-chemistry. I am interested in the action of the digestive juices on certain articles of diet, and wished to carry out tests of my own. I did carry out these tests, and verified certain conclusions which I had formed. That was some weeks ago. The last occasion on which I used the incubator was after my guests had gone on the 14th. It occurred to me that it would be an interesting experiment to ascertain if the potted meat that had been used for the sandwiches was really contaminated or not. I therefore went out to the dust-bin and took a sample from the pot, which I afterwards again threw away. I then prepared a culture to the best of my ability, from the sample of potted meat, of any bacilli which might have been inhabiting it. It was my intention to send a portion of the culture up to some eminent bacteriologist for identification of the bacilli, if any. I have myself no practical experience of bacteriology, but I have a rudimentary knowledge of its principles. I have not the apparatus necessary to effect an identification myself, nor am I competent to separate a particular bacillus; but I thought it an interesting experiment to endeavour to make a culture. I was more than doubtful whether there were any bacilli in the potted meat at all, but I thought it worth trying as an experiment. On the 15th I separated a portion of the culture, which I enclosed in a large capsule, with a view to examining it later under the miscroscope in my surgery to see if I could make out whether it was ready to send away. The idea of enclosing it in a capsule occurred to me because I was preparing another capsule containing a strong dose of jalap and cream of tartar for Mr. Chatford, after I had been called in for a consultation on his case by Dr. Lydston. It occurred to me then that a capsule would form an excellent temporary container for a portion of the jelly holding a certain group of bacilli, as it could be sealed without disturbing the jelly and so prevent contamination from the atmosphere. I had also the idea of making a purer culture of this particular group, which I had not identified, and it was therefore necessary to separate it from the rest before it could be overrun by a more powerful organism. Owing to pressure of work and other matters, I have not yet had time to examine the group. So far as I know, the capsule containing the portion of culture is still where I left it yesterday, in a pill-box filled with cottonwool in the right-hand top drawer of the surgery dresser. I have no reason to suppose that it could be anywhere else.

"'During the night of the 14th I was taken ill. Since my wife died I live alone, and therefore had to attend to myself as best I could. I attributed my illness to having eaten something which disagreed with me, but instead of the abdominal pain, accompanied by violent sickness and purging, which as a medical man I should have expected in such a case, my symptoms were almost entirely of a paralytic nature. This led me to diagnose an attack of botulism. Having recently had a case of botulism under my observation, I am conversant with its symptoms. As soon as I was sufficiently recovered to go downstairs I took a large dose of jalap and cream of tartar, which my experience has shown me is the most effective way of combating this disease. I very soon obtained relief, and by further treatment succeeded in eliminating the poison from my system. Fortunately my attack was a mild one, and by the next morning I was almost completely recovered, though I was unable to eat any breakfast.

"'As soon as I was informed, in the afternoon, that Mr. Chatford had also been taken ill, I sent a message offering my services in conjunction with those of his own medical man. Mr. Chatford, however, having already called in Dr. Lydston, I did not press the point. In the afternoon I called upon Mr. and Mrs. Bourne to make sure that they had not been taken ill, and was distressed to find Mrs. Bourne in bed with symptoms somewhat similar to my own, though unfortunately a little more severe. I was now convinced that these three illnesses must have been caused by something we had all eaten at tea on the 14th at my house, which pointed conclusively to the potted meat. When I heard the next day that Mr. Chatford was really seriously ill I made a special journey into Merchester and again offered my services, this time to Dr. Lydston, feeling that he as a medical man would appreciate the value of the experience in this somewhat rare disease which I could afford. Dr. Lydston considered the matter, and informed me that he could not avail himself of my services without Mr. Chatford's consent. Soon after I returned home, however, he rang me up and asked me to go back for a consultation. I did so, taking with me the large dose of jalap and cream of tartar which I had prepared and put into a capsule for the purpose. I saw Mr. Chatford, and was able to inform Dr. Lydston that he was clearly suffering from botulism. I also gave Dr. Lydston the capsule containing the jalap and cream of tartar to administer to him if he thought advisable. I cannot say whether Dr. Lydston administered this dose while I was in the room or not. I think not, as Mr. Chatford was in a state of considerable collapse at that time, but I did not really notice. It was obvious to me from the lack of improvement in Mr. Chatford's condition that Dr. Lydston's treatment had been on mistaken lines, and I was anxious that he should understand what was the real cause of the illness.

"'In my opinion the potted meat, having become contaminated through natural causes, was undoubtedly responsible for the illnesses of Mr. Chatford, Mrs. Bourne, and myself, and I am unable to throw any further light on the matter.

"'I make this statement quite voluntarily and without being questioned.'"

"There, doctor," said Chief Inspector Russell, almost indecently jovial considering the hour. "That's correct, isn't it? That's exactly what you want to put forward?"

Dr. Bickleigh rubbed his hands gently together. "Quite, I think." They had tried to wear him down by keeping him up so late, but again they'd got hold of the wrong man; a doctor doesn't lose his wits through having to exercise them half the night; he'd soon lose his practice as well if he did.

Superintendent Allhayes smothered a yawn. He had got out of the ways of night-work since reaching his present rank. "Do you wish to make any corrections, additions, or erasures before you sign it?"

"None at all, thank you. I'll sign it now."

Dr. Bickleigh took the Sergeant's pen from him and bent over the table. He was glowing with triumph. There were one or two awkward juxtapositions in the statement, and a few things which he would have preferred to gloss over or perhaps have worded rather differently (in fact the wording all through was absurd; but what could you expect when each single sentence was discussed for several minutes, separately and apart from its context, before being written down?), but nothing to which he could take a real exception. And on the whole the police had been very fair; much fairer than he had expected; that bit at the end was bunkum, of course, just put in to save their faces, but they really had been quite reasonable. Chief Inspector Russell particularly: Dr. Bickleigh quite liked that big, cheerful, paternal-looking man.

No, there were one or two awkward juxtapositions perhaps, but they simply didn't count compared with the marvellous, the utterly glorious way in which he had turned their own traps back on them. There had been only two possible bits of evidence against him, and both of them he had completely demolished. The idea had seemed sound when it occurred to his flogged brain just before dinner. Hearing it read over in the statement, he could have crowed aloud. The incubator and the capsule—absolutely and entirely convincing! The evidence knocked clean out of their hands. Nothing but suspicion left. And you can't arrest a murderer on suspicion. Oh, dear, no. Only felonious loiterers, and housebreakers, and low scum like that. Not an artist in death like Edmund Alfred Bickleigh, Esq., M.R.C.S., L.R.C.P. Good gracious, no.

Dr. Bickleigh had a task not to laugh as he signed his name with an unusually bold flourish, and added the date underneath. Nearly half-past three, and no arrest to compensate them. Well, but of course, they could hardly have been expected to realise what kind of a man they had to deal with; they didn't come up against Edmund Bickleighs every day.

Suspicion would remain, of course: but what on earth was suspicion?

With any luck Chatford ought to be dead by now.

Dr. Bickleigh straightened up. "Well, that's done at last. Now, then, what about that drink you wouldn't have a couple of hours ago? No need to keep your minds sharp any longer now, you know. Say when, Chief Inspector." (And we'll drink a silent toast to a speedy death in the Chatford family.)

"No, thank you. I won't change my mind, doctor."

"No?" said Dr. Bickleigh indifferently. Let him sulk, then, if he wanted to. "Superintendent, say when."

"I think, doctor," said the Chief Inspector, in a strangely gentle voice, "that the Superintendent's got something different to say to you."

The Superintendent seemed to shake himself together. He drew a little nearer to Dr. Bickleigh and fixed him with his rigid gaze. "Edmund Alfred Bickleigh, it is my duty to warn you that anything you say may be taken down and used in evidence hereafter. I now arrest you on a charge of attempting to murder Mr. William Chatford and Mrs. Madeleine Bourne by administering to them poisonous germs at Wyvern's Cross on the 14th September, 1929."

Dr. Bickleigh had been experiencing a curious sensation. A shell seemed to have exploded quite close to his head, as one or two had done in the war. He had undergone once more just that same perception-numbing reverberation, that violent rocking of the brain in the brain-pan which momentarily paralyses the processes of the mind; there was even the old shrill singing in his ears, so piercing as to be physically excruciating.

Slowly, his stunned senses recovered, apprehended, examined, rejected this preposterous mis-statement. "You can't," he said, in a small but very distinct voice. "You've no evidence. No evidence at all."

Chief Inspector Russell laid a huge, not unfriendly hand on the little man's shoulder. "Better not say anything just now, doctor."

Dr. Bickleigh looked up at him. His mouth worked impotently. Only his dry tongue rasped against the parched roof of his mouth with a rustling, scratchy sound. Speech had completely deserted him. It was probably just as well.

"Here, hold up, doctor. Sergeant, give him a chair. Come on; I'll mix you a drink—a real stiff one, eh? No need to chuck up the sponge yet. While there's life there's hope, you know, doctor."

Not a particularly tactful observation perhaps; but Chief Inspector Russell, a kind-hearted man, meant it well.

Chapter Twelve

I

GERM DRAMA
CHARGE OF ATTEMPTED MURDER AGAINST DOCTOR
WIFE'S BODY EXHUMED

From our own correspondent

Merchester (Devonshire), *Friday.*

"That he attempted to murder William Andrew Chatford, of the firm of Shipton, Ogden, Ermehead & Chatford, solicitors, of Merchester, and Madeleine Winifred Bourne, of Wyvern's Cross, by administering poisonous germs to them, to wit, *bacillus enteritidis.*"

These were the words uttered in the old-fashioned Merchester police court this morning, and were the prelude of what promises to be a great drama of the law. The man in the dock was Dr. Edmund Alfred Bickleigh, whose appearance there was the culmination of a series of sensational events during the present week.

Dr. Bickleigh, who wore a blue serge suit and a dark tie, is a slightly built man with a ruddy complexion. He faced the magistrates with coolness, but kept his countenance averted from the public during the short time he was in the dock. He followed with keen and critical interest the evidence of Superintendent Allhayes, Deputy Chief Constable of Devonshire, who arrested him.

"Yesterday evening I went to Dr. Bickleigh's house in Wyvern's Cross, accompanied by Chief Inspector Russell of Scotland Yard," said the Deputy Chief Constable. "I saw him, and told him I was about to arrest him on a serious charge.

"YOU HAVE NO EVIDENCE"

"I cautioned him, and then said:

" 'I now arrest you on a charge of attempting to murder William Andrew Chatford and Madeleine Winifred Bourne by administering to them poisonous germs, to wit, *bacillus enteritidis*, on the 14th of September last.' Dr. Bickleigh replied, 'You can't do that. You have no evidence. No evidence at all.'

"I am instructed by the Director of Public Prosecutions, who has taken the case up, to ask for a remand of a week. I shall offer no further evidence to-day."

Mr. F. L. Gunhill, who represented Bickleigh, said that he did not intend to apply for bail at this stage.

WOMEN CHEER PRISONER

A large crowd that included many women was waiting near the police court in the hope of seeing Dr. Bickleigh. When he appeared, cheers were raised, and many people struggled forward in an attempt to shake his hand. The prisoner smilingly acknowledged the ovation as the police hurried him into the taxi which was waiting, and the cab drove off amid a remarkable demonstration of sympathy with the accused man.

LONG INVESTIGATIONS

The arrest of Dr. Bickleigh is the sequel to investigations which have been in progress in the neighbourhood of Wyvern's Cross for a considerable time. I learn that these investigations were prompted by the Home Office, as a result of communications which were made to London as long ago as last June. Scotland Yard detectives have been pursuing enquiries in the district for several weeks.

Mrs. Bickleigh died in distressing circumstances on the 9th April last year. She had been suffering from a painful illness. An inquest was held, and a verdict returned of accidental death through an overdose of morphia self-administered.

The little community of Wyvern's Cross is in a ferment of excitement. The Scotland Yard officers, working from Merchester, had gone about their enquiries so quietly and unassumingly that nobody except Mr. Chatford and Mr. and Mrs. Bourne had been aware of their presence at all. Indeed, so well had the secret been kept that the news of the arrest came as a veritable bombshell to the villagers, only to be followed by the still greater bombshell later in the day of the exhumation of Mrs. Bickleigh's body. I am informed that when Dr. Bickleigh issued his invitations to tea on the 14th, during which it is alleged that the poison-germs were administered, the officers were hastily consulted and advised an acceptance in order that suspicions should not be aroused by any unneighbourly refusal. The sequel came as unexpectedly to the detectives as to the alleged victims.

I understand that sensational developments are expected.

THE EXHUMATION

The exhumation of Mrs. Bickleigh's body, ordered by the Home Office, took place late this afternoon, and is causing a tremendous local sensation. Digging operations began just after five o'clock, but the coffin was not brought to the surface until after dark. The little churchyard at Wyvern's Cross was closed during the operation to all but officials engaged in the case and the gravediggers.

The scene was eerie in the extreme. The grave which sheltered Mrs. Bickleigh's body lies under an ancient yew. When the coffin had been scraped free of earth, it was laid under this venerable tree to await the arrival of Dr. Sourby, the Home Office pathologist. A few minutes after nine o'clock the headlights of a motor-car ascending a winding hill could be seen, and five minutes later Dr. Sourby alighted, accompanied by Detective Chief Inspector Russell, of Scotland Yard. Policemen carrying hurricane lanterns led them to the graveside.

A dark night, the gloomy sky oppressively overcast; the rising wind moaning through the branches of the ancient yew; the little party standing round the open grave, their shadows distorted into grotesque shapes by the flickering light of the lanterns; the silent knot of awestricken villagers looking on from a distance—such was the impressive solemnity of the spectacle as the handsome oak casket, with brass fittings and name-plate, was hoisted on to a hand-bier and the little procession moved off, led by a constable with a lantern, to a tiny disused cottage, with whitewashed walls and thatched roof, which stands near by.

Only an oil lamp, supplemented by the hurricane lantern, served to illuminate the post-mortem examination conducted by Dr. Sourby. The expert, however, with the celerity and skill born of long years of practice, speedily performed it and removed certain organs from the body.

EXHUMATION LAW

The law relating to exhumations is that a coroner can order the exhumation of a body if he has not already held an inquest; but if he has previously held an inquest, he must apply to the Home Secretary for an order.

ARREST A SENSATION

That the arrest of Dr. Bickleigh has caused a sensation locally is to put it at its mildest. One of the most respected as well as one of the most popular figures in the district, he came to Wyvern's Cross just over fourteen years ago, and since then, by his professional skill and kindness, has endeared himself . . .

A graduate of . . .

His war record . . .

. . .

II

Mr. F. L. Gunhill rubbed his podgy hands together and beamed hearteningly on his client. He looked far too cheerful a little fat man to be a solicitor.

"Oh, you needn't worry about that, Bickleigh. They won't press that charge. They know they couldn't get a conviction. You'll see: the grand jury will throw out the bill, as sure as eggs. Why, they've no real evidence at all."

"I should think not, indeed," Dr. Bickleigh agreed indignantly.

"H'm, yes. Pity you remarked on it, though. Still, no matter, no matter. They have a *prima facie* case, no doubt, and we'll have to get out our answer to it, just in case. But of course they only made the arrest to free their hands for this other investigation. Now that's what we've got to concentrate on."

"It's outrageous," Dr. Bickleigh said thinly. "I could never have conceived such a thing. To lose such a wife is bad enough, Gunhill, but to be put on one's trial for murdering her . . ."

"Yes, of course. Of course. Shocking. We'll go into the matter of counsel more fully, of course, but I strongly advise briefing Sir Francis Lee-Bannerton. Strongly. Just the man for us. If he'll take the case, of course."

"Why ever shouldn't he?"

"Oh, he's a busy man, Lee-Bannerton, you know," said Mr. Gunhill, with something of an evasive air. "Still, we'll go into that later. There are just one or two points I want to examine with you now."

Dr. Bickleigh looked up suddenly. "Look here, Gunhill, they haven't got a case. Have they? I mean, there's even less evidence than in the other. How could there be any evidence against me of such a ridiculous charge? I mean, it's so absurd."

"Oh, they've got hold of one or two small things. Nothing of major importance, I quite agree. In fact, we're quite justified in feeling every confidence. Every confidence. I don't mind telling you, Bickleigh, that I consider an adverse verdict almost unthinkable."

"So I should hope, indeed."

"But that doesn't mean we shouldn't take every precaution," said Mr. Gunhill, with robust sense. "We should, and we must. Of course, if the judge rules out the evidence on the attempted murder charge as inadmissible in the major one, the result is a foregone conclusion. But the prosecution will fight for its admission without a doubt. Still, even there the odds are in our favour. It will depend entirely on the judge."

"They can't possibly find me guilty. It would be too preposterous." Dr. Bickleigh was quite calm. It was impossible that he could be found guilty.

"Exactly. Precisely. I'm delighted to see you so confident. In fact, I'm every bit as much so myself." Mr. Gunhill rubbed his hands and looked extremely confident. "Still, as I said, we must take every precaution. Now, assuming that this evidence is admitted, I have an inkling—yes, indeed, more than an inkling—that the prosecution will make a big point of your conduct in the sick-room. We haven't gone properly into that yet, have we? No. No, of course not. So I should like you to tell me just how it came about that you diagnosed botulism in Chatford's case when he actually had nothing of the sort. How was that, eh?"

Two little tiny points of red appeared on Dr. Bickleigh's cheek-bones, as they had since his arrest whenever he thought of Lydston. "I could hardly be expected to know that I was being deceived by a fellow-practitioner, could I? With the police and a bacteriologist waiting in the next room to try and trap me."

"Of course not. It was—most high-handed. Then you were deceived by Lydston about the symptoms?"

"Most certainly I was. From my own case I had strong suspicions of botulism (as it turned out, I was mistaken; but that's neither here nor there), which I wanted to confirm from Chatford's. I questioned Lydston, and what he told me did confirm it."

"I see. Yes. Of course, you understand the point they'll try to make?"

"Quite," said Dr. Bickleigh disgustedly. "You explained that. And equally that they'll credit me with maliciously substituting the capsule with the culture for the one containing jalap and cream of tartar which they found, exactly as I said, in my surgery. No doubt. I'm supposed to have been trying to commit a murder. We mustn't forget that."

"Yes, yes," soothed Mr. Gunhill. "So Lydston deliberately deceived you. Well, that's quite a good line. Quite sound, in view of the trap they laid for you. Yes, I think we can take that line."

"It happens to be the truth," Dr. Bickleigh said coldly.

"Oh, yes. Oh, naturally. And the capsule: quite sound, quite sound. Yes, I'm sure we can meet that attack adequately. Perfectly. I'm not worried on that head at all."

"Well, as I've told you all the time, Gunhill, I don't see how the case can be sent for trial at all. I've been watching the magistrates pretty closely, and I'm quite sure they don't mean to commit me."

"Possibly, possibly. We haven't had all the evidence yet, but it's quite possible."

"It will be extremely unfair of them if they do," observed Dr. Bickleigh warmly.

"No doubt. Quite so. I'm not sure I don't agree. Because, really, there's only one point in the whole case which gives me the slightest uneasiness. The very slightest. And no doubt you can explain that."

"I'm quite sure I can," Dr. Bickleigh smiled. Of course he could.

"Quite so. Exactly. It's part of the evidence Mrs. Bourne is to give. It hasn't been divulged yet, but I have been given officially to understand that she is prepared to swear that when you called at The Hall on the day of Mrs. Bickleigh's death you informed her that your wife was dead; although you could not possibly have known it so soon yourself unless—well, you see the interpretation that might be made."

Dr. Bickleigh was sitting very stiffly, fighting to prevent the effect of this blow from showing in his face. Good *God*. . . . Yes, of course. He remembered clearly now. Remembered every detail, and how Madeleine had shrunk away from him as if she almost suspected the truth. Perhaps she had. The hag! She was capable of any beastly, horrible suspicion like that.

But this was simply dreadful. How could he have forgotten it so completely, this incredible blunder? And how was he now to explain it?

"That is quite untrue." His mind forced utterance of the words before he could think at all, in blank, instinctive denial.

"Untrue, eh?" Mr. Gunhill did not seem quite so exuberantly confident. "That's good. That's fine. Untrue. You're quite certain, Bickleigh? She's prepared to swear to it. In fact, it was her confiding this to Chatford that really began the whole thing."

"Quite certain. It's an abominable lie."

"I see. *I* see. Then it'll be just your word against hers."

"She's an abominable, malicious woman," said Dr. Bickleigh, with stiff face. "I remember my poor wife telling me what a liar she was. I can give you plenty of evidence on that point. I shall expect you to bring that forward very strongly."

"Blackening the character of an opposing witness, eh?" Mr. Gunhill remarked dubiously. "Risky. Very risky. We shall have to consider that most carefully."

"I should like the truth about that woman to be established, whatever the risk."

"Yes, yes. Well, we must see. We must take advice. We must consult Lee-Bannerton about that. Be guided by him. Well, well. Just your word against hers. I see."

"How is her husband to-day, by the way?" Dr. Bickleigh asked, and hardly troubled to hide his malice behind the question. For retribution at last had followed Madeleine's repeated and mean refusals to improve the sanitation at The Hall. Denny was down with typhoid: he had been taken ill just a fortnight after Dr. Bickleigh's arrest —dangerously ill, Dr. Bickleigh had not been in the least sorry to learn. Conceited young ass! (He had played his part in that hypocritical tea-party, too. God, how Dr. Bickleigh hated that trio.) And, now there was danger of losing him, it seemed that Madeleine had never loved him so well. Typical. Still, there were consolations for her. Widowhood would give her the most marvellous opportunities.

"About the same, I'm sorry to say; about the same," said Mr. Gunhill rather flurriedly, as if he had been not a little discomposed by the peculiar quality of the small smile on his client's face. "Anyhow, no better."

"Really? I'm sorry to hear that. Most sorry," purred his client.

For the first time since his arrest Dr. Bickleigh slept badly that night. His confidence in the issue remained unchecked. The point was a nasty one no doubt, but not damning; besides, it was inconceivable that the jury should not take his word in preference to that slut's. But his loathing for Madeleine was so intense that his mind could not rest. Why, *why* had he not killed her when it was in his power to do so—and damn the consequences! Madeleine was almost worth hanging for.

And the creature had accepted his offers of friendship, broken bread with him in his own house, all the time with her tongue in her cheek, ready even then to swear his life away with her lies. The filthy, hypocritical, murderous vixen!

Well, let her give her slanderous tongue full play. He would see to it at least that she left the court without a shred of decency left her: show her up for the despicable thing she was.

Chapter Thirteen

I

THE trial of Dr. Edmund Alfred Bickleigh for the murder of his wife opened on Monday, the 18th January. It was remarked by the reporters in court that the prisoner walked into the dock with quite a jaunty air, and looked round the court with a slight smile; in their columns the next day they hinted deprecation of such levity on an occasion so critical.

The prisoner did not share their view. He did not find the occasion in the least critical. He found it only a tiresome prelude to liberty.

During the last three months he had, of course, had his bad moments, but they had not been many. His confidence had never been really shaken. Dr. Bickleigh never had any doubt that he was not of the sort that gets convicted. It was, he could not help feeling, rather impertinence to put him on trial at all. Why the grand jury could not have thrown out the bills . . .

And for it all he had to thank Chatford and Madeleine. No, the next time they should not get off so easily.

"Edmund Alfred Bickleigh, you are charged in this indictment that on the 9th day of April, 1928, at Wyvern's Cross, in the county of Devonshire, you feloniously, wilfully, and of your malice aforethought, did kill and murder one Julia Elizabeth Mary Bickleigh. How say you: are you guilty or not guilty?"

"Not guilty." Not guilty of course, you old idiot. Do you think I'd tell a lie?

During the tedious swearing of the jury (no women, thank goodness), Dr. Bickleigh began to speculate on what was to happen next time to Chatford and Madeleine. Something with plenty of pain attached to it. . . . He found himself curiously sustained by such a contemplation.

"Gentlemen of the jury, the prisoner at the bar, Edmund Alfred Bickleigh, is charged in this indictment that on the 9th day of April, 1928, at Wyvern's Cross, in the county of Devonshire, he feloniously, wilfully, and of his malice aforethought did kill and murder one Julia Elizabeth Mary Bickleigh. Upon this indictment he has been arraigned, and upon arraignment he has pleaded not guilty, and has put himself upon God and his country, which country you are. Your duty, therefore, is to enquire whether he be guilty or not guilty, and to hearken to the evidence."

What rot it all was.

However, the jury looked suitably impressed.

Dr. Bickleigh surveyed them benevolently. Twelve good men and true. At a guess, ten farmers and two professional men. Two farmers for certain, for Dr. Bickleigh recognised them. One came from not far outside the Wyvern's Cross district; Dr. Bickleigh had quite a nodding acquaintance with him. He sent a look of recognition across the court now, and the man responded with an embarrassed little nod. Dr. Bickleigh felt more satisfied than ever. Here was one man ready for an acquittal already. What a farce it all was.

He exchanged a smile with Gunhill, and a self-possessed little nod with Sir Francis Lee-Bannerton. Let the fools of spectators stare. They need not think they could put *him* out of countenance.

A sudden hush succeeded the bustle in court. Somebody was getting to his feet.

Of course; that would be the Attorney-General.

How ridiculous, to send the Attorney-General himself down on such a forlorn hope. They must realise how hard up they were for a case. Oratory instead of evidence, it was to be.

II

Sir Bernard Deverell was a tall, thin man with a beaky nose. He began to speak in quite conversational though impersonal tones, addressing a point somewhere on the wall about four feet above the heads of the jury.

Well, now we're off, thought Dr. Bickleigh.

He listened at first with close interest. Of course there was nothing new to come out. He knew exactly the strength, and the weakness, of the case against him. But it was quite absorbing to hear the facts set out in orderly array. On his knee was a pad of scribbling-paper for notes, and his pencil hovered over it alertly.

"May it please your lordship—gentlemen of the jury, it is my duty, in conjunction with my learned friends, to lay before you the evidence in support of the indictment which you have just heard. The unfortunate lady, into whose death we are enquiring . . ."

Dr. Bickleigh's pencil drooped. The quiet voice went on. Morphia symptoms . . . inquest . . . exhumation . . . post-mortem examination. . . . There was nothing to make notes about here. Dr. Bickleigh noticed that Sir Bernard had a habit of bunching his gown up on his left hip as he spoke, rolling it gradually up his thigh till he had got all the slack into a tight ball, and then letting it drop and beginning all over again. Silly.

His attention began to wander.

It was caught again abruptly.

The Attorney-General had dealt with the history of the case up to the time of Mrs. Bickleigh's death. He began to touch on the reasons her husband might have had for rejoicing instead of sorrowing over that death. Motive . . . motive . . . motive . . .

Dr. Bickleigh had not heard the full account of the motive imputed to him. It filled him with sudden horror. They had got the truth—the real, secret truth. That devil Madeleine had . . .

A cold sweat broke out over him as he listened to the measured voice recounting the story of that disastrous passion. This was terrible. Obviously, quite obviously, the motive was overwhelming. He dared not look at the jury. Madeleine was determined to hang him with her lies. Hang him!

He tried to shut his ears to the damning recital, drew little pictures on his pad, grotesque faces, anything to distract his attention. Whatever happened, he must preserve his composure. Let his face for one moment show the terror in his mind, and it was all over. He felt a thousand eyes boring into his forehead, trying to burn their way through to his thoughts. God, this was awful—awful!

In the luncheon interval one enterprising journalist managed to get a look at that page of the pad. He made quite a feature of it in his report the next day. "The prisoner, who preserved a jaunty attitude throughout the day's proceedings, showed his indifference to the Attorney-General's opening of the case by . . ."

When the court adjourned for lunch, Dr. Bickleigh was weak with the strain. Some legal argument had preceded the judge's rising, but he had been unable to attend to it. Something about the admissibility of the Chatford evidence. The jury had been sent out of court. It was important, of course; most important, Gunhill had considered; but its importance had vanished now. He was as good as convicted already on that opening speech alone. Convicted—before the trial had scarcely begun. It was terrible.

Gunhill came to see him in the interval, rubbing his hands as usual. "Well, we can congratulate ourselves so far, I think. Yes, certainly."

Dr. Bickleigh looked at him with haggard eyes. "Congratulate ourselves?"

"Yes, a very fair opening. Scrupulously fair. Sir Bernard let you down quite lightly, don't you think?"

Dr. Bickleigh did not answer.

"It's a pity that Mrs. Bourne's a widow, though," Mr. Gunhill added, shaking his head. "A recently bereaved widow always has an effect on the jury. Invariably. Well, well, let's hope she doesn't cry. But really, Bickleigh, I must say we . . . Yes, every confidence."

III

After lunch the legal argument was resumed. The jury were still absent. Dr. Bickleigh, quite recovered now (how absurd, to be so upset by such a small matter; nerves, of course), listened at first with interest, but soon became bored.

"Rex *v*. Geering (1849), 18 L.J., M.C. 215; Rex *v*. Flannagan, 15 Cox. 403 . . ."

They flourished books about, at the judge, at each other, at anyone who looked a likely person to have a book flourished at him.

Sir Francis Lee-Bannerton made great play with Rex *v*. Winslow, 8 Cox, 397; but nobody seemed very much impressed except Sir Francis himself.

In the end the judge decided that the evidence was admissible.

Dr. Bickleigh was disappointed, but not disheartened. Gunhill and Sir Francis had both warned him that such a decision was extremely probable. Well, it only meant that the farce would be a more protracted one.

Thank goodness that opening speech was finished, though. There had been some nasty moments there.

But it wasn't. The jury came back, and the Attorney-General rose again. Quite chattily, he told them of Dr. Bickleigh's attempts to kill Madeleine and Chatford. The curious thing (thought Dr. Bickleigh, listening with disquiet growing once more) was how right he was. And he spoke as if he knew he was right, too. The most remarkable little details. If the jury realised that he *was* right . . . It began to seem almost impossible that they should not. The fact that he was grew more and more glaringly apparent.

Dr. Bickleigh again found himself unable to glance at their faces, as Sir Bernard made his damning points one after the other. He did not give way to panic again—would not give way; but it was really terrible. To have to sit there and listen silently, helplessly, while this man invited the jury to hang him. . . .

When at last the Attorney-General sat down, Dr. Bickleigh realised that his underclothes were wringing wet. *Had* he still got a chance? He caught Gunhill's eye, and was astonished to notice that it was still as gleaming and jovial as ever. Apparently he had, then. Glancing surreptitiously at the jury, he noticed one of them stifling a yawn. Good heavens!

The calling of the first witnesses was sheer anti-climax. The Attorney-General, as if satisfied with a good day's work, had actually left the court. Dr. Bickleigh watched him go with such relief that he could have laughed out loud (perhaps a little hysterically) at his retreating back. The only two witnesses called that day were examined by

Sir Bernard's junior—and what did their evidence amount to? Nothing! Simply nothing. A surveyor produced plans of Fairlawn (what on earth did they want plans of Fairlawn for?); and Florence, the maid, recounted her impressions of Mrs. Bickleigh's illness and the events of the fatal day. The idea left with Florence was that Mrs. Bickleigh had been very puzzled about her headaches, and could not account for them in any way. Well, so had Sir Tamerton Foliott been. And Dr. Bickleigh himself. There was nothing new there. And as for the rest, Florence's evidence was positively favourable. Obviously she did not believe the doctor guilty, and as one on the spot her opinion must carry weight. And in cross-examination Florence quite agreed that she did not see how it was possible for Dr. Bickleigh to have come back that afternoon without being observed by either her or the cook. Well, you might say impossible. In his re-examination Sir Bernard's junior had to treat her almost as a hostile witness.

When the court adjourned, Dr. Bickleigh had quite recovered his spirits. One must preserve one's sense of proportion: that was the secret.

IV

The proceedings dragged on, with the tedious taking of evidence, examination and cross-examination, ridiculously polite exchanges between counsel, all the flummery of a full-dress trial.

Dr. Bickleigh alternated now between complete confidence and uneasiness; but confidence certainly prevailed. There were nasty moments; several of them; far too many of them. But Gunhill was always very reassuring afterwards; and, though sometimes quite appalled at the time, Dr. Bickleigh was always able to call proportion to his aid before too long.

Madeleine's evidence, for instance.

To Dr. Bickleigh's cynical perception, Madeleine was revelling in the situation; in the notoriety, the limelight, the sympathy, even in her widowhood. But, knowing how he himself had been taken in, he realised that it was too much to hope that the scales could be stripped from the other male eyes in court. He settled himself down not to listen, and began to draw a very elaborate and meticulous study of a galloping horse. The reporter, who was featuring Dr. Bickleigh's artistic efforts for the benefit of his readers, hastily jotted down: "Ashamed to face old love testifying against him, prisoner pretended to be absorbed in his sketching."

In low, candid tones Madeleine revealed the hideous pursuit to which she had been subjected. By innuendo rather than by any direct statement, Dr. Bickleigh was shown as a ravening beast endeavouring to get his claws into pure and innocent maidenhood. The reporters sharpened their pencils. Here was the goods. There would be strong coffee and wet towels that night for the headline merchants. Madeleine, a figure of infinite pathos in her widow's weeds, noticed the sharpening of pencils and promptly wept a little. The judge, the Attorney-General, the jury, even Sir Francis Lee-Bannerton, looked their consternation. Dr. Bickleigh, quite unable to stop himself listening, abandoned his horse and writhed in the dock with impotent rage.

"Now, Mrs. Bourne, you've told us that the prisoner forced his way into your bedroom and there proposed marriage to you. You naturally referred, as you say, to the fact that he was already married. Kindly tell us what he replied to that."

Madeleine hesitated, in gentle, feminine reluctance. Then with quiet courage she did her duty. "He said: 'Julia is dead.'"

As every newspaper on the following day remarked: sensation.

Dr. Bickleigh glared at Madeleine. On this point, he knew what chance there was of losing the case depended. In spite of the sinking feeling in his stomach, he strove to give an impression of a man righteously indignant at being faced with a foul lie.

The Attorney-General sat down.

As the cross-examination proceeded, Dr. Bickleigh's heart sank lower and lower. In spite of his warnings, it was clear that even Sir Francis Lee-Bannerton had been taken in by Madeleine. He handled her gently, openly sympathised with her, played up to her own play-acting. Dr. Bickleigh, almost frantic, began writing passionate little notes addressed to his counsel. Sir Francis would not even look at them. Dr. Bickleigh could have shouted at him with fury.

The worst of it was that Sir Francis had all along refused point-blank to attack Madeleine. He had considered it thoroughly bad policy, in view of her recent widowhood and the effect she would undoubtedly make on the court. He had said, with the utmost casualness, that he intended to leave his line of cross-examination till the time came; he would consider Madeleine when she gave her evidence, and decide then and there what line to take with her. And now he was taking no line at all. Simply giving the case away. Good God, leading her on to more and more outrageous statements and innuendoes against himself; that was what he was doing. Dr. Bickleigh grew more and more frantic.

It was a glimpse at the Attorney-General's face that made him think. Sir Bernard was leaning back with his eyes on the ceiling and an expression of such utter blankness that it must have been concealing some inward sorrow. Dr. Bickleigh gazed at him for a moment in astonishment, for Sir Bernard ought to have been looking extremely happy at having his case won for him like this; yet undoubtedly Sir Bernard was not. Dr. Bickleigh turned his attention back to his own counsel, and began to listen with reason instead of emotion. The next moment he understood—and in the reaction of the moment uttered a sharp little laugh. The judge frowned on him, but Dr. Bickleigh did not care. For once Madeleine had overreached herself.

"Now, Mrs. Bourne, it distresses me to have to intrude on your recent great sorrow," Sir Francis had said diffidently (he had a curiously diffident manner which was rather charming), "but it is my duty to ask you this: were you and your husband a few months ago not contemplating a divorce?"

"Certainly not," said Madeleine indignantly, while ears everywhere were pricked up.

"You swear to that?"

"Really, Sir Bernard," interposed the judge, "is this relevant?"

"Quite, your lordship. It will be apparent in a moment. You swear to that, Mrs. Bourne?"

"Certainly I do," Madeleine replied, with womanly dignity.

"But—well, to put it bluntly, you and your husband did not get on well together?" apologised Sir Francis.

"My husband and I loved each other very dearly." Madeleine rolled her eyes at the judge in mute appeal.

The judge rolled his eyes at Sir Francis, but without effect.

"But, like most married people, you had your quarrels?" suggested Sir Francis, with a deprecatory smile.

"We had only been married eighteen months."

"If you wouldn't mind answering my question, Mrs. Bourne?"

Madeleine drew herself up. "If I must, the answer is 'No.' My husband and I had never quarrelled."

It was at this point that Dr. Bickleigh laughed. Never quarrelled, when it had been notorious in Wyvern's Cross that . . . But no doubt the woman really believed it. Her powers of self-deception were incredible. Yes, no doubt she had already, in the brief weeks of her widowhood, persuaded herself that her short married life had been idyllic. Now he saw what Sir Francis was getting at.

"But, like most women," pursued Sir Francis diffidently, "you had your moments of jealousy?"

"Certainly not. My husband had never given me cause for such a thing."

"Oh, not after your marriage, no doubt. But before it. You never expressed jealousy of the women your husband had been fond of before he met you?"

Madeleine hesitated. The judge shuffled his papers uneasily.

"I'm afraid I must press you for an answer, Mrs. Bourne."

"No, never!"

Sir Francis suddenly shed his diffident manner. He glared at her. "Perhaps you will tell me that you did not keep him up till four o'clock in the morning for nights—for weeks on end, till his health was seriously affected, while you raved at him over the women he had loved before he even knew of your existence?"

Madeleine shrank back in the box and went sallowly pale. Her mouth set like a rat-trap.

The judge leaned forward. "Sir Francis, I must ask you to justify this remarkable line of cross-examination. I have allowed you considerable latitude, but I cannot see that the examination of this witness has made it relevant for ——"

"Certainly, my lord," snapped Sir Francis, leaping for

this opportunity. "My cross-examination is directed to establish that the evidence given by this witness is totally unreliable: that she is notoriously untruthful, malicious, and mentally unbalanced. And I intend to call evidence of my own to prove this."

As the newspapers again had it: sensation.

Dr. Bickleigh leaned over the dock, his face blazing with joy. He could have embraced his counsel on both cheeks. For the third time in his life that unbodily exaltation lifted him into a sphere of delirious happiness.

"You realise, of course, what you are doing, Sir Francis?" The judge had recovered himself, if others had not.

"Perfectly, my lord. My client is prepared to face any cross-examination of a personal nature. He has nothing to conceal."

The judge glanced at the clock. The time was a quarter to four. "Nevertheless, I think I will adjourn the court now, to give you an opportunity to think things over."

"That is very kind of your lordship. I am much indebted."

V

Gunhill was nearly as excited as Dr. Bickleigh himself. "The case is as good as won. He led her on, you see, till she'd contradicted herself on a few small points, and then established her in the mood he wanted. Naturally she played up. Then he came out into the open."

"But you haven't got the evidence about . . ."

"Oh, yes, we have. Indeed we have. Most certainly. I followed up that line of enquiry very closely indeed, you may be sure of that. Mrs. Bourne's evidence was the only really damaging thing against you, and if we could discredit that . . . You may be sure I concentrated on that line very closely."

"But you said—Sir Francis pretended . . ."

"He didn't want you told, in case he changed his line at the last minute. He wanted to get the exact impression she made on the jury first. Now we can go ahead. I can tell you now, Bickleigh, we've got the most conclusive evidence both of her untruthfulness and her lack of balance too, to say nothing of her downright malice towards yourself."

"I've always said she was mad," exulted Dr. Bickleigh. "Not certifiable, unfortunately; but certainly over the border-line. I told you so dozens of times."

"Exactly. Precisely. And very fortunate that you did so. And the beauty of the position, you see," said Mr. Gunhill, rubbing his hands so vigorously that they positively rasped, "is that, though they're entitled now to attack your personal character, to do so will only damage their own case. If you've been frank with me (and of course you have, of course), there's nothing for them to attack you on except your somewhat—well, shall we say indiscriminate relations with women? And it won't benefit them at all to show you as indiscriminate. Their whole case rests on your affection for one single woman. The more women, the less motive."

"Of course," Dr. Bickleigh grinned. "Very funny."

"Anyhow I think—yes, I think that will be the end of Mrs. Bourne."

It was.

The next morning, in place of Madeleine a medical certificate arrived to the effect that Mrs. Bourne was in bed, suffering from nervous prostration and shock, and was not in a fit state to attend the court. Sir Francis looked at the jury so meaningly that they felt quite uncomfortable.

Dr. Bickleigh sat back in his chair in the dock and prepared to listen to the evidence of Chatford with nothing but an academic interest. As Gunhill said, the case was won already.

Chatford certainly did not advance the cause of the prosecution very much. His evidence was limited to his own participation in the attempted poisoning case, the tea-party, his own subsequent illness, Dr. Bickleigh's attempts to see him, and their sequel. It was all very vague. Dr. Bickleigh's serenity grew. Really, if this was the best they could do . . . Why, it was all innuendo and inference; nothing definite at all. Sir Francis handled Chatford very nastily in cross-examination too. Hinted at his jealousy and malicious feelings towards the prisoner, just eliciting enough to be able to damage the value of his evidence; leaving the suggestion that Chatford was a vindictive busybody. It was all very clever.

The medical evidence came next, headed by Lydston. Even Lydston Dr. Bickleigh found he could listen to without anger—Lydston reciting in his precise tones the unprofessional conduct of the prisoner, his diagnosis without any examination at all, the startling nature of that diagnosis, and the way he and Chatford had conspired to do their piece of play-acting. That play-acting—well, talk of unprofessional conduct! Towards the end of all this Dr. Bickleigh did begin to feel a little uneasy. Lydston was damnably convincing. But the cross-examination, eliciting Lydston's admission that he had wilfully deceived the prisoner as to Chatford's symptoms and so could not be surprised at whatever he diagnosed, went some way to restore the balance.

Sir Tamerton Foliott's evidence confirmed this restoration. It was most impressive, but did not amount to much; however, what was there was almost more helpful to the defence than to the prosecution.

Sir Tamerton was followed by the various experts. Dr. Ryder, bacteriologist to the Home Office, came first—a large man with a big black beard, who spoke with extreme confidence. Invited by the Attorney-General to tell the court what he had discovered with regard to the culture submitted to him for examination, he did so with gusto.

"The medium submitted to me for examination was an ordinary gelatin plate. There were several colonies on the plate, all presenting the thin, notched, irregular appearance of the colon-typhoid group. I carried out the usual processes, and identified the different organisms. I identified *bacillus coli communis, bacillus enteritidis, bacillus paratyphosus B., bacillus typhosus, bacillus aertrycke,* and others of this same group. *Bacillus enteritidis,* or Gaertner's *bacillus* very decidedly predominated."

"Thank you, doctor. And as regards the contents of the capsule, which you also examined?"

"This contained a small portion of gelatin which corresponded in shape and size with a gap on one edge of the gelatin plate. On this portion was a group of *bacillus enteritidis* only; no other organism was present except *bacillus enteritidis.* This applies equally to the residue of the potted meat, which was also submitted to me for examination. This contained *bacillus enteritidis* only."

"I see. To the layman, *bacillus enteritidis* means the german which produces typhoid fever?"

"That is so."

"Perhaps you would explain to the jury the leading characteristics of this *bacillus*?"

"Certainly," agreed Dr. Ryder heartily, and turned to the jury. "*Bacillus enteritidis,* or Gaertner's *bacillus*, is a leading member of the large colon-typhoid group. As regards its morphology, it is actively motile, carries several flagellæ, forms no spores, and is Gram-negative. Like all others of this group, it is aërobic; it grows well on ordinary media and is easy to cultivate. So far as concerns its cultural characteristics, it ferments glucose, lævulose, maltose, glactose, arabinose, raffinose, mannite, sorbite, dulcite, and dextrin, with production of acid and gas, but has no action on saccharose nor, as a rule, on salicin and glycerin. It gives very little or no indole, and does not give the Voges-Proskauer reaction. In litmus milk ——"

The Attorney-General managed to stem this flow. "Yes, but if you could manage to put it a little less technically, doctor. And I was meaning, more particularly, its effects on the human frame?"

"Oh, I beg your pardon. Well, it is established now that *bacillus enteritidis* is the most frequent cause of meat poisoning. It has been discovered in meat from pigs, cattle, horses, and fish. Symptoms are due to action of the toxins, and their onset is generally rapid, not to say sudden."

"And these symptoms are?"

"Usually, vomiting, diarrhœa, pains in the abdomen and head, prostration, collapse, cold sweats, rigors, cramps, rashes, and furred tongue," replied Dr. Ryder with gusto.

"Exactly. Now, you have heard Mrs. Bourne's and Mr. Chatford's symptoms described in court here. Is it your opinion that these are consistent with poisoning by *bacillus enteritidis*?"

"Entirely consistent."

"And you actually identified this organism in Mr. Chatford's eliminations?"

"I did."

"You have no doubt that Mr. Chatford's illness and Mrs. Bourne's indisposition were caused by this typhoid *bacillus* having found its way into their systems?"

"None at all."

"Now, you examined the gelatin plate also for *bacillus botulinus*, the germ which causes the disease known as botulism? Did you find any?"

"None."

"Could you have expected to do so?"

"No, I could not. *Bacillus botulinus* is anaërobic. In other words, it dies if exposed to the air. The medium as prepared was suitable for aërobic organisms only. *Bacillus botulinus* could not have survived. Nor were there any traces of this *bacillus* in the eliminations."

"Are the symptoms of botulism similar to those produced by *bacillus enteritidis*, which is the germ of typhoid, or enteric fever?"

"Certainly not. They are totally different. In the case of botulism the symptoms are headache, dizziness, followed by diplopia, partial ptosis of both eyelids, dilated pupils, paralysis of the facial muscles, the larynx and the pharynx, with stasis of the intestines, giving rise to constipation. Vomiting is usually absent."

"So that in many ways the symptoms of botulism are directly opposite to those produced by *bacillus enteritidis*?"

"That is so."

"In your opinion would it be possible for a medical man, judging the case on the symptoms alone, to diagnose a case of poisoning by *bacillus enteritidis* as botulism?"

"Not if he was in his sane senses," replied Dr. Ryder robustly.

The Attorney-General went on to persuade his witness to translate some of his earlier technicalities into language more fitted to the comprehension of ten farmers and two professional men.

Dr. Bickleigh was amused how useful his blunders in bacteriology were proving. In his case a little knowledge was a blessed thing. If he had made his culture of *bacillus botulinus* properly, instead of managing to cultivate apparently every possible other *bacillus* that had been present in the Sampford boy except this particular one, it might have looked very nasty for him indeed. He also congratulated himself most warmly on the artistic feeling which had caused him to infect the residue of the potted meat with such admirable results.

The Attorney-General proceeded to dispel this complacency. Reverting to the gelatin plate, he asked blandly whether the cultures on that might have been obtained from the potted meat. Dr. Ryder was emphatic that they could not. Only one organism was present in the potted meat; this would not account for *bacillus paratyphosus B., bacillus typhosus,* and the rest on the plate. How then, in his opinion, might such a plate have been prepared? Sir Francis objected, and the judge allowed the objection; such a very speculative question could not be permitted. The Attorney-General contented himself with getting his witness's repeated assertions that such a possibility was untenable; the infection of the potted meat might have come from one of the cultures of *bacillus enteritidis* on the plate; the plate could not have been infected from the potted meat alone.

Naturally the defence had had their eyes opened by their own experts to this fact, but Dr. Bickleigh did not at all like the Attorney-General's very emphatic handling of it.

In cross-examination the explanation was put forward, and Dr. Ryder quite admitted its feasibility. The predominance of *bacillus enteritidis* showed that the greater part of the cultures did, in fact, come from the potted meat; the remaining organisms which, though present in quantity, were so much less prevalent, were due to another experiment which Dr. Bickleigh had made at the same time on the same gelatin-plate with eliminations from the district isolation hospital. (Fortunately Dr. Bickleigh had had a patient in the isolation hospital at the time to account for a visit there.) In re-examination, however, he quite agreed with the Attorney-General that it was exceedingly odd to make two different cultural experiments on the same plate, and not to say valueless, for the more powerful organism would only overrun and destroy the weaker one; moreover he would, in this case, have expected to find the cultures in a decidedly less advanced state. In further cross-examination he could not be made to retract this, but only to repeat that nevertheless the explanation of the defence was quite consistent with the facts as he observed them.

On the whole a witness by no means helpful to the defence, felt Dr. Bickleigh, as he watched the broad back disappear with considerable relief. It had been a nasty couple of hours.

The evidence of Dr. Sourby, the Home Office pathologist, who followed, though lengthy, amounted to nothing more than that he had been able to find in the body of Mrs. Bickleigh no traces of natural disease: certainly nothing to account for her headaches and ill-health: no, there had been no neoplasm on the brain. In cross-examination, he agreed that not only was death perfectly consistent with an overdose of morphia, but that the post-mortem appearances which he had heard described this was almost certainly the cause. Dr. Sourby was confirmed in this opinion by Sir James Clerihew, Medical Adviser to the Home Office. As, however, the cause of death was not in question, this did not advance matters much either way. Dr. Bickleigh grew more and more bored. He was rather proud of being bored. Had anyone ever been bored with his own trial for murder before? Hardly. But, really, there seemed nothing to go on with, now that Madeleine had been so effectively quashed. Compared with that, nothing else seriously counted.

The next witness, however, imported a little more interest into the proceedings. This was Mr. Pymm, the Senior Official Analyst to the Home Office. He had to admit that in the organs handed to him for examination by Dr. Sourby he had been unable to find traces of any poison at all. The morphia, which it was in evidence that Mrs. Bickleigh had been taking in such large doses, would in any case have disappeared after such a lapse of time, as would any other vegetable poison; but of any metallic poison, such as arsenic, there was no trace at all. The only unusual substances which he had discovered were vanadium, present in surprisingly large quantities, and a very little gold. He had been quite unable to account for the presence of these two, so rarely used in medicine.

Dr. Bickleigh smiled inwardly. He knew where the vanadium and gold came from.

Unable, that was (proceeded Mr. Pymm), up till only a few days ago. Had the combination then suggested something to him? Yes, it had.

Dr. Bickleigh sat up alertly. This was something new.

By a curious chance, there had then occurred to Mr. Pymm's memory a proprietary preparation which had appeared a few years ago, and which, in the course of his duties, he had had to analyse. This preparation was known as Farralite, and it was one of the many proprietary medicines designed to correct uric acid diathesis, of which samples are circulated from time to time among members of the medical profession. This particular preparation had not been a success, owing to its high cost and to the fact that it induced violent headaches, and it had not been taken up by the profession.

A sick feeling took possession of Dr. Bickleigh. They were going to disclose everything, show exactly what he had done, expose to the glare of expert examination that secret plan which he had thought so undetectable. This was disaster.

By calling on every atom of his self-control, he was able to sit impassively through the terrible evidence that followed, listening to his method being described in the minutest detail (only as a theory, of course, but the way the man spoke showed that he had not the faintest doubt of the truth of it); hearing Mr. Pymm give it as his unalterable conviction that this preparation could certainly have induced such headaches as Mrs. Bickleigh suffered from and he could think of no other drug which would; hearing Mr. Pymm quite unshaken in cross-examination; realising the prosecution's point being made more and more dependent on proof that Dr. Bickleigh had had access to this preparation, and watching the feeling in court becoming more and more tensely crystallised on this one question; then listening to a representative of the firm in question detailing, with the ledger in front of him, that on this date, on that date, on the other date, Dr. Bickleigh had ordered supplies of Farralite, and hearing the Attorney-General asking, in tones undisguisedly triumphant, that the ledger be put in as an exhibit in the case.

There was no doubt about it. The prosecution had managed to close up a link in the chain which more than made up for the one that Madeleine had snapped. The last secret of the way he had killed Julia had been snatched from him and held up like a conjurer's handkerchief before the jury—turned this way and that, left with no further possibility of deception. Dr. Bickleigh, turning for a moment unguardedly harassed eyes upon them, looked hastily away again as he saw how they avoided his look.

The recalling of Dr. Sourby and Sir James Clerihew to confirm Mr. Pymm's conclusion was hardly necessary; but the prosecution would leave nothing to chance; they meant to hang him.

At last the medical aspect of the case was finished. And with it went Dr. Bickleigh's buoyant hopes. He hadn't a chance now.

Only one witness of any importance remained to be called—Ivy. She entered the box shrinkingly and timidly, keeping her eyes turned from her lover in the dock. Dr.

Bickleigh, too depressed almost to keep up appearances, looked at her dully.

They were kind to her. Everybody on counsel's and solicitor's benches, almost everyone in court, knew that she had been the prisoner's mistress, but no reference was made to the fact. It was not necessary to the prosecution's case. But something else was. As Ivy quaveringly told her story of meeting him on the fatal afternoon, Dr. Bickleigh had a flash of terrible premonition. He saw with sudden, awful clarity, the ghastliness of a blunder he had made. In his anxiety to show Chatford's interested maliciousness he had shown, too, Ivy's unreliability as a witness against him. The case for the prosecution depended entirely on being able to prove that he had had time that afternoon to get back to Fairlawn between the time of his meeting the two villagers in the road and being seen by Ivy. On Ivy alone hung his chance of proving that he could not—Ivy and her evidence as to the time when she gave it to him. But now Ivy was suspect. They would press her, hint that she was wrong, hint even that she was wilfully altering that time to help her old lover.

Dr. Bickleigh listened, with face set so rigidly that the muscles of it quite ached; his jaws were clamped tightly together.

Ivy knew.

Ivy knew that he had killed Julia, that he had tried to kill Chatford and Madeleine. Dr. Bickleigh felt her knowledge instinctively and surely. Ivy knew, but—she was not going to give him away. Oh, bless the girl: bless her. When he was free, *if* he ever was free, he would make it up to her. She loved him in spite of what she knew he had done, loved him and still wanted to marry him. She should marry him. Next time there should be no mistake. By God, no! He owed her that, and he would pay—with Chatford's life.

His face relaxed; the set lines of his jaw lost their hardness. His lost hope began to creep back.

The Attorney-General bunched his gown a little higher on his hip. He scratched very delicately with his forefinger at the extreme point of his nose. His junior sat up. He recognised the nervous habit which meant that his leader was going to make a very special effort.

Ivy! What a slender thread (Dr. Bickleigh felt) on which to hang his last chances of escape from the hangman's rope. And yet the thread had held.

During the next few minutes Dr. Bickleigh watched, with mask-like face, the thread chafe, fray, and snap. With the tears streaming down her face, Ivy at last admitted to the Attorney-General's persistence that the time had not been as she had given it. It was a quarter of an hour later. The prisoner had told her, long afterwards, that her watch must have been wrong.

It was all up.

VI

When his own counsel rose to open to the court the case for the defence, Dr. Bickleigh had no hope left at all. One by one his props had been knocked away from under him. Sir Francis was fighting a hopeless case. Dr. Bickleigh listened with complete apathy.

It was not for quite an appreciable time that it dawned on him that, if the hope was a desperate one, Sir Francis himself seemed unaccountably ignorant of the fact. He spoke with confidence. His diffident manner of cross-examination, which had led so many unsuspectingly superior witnesses to let out things which they bitterly regretted afterwards, had given place to a resolute and finely tempered indignation. Dr. Bickleigh began to understand that it was a cruel and scandalous thing that he had been put on trial at all, to answer a charge of mere possibility of opportunity and imputed motive, without a shred of real evidence to support the case against him. He was so surprised to learn that there was no real evidence against him, in spite of what had undoubtedly gone before, that his apathy began to melt.

It melted faster and faster. There *was* no evidence against him. That was astonishing, but it was perfectly true; Sir Francis showed it quite clearly. What he had considered the most damning facts, conclusively proved, turned out to be neither facts at all, nor proved, but one and all capable of the most innocent and far more probable explanations. Of course Dr. Bickleigh had ordered Farralite—openly, in his own name, without concealment. Why ever not? He had nothing to hide in doing so. Farralite was known to him as having obtained the most remarkable results in the complaint for which he required it for Mrs. Bickleigh, namely, excess of uric acid; that it had given rise to headaches his client neither knew nor even now believed. In any case, he had certainly not connected Mrs. Bickleigh's headaches, which no less an authority than Sir Tamerton Foliott had agreed must be due to quite other and perfectly natural causes, with Farralite at all. Why should he? After all, one can hardly open the human brain to discover whether there is a tumour on it or not. When all the facts known to medical science point to the supposition that there is, an ordinary general practitioner must accept the verdict.

As for Ivy—well, somehow or other Sir Francis showed quite kindly but very plainly that Ivy simply did not matter one way or the other. Mrs. Chatford and Mrs. Bourne . . . Interested witnesses. . . . Very painful to have to impugn a word given in such solemn circumstances, but really his duty compelled him to . . . Ivy and Madeleine simply did not count.

As for the rest of the case for the Crown—pure guesswork! *Pure* guesswork, from beginning to end; guesswork, guesswork, guesswork, guesswork, *guesswork*, GUESSWORK. . . .

As for the secondary charge, well really . . . Sir Francis just smiled. Obviously there was nothing else to do. The potted meat had been found to be infected. That was the whole point, was it not? Found—by the police themselves—to be infected—just as it would have been if the prisoner's story were true—just as it would not have been if the prisoner's story were untrue. . . . Infected—infected—infected—*infected*—INFECTED! There was simply no case to answer.

"I call the prisoner, Edmund Alfred Bickleigh."

Dr. Bickleigh felt as if somebody had suddenly hit him a violent blow in the stomach.

He walked, on shaking legs, from the dock to the witness-box.

Even in his moments of highest confidence he had dreaded this ordeal: even when he had considered it only part of the whole unpleasant prelude to liberty. Occasionally he had tried to persuade himself that it would be fun to cross rapiers with no less a person than the Attorney-General himself, and beat him at his own game (and secretly he had, in spite of his fears, been sure that he would beat him), but it was only an effort to fight the remains of that strange inferiority complex of his which made him dread the battle while still not doubting the ultimate victory. Now that the ordeal had come, he felt sick and faint with terror.

But he must control himself. He must not show it. An innocent man would never show fear.

He gripped the edges of the witness-box till his knuckles showed up starkly white.

Sir Francis saw his agitation so desperately concealed

and pretended to be busy for a moment with his brief, to give him time to recover. Then he smiled at him, in a perfectly charming and friendly way, and said: "Dr. Bickleigh, did you administer to your wife the dose of morphia which killed her?"

"No, I did not," said Dr. Bickleigh indignantly; and with the words his fear fell completely away from him —so completely that he was quite astonished. Stage-fright—that's what it must have been. Simply stage-fright. And now it had gone. Besides, he was sure now that he could detect a friendly feeling in the court towards him. They were on his side. Even the jury. It was Sir Francis and himself and the spectators and the jury and everyone against the Attorney-General, with his beastly insinuations.

Dr. Bickleigh went on to delight Sir Francis by being a perfect witness.

He had been thoroughly rehearsed, of course, as to the line his examination would take, though not as to its exact questions; the right answers fell from him one by one, delivered in just the right tone. Beforehand he had spent nerve-racked hours debating his attitude in this witness-box. If too calm and collected, might not that be construed as the brazenness of the criminal? If flustered and anxious, as a guilty conscience? Now he did not worry. The right attitude had come to him instinctively. He just knew it was the right attitude.

Even when the Attorney-General rose to cross-examine, that nauseating fear did not return. He felt no fear at all. His wits were all about him. He *was* going to beat the man at his own game, and it *was* going to be fun.

And it was fun.

The Attorney-General pressed him hard. About Madeleine, about his alibi, his opportunity of getting back to the house, his wife's illness, the Farralite, and on top of that about the still more dubious (yes, really, the far more dubious) circumstances of the attempted murder charge, the germ-culture and all the rest of it. But Dr. Bickleigh never lost his head for a moment. Not a moment. His formidable opponent got no change out of him at all. The few points on which it was impossible to avoid being more or less equivocal were put right in cross-examination, and Dr. Bickleigh returned to the dock hard put to it not to grin derisively in the Attorney-General's face. It would be nice to know that he had had no small part in obtaining his own acquittal. Dr. Bickleigh had seldom felt so intensely pleased with himself.

Sir Francis called his other witnesses.

Ever so many people were anxious to save Dr. Bickleigh's neck. There were witnesses to his character, his amiability, his popularity, his affectionate relations with his wife. There were even the Crewstantons. There was Mrs. Holne, a most whole-hearted witness, to swear indignantly that the sandwiches had never been out of her sight for a single instant. There was a handwriting expert, to swear just as firmly that the prescription and its signature *was* a forgery, and a most obvious one too. There were expert medical, bacteriological, and pathological witnesses, all prepared confidently to contradict the expert medical, bacteriological, and pathological witnesses for the Crown (simply and solely, of course, because the latter were mistaken, not for a moment because the former disliked them); names just as eminent, too. More so really, because unbiased.

Then there were witnesses to prove Madeleine's predilection for lies: maids from London and Devonshire, to prove hearing their mistress sobbing and howling at four o'clock in the morning at her unfortunate husband because he had been rash enough to look fondly on other women before he ever so much as knew that she herself existed. ("Yes, sobbing and 'owling—well, like a wild beast it was," admitted a fat and motherly cook whose very appearance amounted to a certificate of character in Dr. Bickleigh's favour. "Yes, like a wild beast. You could 'ear it all over the 'ouse. Scream, too, she would. Well, you couldn't 'elp but 'ear it, try as you would. Made me and the other maids feel quite ashamed, it did, and that's a fact.") People came from Wyvern's Cross, too (people who liked the doctor more than Madeleine, and there were plenty of them), to prove Mrs. Bourne's malicious stories against the doctor, and the palpable lies she had told. Sir Francis offered to call sixty-five different witnesses on this point alone, till the Attorney-General had to accept the evidence as given.

But even then nothing was left to chance. Expert witnesses in yet another branch were called to prove that Madeleine was suffering from a not common but certainly not rare neurotic complaint which in this case had had its outlet in this insane retrospective jealousy, but might have taken, or still take, any other similar form. Insane? Well, in a way, really, yes: a form of mental unbalance almost amounting to insanity; not certifiable, though, of course; just on the safe side of the borderline. Giving rise to delusions? Oh, certainly. Such as that people were in love with her who were in reality nothing of the sort? Precisely; the exact kind of delusion which would occur. A lack of proportion, in fact, about everything in any way concerning herself which touched, in some respects, genuine megalomania, and meant a complete disregard of truth and fact. Conceit gone mad. Very sad, very sad. But sadder still for any unfortunate man who happened to marry one of these raving creatures. And decent parents, of course, would prevent such a daughter from marrying (oh, yes, they would know her to be unbalanced, certainly), but of course in this case . . .

Nobody mentioned Madeleine any more. A prosecution's chief witness can never have been more effectively disposed of.

The trial dragged on.

Dr. Bickleigh's confidence was now unshakable. He knew, just *knew* now, that an adverse verdict was impossible. So did Gunhill. So did Sir Francis himself. Every evening, after the expenditure of a few more thousand pounds in the day's proceedings, they would meet in Dr. Bickleigh's cell for a few minutes before he was taken back to the prison, rub their hands vigorously, and smile at each other. It was a foregone conclusion. Sir Francis told Dr. Bickleigh frankly that he had never been so confident of a verdict in the whole of his career before.

Even the Attorney-General's closing speech did not shake Dr. Bickleigh's settled optimism. The man was simply making the worst of a bad job. No one could fail to see that, not even the jury. The unfairness of allowing him to speak last, after Sir Francis, did not really matter. Dr. Bickleigh simply smiled openly at the ludicrous imputation that he had committed one murder and tried to commit two others. One simply did not do such things.

The judge was not at all bad. Not at all bad. Dr. Bickleigh, listening critically to the summing-up, was quite prepared to admit that. On one or two points perhaps he did not emphasise as strongly as he should have done the absurdity of the suggestions of the prosecution, and it was annoying of him to appear to attach quite as much weight to the evidence (such as it could be called) against Dr. Bickleigh as in his favour. Still, on the whole he really was quite fair. But far too long. Far, far too long. Good heavens, how that measured, unemotional voice droned on and on and on. Would it never come to an end?

It did. The jury filed out to consider their verdict. Dr. Bickleigh retired from the public's gaze.

He was very chatty with his warders during the time of waiting. They were not bad fellows at all. He must look them up when he was free, and they would all have a good laugh over this business. He told them quite plainly that a verdict of guilty was utterly out of the question. They were inclined to agree with him.

The jury was only absent a bare forty minutes.

"I told you so," Dr. Bickleigh smiled, as they went up the stairs into the court-room together. One of the warders, with gloomy leanings, had said that under the hour in a doubtful case like this always meant an acquittal.

Dr. Bickleigh was not in the least nervous. Not even perturbed. His confidence was undiminished as he looked over the faces of the jury in a kind of proprietary way. Twelve good men and true.

Sir Francis was not even in court. Gunhill had told Dr. Bickleigh that he had an urgent engagement elsewhere, which he had left to keep as soon as the summing-up was over. To wait for the formality of the verdict, Sir Francis had felt, was a mere waste of time.

"Gentlemen of the jury, have you all agreed upon your verdict?"

"We have."

"Do you find the prisoner at the bar, Edmund Alfred Bickleigh, guilty or not guilty of the wilful murder of Julia Elizabeth Mary Bickleigh?"

"Not guilty."

Well of course.

"Is that the verdict of you all?"

"It is."

But for all that Dr. Bickleigh drew a huge breath of relief, and felt rather weak about the knees as he turned to the judge and waited to be formally discharged.

Well, that was the end of everything. Eight whole days of it, and now—free at last. Well, not technically free. He was still in custody, of course, on that ridiculous attempted murder charge. That would be taken almost immediately, a mere formality. Everyone knew that, having failed on the major charge, the Crown could never hope to get a verdict against him in the minor one; really the trial just finished had been a trial, in a way, upon the other charge too. Quite possibly (thought Gunhill) the Crown would enter a *nolle prosequi*. Anyhow, he had nothing to worry about now.

The judge said a few words to him, and Dr. Bickleigh, who had not heard one of them, beamed back vaguely. People pressed forward to shake his hand as he stepped out of the dock, Gunhill and the rest. There was even some attempt at cheering. Dr. Bickleigh felt a hero. Damn it all, he *was* a hero. There were precious few people who could get away with a killing like that. And now he was out of danger. Ruined, of course. Every halfpenny he had in the world had gone into his defence: he would possess little more than the clothes he stood in; a nice system, that allows that sort of thing to happen to an innocent man. Yes, ruined right enough, but out of danger for good and all. And as for being ruined—well, Chatford had ruined him, and it was only fair that Chatford should be forced to make restitution. And, by God . . .

As with smiling face and nodding head he accepted the congratulations of those round him, and shook hands that were being continually thrust towards him from all sides like a *cheval de frise*, a little spot deep down in Dr. Bickleigh's consciousness glowed and burned with a fierce hatred of Chatford and a determination for vengeance.

Chatford! Chatford, to set himself again *him*. . . .

Somebody tapped him sharply on the shoulder, and he looked round into the unsmiling face of Superintendent

Allhayes. "Better come this way, I think, doctor. Must remind you, still in custody, until . . ."

"Yes, of course," Dr. Bickleigh laughed gaily. "Still got your clutches on me, haven't you? Like me so much you can't let me go, eh? All right, Superintendent."

Still laughing (for, after all, it was rather amusing, after being acquitted of murder), Dr. Bickleigh accompanied the Superintendent into another room. It was empty, except for two constables and a sergeant.

"Well, lead me to the Black Maria," giggled the little man. "Or are you going to give me a drink first, Superintendent? I can tell you, I wouldn't mind one a bit."

The Superintendent's moon-like face did not alter its expression by a millimetre. "Edmund Alfred Bickleigh, I now arrest you for the wilful murder of Dennis Herbert Blaize Bourne, by administering to him the germs of typhoid fever on the 14th September, 1929, and I warn you that anything you say may be taken down and used in evidence hereafter. Hi, stop that, you —— Sergeant, get hold of him, can't you? Barrows! Spreyton! Don't stand there like stuffed dummies. . . ."

Epilogue

ON MONDAY, the 24th April, the trial opened of Dr. Edmund Alfred Bickleigh for the wilful murder of Dennis Herbert Blaize Bourne by administering to him poisonous germs, to wit, *bacillus enteritidis*. The trial lasted four days. Late in the afternoon of the 27th the jury returned a verdict of guilty.

In passing sentence the judge said: "Edmund Alfred Bickleigh, yours was a commonplace, sordid crime for which I can find no extenuating circumstances whatever. It only remains for me to . . ."

On the 15th May, Dr. Bickleigh's appeal against this verdict was heard in the Court of Criminal Appeal by the Lord Chief Justice, sitting with Mr. Justice Darlington and Mr. Justice Parbury. The grounds of appeal were (*a*) misdirection by the learned judge in his charge to the jury, and (*b*) that the verdict was against the weight of the evidence. The appeal was dismissed.

On the 2nd June, Dr. Bickleigh was executed for the murder of Dennis Herbert Blaize Bourne. He protested his innocence to the last.

THE END

THE PERENNIAL LIBRARY MYSTERY SERIES

E. C. Bentley

TRENT'S LAST CASE
"One of the three best detective stories ever written."
—Agatha Christie

TRENT'S OWN CASE
"I won't waste time saying that the plot is sound and the detection satisfying. Trent has not altered a scrap and reappears with all his old humor and charm." —Dorothy L. Sayers

Gavin Black

A DRAGON FOR CHRISTMAS
"Potent excitement!" —*New York Herald Tribune*

THE EYES AROUND ME
"I stayed up until all hours last night reading *The Eyes Around Me*, which is something I do not do very often, but I was so intrigued by the ingeniousness of Mr. Black's plotting and the witty way in which he spins his mystery. I can only say that I enjoyed the book enormously."
—F. van Wyck Mason

YOU WANT TO DIE, JOHNNY?
"Gavin Black doesn't just develop a pressure plot in suspense, he adds uninfected wit, character, charm, and sharp knowledge of the Far East to make rereading as keen as the first race-through." —*Book Week*

Nicholas Blake

THE BEAST MUST DIE
"It remains one more proof that in the hands of a really first-class writer the detective novel can safely challenge comparison with any other variety of fiction." —*The Manchester Guardian*

THE CORPSE IN THE SNOWMAN
"If there is a distinction between the novel and the detective story (which we do not admit), then this book deserves a high place in both categories." —*The New York Times*

THE DREADFUL HOLLOW
"Pace unhurried, characters excellent, reasoning solid."
—*San Francisco Chronicle*

(Nicholas Blake continued)

END OF CHAPTER
". . . admirably solid . . . an adroit formal detective puzzle backed up by firm characterization and a knowing picture of London publishing."
—*The New York Times*

HEAD OF A TRAVELER
"Another grade A detective story of the right old jigsaw persuasion."
—*New York Herald Tribune Book Review*

MINUTE FOR MURDER
"An outstanding mystery novel. Mr. Blake's writing is a delight in itself."
—*The New York Times*

THE MORNING AFTER DEATH
"One of Blake's best."
—Rex Warner

A PENKNIFE IN MY HEART
"Style brilliant . . . and suspenseful."
—*San Francisco Chronicle*

A QUESTION OF PROOF
"The characters in this story are unusually well drawn, and the suspense is well sustained."
—*The New York Times*

THE SAD VARIETY
"It is a stunner. I read it instead of eating, instead of sleeping."
—Dorothy Salisbury Davis

THE SMILER WITH THE KNIFE
"An extraordinarily well written and entertaining thriller."
—*Saturday Review of Literature*

THOU SHELL OF DEATH
"It has all the virtues of culture, intelligence and sensibility that the most exacting connoisseur could ask of detective fiction."
—*The Times* [London] *Literary Supplement*

THE WHISPER IN THE GLOOM
"One of the most entertaining suspense-pursuit novels in many seasons."
—*The New York Times*

THE WIDOW'S CRUISE
"A stirring suspense. . . . The thrilling tale leaves nothing to be desired."
—*Springfield Republican*

THE WORM OF DEATH
"It [The Worm of Death] is one of Blake's very best—and his best is better than almost anyone's."
—Louis Untermeyer

George Harmon Coxe

MURDER WITH PICTURES
"[Coxe] has hit the bull's-eye with his first shot."
—*The New York Times*

Edmund Crispin

BURIED FOR PLEASURE
"Absolute and unalloyed delight."—Anthony Boucher, *The New York Times*

Kenneth Fearing

THE BIG CLOCK
"It will be some time before chill-hungry clients meet again so rare a compound of irony, satire, and icy-fingered narrative. *The Big Clock* is . . . a psychothriller you won't put down." —*Weekly Book Review*

Andrew Garve

A HERO FOR LEANDA
"One can trust Mr. Garve to put a fresh twist to any situation, and the ending is really a lovely surprise." —*The Manchester Guardian*

THE ASHES OF LODA
"Garve . . . embellishes a fine fast adventure story with a more credible picture of the U.S.S.R. than is offered in most thrillers."
—*The New York Times Book Review*

THE CUCKOO LINE AFFAIR
". . . an agreeable and ingenious piece of work." —*The New Yorker*

MURDER THROUGH THE LOOKING GLASS
". . . refreshingly out-of-the-way and enjoyable . . . highly recommended to all comers." —*Saturday Review*

NO TEARS FOR HILDA
"It starts fine and finishes finer. I got behind on breathing watching Max get not only his man but his woman, too." —Rex Stout

THE RIDDLE OF SAMSON
"The story is an excellent one, the people are quite likable, and the writing is superior." —*Springfield Republican*

Michael Gilbert

BLOOD AND JUDGMENT
"Gilbert readers need scarcely be told that the characters all come alive at first sight, and that his surpassing talent for narration enhances any plot. . . . Don't miss." *—San Francisco Chronicle*

THE BODY OF A GIRL
"Does what a good mystery should do: open up into all kinds of ramifications, with untold menace behind the action. At the end, there is a bang-up climax, and it is a pleasure to see how skilfully Gilbert wraps everything up." *—The New York Times Book Review*

THE DANGER WITHIN
"Michael Gilbert has nicely combined some elements of the straight detective story with plenty of action, suspense, and adventure, to produce a superior thriller." *—Saturday Review*

DEATH HAS DEEP ROOTS
"Trial scenes superb; prowl along Loire vivid chase stuff; funny in right places; a fine performance throughout." *—Saturday Review*

FEAR TO TREAD
"Merits serious consideration as a work of art."
—The New York Times

C. W. Grafton

BEYOND A REASONABLE DOUBT
"A very ingenious tale of murder . . . a brilliant and gripping narrative."
—Jacques Barzun and Wendell Hertig Taylor

Edward Grierson

THE SECOND MAN
"One of the best trial-testimony books to have come along in quite a while." *—The New Yorker*

Cyril Hare

AN ENGLISH MURDER
"By a long shot, the best crime story I have read for a long time. Everything is traditional, but originality does not suffer. The setting is perfect. Full marks to Mr. Hare." *—Irish Press*

(Cyril Hare continued)

TRAGEDY AT LAW

"An extremely urbane and well-written detective story."

—*The New York Times*

UNTIMELY DEATH

"The English detective story at its quiet best, meticulously underplayed, rich in perceivings of the droll human animal and ready at the last with a neat surprise which has been there all the while had we but wits to see it." —*New York Herald Tribune Book Review*

WHEN THE WIND BLOWS

"The best, unquestionably, of all the Hare stories, and a masterpiece by any standards."

—Jacques Barzun and Wendell Hertig Taylor, *A Catalogue of Crime*

WITH A BARE BODKIN

"One of the best detective stories published for a long time."

—*The Spectator*

James Hilton

WAS IT MURDER?

"The story is well planned and well written."

—*The New York Times*

Francis Iles

BEFORE THE FACT

"Not many 'serious' novelists have produced character studies to compare with Iles's internally terrifying portrait of the murderer in *Before the Fact,* his masterpiece and a work truly deserving the appellation of unique and beyond price." —Howard Haycraft

MALICE AFORETHOUGHT

"It is a long time since I have read anything so good as *Malice Aforethought,* with its cynical humour, acute criminology, plausible detail and rapid movement. It makes you hug yourself with pleasure."

—H. C. Harwood, *Saturday Review*

Lange Lewis

THE BIRTHDAY MURDER

"Almost perfect in its playlike purity and delightful prose."

—Jacques Barzun and Wendell Hertig Taylor

Arthur Maling

LUCKY DEVIL
"The plot unravels at a fast clip, the writing is breezy and Maling's approach is as fresh as today's stockmarket quotes."
—*Louisville Courier Journal*

RIPOFF
"A swiftly paced story of today's big business is larded with intrigue as a Ralph Nader-type investigates an insurance scandal and is soon on the run from a hired gun and his brother. . . . Engrossing and credible."
—*Booklist*

SCHROEDER'S GAME
"As the title indicates, this Schroeder is up to something, and the unravelling of his game is a diverting and sufficiently blood-soaked entertainment."
—*The New Yorker*

Julian Symons

THE BELTING INHERITANCE
"A superb whodunit in the best tradition of the detective story."
—August Derleth, *Madison Capital Times*

BLAND BEGINNING
"Mr. Symons displays a deft storytelling skill, a quiet and literate wit, a nice feeling for character, and detectival ingenuity of a high order."
—Anthony Boucher, *The New York Times*

BOGUE'S FORTUNE
"There's a touch of the old sardonic humour, and more than a touch of style."
—*The Spectator*

THE BROKEN PENNY
"The most exciting, astonishing and believable spy story to appear in years.
—Anthony Boucher, *The New York Times Book Review*

THE COLOR OF MURDER
"A singularly unostentatious and memorably brilliant detective story."
—*New York Herald Tribune Book Review*

THE 31ST OF FEBRUARY
"Nobody has painted a more gruesome picture of the advertising business since Dorothy Sayers wrote 'Murder Must Advertise', and very few people have written a more entertaining or dramatic mystery story."
—*The New Yorker*